ACCLAIM FOR JAMES PATTERSON'S HOTTEST SERIES!

MISSING: A PRIVATE NOVEL

"*MISSING* IS, IN A WORD, TERRIFIC. This is a one-sit, fast-paced read that fully satisfies but nonetheless will leave you wanting more." —BookReporter.com

THE GAMES

"FAST-PACED...THERE IS NO DOUBT YOU CAN FINISH THIS BOOK IN ONE SITTING."
—Blograma.com

PRIVATE PARIS

"THERE'S NO FLUFF OR DEAD WEIGHT, AND REVELATIONS COME FAST AND HARD...This story is drenched in realism and really strikes a chord, proving to be a worthwhile read."
—matthewrbel.blogspot.com

PRIVATE VEGAS

"NEVER A DULL MOMENT IN THIS ACTION-PACKED PAGE-TURNER."
—Writerswrite.co.za

PRIVATE INDIA: CITY ON FIRE

"IT IS UNPUTDOWNABLE AND DEFINITELY A PAGE-TURNER...ONE IS FORCED TO KEEP READING 'TIL THE END, THOUGH THE END IS OVER 450 PAGES AWAY."
—Winnowed.blogspot.com

BOOKS BY JAMES PATTERSON

The Private Novels

The Games (with Mark Sullivan)

Private Paris (with Mark Sullivan)

Private Vegas (with Maxine Paetro)

Private India: City on Fire (with Ashwin Sanghi)

Private Down Under (with Michael White)

Private L.A. (with Mark Sullivan)

Private Berlin (with Mark Sullivan)

Private London (with Mark Pearson)

Private Games (with Mark Sullivan)

Private: #1 Suspect (with Maxine Paetro)

Private (with Maxine Paetro)

A complete list of books by James Patterson is at the back of this book. For previews of upcoming books and information about the author, visit JamesPatterson.com or find him on Facebook.

Missing: A Private Novel

James Patterson

<small>AND</small>

Kathryn Fox

<small>VISION</small>

<small>NEW YORK BOSTON</small>

Copyright © 2015 by James Patterson

Cover photograph by Stephan Carroll/Arcangel
Cover copyright © 2017 by Hachette Book Group, Inc.

Grand Central Publishing
Hachette Book Group
1290 Avenue of the Americas, New York, NY 10104
grandcentralpublishing.com
twitter.com/grandcentralpub

This book was previously published as *Private Sydney* in the UK by Century and in Australia by Century Australia, part of the Penguin Random House group of companies, in 2015.

Published in hardcover and ebook by Grand Central Publishing in October 2016.
First mass market edition: June 2017

Grand Central Publishing is a division of Hachette Book Group, Inc. The Grand Central Publishing name and logo is a trademark of Hachette Book Group, Inc.

The publisher is not responsible for websites (or their content) that are not owned by the publisher.

The Hachette Speakers Bureau provides a wide range of authors for speaking events. To find out more, go to www.hachettespeakersbureau.com or call (866) 376-6591.

PRIVATE is a trademark of JBP Business, LLC.

ISBNs: 978-1-4555-6812-3 (mass market oversize), 978-1-4555-6813-0 (ebook)

Printed in the United States of America

OPM

10 9 8 7 6 5 4 3 2 1

Missing: A
Private Novel

Chapter 1

BRANCHES FROM THE eucalypts and blue gums cracked as they whipped the electrically charged air.

A storm from the east would hit soon and cover his tracks through the dense bushland. The cabin was isolated and close to a river, with a 270-degree vantage of the valley below, but that was in daylight.

Every sense on heightened alert, he scanned the door frame with his night-vision goggles for the two strands of hair he'd positioned in the jamb days before. Locating both, he exhaled as the door eased open.

The urn over the fireplace was exactly as he'd left it too, the tiny notches in the wood lined up precisely with its rim. He checked his watch. Ninety seconds.

He unscrewed the base of the urn and located the USB device, which he secured inside his zippered jacket pocket.

His watch buzzed with a slow pulse. Someone had infiltrated his perimeter. With no road access from the north, they had to be on foot.

The pulsing sound doubled. Now two people headed towards the cabin. *Cleaners.* Men whose job it was to clean up messes and make sure nothing was left behind.

It confirmed he was a priority. If they had made it here, a hell of a lot of manpower was being invested in hunting him down.

He snatched his backpack and headed for the bedroom. Sliding back a rug at the foot of the bed exposed the trapdoor.

With the alarm pulsing on his wrist, he grabbed a bowie knife from his pack and dug it into the narrow space between the hatch and floor, dislodging caked dirt.

Summoning all his strength, he grunted and yanked. The hatch gave way. He squeezed through and lowered himself feet first. With a hook and wire he'd screwed into the cavity years before, he reached up, replaced the handle in its recess, and repositioned the rug before lowering the hatch.

Sweat dripped from his forehead. He checked his watch again and listened.

No other sensors had been tripped. Instinct told him there were still just two men out there.

On his elbows and stomach the fit was tight, but at least he could propel backwards. After a few meters he removed a rope and screw-top tin from his pack. He unwound the line of rope before topping it with a thin layer of magnesium powder.

Fifteen more meters back and his boots should reach the removable panels at the rear of the wood shed.

The sound of feet clomping inside the cabin was suddenly paralyzing. There were two male voices, then glass smashed.

He lit the rope and reverse commando-crawled as fast as his elbows, toes, and knees could manage.

Flame ripped along the tunnel to the base of the cabin. As he kicked out the shed boards and escaped the tunnel, yelling pierced the night.

By the time they'd dealt with the flaring caused by the water, he'd be long gone.

Goggles fixed and backpack secure, he jogged along one of the paths he'd previously mapped out, careful to stay close to the gully on his left.

Fifty meters along, one of his motion detectors was attached to the base of a tree. It had already saved his life and could come in handy next time.

As he bent down and unstrapped the cord, something brushed his right wrist. Instinctively, he slapped it hard with his other gloved hand before pocketing the device and running on.

Within minutes, pain tore through his wrist, like a nail had been hammered into it.

He could hear voices in the distance.

Sweat poured from his face as the burning in his wrist intensified. Nausea rose in his gullet but he had to keep moving. He was light-headed.

Wind howled as the storm moved in. The sooner it came, the less likely they'd find him before daylight. He headed off again and stumbled on a rock formation. Reeling back, he staggered, unable to maintain his footing. He reached for something to grab. Anything.

Agonizing pain shot through his side as he hit the rocks below. The world went black.

Chapter 2

THE EARLY MORNING temperature was crisp as I stretched aching muscles. Even a punishing run couldn't lessen the grief that today brought. I watched the flaming sun rising above the north and south heads, as a mammoth cruise ship glided into Sydney Harbour. It took me back to my honeymoon when Becky and I sailed home from Noumea.

The spectacle of passing through those heads as the sun lit the city was one of our most treasured memories. It was the moment she told me she wanted to be known as Mrs. Craig Gisto.

It had been eight years now, and a song, a smell, even a sound, could still trigger a volcanic release of pain from my core.

If Cal had lived, he would be eleven today.

The car accident that took their lives trapped Cal as an eternal three-year-old and me as a widower. I wondered why there was a word for children who lost parents, but not one for parents who had suffered the greatest loss of all.

After a quick shower and breakfast, I was comfortably

heading to the city in my Ferrari Spider. On Military Road, I stopped at the traffic lights just before the turn-off to Taronga Zoo. Cal's favorite place.

Memories of him hanging off a gorilla statue were interrupted by a call. Jack Morgan. It had to be late morning on the west coast.

"Hi, Jack, what can I do for you?"

The LA-based owner of Private spoke quickly. "Craig, I'm on a helicopter so we may lose connection. I'm asking for a favor. Eric Moss is the CEO of a company named Contigo Valley." The background noise made it difficult to hear.

"You're fading," I said into the hands-free microphone.

He shouted over the din. "He and his daughter are old friends. Moss was at the top of his field and disappeared two days ago. E-mailed a resignation with no explanation."

"Do you suspect foul play?"

Jack gave directions to the pilot then returned. "This is a billion-dollar company with international contracts. It needs Moss."

I knew some of the work the company did with safety and medical equipment. So the CEO resigned on Friday and hadn't been heard of over the weekend. He could have been drinking away his sorrows or celebrating with a young fling.

I braked as a BMW cut into my lane on the approach to the Harbour Bridge.

"Is the daughter high-profile?"

Most of Private's clients were either famous, wealthy, or both, and wanted scandals kept out of the tabloids.

"She's special, Craig. I'm asking you to do this for her. Her name's Eliza Moss. She owns Shine Management."

The phone crackled again.

"I've been a big supporter of Eric Moss," Jack continued. "Trust me, this isn't like him. Eliza and the company are his life. He wouldn't walk away without a fight. And he'd never do this to his only child."

I wondered what sort of daughter panicked when her father didn't contact her over the weekend. But if Jack thought it worth looking into, I'd do it, despite this week's heavy workload.

"Thanks, Craig," he finished. "Let me know if I can help in any way."

When the line went silent, I replayed the conversation in my mind. Jack mentioned Eliza was special to him. I wondered how special.

After pulling into the car park just after seven a.m., I took the stairs to street level.

First thing I saw was shattered glass.

The ground-to-ceiling door to Private had been smashed.

Chapter 3

I STEPPED PAST the two young men working on the glass repairs and was greeted by our receptionist thrusting forward a handful of messages. Collette Lindman hadn't been with us long, and seemed overly eager at times, but had skills that I believed would come in handy one day.

"These are the important calls on the machine. And there's a married couple waiting in your office. They were supposed to see Johnny at eight but came early to beat the traffic and had a good run. I couldn't leave them in the waiting area with all that broken glass and without the door, it's been pretty breezy—"

Collette barely drew breath. First thing was the door, which she still hadn't explained.

"What happened? I didn't get a call."

"Oh, that? I didn't want to bother you. The security company phoned me at home and said our door had been smashed by vandals. Anyway, I rang the glass repairers, who came straight out. They said other businesses had breakages too. I hope it was the right thing to do. Before you ask, the door was shattered but unopened. No one got inside."

Given the amount of high-tech equipment in the place, that was one positive. It was difficult to take it personally when other businesses had been affected.

I stepped farther inside so the workmen couldn't hear. "Who exactly are the people in my office?"

"Mr. and Mrs. Finch. It's heartbreaking what they've been through. I didn't think you'd mind, under the circumstances."

Getting to the point was not Collette's strong suit. "That's fine. What are they here for?"

"A background check. I assured them the name 'Private' means their information stays that way, 'cause they seemed pretty nervous about confidentiality."

I felt a pounding in my head. "You did the right thing, Collette. The police will need the security footage from last night. We'll have good images of the door being hit and who did it."

She hesitated. "That's another thing I didn't want to bother you with yet."

"Tell me now."

"The computers are down. I mean, that might be why there isn't *actually* any vision of what happened overnight." She touched my arm. "Don't worry, I've called the technicians. They'll be here in a couple of hours."

Technicians would take far too long. Without computers we couldn't work.

"Get Darlene to come in early. If she can't fix the problem, she'll know who can."

I took stock of Monday morning so far: a favor for Jack Morgan, a smashed door, no computers, and an anxious couple in my office, all by seven a.m. Cal's birthday was shaping up to be one hell of a day.

Chapter 4

I COULD SEE the pair through the glass wall to my office. The man paced while his wife sat twisting the rings on her left hand.

I entered, introduced myself. The husband was late forties. The cut of his suit, along with the white shirt and pale blue tie, suggested middle management, or a small business operator.

"Gus. Finch." He shook my hand vigorously. "And this is my wife, Jennifer."

I greeted the woman, who wore a crimson silk shirt with a black skirt. She had to be at least ten years younger than Gus.

I took a seat at my desk. Finch sat next to his wife and held her hand.

"How can we help you?" I asked.

"We want a background check on someone. A potential employee."

With the computers down, I opened a journal and started taking notes as Finch began rattling off his requirements.

"You should check she is healthy, no mental illness,

has no criminal past, and that includes charges for DUI. I don't just mean convictions in case she got off on some technicality, I'm talking charges, any history of affairs..." He ticked off the list on his fingers. "Doesn't abuse drugs or alcohol, is clear of any sexually transmitted infections, has a mortgage to show she's committed to staying locally, and isn't in more than $200,000 debt."

This was clearly no ordinary pre-employment check, unless the job was for a child-care worker. The mortgage question threw me. Not many nannies in Sydney had paid off mortgages to the last $200K. Nannying jobs were something students or new graduates sought.

His wife added, "And we have to know she's a good mother." She squeezed her husband's hand, pale gray eyes boring into mine.

"Yes," Finch confirmed. "If we're going to trust her with our children." The inflection in his voice went up a notch at the end of this comment. He was lying, and he wasn't very good at it.

Today, I didn't really care to know why. "Agencies routinely do employment checks and they charge a lot less than us. To be honest, you'd be better going through one of them."

Finch slapped an envelope on the table. Hundred-dollar notes spilled out.

"We want *you*, not anyone else, to do the check. You guarantee confidentiality."

I didn't like people assuming I could be bought. Not everyone has a price. Whatever they wanted kept secret didn't sit right.

Maybe it was just my mood, but it didn't seem worth the hassle.

"That isn't how we do business, Mr. Finch. I'm afraid we can't help you."

I stood to usher them out the door.

They remained seated.

"Walk away and you'll regret it," the man said calmly. "You do the right thing by us and we can boost your business. Turn us away and I can guarantee Private will suffer."

Chapter 5

I SWUNG AROUND. This guy had picked the wrong day to tick me off. "I don't answer to threats." I took a step forward. "Or deal with liars."

Finch now stood and his wife quickly stepped between us. The guy was volatile and she knew it.

"I'm sorry," she interjected. "We're not being truthful. I—we—can't have children so we're looking at a surrogate."

Suddenly the couple's questions made sense. I relaxed a little.

Finch's bluster evaporated. "We didn't know if you'd agree to help us if we told you the truth. We have to know if she's likely to extort us for more money, and that we won't be dragged into legal fights down the track."

This was obviously difficult for them, but there was no point continuing the conversation. Commercial surrogacy was illegal in every Australian state. Carrying a baby out of kindness, known as altruistic surrogacy, *was* permitted but fraught with potential legal complications.

"We didn't mean to threaten you," she added. "It's just that there are many of us in the same situation and we could bring you a lot of business. Most of us would pay whatever it took to have our own children."

"We work closely with law enforcement," I explained, "and what you're proposing is illegal. You're obviously planning on paying for this baby. I'm sorry."

"Mr. Gisto." The woman touched my arm. "Do you have children?"

The question stopped me cold.

"I've had eight miscarriages and we had a daughter, Caroline..."

"Stillborn," the husband almost whispered.

She held my gaze. "We've tried everything natural, multiple rounds of IVF. And now my husband's too old at forty-eight to adopt. This isn't a whim. We can give a child a wonderful life."

It was impossible not to feel for what they had been through, but I was responsible for this business. I certainly couldn't let emotion sway my decision.

She paused. "Doctors have told us it isn't possible, so we are turning to a surrogate who says she just wants medical costs covered. That's all."

A stranger becoming pregnant and not wanting anything in return sounded risky.

"We could have gone to somewhere like India or Thailand, but that doesn't seem right."

Not to mention the practice was outlawed there now too, I thought. We moved back inside the office. "How did you hear about this woman?"

"Her name's Louise Simpson. She advertised on a surrogacy website. We just want to know if she's genuine."

A background check could only give her credit rating and criminal history. She would have to approve of them accessing her medical information, and I told them that.

"We understand. But this is our last chance," Mrs. Finch pleaded.

Despite reservations, I agreed to help.

Chapter 6

HE WAS WOKEN by burning in his wrist and forearm, and a deeper, bone-like pain in his right shoulder. He took a gasp and inhaled smoke, as sun peeked through the canopy directly above.

Disoriented, he struggled to sit up. Sweat dripped off him. He cradled his right arm, which provided some relief. The shoulder was out of its socket, down and forward. Then he remembered something had brushed him when he'd reached for the sensor device.

Peeling off the right glove, he saw the curled-up body of a spider. A centimeter long, black with a red patch on its back. A red-back.

The welt on his wrist was unlike anything he'd experienced before. Hospitals had antivenom, but it had to be administered quickly to be effective. That wasn't an option given the nearest hospital was two hours by road. He moved his other limbs and ankles. The shoulder had taken the brunt of the fall. It had to be put back in place. Then he could at least get to safety and take his chances with the bite.

The sound of a distant siren echoed in the valley. The

cabin had gone up in flames and the flames must have spread to surrounding bush. The "cleaners" should be long gone, but the area would be swarming with locals and emergency services volunteers, and the police.

He pulled himself to his feet and took some breaths. It was now or never. With all the strength he could muster, he ran and slammed his shoulder into a tree. Pain exploded through his shoulder and arm as he suppressed a scream. A few seconds later, it eased. The shoulder was in place but he could feel the lymph nodes under the arm were swollen and tender. The poison was spreading.

Using a spare shirt as a sling, he struggled to recall everything he'd ever learned about red-back spiders. No one had died from their bite in years. But if the toxin didn't kill, it could debilitate and affect nerves for up to a week.

Either way, the odds of making it through today were worse than even he'd imagined.

Chapter 7

WITH THE FINCHES sorted, I could concentrate on more pressing issues. Johnny Ishmah had begun trying the computers and backup systems, starting at reception.

The young investigator was completing a degree in criminal psychology. Brought up in a rough part of the western suburbs, his schoolmates included the son of a leading underworld figure. Those contacts had proved helpful more than once.

Dust swirled into the entrance as two men maneuvered a large pane of glass towards the door.

I asked Johnny what he had so far.

"I ran a virus scan on the entire system. Nothing showed up. The cameras didn't record because Collette's computer was shut down."

The video feed was accessed on her station. One of her tasks was to fast-forward through the footage each morning.

I turned to Collette, who was anxiously picking at bright red fingernails.

"Could you have accidentally shut it down instead of logging off last night?"

"No. I did what I do every night. Log off."

Whatever happened, the footage didn't exist.

Next to arrive was Darlene Cooper, her usual immaculate ponytail and wrinkle-free shirt and jeans replaced with a baggy top and crinkled pants. Nothing about today seemed routine.

"Sorry, boss. I came as quickly as I could."

I explained the situation and she told us not to turn anything on until she'd had a chance to update the virus library. Meanwhile, I went to find Mary in her office. She could start on the Finch job.

After filling her in, I suggested she use her phone until online access was restored. Instead, she stood, arms folded across her chest. The former military police officer and kickboxer was formidable at the best of times. The stance emphasized her biceps and was designed to intimidate. "You can get someone else."

Her reaction took me completely by surprise. My most experienced investigator and right hand in the business, Mary Clarke pulled more than her weight in the agency.

"Today's not started well. We need to function even more efficiently as a team. None of us gets to pick and choose cases. The others are tied up with the computers—"

She stood, arms still folded, like a bouncer blocking a nightclub entrance. "You don't need to remind me about teamwork."

That was true. Mary had put herself on the line many times, including for my safety. I closed the door so we could speak in private.

"Is there something going on I need to know about?"

"I don't want to be a part of this. Johnny can do it."

Darlene interrupted with a knock. "Thought you'd want to know. I updated the virus library and tracked the source to Collette's computer. Going through the log files, the system shut down at midnight."

"It was programmed to switch us off in the night?" I asked.

"Could have been in an e-mail attachment or a bogus web link. I'm still running diagnostics, so if you give me an hour, I'll do a full sweep of the backups too."

I wondered how long it would have taken if Darlene wasn't on the job. And what sort of thrill led people to design viruses which destroyed strangers' computers. Our business relied on confidentiality and with high-profile clients we needed to guarantee information security.

Right now, that was at risk.

"Can you double-check for spyware? We can't afford to have anyone access the systems."

Darlene looked from Mary to me, obviously sensing the tension. "On it."

I thanked Darlene and watched her leave.

Mary's finger was already poking my chest.

"You ever dare question my loyalty again, I'm out."

She pushed past me and slammed the door.

Chapter 8

MARY'S REACTION LEFT me stunned. She was the calm, measured one of the team.

I followed her into Kent Street, where she continued to weave through workers heading to their offices.

I just missed colliding with a man in a suit, eyes down on his phone. "What's really going on?"

She kept walking. "I won't be a party to buying and selling babies."

"What the hell is that supposed to mean? It's one background check, an hour's work, maybe two."

The pedestrian lights went green and we crossed, passing behind a taxi blocking the intersection. She stopped at the other side.

Frustration mounting, I tried to understand her problem. "What am I missing here?"

"You let Cal affect your judgment."

Mary could hit hard, and with precision.

We stood on the curb in silence as a wave of people swept past, juggling coffees and briefcases.

Mary spoke first. "I know today is his birthday."

We were on the corner outside the Queen Victoria

Building's Market Street entrance. A homeless man with a cardboard sign sat begging for spare change.

"I'm not seeing your point, Mary."

"This couple come to you with a sob story about wanting a child. Like they have a God-given right to breed."

So that was it. Mary had a problem with surrogacy.

A woman with twins in a double stroller approached. We stepped out of the way, beside a cart that sold snacks and magazines. I ordered two coffees and some fruit.

Mary wasn't finished. "What happens if the surrogate is carrying twins? These people target poverty-stricken women in Southeast Asia. They act like it's mail order, and they have every right to a refund if the result isn't to their liking—"

I'd never seen Mary so worked up about a single issue, and she hadn't even met the Finches to form an opinion of them.

"I get it. And it's tragic when that happens. Sometimes you have to trust your instincts and believe in the good in people. A woman is volunteering to become pregnant, for no profit. Isn't that between her and the Finches?"

"Do you really think a stranger will risk her health and her own family for nothing? This is baby trading no matter how you spin it."

"OK. You don't agree with what the couple is doing. But if we only accepted clients whose life choices we agreed with, we'd be out of business."

"Today you let emotion override reason. Once you start doing that, Private will suffer."

"Mary, this is one background check."

The vendor handed over the coffees. Mary took a cup, a concession of sorts towards peace.

"I just hope this one doesn't come back to bite us." She had the final say and headed back to the office.

I gave the other coffee, banana, and apple to the homeless man and looked up Eliza Moss's company on my smartphone. She worked just a block away.

I decided to make a detour there before facing any more complications at the office.

Chapter 9

SO FAR, I hadn't found much on Eric Moss, CEO of Contigo Valley. The name sounded more like an orchard than a development and training organization. From a quick search, again on my phone, there were no public scandals. Moss had never married.

I headed into the Market Street building, scanned the directory, and took the elevator to the thirty-fifth floor. Inside double doors to the left was a glass desk with a twenty-something woman poring over photo proofs.

Behind her was a giant canvas print of female rock climbers, giving those below a hand up.

The young woman looked up.

"I'm here to see Ms. Moss."

"You must be the private detective." She gave a megawatt smile as she came out from behind the desk. "Eliza's working in the conference room. At the end there. You can't miss it."

I moved to where she'd pointed. In the room, two women sat at one end of a long wooden table surrounded by computers and diaries. The one at the end spoke assertively into a phone.

"There is *no way* the budget can reach to ten! Eight thousand or we'll have to cancel." After a pause, she nodded and gave the thumbs-up to her colleague, who smiled. "Ramone, you are a genius. I'll make sure all our members know how incredible you are."

I wondered if Ramone would stay in business long if he dropped his prices so easily.

Off the phone, the pair high-fived and paused when they saw me.

I entered the room. "Craig Gisto. Jack Morgan said we should speak?"

The negotiator tapped the other lightly with a finger. "Can you give us a few minutes?"

"Of course." The colleague collected some paperwork and excused herself. "If you need anything…"

"We'll let you know." Eliza remained sitting and gestured for me to have a seat. There was no hint of despair or anxiety about her father.

"Thank you for coming. Jack speaks highly of you."

"He mentioned you were concerned about the whereabouts of your father."

She stroked the face of a diamond-encrusted watch on her left wrist. The only other piece of jewelry was an infinity ring on her right hand.

"He is supposed to have resigned—by e-mail—last Friday and hasn't been seen since. He would never leave Contigo. He turned it from a handful of search-and-rescue volunteers into a multibillion-dollar organization with an international reputation."

I studied her face as she spoke. Blonde, shoulder-length hair with a cowlick on one side of her fringe, pale green eyes, enough makeup to look natural but highlight her fine features.

The woman from the front desk interrupted us with

a document in hand. "I'm sorry, but the florist wants to know—Singapore orchids dyed blue or violet?"

Eliza Moss waved her in.

"Blue." Eliza initialed the page and clicked off her pen. "We recruit for over a thousand companies, working to increase women's representation at executive and board levels."

"Dyed orchids?" I asked.

"We're holding a major charity fund-raiser at the Park Hyatt tonight and I need to make sure it's a success. A lot of people are taking note of how we do."

Being the boss meant traveling a fine line between delegating and micromanaging. I wondered if she was an overly protective daughter or justified in raising the alarm.

"Is it possible your father simply went away for a few days? Wanted to have some time out after making a rash decision? Or maybe spend time in a new relationship?"

The list of possibilities was endless, especially with middle-aged men who had resources at their disposal.

"There's no woman." She was adamant. "He'd have told me. His work is everything. He even sleeps at the company base, near the Blue Mountains."

I sat forward. "Does he have any medical history or a condition that worries you if he goes without treatment? Physical or—"

"Why does everyone assume someone who commits themselves to work is either lonely, depressed, or suicidal?"

I suspected she was referring to comments made about her. "You've already flagged this as aberrant behavior, for him. We need to know his routine before pinpointing when and what changed."

"And how to find him. I'm sorry. This is just…He's very private. We both are."

In my business, *private* was a euphemism for keeping secrets. Eliza obviously idolized her father. If I started digging…

"I need to explain something before we start. In the course of an investigation, we may discover information you didn't expect. It could change your impression of him and possibly alter your relationship."

She thought for a moment and came back to the watch.

"He knows I'd worry, so do what you have to. Keep me completely informed. I'll pay whatever it takes. Just find him."

Chapter 10

"I'LL NEED MORE than we have so far," I said as there were further interruptions by staff. I wanted her complete focus. "Is there anywhere quieter we could speak? To clarify personal details."

"Here suits me better," she said, matter-of-factly. "I can handle any last-minute issues. Like I said, tonight's important."

I didn't have a choice. Over the next half hour, punctuated with queries about song lists and raffle items, I gained a picture of Eric Moss. An only child, focused and driven by the desire to excel in his field.

I was surprised to learn that Contigo Valley was a nonprofit organization. And tax exempt. There weren't many with turnovers in excess of hundreds of millions. Greenpeace was the only one that came to mind.

Funded by donations, loans, and occasional government grants, Contigo raised revenue by developing and selling new trauma devices, safety equipment, and retrieval vehicles. They were awarded large supply contracts both in Australia and overseas.

"Bushfires, tsunamis, floods, landslides, man-made

disasters. My father increased survival rates for victims and emergency service workers. A device for giving life-saving fluids to injured soldiers has changed protocols in emergency departments and the combat field. Contigo even trains soldiers from China and the USA."

I could see why Jack Morgan, a former US marine, had invested in the company. It was a cause close to his heart. Still, I needed more about Eric Moss the man.

According to Eliza he was fit aside from a few extra kilos, didn't smoke or drink, and only reluctantly attended work functions. He avoided the media, leaving that to the chairman of Contigo's board, Sir Lang Gillies. It sounded as if Moss enjoyed his own company more than other people's. At fifty-eight, he was a workaholic.

"Any conflicts with colleagues or subordinates?"

"Only with Lang Gillies. Dad's been feeding his ego for decades. The old man spends his life on company junkets, in the social pages, collecting awards for work Dad did."

"Why keep someone like Gillies on?"

"He has influential friends and Dad prefers life out of the spotlight."

That made sense. Sir Lang and his third wife were regulars on Sydney's social circuit. Lang was politically connected, having made his money as a property developer in the most corrupt period in the state government's history.

I took notes. "So Gillies received the resignation e-mail on Friday?" Moss's departure should have been big news in the business community.

Eliza's eyes shone with a new intensity.

"The old man is lying. Lang told me Dad felt like a change. And how he'd wished Dad well."

"You don't think that's what happened?"

"No way. Dad would never have left, let alone like

that. Besides, Lang knows that without Dad the organization would fail. And..." She poked the table with her index finger. "No one else has seen the resignation e-mail."

I agreed that Gillies's disinterest in Moss's plans was questionable.

The receptionist interrupted again, this time for a call. Eliza held out her hand for the phone and covered the mouthpiece.

"I've put together a list of places Dad goes, where and when he was born, where he lived, anything that might help."

As she took the call, I flicked through the two-page document. It made Moss sound like a saint.

"No trappings of wealth despite the potential to command millions in salary." I read further. "Drives an eight-year-old Toyota four-wheel drive."

Eliza put the phone on the table with a thump. "Dad has never gone more than a few hours without calling back. No matter where he is. If he's on a training exercise, he has a satellite phone with him." She bent lower to lock eyes with me. "Something's really wrong."

Clomping heels rapidly approached. Another young woman tapped a clipboard and Eliza nodded.

"I'd appreciate if you keep me informed, regularly. Is that all?"

I was taken aback by the curt end to our conversation. She'd just raised the issue of foul play involving her father then closed off any chance of further discussion. As I stood and pushed my chair back in, she remained seated. A queen holding court with minions at her disposal.

"Thank you, Mr. Gisto," she said, shaking my hand.

I was unceremoniously dismissed.

Chapter 11

BACK AT THE office, Darlene had managed to restore all computer function. The virus had been isolated to the reception computer, which was lucky in the grand scheme. The new glass was fitted and Collette had cleaned the foyer. It was as if the morning's distractions had never happened.

I found Johnny in his office. The check on Louise Simpson was straightforward. An insurance company was stalling on compensation for an industrial accident that killed her husband, Vincent, eight months ago. She had two kids and lived modestly in Killara, in a home with a mortgage currently paid by her late husband's parents. She was a cleanskin, without even a parking ticket to her name.

My one concern was the group where Louise Simpson advertised.

"What about the surrogacy site the Finches found her on?"

Johnny flicked through some papers. "It has a firewall up, so I couldn't find out who runs it. If you want me to, I can, but it'll take more time."

"There must be legitimate organizations you can run it by."

Johnny was already ahead. "I contacted the two best-known surrogacy groups, whose reps work with state governments on clarifying the laws on overseas surrogacy that at the moment differ in every state. They both vouched for the content and advice on the site." He pulled it up on his 24-inch screen.

"Apparently it's the only one that offers to connect people with altruistic surrogates in this country. It also connects couples to agencies overseas that deal in commercial pregnancies and navigate visas, birth certificates, documentation of legal parents, and other bureaucratic nightmares. From what I can see, the hopeful parents are pretty vulnerable every step in the process."

I wondered if the Finches had been burned overseas, which was why they were turning to a local surrogate. Either way, it didn't matter. Johnny could send through the information he'd collected and invoice the Finches. We need have nothing more to do with them or their life choices.

I was relieved. At least something today had been straightforward. I needed Mary on the Moss case right away. We'd start at Contigo's city office in Martin Place. If Lang Gillies had lied about the resignation, Eric Moss's disappearance had just become our top priority.

Chapter 12

THE WALK TO Martin Place was quick and silent. On our way to the MLC Centre, Mary stopped short of the revolving door and looked back at a memorial to the victims of the 2014 siege.

She had been directly across at the Channel Seven studios interviewing a client, an hour before the gunman entered the café.

"You couldn't have changed the outcome," I said, "if that's what you're thinking."

She shrugged and pushed through the door.

Contigo Valley's central office was on the sixty-fourth floor of prime Sydney real estate. Prominent legal chambers, international finance corporations, a Russian bank, and the US Consulate all shared space in the building. It was a stone's throw from State Parliament as well.

We were greeted at reception by Eric Moss's personal assistant. In his mid-twenties, Oliver Driscoll was around 170 centimeters with hair shorter at the sides than on top and dark-rimmed glasses. He quickly led us to an outer office with an interconnecting door.

"This is where we work." He opened double doors

into a larger room. A white shag-pile rug filled some of the void between a nondescript desk and sofa. The desk was conspicuously clear apart from a closed A4 portfolio diary in its center.

"How long have you worked with Mr. Moss?" I asked.

"Two years." He seemed focused on the piece of rug. "I can't believe he just walked out. Without telling me."

"Have you cleared out his things or is this how Mr. Moss likes to keep it?"

"Eric's fastidious. He writes everything in the diary. Calls, meetings, functions. I don't get why he'd ever leave it behind."

Mary wandered around the room. "Does he have a problem with computers or smartphone calendars?"

"He's just old-school and likes to have everything written down."

Mary wondered, "Doesn't that reduce efficiency?"

"In the afternoons I fill in his upcoming appointments. If he's at the base, I phone him and he writes it all down. He always has it with him."

I moved around to the desk. "May I?"

"Sure."

I opened the diary. It had functions organized for the next six months. Fund-raisers, training courses, and a list of everyone he called. From the volume of calls listed each day, Moss seemed averse to e-mails as well, yet that was how he'd chosen to resign.

The assistant hovered. "If Eliza is asking you to help, she must be worried too."

"Too?" I looked across at Driscoll.

"Something stinks. Eric would never walk away. This was his life, and we were like family. He'd work from six in the morning until midnight. Even slept on the fold-out couch when he was in town." Driscoll moved to the other door and opened it. "This is his bathroom."

A toothbrush and razor were still in place in the shower recess.

Mary quietly checked out the bookshelf then tried to open a credenza beneath the desk. It was locked.

"Do you have a key?" she asked.

"No. Eric is the only one with that. Why would he keep an office key and leave his personal belongings? None of this makes sense." Driscoll sat on the sofa, face in his hands. I had to wonder about how close the assistant was to his boss.

"Did Eric have problems or disagreements with any of the staff?"

Driscoll shook his head. "He gets on with everyone, knows everyone's names. Even kept paying one woman who had cancer and ran out of sick leave."

He smoothed his skinny trousers. "Eric believes you can tell a man's character by the way he treats people who can't further his career."

It sounded as if Moss and his daughter shared philosophies.

I sat beside him.

"How are the staff taking the news?"

"Donors are panicking, groups are canceling training camps...It's exactly what Eric wouldn't want to happen. And none of us wants to work for—"

"Driscoll!" a voice snapped.

The assistant sat to attention. "Quick, hide Eric's diary," he whispered.

Mary dropped it to the floor and pushed it under the desk with her feet.

Chapter 13

I RECOGNIZED THE distinctive cravat and striped jacket from the social pages. Sir Lang Gillies, chairman of Contigo's board.

"You should have told me Eliza sent visitors." He made no attempt to hide his disdain.

"Craig Gisto, Private Sydney, and this is Mary—"

"I know who you are and you have been misled." He turned and limped on what looked like a bad hip. Mary and I followed with the assistant close behind.

"Mr. Moss's daughter has asked us to find her father. If you know where he might be—"

"The Bahamas, Noumea? Have you tried Tasmania, the Midlands?" He waved arthritic fingers in the air. "He always talked about going there for a holiday."

I stepped into line with him, past a couple of offices with staff answering phones.

I decided to be noncombative in my approach, despite the obvious animosity towards us. "We understand the timing and manner of his resignation was surprising."

"How so? The man was free to leave without notice. He's no doubt taken up a more lucrative offer. And before you ask, it wasn't my place to question him. I didn't care to know."

"How many years was he with Contigo?"

"I've been on the board for twenty-seven years. So a couple more than that. We built this organization into what it is today..."

If that was the case, it was unusual; no golden hand-shake, no farewell, no drinks. Not even a media release.

"...into a world-class research and development center."

We moved into an office. Mahogany bookshelves housed rows of photos, reaffirming Sir Lang's importance to the world. Framed images of him with prime ministers, celebrities, and a US president.

Gillies made sure we noticed. "Impressive," I said for his benefit as he plonked himself into a high-back leather chair behind a desk the queen would have been proud to own. The assistant and Mary lingered in the doorway.

"Is there any other reason you can think of that might have prompted Eric Moss to change jobs so suddenly? I mean, a quarter of a century with no changes, then," I snapped my fingers, "he's gone in a flash. Without telling the people he's closest to."

Gillies opened the financial newspaper on his desk and looked up, as if bored by our presence.

"I cannot discuss Moss's work with you due to com-mercial confidentiality." He reached into a drawer and pulled out some glossy brochures. "These should tell you all you need to know about what we do. Now, I have an organization to run. Oliver will show you out."

I took the promotional material and entered the cor-ridor.

"And, Oliver, bring me Eric's diary. I'll be personally handling all his appointments and calls."

"I'll have to search for it, Sir Lang." The assistant seemed defeated. "Is there anything else?"

"There'll be significant restructuring in this office. Let the staff know that anyone breaching confidentiality by speaking to these people will be the first to go."

Gillies really ticked me off. He was beyond arrogant. Anyone with a heart would want to make sure Eliza's concerns were allayed.

Unless he had something to hide.

Chapter 14

I WASN'T ABOUT to be railroaded by Lang Gillies. I popped my head inside his door and asked if he objected to my using the bathroom on the way out. He grunted, but could hardly refuse.

Mary seized the opportunity to distract the old man by pointing to a photo of him in military uniform proudly displayed on his desk. I stepped back into the corridor and left her standing at ease by the picture, hands clasped behind her back.

"Where did you serve, sir?"

The old soldier couldn't resist the urge to brag. And Mary could keep him talking with her knowledge and experiences in the military. It bought me a few minutes with Oliver.

"If Eric's in some sort of trouble, maybe I can help," he volunteered.

Thankfully, Gillies's threat hadn't intimidated the man who worked closest with Moss.

"Any idea what sort of trouble Eric could be in?"

Oliver scratched his neck. "The guy's a monk. Doesn't drink, smoke, gamble, take drugs, or date. It's offensive the way Gillies's acting like he didn't ever exist. He's *got* to know where Eric went."

This could be the only opportunity I had to ask. "Were you two having an intimate relationship?"

The assistant smirked. "You think Eric and I were an item? God, no, he's way too serious for me. Besides, he was married to this place. From what I can tell, he wasn't interested in either sex. It was like he was asexual."

I asked Driscoll if he could tell me who looked after the accounts.

He hurried back to his office and wrote down the name of the chief financial officer whom Moss dealt with. "She's fond of Eric and due to retire in a few months. She won't have much to lose by talking to you."

He collected Moss's diary. The information was only in hard copy, nothing electronic. Once Gillies got it, any leads would be kept from us.

"Any chance I can get a quick look before you hand that over?"

"Better than that." He glanced around to ensure no one was in earshot. "I'll photocopy it first." He held the diary to his chest.

I couldn't walk out with papers now and it was unlikely I'd ever be allowed back in.

"Can you courier the copies to our office?"

"I can't see me getting away until late. Maybe I can drop them off before I check in with Eliza."

"How well do you know Miss Moss?" I asked.

"Sometimes when we were working late, Eliza would bring dinner and eat with us. They're both really good people."

We left the office with the diary still in Oliver's hands.

As he closed the door behind us the assistant said, "Lang Gillies may come across as a buffoon but he has a lot of powerful friends. You'd never want to cross the vindictive SOB."

Chapter 15

FROM THE FOYER, I called the financial officer's number.

Renee Campbell listened as I introduced myself and explained that there were concerns about Eric Moss's whereabouts.

Oliver Driscoll, however, had beaten me to it.

She agreed to meet us in Martin Place in five minutes and suggested a café that made great flat whites.

As the coffees arrived, a small woman in her late sixties approached. She had short, wispy gray hair and wore a pink crocheted vest over a navy skivvy and skirt.

She took a seat and thanked us for meeting her.

"I can't believe he's gone."

"It sounds like his leaving shocked almost everyone. Do you have any idea where he went?"

She stared at the coffee. "No. I couldn't believe it when I heard he'd resigned. We were supposed to meet that afternoon."

"Was there a problem with accounts?"

She wrapped both hands around the cup and took a sip before answering.

"Not really. I couldn't locate the receipts for a table at a charity ball. I happened to mention it to Eric in passing. He said he had them in his office and told me to come at four o'clock the next day. He's so lovely; he put half an hour aside so we could catch up over a cuppa."

Mary glanced at me.

"How much were the tickets for?"

"Ten thousand dollars. It's like petty cash. Last year we turned over four hundred and seventy million dollars from donations and revenue."

I downed my drink and asked if Moss had much to do with the finances.

"Not routinely. Although he was adamant he handle some of the accounts himself, which he kept locked in a safe in his office."

"Didn't that seem odd to you? No checks and balances?"

"Not for us. Some of Contigo's contracts deal with defense departments and international governments. They involve issues of national security. Oh, and Eric kept watch over Sir Lang's expenses. The old man takes his wife on every imaginable junket, first class all the way, claiming he's promoting the organization around the world."

Donors may not be thrilled about all the first-class travel in a nonprofit organization. I asked if Moss ever confronted Gillies about the spending.

"No, but he kept his own record. It was easier to run the place efficiently without Sir Lang around to interfere. Gillies is a figurehead but he does bring donations in through his rich cronies."

I wanted to know about Moss's salary package and what sort of payout he would receive after that many years of service. It was all conjecture at this stage but I had to consider the common reasons for sudden resignation. If he took a better offer, that salary could narrow the companies who could afford him.

"Could Eric have been headhunted by another company?"

Renee Campbell scoffed. "You obviously don't know the man. Money means little to him. He costs Contigo about forty thousand dollars a year and doesn't even receive it."

"In expenses?"

"No," the older woman chortled. "That was supposed to be his salary. He has every cent of it put into a trust for Eliza. She'll have access to it on her fortieth birthday, or her father's death. Whichever comes first."

It sounded like an odd arrangement. I was curious. "How much is in it now?"

"Due to investments, it's around one and a half million, I believe."

I had to wonder about Eliza now. Family members had killed for a lot less. The devoted daughter could have been an act. If Moss had been killed, and I could prove it, she was suddenly a lot wealthier.

Chapter 16

BACK AT THE office, Mary went over the Contigo brochures.

It was all we had until we got hold of the diary photocopies. The locked cabinet in Moss's office could answer a lot of questions. That was, if Moss or Gillies hadn't emptied it first.

As far as I was concerned, the circumstances of Moss leaving were suspicious. Lang Gillies was determined to make sure our access to all of Contigo's records was blocked. There had to be something significant in the organization's books. Why else would Moss disappear after a minor discrepancy was discovered? Were the two events even related?

I decided to look into Contigo's contracts. The website looked like it promoted an exclusive resort. Situated on thirty-five hectares just west of the Blue Mountains, it could have been a stunning rural retreat. There was little practical information apart from mention of training facilities for rescue workers, emergency retrieval operations, and disaster simulations.

I ran a check on Lang Gillies first. Gut instinct said

he was hiding something. On top of that, he was the last person known to have seen Eric Moss.

Gillies held dual UK and Australian citizenships and was knighted two years earlier for a life of service to the community. Prior to that, he used the title "Dr." after being awarded an honorary doctorate in humanities from the University of Wollongong. The son of a High Court judge, he joined the air force and flew cargo planes. Interestingly, there was no record of him serving in Vietnam, despite his *Who's Who* entry citing him as a pilot during the war.

My guess was that his father's connections had kept him far away from conflict zones. Marrying the daughter of the state's longest-serving governor wouldn't have hurt either.

From what I could gather, Lang started a cargo business in the 1970s then found his way onto the boards of charitable organizations. Ones his father-in-law happened to be patron of. He joined Contigo's board twenty-seven years ago and had benefited ever since.

And Gillies had not only picked up a knighthood but also collected an honorary doctorate on the back of Moss's work.

From what Oliver Driscoll had said, Moss was private and married to his job and wanted little remuneration or acknowledgement. The men couldn't have been more different.

I wondered how Gillies's expense account sat with someone like Moss. The CEO had to be independently wealthy to sacrifice a salary for all those years. More than that, he had to be very committed to the work they did there. I couldn't help suspecting he'd had a falling-out with Gillies. The old man certainly wasn't mourning Contigo's sudden loss.

And then there were the secret contracts and accounts in Moss's safe. What could be so confidential that no one else in the organization was permitted to know about it?

Chapter 17

I CALLED JACK Morgan and left a message for him to ring me, then I went to check on the rest of the team. Darlene was extracting DNA from a series of forensic rape kits for the police. It was a service I wanted Private to supply for free as the police laboratories were often backlogged for more than six months at a time.

Johnny was involved with the case of a trade union official accused of using work funds for brothel visits. A few of the credit card receipts resembled the official's. Others were nothing like it. He was scanning the signatures of all the union executives and superimposing handwriting to identify potential suspects.

I stopped in on Mary, who had the Contigo brochures open across her desk.

"Sir Lang Gillies made my flesh crawl," she said. "No wonder he's so close to the power brokers in both political parties."

I turned around a chair and straddled it. "What have you got?"

"I've been looking into his family-owned companies.

He and his wife are silent partners in a series of shops in Circular Quay with Alby Slade."

That made Gillies a lot more powerful than I'd imagined. Slade was one of the "silent puppeteers" behind a number of politicians. Rumor had it he was responsible for deposing two state premiers who dared question the legality of his business dealings.

"Slade's been up before the Integrity Commission and the Independent Commission against Corruption; he's alleged to have threatened investigative journalists among others." Mary added, "And Gillies is in business with him."

"Maybe Moss thought the Slade business would tarnish Contigo."

Mary sat back, hands clasped behind her head. "The work Moss did was top-notch." She swung a notepad around. "These are some of the things his team has produced."

One was a device that injected fluids directly into bone.

"This lifesaving device can be used by soldiers in the field. It goes into the shoulder or shin, and can deliver liters of fluids, like plasma, in minutes. They've been snapped up by armies from just about every nation. Victorian paramedics and hospitals are trialing them next month."

Sales like that were lucrative. "Does Contigo own the patent?"

"Yep. Its returns have already paid off bank loans used to develop it."

Moss's work wasn't limited to small items. His team modified the capacity of aerial-firefighting helicopters, credited with saving thousands of houses in bushfires over the last decade.

"Flame-retardant clothing, emergency retrieval training. They even came up with a new foam formula for the helicopters to dump on chemical fires."

Mary was justifiably impressed.

"Any idea what those secret contracts were about?"

She took back her notes. "Contigo was contracted to work with the government on something highly secret. A buddy in Defense said it was so secret, rumors were circulating about everything from digestible drones to transformer tanks. He seemed to think it involved counterterrorism."

"How much was the contract worth?"

"My contact thinks it had to be over eighty million."

I blew out a whistle. "That's a lot of money to keep track of in a paper ledger."

"Another source, at the fraud squad, says they've been asked to investigate a number of not-for-profit organizations."

"Contigo Valley's on their list?"

"Yep, but they're being pressured to hold off on that one. Someone in the government doesn't want them investigated. They're tendering for a number of federal defense contracts. Any hint of scandal will affect Contigo's chances."

"And boost any rival's." I stood up and stretched my back. "Do you know how they got on the fraud squad's radar?"

"You'll love this. An anonymous caller phoned their office."

We needed to find out who had reason to want Moss out of the picture. With government subterfuge, this case just got a lot more complicated.

Chapter 18

I STOOD AND turned the chair back around. Mary cleared her throat.

"Craig, about this morning—"

I raised a hand. "You don't have to—"

"No, I was way out of line."

She got no further as Collette burst in, red-faced. "You two need to see this!"

We moved quickly into the conference room and Collette turned on the curved screen.

A news bulletin showed crime-scene tape around a suburban home. A woman had been brutally murdered in Killara.

A banner across the bottom read Fiddens Wharf Road. "It's the same street as Louise Simpson," Collette said.

The potential surrogate for the Finches. I noticed Mary's body tense.

Johnny and Darlene joined us as an image of a blue

Toyota Corolla in a carport appeared. Its number plate was pixelated.

My heart began to pound as I asked Johnny what car Louise Simpson drove.

Johnny's eyes fixed on the screen. "That exact make and model."

Chapter 19

THE YOUNG REPORTER pressed her earpiece and relayed what she knew. "We understand that at approximately four-twenty this afternoon, a woman's body was found inside the home by an elderly neighbor. This gentleman noticed the front door was wide open. That's when he made the shocking discovery."

The network's "serious" news anchor, Bruce Davitt, pushed for details. "Has the man been able to help police piece together what happened?"

"Bruce, ambulance officers are on the scene and we understand they're treating the neighbor for shock. Police are standing by to interview him."

"Do we know anything about the victim or how she died?"

"As yet, the victim's name hasn't been released but I can tell you that homicide detectives have arrived."

On her laptop, Darlene had pulled up the Google street images of Louise's address. My heart sank. The reporter was across and down the road, but the house looked similar to the one on Darlene's screen.

Bruce Davitt announced that residents in the suburb

of Killara were shocked at the gruesome discovery. As we watched people walking dogs recoil with predictable horror at the mention of murder in their neighborhood, I phoned Deputy Commissioner Brett Thorogood.

His phone went straight to voice mail. I asked him to ring me urgently about the Killara homicide victim. Johnny, meanwhile, tried to reach the Finches. His olive skin blanched when he heard a prerecorded announcement. The number was not connected.

"I e-mailed them a couple of hours ago with the information," he said. "It had the Killara address in the report." He tried e-mailing again. This time his message bounced straight back.

My phone rang. It was Brett Thorogood.

He immediately confirmed the dead woman's name.

Louise Grace Simpson.

Chapter 20

TWENTY MINUTES LATER, Darlene and I were at the scene. Thanks to Private's arrangement with the police to share resources, we were allowed in.

Darlene donned plastic overalls and headed in first with her collection kit. I assessed the scene from the outside. The front yard contained potted native plants. A wooden carport housed the Corolla. Around the side of the house, a bathroom window was slightly ajar. The soil was damp but there were no footprints or signs of entry.

The backyard was larger, with a glassed-in veranda. A magnetic board on an easel stood beside a small plastic table and chairs.

My throat tightened. Two innocent children were now orphans. And my decision this morning may have gotten their mother killed.

Mary had been right. We should screen clients before working for them.

Through a line of pines, I could make out a golf club's fairway. Squeezing through gaps in the trees, I reached the back fence. On the right-hand corner, on a hinged gate, were dark smears. Blood.

The killer had escaped over the back fence. Someone on the golf course could have seen him. I called Johnny to find out who could have been playing those holes in the hours before the body was found.

I photographed the area with my phone. Darlene should swab here when she'd finished. With crime scene officers still inside the house, I told the constable standing guard by the car not to let anyone traipse through the yard. All we needed was for inexperienced officers to tread all over what could be the only evidence to help find the killer.

I pulled shoe covers on and entered through the front door. The lock was intact, with no signs of forced entry. In the corridor a hole had been knocked through the plasterboard wall with blood spatters on the floor. Dark red smears marked the way to the lounge room. It looked like the victim had been hit or shoved into the wall and had bled onto the floor, then been dragged farther inside.

The first room on the right contained a neatly made double bed with a floral bedspread. A pine tallboy held silver-framed family photos. Above the bed hung a large wedding photo of the couple gazing into each other's eyes at the beach. The wardrobe doors were open. Female clothes filled only half the space.

The horror had unfolded in the kitchen. The body was slumped forward in a chair. Long brown hair was matted with blood.

The stench in the room was one I'd inhaled too many times. Body odor almost masked the metallic aroma of blood. I wished we could bottle it. Every individual left a unique and identifiable scent at a scene.

Dr. Rex King greeted me. I was grateful that a pathologist friendly to us was in attendance. Rex had no problem sharing the work and respected Darlene's abilities. There would be no pissing contest between organizations here.

"Cause of death looks like a knife wound to the lower abdomen," he said. "She took a beating first."

A female detective stood, hands on hips, observing. She introduced herself as Detective Constable Kristen Massey.

I needed to know. "Where are the kids?"

"How'd you know she had any?" Detective Massey asked.

"She had a four-year-old girl and a three-year-old boy. Husband died in a work accident about six months ago."

"Then, Mr. Gisto, you know almost as much as us. They're still in day care. If we can't locate a relative, they'll spend tonight in the care of the state."

Darlene looked up at me. "No signs of a break-in. She either knew the killer or unsuspectingly opened the door."

The detective said, "So far, there's no sign of robbery. Her purse and phone are still on the lounge."

A microwave sterilizer with upturned baby bottles sat on the bench. It seemed odd to me she would be sterilizing bottles for a toddler and preschooler.

Rex King stepped back. "I suspect she was systematically beaten before being stabbed—once. I'll need to check on the autopsy table but the blade appears to have passed downward through the lower abdomen."

Darlene and the forensic technician took more photos of the wound, as I confirmed, "No signs of sexual assault, then?"

Rex nodded. "From the position and angle of the blade entry," he examined the stab wound more closely, "it's likely our victim suffered a perforated uterus."

The words hit like a mallet to my chest.

Chapter 21

"WHAT THE HELL do you think *you're* doing?"

I turned to face Local Area Command Detective Mark Talbot. My cousin and I had a torturous history but I thought we'd made peace last year.

"Dr. King, if these people are disturbing the scene, I'll—"

"The opposite. They're proving invaluable. Darlene's helping and we'll get faster turnaround if she can put the samples through Private's lab."

Detective Massey added, "Mr. Gisto knows the background."

My cousin surveyed the scene and I caught a glimpse of repulsion on his face at the state of the body.

The crime scene technician was now photographing the kitchen. The small space was becoming more crowded by the minute.

Mark bent down to view the body. "She's wearing a wedding ring on her left hand. I was told she was a single mother."

"Widow," I added. "Kids are in day care apparently."

Mark glanced around the room. "You work all that out gawking at a body?"

He was in one of his moods. Even the other detective seemed wary of him. He turned his attention to Rex King.

"Doc, what do you know so far?"

Rex nudged half-glasses farther up his nose with the back of his wrist.

"She sustained a head injury to the frontal region and nose, and there is bruising around her neck. It looks like she was grabbed and slammed into something solid."

"Like a wall." I pointed to the hole in the hallway.

"And then she was dragged in here," Mark commented.

"Tied to a chair and beaten," Rex explained. "I can't say whether she was conscious or not, but she was alive when the knife penetrated her lower abdomen. Lividity and body temperature put time of death between one and three hours ago."

Mark checked his watch. "That makes death somewhere between one-thirty and three-thirty." He turned to face me and sighed. "Why are you here?"

With an index finger theatrically tapping his chin, he delivered his best. "Oh no, don't tell me. She's one of your conquests."

Anger surged through my veins. I wanted to ram the smirk on his face right to the back of his head.

Darlene was quickly between us. "For God's sake. Are you still going on about Becky marrying Craig? This is about *Louise Simpson*, not you."

Mark stood intimidatingly close to Darlene. "I can get you kicked out of here in a flash," he snapped. "This is between Craig and me."

I had no idea what had inflamed him again. "What's

your problem? A woman has been murdered and you are attacking *me* over old history."

"Are you going to tell me how you knew the victim?"

I took a slow breath and explained about Gus and Jennifer Finch. I thought I could see a faint smile appear on Mark's lips, then just as quickly disappear.

"I see." Mark rocked on his heels. "You provided two strangers with intimate details of our victim—for payment, of course—hours before she was found brutally murdered. And now you can't tell us where to locate these people." He moved even closer. "Hope you get good job satisfaction."

I lunged at him and Darlene was on her feet again, the other detective blocking us. Mark raised his hands in the air as if surrendering.

"He's not worth it, Craig. He wants you to hit him. Right here, in front of witnesses," Darlene warned.

I swallowed back the rising bile. Darlene was right. Mark would love nothing more than to report I'd started a fight at a crime scene so we'd never be allowed on one again. Finding Louise's killer had to be our priority.

Rex spoke calmly. "Detective, a knife is missing from the set."

A magnetic strip attached to tiles on the wall above the stove contained a series of knives increasing in size. There was a space between the first and third.

That meant the killer may not have planned to murder Louise. Maybe she refused to be their surrogate and things turned sour.

"Right, that place of yours is filmed 24/7. I want the video footage of the couple you saw this morning."

I sighed. This was going to sound like we had no intention of cooperating.

"The computers went down overnight and we have no vision from midnight until after the couple had gone."

Mark nodded. "That's the way you're playing this?"

"Look, we came here to help with the investigation."

"Or to cover your butt." He stepped menacingly close. "You better get a good lawyer, cuz. You're facing charges. Conspiracy to commit murder."

Chapter 22

A WOMAN'S SCREAM stopped everyone. It was primal, guttural.

Mark and Kristen Massey headed for the open front door. I stayed close behind.

The female detective stopped the woman, who was in her late twenties. "Ma'am, this is a crime scene. I'm afraid you'll have to—"

"My baby! Where's my baby?"

Mark flicked me a look as if I might know what she was talking about. I remembered the microwave sterilizer and my heart drilled.

A young constable was trying to restrain the woman. "Ma'am, you can't be here."

She buckled to her knees. "Zoe needs me. She's just a baby."

"Wait!" I pushed through as the woman continued shouting for someone to listen to her.

I knelt down with her. "Was Louise minding your child?"

The woman dug her fingers into my arms. "Zoe, she's eight weeks old." Her voice became higher-pitched.

"Why won't anyone let me see her?" She locked eyes with mine. "I just need to get my baby."

"Something's happened to Louise." I spoke calmly, and slowly released her grip. "We didn't know she had Zoe with her."

Kristen Massey put her arms around the mother while Mark and I raced back inside.

We checked cupboards, drawers, a toy trunk, even the washing machine in case Louise had hidden the child to protect her. The search proved futile.

The baby was gone.

Chapter 23

MARK AND I moved outside, now united in our task. The mother was sitting on the brick wall, shaking. She still had the wide-eyed look of hope when we returned.

Her name was Courtney Ruffalo, Detective Constable Massey explained. Louise had been babysitting once a week for three weeks. "To give her a break. Her husband's a fly-in, fly-out miner in Queensland. He isn't due back until Friday night."

Courtney nodded, holding back tears. "Is my baby all right?"

Mark said, "Is there anyone else who might have picked her up for you?"

There was no proof Zoe had been in the house when the murder took place. Then again, anyone who routinely collected the child would have known to take the sterilizer and bottles too.

"Geoff's away. I have a sister. She works at Westmead Hospital and doesn't finish until after three."

That was at least forty minutes away by car.

We had to consider the possibility that Louise had been killed in order to abduct Zoe.

It could have been unrelated to the Finches' visit. But I had to face reality. The Finches may have killed Louise for the baby.

Mark pulled me aside. "We'll put out a statewide alert for the missing child. I'll let the powers know to prepare a media release. We'll need a photo and description of what the child was wearing."

Courtney Ruffalo had a photo on her phone, taken that morning. Zoe had on a pink cotton jumpsuit with a yellow-and-white flower embroidered on the chest.

Detective Constable Massey spoke quietly to me as I passed her the phone with the baby's image.

"Mark was out of line but he's damn good at his job. He's…" She glanced around to make sure no one else heard. "Just going through a rough time. I'm trying to cut him some slack."

Today was no joy ride for any of us. Even so, nothing matched what Louise Simpson had been subjected to. "Are you making excuses for him?"

"No. But he just found out the woman he was seeing was two-timing him. They were about to move in together."

At least that explained the change in my cousin's attitude. He'd never taken rejection or betrayal well. Seeing me now was like ripping the scab off a deep and painful wound.

"Priority for all of us is finding the child and Louise's killer," I stressed.

"Let's hope Zoe's still alive," she added, out of the mother's earshot.

We needed to get a break quickly. The more time that passed, the less chance we had of finding baby Zoe—alive or dead.

Chapter 24

I RANG TO let Mary and Johnny know about the missing baby.

Right now they needed to utilize every possible resource, anything that could give us a lead on the Finches, or the Ruffalo family.

Meanwhile, Darlene began photographing and swabbing the back fence.

Mark and I jumped to the neighbor's side and tried to follow the trail. From what we could tell, the killer had Louise's blood on his torso. In a hole, stuffed beneath some rocks, was a blood-stained gray hoodie. Generic Target brand. One of thousands sold around the country.

We followed the trampled grass until it stopped a few houses down. On the other side of the fence was a red smear. The killer had climbed over the fence here, somehow carrying the baby.

"I'll get the uniforms to canvass the street," Mark said, frustrated the trail was lost.

I rang Darlene and told her about the hoodie and the extra fence marks. She'd get onto them as soon as she'd finished in the Simpson yard.

An elderly woman peered through the back screen door.

"Excuse me, ma'am." Mark was in full professional mode, ID in hand. "Can we have a word with you?"

The slippered woman shuffled down the back path and stopped at a gate that opened onto the course.

Mark explained that there'd been an incident a few houses down and asked if she'd seen anyone in her yard or noticed any damage to windows or doors.

She gripped the top of her blouse and looked back at the house, explaining she'd been to bingo at the local club and only been home half an hour. Everything was as she left it.

"My children complain about me living so close to the golf course, but this has been my home for over forty years."

Cutting short her conversation, Mark gave her his card and asked her to call him if she remembered seeing anyone or anything out of place.

She toddled back to the house, muttering something about what the world was coming to. We entered through the gate and examined the yard. On the concrete drive was a dark crescent-shaped mark. It could have been blood from the killer's shoe.

Mark ordered one of the officers to cordon off the yard.

"This could be how our killer escaped," he said. "We need to test the stain for blood."

We walked along the street to the Simpson house. Crowds had now gathered outside the crime scene perimeter.

DC Massey had established that Louise's parents were touring the Northern Territory in a Winnebago. Her brother lived two hours north, outside Newcastle. He was trying to call the parents, who could be out of phone range.

"What about the children?" I asked.

"The brother's driving down to get them. Day-care staff will stay until he gets there."

"Zoe's father?"

"Flying back, gets in at eight."

I checked my watch. If Louise's parents didn't answer their messages or get to somewhere with phone service, they'd be hearing about their daughter's death on the nightly news.

Vans from all the major stations now blocked the street, with reporters jostling for the best position. Louise Simpson was already a ghoulish spectacle.

There was nothing more for me to do here. Running the gauntlet, I returned to the car without making a comment.

The only way to assuage the guilt I felt was to do everything possible to find that baby alive.

And catch whoever was responsible.

Chapter 25

BACK AT PRIVATE, Johnny and Collette were already working on a computerized composite of the Finches.

It can't have been a coincidence that the security cameras had been down when the pair came in. If they were behind it, the plan to avoid being photographed was elaborate. Planting a virus and smashing a door suggested they knew the layout of our building and which computer operated the cameras.

They could have met us anywhere. In a park, another office, or a shopping mall. Something didn't fit.

I racked my brain to recall even the slightest detail. The man was volatile and reacted badly when he thought he was being called a liar. Then again, he backed down with little persuasion. The woman was either genuine or a brilliant actress. She knew exactly what to say to garner sympathy.

Had they deliberately chosen me, today of all days? That meant they knew my personal history and planned to use me to get the information on Louise. But if they were that computer savvy, they could have found all the information on Louise themselves.

Had someone set me up? Someone who wanted me arrested for conspiracy to commit murder. I kept seeing the Simpson children's playthings through my mind and images of their mother's battered body.

Mary tapped on the doorjamb, with a coffee cup in hand and a ziplock bag of trail mix.

"Thought you could use these."

I hadn't eaten all day and was beginning to feel the effects. My headache was back.

"It's probably fake but we need to check out the address the Finches gave us," I said, before sucking back the coffee and popping a handful of nuts and seeds.

Mary slumped in my lounge. "Already did. It's a vacant block. And there isn't anyone called Gus or Jennifer Finch either. I also tried Angus and Gustav. Nothing comes up on the usual databases."

It figured. The couple had lied about everything.

The only other lead was the e-mail address used to contact Louise through the surrogacy website.

"They said they contacted Louise through that, which is how they found out she lived on the North Shore." I sat straighter. "Could you trace the address the e-mail was sent from?"

Mary pressed both hands on her knees and stood. "Whoever owns that site is hiding behind a firewall. I couldn't get through but we can try working backwards from Louise's e-mail account."

"Thanks. Keep me posted. I want to hear any news, no matter how insignificant it may seem."

I sounded desperate. I was.

Chapter 26

I FOUND DARLENE in our lab.

"Anything solid from the fence or kitchen?"

Her blue eyes had a spark as she pulled on a white coat over her jeans and baggy shirt.

"Good palm print on the fence, and the aglet on the cord of the hoodie has potential. Same with DNA from the print on the body's neck." She placed her camera on the desk. "I'm more hopeful about what we got with the ALS."

You could always rely on Darlene. She found evidence that seasoned crime scene technicians missed. Fingerprints on skin were notoriously difficult to capture, which is why she had been using the forensic Alternative Light Source, or ALS, when the opportunity arose.

"Got the best result at 450 nanometers. Amido black's risky but Rex agreed to try it on one of two bloodied prints on Louise's arms. It washed away the first, but we got lucky with the second. Blood on the ridges darkened for what I hope is enough contrast to get a good image of the print. I promised to send through our copies ASAP."

"Did they fingerprint the neighbor who found the body?"

"I asked them to. Even though he couldn't remember touching the body, these could turn out to be his. He was pretty shaken up."

If the killer acted impulsively, I hoped he or she had been sloppy.

"Any sign of the murder weapon?"

"Not yet. The police are searching bins, drains, and yards in the area."

She scrubbed her hands and put on fresh gloves. As she wiped down the benches with antiseptic, she thought out loud, "If the baby was the target, why beat and then stab Louise? I get that she saw the killer's face. But if our clients did it, you and Collette could already identify them."

As usual, Darlene spoke good sense. The knife perforating the abdomen had to be key. That made the attack personal. Maybe we were missing something. What if another couple had wanted her to be a surrogate and things had gone sour?

I texted Johnny to join us. He was there almost instantly.

"We need to look into Louise's surrogacy experiences, her background," I explained. "Zoe's parents need to be checked as well. Make sure the husband was in Queensland and find out if there was any tension in the marriage or questions of paternity, custody, anything you can think of. And anyone who might have wanted either woman to suffer."

"I'm on it," he said, looking to Darlene.

She nodded, as if giving him permission to leave. There seemed to be a new dynamic between the two.

Darlene laid out the evidence samples on the clean benches and I left to help Johnny. Mary caught me outside the lab.

"Mark Talbot's here. He's got a warrant."

Chapter 27

MARK AND DETECTIVE Constable Massey stood in the entrance with two uniformed officers.

Mark handed over the search warrant. It was for video footage from the last twenty-four hours along with files pertaining to Gus and Jennifer Finch: addresses, e-mails, invoices, payments. They also wanted my personal notes.

I explained again how the video had failed to record anything from midnight on. But they were welcome to the footage we did have.

"Still find it all pretty convenient," sneered Mark. "Mystery couple visits you; you assist them with surrogacy, which is illegal in this state—"

"It was to be an altruistic surrogacy," I interrupted.

"Unfortunately, Louise Simpson isn't around to verify that," he retorted.

Clearly, his mood hadn't improved since we'd left the crime scene.

He stepped aside to have a quiet word with one of the uniformed officers. No doubt a power play to make me sweat.

The conversation seemed to amuse him.

When he returned his smug expression confirmed it. "Your story about other businesses being vandalized doesn't seem to hold true. It appears no one else had any damage last night. Just your office."

Our receptionist jumped to my defense. "The repairmen said they had a number of windows to fix in the building."

I hadn't recognized the glass company as one we would use. "Collette, where did you get the number for the repairers?"

"In a card that was under the door. I thought they were like, you know, tow trucks. My uncle drives one. He listens to police radio so he can get to an accident first."

It became clearer now. We'd been deliberately targeted. But by whom? The glass repair company drumming up business? That didn't explain the computer virus.

Mary offered to show Kristen Massey the video recordings we had up until the shutdown. Mark stayed with me.

"You look tense, Craigy boy. Might as well have a seat. This could take a while."

It was how he worked. Pressing buttons to get a reaction. Just like he did when we were teenagers in the same house. Back then he had the advantage of size and mates to belt me around.

Now he had a police force on his side.

"Don't think this is personal. Try seeing it from where I stand. You meet this couple, who could be serial killers for all you know, then you give them personal info on a young mother who's struggling to bring up small kids while grieving for her dead husband." He sucked air in through his teeth. "Within hours she's dead. And a baby she was minding vanishes."

He wasn't saying anything I hadn't already told myself.

"Work with me," he goaded. "There's more. By some dumb luck, you don't seem to have anything to help us identify them." He waved a hand in the air dismissively. "The most expensive, highest-tech security cameras conveniently don't record the crucial moments."

"That's exactly what happened," Collette argued. "You're making it sound like—"

"You are deliberately obstructing justice? Or conspired to kill Louise Simpson? That would make you an accessory, Ms...."

"Lindman," she answered, voice wavering as her eyes appealed to me.

I needed to stay controlled. "He's trying to upset you. We haven't done anything wrong."

Johnny appeared with all the information we had on the Finches, along with everything he'd collected on Louise Simpson. His presence eased some of the tension.

He explained, "The address and names they provided are fake, the number's disconnected, and the e-mail bounces. They didn't pay us. The invoice didn't go through."

"No surprises there," Mark mumbled.

Thankfully, Johnny didn't mention the envelope of cash Gus Finch had produced, as there was no proof I'd given it back.

Collette printed out a dozen copies of the computerized profile of the suspects she and Johnny had compiled. They were amazingly accurate.

She also provided the files on a memory stick.

"Is there anything else?" I asked, trying to appear unfazed.

Mark dumped a number of photos on the reception desk.

"I want you to look at these and never forget Louise Simpson's lifeless face." He turned to his team. "That's about it. *For now.*"

Chapter 28

THE THOUGHT I may have helped the killer find Louise Simpson began to fester.

I studied the photos back in my office. Mark had done me a favor by leaving them. I could go over the scene and see if we missed anything at the time.

I heard a noise and looked up. Mary was leaning against the door frame.

"That could have been worse," she said.

"He's threatening to charge me with conspiracy to commit murder, obstruction of justice." I rubbed the back of my neck, feeling a wave of fatigue.

"You haven't been arrested yet. We can still prove him wrong."

I sat back and focused on the ceiling. "Trouble is, I may be guilty."

Mary came around and propped herself against my side of the desk, arms folded.

"You didn't beat that woman or stab her to death. If you hadn't given them the address, they could have got it from any computer geek or hacker. If the killer plucked the number from the White Pages, you wouldn't blame Telstra."

Mary was right. Again.

"This morning I did let emotion overtake logic. Look what it did to Louise Simpson, her kids. And it could cost all of us here at Private our jobs and reputations. Maybe more."

"All I know is, if you're looking back, you're going in the wrong direction." She leaned closer. "A mother wants her child back. Louise's family needs justice. We can deliver both. Deal with the rest later."

I splayed my fingers on the desk and stood, grateful to be working with such a professional team. Mary had made it clear this was no time for regrets.

"You're right. We put everything into finding baby Zoe. Non-urgent cases go on the back burner. We'll refund any clients who aren't happy about it."

"One more thing," Mary added. "Collette could use one of your pep talks."

I'd known Mary long enough to understand what that meant. Mary had noticed that Collette was upset, but talking emotions with a colleague wasn't her forte.

"Thanks for the heads-up—I'll go see her. And we need everyone in the conference room. Five minutes."

Chapter 29

I FOUND COLLETTE in the kitchenette. When I walked in, she quickly fussed over the coffee machine.

"Thought we could all do with a caffeine hit," she managed.

The red, puffy eyes were impossible to hide. It was easy to forget Collette was only twenty-two and had no experience on the force or in the legal profession. She had knocked on the door with enthusiasm and what Becky would have called "loads of gumption."

She had drive, and a strong will to learn and take on extra tasks. And she was a good public face for the business. Caring, an attentive listener, and a keen observer; the precision of the profile images confirmed that.

"Rough day," I said, popping a pod into one of the two machines. "We've got a staff meeting in the conference room in five."

She avoided eye contact. "I'll make sure everyone's hydrated and fed."

Her hands were shaking, so I offered to help.

"You have a seat at the table and I'll get this going."

The simple offer was enough to break her resolve.

"I'm so sorry about that poor woman. I keep seeing her face…What those people inflicted." Her voice rasped. "And the baby."

Like a pressure valve releasing, she erupted into tears. I handed her the cup I'd made and grabbed some milk from the fridge. So far, I'd been careful to shield Collette from graphic crime scene photos. There was no need to see them in the jobs she did. But Mark leaving the photos had delivered the desired effect.

"The Finches looked so harmless. I mean, I was totally taken in by the story. About how they lost all those pregnancies."

You and me both, I thought.

I placed a hand on her shoulder. "You aren't responsible. None of us is."

She stared at the milk carton. "That detective thinks we are."

I didn't want to go into the background, just gave her the essentials. "Mark Talbot and I have history. It's policing 101. Shake a tree and see what falls out."

Collette looked up, her brown eyes wet.

"Are we the only tree he's got?"

"So far. Which is why I need you to step up. We all have to."

She sniffed and wiped her eyes with a hankie.

"I thought you were going to fire me."

I moved my hand from her shoulder. "The virus could have happened to any of us, and we both fell for the couple's sob story."

"I'm sorry it happened to you, today."

The comment was unexpected.

"Why would you say that? Have you been talking to Mary?"

She waved both hands. "No. Before I came here the first time, I did some research. There were articles in the papers about the . . . I mean, your . . . terrible accident. I'm sorry you lost your family."

I didn't know whether to be offended or impressed by her initiative. I opted for the latter.

"We can't change what's happened."

"I know." Her eyes were dry now.

"We're all going to be tied up with finding Zoe and Louise's killer. I need you to get to work on Eric Moss. Everything you can get on him will be helpful. His daughter didn't give me much to go on, just where and when he was born. Johnny can help you access all the relevant databases. If you can get me the basics, birth certificates, passports—"

"I know exactly what you're after." She smiled nervously. "I hope I don't let you down."

Chapter 30

THE TEAM WAS keen to be briefed. I kicked off.

"Finding the baby is, obviously, our top priority."

I made no mention of the search warrant or police visit.

"Darlene. Anything so far in the evidence?"

She spread out the crime scene photos.

"Louise put up a fight, despite being taken by surprise."

Johnny scribbled notes. "Are we thinking she knew her killer then?"

Darlene continued, "She was in a quiet neighborhood. No grilles on windows or security doors. My guess is she was pretty trusting and opened the door."

That didn't help us narrow the suspect list.

"What else?" Mary asked.

"I thought this was interesting." Darlene referred to images of the face. "The victim's face doesn't appear to have been fractured." She pointed to the whites of the eyes. "Cheek fracture would cause hemorrhages in the lateral sclera."

We all appreciated that was why one punch, or a "coward punch" as it had become known, was so dangerous. The face and skull weren't designed to be hit with such blunt force.

"The cheeks, the left one in particular, is reddened and swollen," Darlene explained. "There are a couple of parallel scratches on the left cheek too. I swabbed them, which is our best chance for DNA so far."

Collette appeared with a tray holding a coffee pot, milk jug, sugar, and spoons, which she placed on the sideboard, alongside a box of pastries and upturned mugs.

She'd reapplied her eye makeup. You couldn't tell she'd been upset. Johnny winked at her as she sat beside him.

"What did I miss?" she whispered.

Darlene recapped. "I think Louise was slapped multiple times, not punched, and the killer may have left behind DNA in scratch marks on that left cheek."

Collette volunteered, "The woman this morning had long, manicured nails. She kept clicking them as she waited."

"I didn't find any broken nails at the scene," Darlene said. "That could explain the slapping. It's something a woman with nails might do."

"Or a man who wanted to inflict pain without leaving obvious bruising," Mary added. "Typical in domestic violence."

We needed to concentrate our efforts to be most efficient. I listed tasks in order of importance. "We can't rule out two people at the scene. Mary, can you talk to Louise's brother and track down her close friends? See if she had any previous surrogate pregnancies, and if she told anyone about using that site."

"On it," Mary said. "And if there was a man on the scene, requited or otherwise. Young widows are pretty vulnerable."

"You read my mind," I said. "Johnny, can you go through Louise's phone and bank records? E-mails too. Check whether she contacted our couple, visited outside her area. Anything to help us narrow the part of Sydney we're looking at."

Johnny raised another issue. "If Zoe Ruffalo had been at the Simpson house on three consecutive Tuesdays, it's possible the baby was the target and Louise was collateral damage."

I agreed. "We can't afford to narrow our thinking too early."

"While I'm at it, I'll look into the Ruffalos and their finances," he said. "Miners make good money. It's possible there'll be a ransom demand."

The police, I knew, were preparing for that possibility.

Mary raised an index finger. "What about Eric Moss? Can we risk losing time on that one?"

I gestured towards Collette. "We've got it covered."

Our receptionist stared at her notebook. No one batted an eyelid.

"How far are we on identifying the origin of the e-mail sent to Louise Simpson? If the surrogacy site is protected by a firewall, can we trace the e-mail?"

Darlene was the one to speak. "Johnny and I tried that a few minutes ago. Our suspects used a VPN address, so the IP turned up as coming from America."

"So they're *au fait* with hiding?" Mary commented.

"Not necessarily," Collette offered. "Heaps of people use VPNs. It's how you download shows from American Netflix and Hulu."

All I wanted to know was whether they could work

backwards from the VPN to pin down the local address. Darlene knew that was what I wanted to hear.

"There's a guy I know who can try it for a grand."

Darlene had some "interesting" contacts who often challenged technical boundaries of the law.

"Let's get him on it."

Unless someone identified the Finches from the profile images soon, the mysterious computer expert was our best hope of finding baby Zoe.

Chapter 31

TWO HOURS LATER, there'd been no word about Zoe and no ransom call. The police had set up at the Ruffalo home, around the corner from the Simpson scene.

Our friendly deputy commissioner had given us the information gleaned from Zoe's mother. We took that and collected more. Nothing stood out as particularly useful.

Geoff and Courtney Ruffalo appeared happy to their neighbors, owed six hundred thousand on a mortgage, but paid their credit cards off on time. There were no withdrawals from bank accounts apart from small, consistent amounts of cash each week and direct deposits to pay the regular bills. The husband wasn't in debt. There was always the possibility of an affair with a colleague at the mine.

They'd been together eight years and married for three.

Courtney Ruffalo and Louise Simpson met at the local park and struck up a friendship. When Zoe was born, Louise offered to babysit while Geoff was away. The new mother used that time to attend a postnatal yoga class.

The instructor confirmed Courtney was in class at the time Louise's body was found.

I remembered how challenging Cal's first few months were, especially for Becky. When days and nights all blurred into one.

I felt a deep ache in my chest and took a slug of Chivas Regal that lived in the locked top drawer of my desk, in the flask Becky had given me on our wedding day. Right now it was the closest I could get to her and Cal.

But we still had to find baby Zoe.

I placed it back in the drawer.

In the lab, Darlene was busy processing samples. There was no word yet from her mystery friend.

Johnny and Mary were collating information. I decided to see how Collette had fared with her assignment.

I found her at her desk, face red and flustered.

"Everything all right?" I pulled up a chair by her side.

"I don't know," she said. "You may want to sack me now."

Before I could ask why, she blurted her explanation. "I haven't found anything yet." She nervously checked her watch. It was nearing nine o'clock.

"You must have found something in two hours." I couldn't hide my frustration. Time was critical and I'd given her basic facts to gather.

"I couldn't even find a clear photo." She began to tear up again. "I promise I tried. I promise, I'll be in super early tomorrow."

Today had been tough on all of us, including Collette.

"You should go home and get some rest."

Collette looked relieved. She picked up her phone and bag and let herself out the new glass door, locking it behind her.

The pounding in my head returned. Collette's task had been simple. Any of the others would have had a dossier on Moss by now. I began to wonder if I'd overestimated her potential.

I checked my phone for any messages from Brett Thorogood or Jack Morgan. Nothing so far.

Sitting at reception, I started with the list Eliza Moss had provided. Friends of her father, where he'd lived, been born.

Movement on the surveillance monitor caught my attention. A man greeted Collette. He was stocky, muscular. He had his back to the camera so I couldn't see his face, only the bunch of roses he was hiding. He reached forward and kissed her on the cheek as he presented the bouquet.

As far as I'd seen, Collette's relationships were frequent and short-lived. This one appeared to be in an embryonic stage.

I flicked through what Collette had recorded so far. There were question marks against passport, registration of birth, bank account.

While the others worked on identifying the mystery pair, I made a strong black coffee and prepared for a long night.

Chapter 32

I STARTED WITH the usual databases. There was no one with a name even resembling Eric Moss born on or around the date Eliza provided.

Even allowing for misspellings, typographical errors, and flawed transcribing, his birth wasn't registered in New South Wales. Definitely not in the small town of Jerilderie or the nearby, larger town of Deniliquin. Jerilderie, in the state's west, was famous for being raided by the country's most notorious bushranger, Ned Kelly.

Searching the electoral rolls, there was no Moss registered in Echuca, Victoria, or Moama across the border, for the decade he and his parents supposedly lived there. Eliza had made a note about her grandfather drowning in the Murray River when the paddle-steamer he crewed for the sawmill caught fire. A quick search of cemeteries in the area proved futile. There was no record of Eric's mother, Margaret, or grandparents living or dying in the area.

Eric Moss didn't appear on the current electoral roll. He hadn't requested a silent listing. From what I could tell, he had never voted, enrolled, or been married.

He wasn't listed in *Who's Who*, despite being CEO of the largest Australian-based nonprofit organization. Infopedia only mentioned him in a page on Sir Lang Gillies, with no accompanying link to his name.

I began to wonder if records for Moss had been wiped. Or if they had ever existed. No tax file number, no Medicare number, and no digital imprint. Scores of articles on Contigo Valley quoted Gillies and mentioned Moss in passing. He was rarely photographed without dark glasses.

What struck me most was he didn't have a passport or driver's license.

The man known as Eric Moss was a ghost.

Chapter 33

I DECIDED TO do what I should have done with Gus and Jennifer Finch and double-check who our clients were and what they claimed to be.

I refused to be played again so this time I searched for Eliza Moss. An abundance of photographs of her appeared in business and social pages. She talked with pride about her father, but there was no mention of a mother.

She claimed she'd been born in Lithgow, not far from Contigo Valley. Only there was no birth record for Eliza Moss. By now, my patience was at breaking point.

What were these people playing at? If they wanted their true identities to be secret, it was beyond bizarre that they would both hold high-profile jobs. I had to wonder what sort of fraud the two could have been perpetrating. Was Moss siphoning money from Contigo or its donors? One thing was certain: I wouldn't be party to it.

I headed back to the lab to check on Darlene's progress. She was in the middle of attempting to highlight a fingerprint on the aglet from the blood-stained hoodie.

"I tried cyanoacrylate in the fume cupboard," she said. "It didn't pick anything up. Now I'm adding a fluorescing agent."

The fume cupboard was a way of highlighting latent fingerprints. The work was tedious and fiddly. It took someone with Darlene's patience and experience to develop new ways to improve the technique.

"If there's a partial, you're hoping ultraviolet light will show the definition?"

Darlene smiled, the full-dimpled version that was reserved for someone appreciating her ingenuity. "You *so* get me." Her attention quickly turned to the remaining specimens. "I'll let you know the second I find something."

Next stop was Mary and Johnny. They hadn't made much progress on the IP address. I suggested they go home, get a few hours' sleep, and come back early.

Mary stood up and stretched her back, cracking the joints in her spine and neck. "You should grab some kip too," she said.

"I'll stay here on my office couch." It wouldn't be the first time. Anyway, after the door being smashed last night, I'd be more comfortable if Darlene had someone with her in the office.

Johnny offered to stay but there was little point. He agreed to keep working a couple more hours, though. There was something important I needed to do.

I headed out to confront Eliza Moss.

Chapter 34

I PARKED BY The Rocks at Circular Quay and walked along the promenade. The night was clear with a slight hint of a breeze. Summer crowds were out enjoying the best of the harbor. It still amazed me how stunning the city could look, particularly at night with the iconic bridge and opera house lit up.

I'd lived in a few great cities but this one always felt like home.

It was almost ten. Eliza's function would be in full swing. I was now calm enough to challenge her without emotion.

I breathed in the sea air and entered the Park Hyatt through the bar.

The noisy ballroom was decked out in full Mardi Gras splendor. Colorful streamers, ornate masks, beads, and brightly colored candles adorned the banquet tables. The residual aroma of spicy Cajun wafted from the "Spice Palace" buffet as a jazz band played to a full dance floor. On the perimeter of the room, people jostled around carnival stalls offering temporary tattoos, fortune-tellers, and voodoo instruction. The atmosphere was electric, not the usual dull charity event.

I spied Eliza at a table near the center of the ballroom and wove my way through overly merry revelers. A street magician I passed seemed affronted that I wasn't interested in his card tricks.

My client sat amid a sea of wealth, at a table with a couple of recognizable faces, and some barely identifiable ones thanks to overzealous cosmetic work.

She saw me approach and interrupted her conversation without getting up.

"You have news?" Her piercing green eyes looked up at me.

"We need to speak in private."

A minion delivered her a glass of wine. "Things wrap up in about half an hour. Can this wait till then?"

I wondered what the hell this woman was playing at. She seemed more interested in holding court than finding her missing father. I didn't like being used or made a fool of. She'd contacted Jack Morgan and misled both of us. Given she was going to profit in the event of her father's death, she could leave her workers to "wrap up" for her.

"I need to see you in private. *Now.*" I was sharp, exactly as I'd intended.

She suddenly seemed rattled. "OK. There's a staff room we can use."

As I waited, she pushed back from the table and led the way out of the ballroom—in a wheelchair.

Chapter 35

ELIZA TOOK US to a room provided for her event staff. A four-seater table and a television mounted on the wall were all it could accommodate. The TV was on with the sound muted.

Inside the room, she moved straight for a bar fridge and pulled out two small bottles of beer.

She maneuvered to the table and offered me one. I declined and sat opposite, regretting judging her for "holding court" when she was wheelchair-bound. Still, I was reeling from the day's events with the nonexistent Finches, and now the phantom Eric Moss. My pulse raced with anger at having been conned—again.

She twisted the cap of her beer and drank from the bottle before ripping open a bag of corn chips on the table. "Help yourself." She took a couple of chips and waited for me to speak.

"There's no word on your father." I placed both elbows on the table. "But you probably already knew that."

She swallowed hard. "You must have something by now."

"I get the feeling I wasn't expected to, given the 'facts'

you provided. About yourself and the man you call your father."

There was a moment's silence. "Are you serious? What's got into you?" She slammed the bottle on the table. "Is this about my chair?"

"I don't appreciate being lied to."

She threw her head back and laughed. "That's pretty rich, calling me a liar because I don't wear my disability like some neon sign. Shock, horror. I acted normal and you treated me like I was. Now you sit there, all sanctimonious, accusing me of being dishonest." She looked me up and down, exaggerating every movement of her upper body. "We're all disabled. You hide your emotional scars with swagger and self-importance. Let me guess. Your parents divorced, leaving you with commitment issues—"

My anger seethed. She had no right to lecture me on family. Attacking me just proved her dishonesty. I'd wasted enough time on Eric Moss, whoever he was. I stood to leave.

"Lies have a way of unraveling." I didn't bother to hide my irritation. "Did you think I wouldn't find out the truth?"

"You assumed I was like you. I just didn't assault you with my differences." She took a few more slow sips. "People treat me differently once they know. Case in point, you."

"This has nothing to do with your wheelchair."

"Now who's the liar? Why is it an issue then?"

"Because you and your father both seem good at covering up who you really are."

"If you want to know, I act that way so people will take me seriously. I wanted to prove to my father I was independent. It's why I started my own business, to show everyone I could be a success." She gulped what was left of the beer and wiped her mouth with a serviette. "Well, actually, that part's not entirely true."

The comment took me by surprise. Judging by tonight, she excelled at what she did.

"I have a master's in business studies and my résumé landed me countless interviews. Only the moment a prospective employer saw the chair, they'd start mentioning someone they knew who had cancer, or a footballer who'd become a quadriplegic in an accident." She picked at the label on the bottle. "I could see them suddenly panic about insurance, workers' comp, and whether the toilet in their inner-city terrace office would have to be refitted.

"Now, I ditch the chair for meetings with clients so they treat me like an AB person."

"AB?"

"Able-bodied." She made a point of enunciating the phrase.

"Which is why your staff keeps coming to you for signatures and advice." I felt foolish for misreading her manner. Even so, I still had to confront her about the lack of documentation for her and Eric Moss.

"There's something we need to get clear. Your father isn't who you claim he is. He doesn't exist in terms of Medicare, the electoral roll, or any other usual records." I ticked them off on my hands. "No passport, no bank account, nada, nothing. I couldn't find a single identifying document."

"Really?" She landed the empty bottle in the rubbish bin by the wall. "Tell me. How can someone as brilliant as Jack Morgan be so wrong about you?"

Chapter 36

ELIZA MOSS PULLED no punches in what she thought of my incompetence. I let her vent. In my experience, anger usually stemmed from fear or guilt.

"Jack is *not* going to be happy," she said, scrolling down her phone contacts. "I need professionals to find him, not some two-bit amateur. He could have been in the fire for all you know."

"What fire?"

She looked exasperated. "You really have no idea?"

I'd been so caught up in the events of the day, I hadn't seen any other news. "I've been working with the police on another urgent case."

She pulled up a photo and held the phone so I could see. "It's off Evans Road, between Katoomba and Blackheath. It made the news because firefighters were concerned it might take Jemby Rinjah with it. Luckily, it didn't."

I knew of the award-winning ecolodge that backed onto the national park. I took the phone. The cabin was a burned-out shell.

"They think it was arson."

I scrolled through a series of photos. Surrounding bushland had been incinerated as well.

"Who owns it?"

"A friend of my father. Dad would go up there sometimes for the weekend, or take the occasional overseas visitor there. He loves all that area."

"Was anyone hurt?" What I was really asking was if any bodies were found.

She shook her head. "Reports said no. I just don't think it's a coincidence. It's as if everything he values is being destroyed. His job, his friend's cabin."

"I'll look into it."

"Don't bother," she said. "I'm getting someone else."

A TV news update caught my attention with the photo of a baby in pink. The commentary wasn't necessary, given the Crime Stoppers number scrolled on a loop across the screen.

Eliza looked up at the TV. "That poor baby and mother." She glanced back at me, and must have read the pain on my face. "How long's she been missing?"

"Eight hours," I answered, without looking at my watch.

Her tone was subdued. "That's the other case you're working on, isn't it?"

I rubbed my neck again. "Let's just say it's been a full day and I can't afford to be messed around with. There's no one with the name Eric Moss born anywhere near where you said, or when."

She leaned forward. "I don't understand. That *is* Dad's full name, date of birth. I even gave you his parents' names, everything I knew."

I watched her carefully for any hint of lies. "There's no birth registered for Eliza Moss either."

She threw her head back again. "You've investigated me? If you'd told me earlier, I could have saved you the trouble."

Chapter 37

ELIZA MOSS TOOK a swig from the second bottle of beer before explaining that she was born to a teenage girl who worked in the canteen at Contigo's rural base. The girl had no money or support and no skills to look after a child, let alone one that was—she used her fingers as quotation marks—"abnormal."

"In what way?"

"I was born with an unusual neurological condition. My mother was pressured to put me in an institution. Eric didn't want that to happen. He offered to pay for all my medical care, physiotherapy, and even new trial therapies. Not long after, he adopted me and my mother left town. No one's heard from her since, not that you can blame her. Unmarried mothers in rural areas were social outcasts back then."

One of the women I'd seen earlier in Eliza's office popped her head through the doorway.

"Sorry, but I thought you'd want to know. After costs, the night raised..."

Eliza's eyes widened. "Give it to me straight."

"A hundred and twenty-seven thousand dollars!"

Eliza smiled broadly. "That's brilliant. As usual, a great job done by all. And thanks for your help, Jules. You are a wonder."

The colleague blushed and looked at me, then back at Eliza. "You may as well head off. I'll finish up here."

"Appreciate it." Eliza slumped after the assistant left. "Where were we?"

"You were telling me why I couldn't find your birth certificate."

"The certificate had my mother's name on it; the father's name was left blank."

As far as she was concerned, Eric Moss was her father. There was little doubt she also saw him as her savior. Without him she may well have been left to rot in an institution.

I began to believe she had no idea her "father" didn't officially exist.

Chapter 38

ELIZA MOSS SEEMED blindsided by what I had to say. She explained that Eric avoided overseas trips. Even so, she'd assumed he had a passport. Her father had always been private about his own family and childhood but once talked about the accident in Echuca and his mother's grief. He'd never mentioned it again.

Eric and Eliza had each other and didn't seem to need anyone else.

In one of their holidays together, Moss hired a boat and crew. They sailed the Whitsundays for a couple of weeks and talked about politics, history, and everything else but his past.

"The few times I asked about his childhood, or even my mother, he'd fob me off by saying, 'It's not where you're from that counts. Where you're going and how you get there is all that matters.'"

Apart from a handful of trips and cabin visits, people usually traveled to see Moss in Contigo Valley. There they could see the facilities and equipment in action. Canberra was a favorite for the pair during school holidays. The museums, galleries, and exhibitions were an easy drawcard.

It made sense that Moss didn't have a passport. Even so, it was unusual for a CEO to negotiate major international deals without venturing outside the country.

A text interrupted. I excused myself to check. It was from Johnny.

Gone over Ruffalo's and Simpson's bank/ phone statements. No leads so far.

I needed to relieve Johnny so he could go home. Darlene would be working for a lot longer. The broken door still unnerved me. I didn't want my staff put at any risk.

I stood and pushed the chair towards the table. "I'm sorry but I have to go. Can we talk more tomorrow?"

She placed the second beer bottle on the table and nudged aside the half-eaten chips. "Of course. I hope it's good news about the baby."

"How are you getting home?"

Those green eyes challenged me. "Would you ask an AB woman that?"

I had to concede, "Probably not. I just know how difficult taxis can be at this time of night."

"I have a room upstairs as part of the hotel package." She reached out her hand and we shook again. "Thanks for the thought, though."

I felt like we needed to tread carefully finding Moss.

Eric wasn't who he claimed to be and I had a bad feeling his daughter was going to be hurt when we unraveled whatever secrets he was keeping so well hidden.

I texted Johnny to go home and get some sleep. I'd be back in ten.

Chapter 39

JOHNNY HANDED OVER the Simpson file first. Thanks to Darlene, we had the data from Louise's mobile phone and computer. There was no landline in the house.

Some days she made few calls; others were spent in a series of long conversations. Johnny had written "day care" beside the dates they tended to occur. Louise's brother, the compensation lawyer, and her mother were frequent numbers on those days.

There were only occasional calls made to or from the phone after eight-thirty at night. All online activity usually ceased by ten.

Supermarket groceries were home-delivered every Wednesday. A single mother, she kept a routine. Good for the kids, but it made her predictable. And as a result, an easier target for a killer.

The husband, Vincent, had fallen from scaffolding on a construction site and died from a brain hemorrhage two days later. The insurance company alleged that a preexisting medical condition contributed to his death. Vincent Simpson had contracted hepatitis A while on holiday in New Guinea years before. His liver function was slightly raised at the time of admission. It sounded like a stretch to me, but insurance companies paid doctors big dollars to mitigate payments on medical grounds.

However, their strategy was more likely to be to wear down a widow pursuing a claim. Not torture and murder her.

Still, the payout could exceed three million. Johnny had included a printout of a newspaper article that mentioned the potential amount. That could have made Louise a target for extortion. What if the killer thought the baby was really Louise's and the plan changed when she revealed Zoe wasn't her child?

Possibilities raced through my mind.

Her Internet settings were private, and she had fewer than a hundred "friends" on social media.

I logged in with the password Johnny had guessed. The kids' names and years of birth.

Photos of two smiling kids filled the posts, taken at parties, swimming, and day care. In every one, she held the children close.

One image stood out. Her husband kissing her expanded belly. The comment beneath read "Missing Vince so much. Happiest time of our lives."

I went straight in to Darlene to see if she had any results.

She was magnifying images on an electron microscope.

"This hair sample is different from Louise's. They're both brown." She enlarged the slide further so I could compare them. "The longer one was broken off. No root. We could only get mitochondrial DNA from it. I took the other from Louise's head. It will take a couple of days to extract."

I studied the hairs. The broken one was more coarse, and thicker in diameter.

At this stage any DNA was better than none. If we could narrow it down to members of the one family, we'd exclude about four million people in the city.

"Good pickup," I said and meant it.

Darlene had managed to enhance a partial print on the aglet from the hoodie and had a striking image of the palm print from the back fence. She was still working on one of the prints from Louise's neck.

"Rex called a few minutes ago," she said. "Gross examination's done but the histopathology will be a while longer."

I braced for what I suspected was coming.

"His first impressions were right. She died of acute blood loss. The stab wound was deep and severed an artery on the way through. It entered above the pubic bone and perforated the uterus, passing above the bladder."

I said what Darlene didn't. "Chances are, whoever did this knew what they were aiming for."

This was no random killing. Louise's murder was deliberate and extremely personal.

Chapter 40

AFTER GOING OVER the files again hoping to find something we'd missed, I managed an hour of fitful sleep on the couch in my office.

Darlene woke me at six a.m. She was heading home for a shower. As she let herself out, Brett Thorogood slipped in. The deputy commissioner was in dress uniform, cap in his hand, ready for a press conference.

"Rough night for everyone," he said, knocking my socked feet off the couch and sitting in their place.

I sat up slowly. "Please tell me you've got good news."

His face was stony. "Radio and TV stations are putting out hourly bulletins. Crime Stoppers has been flooded with calls overnight after people saw the couple's composite pictures."

I knew that wasn't all positive news. There would be hundreds, possibly thousands of false leads to keep the police busy for months. Valuable time would be lost chasing crank calls.

"This couple," he asked. "Is there anything else you can tell me?"

I'd racked my brain all night for any more details about the pair.

"Craig, give me something to work with."

I stood up and faced him. "You know I want to find this child more than anyone else. My team worked through the night."

Brett calmly rotated the cap in his hands. "Darlene's contribution was invaluable. I'm trying to protect Private, but you know you aren't the commissioner's favorite. There's going to be a backlash once the shock jocks call for mandatory homicide sentencing and senior heads on platters."

He didn't have to remind me. A breakthrough could not only save baby Zoe, but also our reputation.

"Her face had minimal trauma," I explained. "Gut tells me someone wanted information from her. If they wanted to torture her, they were pretty amateur. Stabbing of the uterus was very specific."

Brett remained focused on his cap. "The surrogacy motive is the best we have?"

"Right now it's all we have."

"Then I'll get the taskforce to hone in on the surrogacy organizations. See if anyone admits to knowing this pair or meeting with them at some stage."

He stood and I thanked him. Before he left I had one question.

"What do you know about Eric and Eliza Moss?"

Chapter 41

BRETT COCKED HIS head. "Why would you ask?"

"Eric Moss walked out of Contigo four days ago and no one's heard from him since. The daughter suspects foul play."

"And you're investigating him?" Brett dropped his cap on the desk. "The Simpson murder is nothing compared to the Pandora's box you'll rip open with this one."

The comment was not what I expected. What did the deputy commissioner of police know about Moss going missing? "How about I make you a decaf while you explain?"

We headed to the kitchenette. Brett had suffered heart palpitations and his doctor had recommended cutting back on caffeine. Greta, his wife, enforced it religiously in addition to a low-cholesterol, low-salt, and organic diet.

"Make it a latte and we're on. I've got forty minutes before a briefing."

I made the coffees while he stood against the bench, talking freely.

"From memory, Eliza spent some time in the US,

about three years ago. She and Jack Morgan had a thing for a while, I think, but it fizzled out."

Brett knew Eric Moss and considered him a decent guy who connected well with people. "He could have talked the Middle East into peace." Committed to his business, he'd turned down jobs running a number of organizations for much better pay.

"I had some dealings with him over police training with the retrieval squads. He was spot-on and had innovative ideas about improving our efficiency. From what I could tell, he was a golden boy for ministers, police, and defense brass. Sending equipment overseas to help with disasters was great PR; kudos for the state and federal governments to get mileage from, especially at election time."

He opened a white box and picked up a pastry left over from yesterday. Half went straight into his mouth.

I handed him the coffee.

"Thanks," he managed, savoring his treat and picking up a chocolate croissant. "Greta—"

"What happens in Private…"

"You always could keep a secret," he said and took another large bite.

I asked if there was any hint of corruption at Contigo. He stopped chewing. "Is that what you suspect?"

I explained how Moss resigned with no warning after the finance officer questioned a small discrepancy. And how Gillies didn't seem keen to have anyone sniffing around the company. He certainly didn't care that Moss had left without any explanation.

"Lang's a classic corporate parasite. He often travels with his wife, only they stay in separate hotel rooms. He orders porn movies and when it comes to checking out, acts outraged at the false charges on his credit card, threatens to tell the media about the hotel scam…"

"And gets the charges wiped."

"Every time." He drained his mug and placed it in the sink. "You say Gillies wasn't fazed by Moss leaving?"

"Made out he didn't care to know why. As if Moss was easily replaced."

Brett frowned. "Doesn't add up he'd be happy to see his meal ticket walk away. Unless, of course, Moss had something that could bury Gillies."

That's what bothered me. No one had seen or heard from Moss, and no one but Lang had seen the resignation e-mail.

Brett continued as I walked him out. "Lawyers, police, defense forces, and governments have a lot invested in Contigo Valley. If Moss uncovered corruption, you don't want to be around when that powder keg blows."

Chapter 42

A COURIER ARRIVED at seven-thirty a.m. with a box on a trolley and instructions to deliver it straight to Darlene Cooper. His shirt had a logo on the pocket: Gene-IE Path Systems. They imported the latest in scientific machines.

Darlene returned with wet hair, and beamed when she saw the delivery.

"I'll explain once we get it in the lab." She led the way to where she wanted it. The delivery man obliged.

In the conference room, Johnny looked remarkably rested for someone who had managed a few hours' sleep at the most. Mary was sucking on a protein shake she'd brought from home. True to her word, Collette had arrived early, already having collected coffees along with eight egg-and-bacon rolls from a café down the street.

The smell of the bacon made me realize how long it had been since I'd eaten. We took our seats and I told them first about Brett Thorogood's visit. I didn't need to remind them how much we needed to get a break today.

Johnny was the first with an idea. He wanted to go back to the street address the Finches had provided.

"It's a vacant block," Mary reminded him.

He wasn't swayed. "That isn't a coincidence. I really believe they're familiar with the area. I can take copies of the images we made and canvass the streets in daylight."

It was a good idea. "You might just get lucky. If you go now, you can catch the neighbors before they head to work."

Johnny grinned, grabbed copies of the images, and squeezed past Darlene on his way.

Darlene pulled on her lab coat, her hair now tightly looped into a bun. "I'm hoping that machine will help." She picked up a roll. "It's a Swift Gene-IE machine that can process DNA in ninety minutes."

It normally took days to get a DNA analysis with our equipment, which was more advanced and faster than the police labs.

"I didn't think they were available yet," said Mary.

"Well, not widely," Darlene declared. "It's one of only two in the country. And we have it on permanent loan."

"What's the catch? Does speed leave a wider margin for systematic error?"

"No," Darlene said. "But you're right about limitations. It can't extract individual DNA from mixed fluids so isn't any good for rape kits, and it can't detect gender or race at this stage."

"When will you get a result?" I appreciated that Darlene needed time to learn how to use it.

"The tech's calibrating the machine now. After the printout, the machine compares the DNA to all the others in the database." She dumped two sugars into her coffee. "Should have something by ten this morning."

"How did you manage to pull this off?" I was amazed.

"Quid pro quo. If we like it, we can recommend it to each of the other Private offices for a bulk discount." She grabbed a serviette and excused herself to get on with the analysis.

For the first time, we had widened our edge on the police resources, and we had our tech marvel to thank for it.

Chapter 43

JOHNNY PULLED UP outside the vacant block. The address may have been bogus but the street existed. Two blocks back from the nearest main road and quiet, even for this time of day. Down the road, the shell of a service station had been fenced off. Within a hundred meters, the yards of three dilapidated houses displayed For Sale signs.

He tried the side with an overgrown jacaranda first. In the drive sat a white ute. *Top Job Pipes and Plumbing*. A 1-800 number was printed on the back and side.

A man in a blue workman's shirt answered the door. He had a piece of toast in one hand and took the chance to slip past a crying toddler. As the door closed, the child began to scream from inside. The man unlocked the vehicle and placed the toast on the dashboard before turning to Johnny.

"Hi. My name's Johnny Ishmah. I'm investigating Zoe Ruffalo's kidnapping."

"Yeah, I saw that on the news. Makes you think no one's safe anymore."

"The police are keen to interview this couple. I was wondering if you could take a close look and see if you recognize one or both of them."

The man wiped both hands on his shirt before taking the first profile. "So you think they live around here?" He looked carefully at the face then shook his head.

"How about the woman?" Johnny swapped the pictures.

"Sorry, mate, haven't seen either of them. We only moved in three months ago. If she is from around here, the codger across the road'll be your best bet. He's about ninety in the shade and sits out there every day." He pointed towards a red brick house with a half-veranda diagonally opposite. "Reckon Frank knows all the neighborhood's little secrets." He climbed into the ute and wound down the window. "Hope you find the bastards that did it."

Johnny was relieved that the public appeals had at least made an impact. Overnight, as a long shot, he had scanned the images into facial recognition ID software. It hadn't paid off. The sketches may have looked accurate but lacked the exact dimensions of mouth to nose, ear contours, and forehead size.

He crossed the road and walked into the elderly man's yard. A cat took off from the front veranda, leaving white hairs in the cushioned cane chair it had been curled on. Beside that was a wooden chair with tattered tapestry cushions. Against one of the chair's arms, a full metal ashtray stood on a spiral wooden stem base. It had to be from the 1950s. Johnny's grandparents had one similar. The smell reminded him of that house, where smoke had darkened the walls and embedded in all the furnishings.

Above, an abundance of spiderwebs hung from the

guttering. Johnny knocked loudly on the closed screen door. There was no answer. He tried again.

This time he walked around the house, hoping the gentleman was in his backyard. Through the rear window, he saw a still figure.

Slumped across the breakfast table.

Chapter 44

JOHNNY TRIED THE back door. It was locked. He raced around the front of the house and entered through the screen door.

The man was facedown on the table, a radio playing by his side.

Johnny tried to feel a neck pulse when suddenly the man took a gasp and snorted. He was asleep.

"Sir! Frank!" Johnny shouted.

He sat up and Johnny stepped back.

"Who the hell are you?" he demanded. There was no sign of fear or concern about a stranger in his home.

"Johnny Ishmah. I thought you were...You didn't seem to be breathing."

"I was trying to hear the race results. Must have nodded off." He rubbed the stubble on his chin and licked his lips. "Are you my new carer?"

"No, I was knocking. You didn't answer."

"Funny thing about screen doors is you can *hear through 'em*."

Johnny suppressed a smile. "Sorry, sir."

"Just a minute..." He adjusted something on his

hearing aid. "No point wasting batteries when I'm on my own. Now what are you here for again?"

Before Johnny could answer, the elderly gentleman picked up a walking stick and slowly lifted himself from the chair. He was stooped, and he shuffled to the front door.

"Well?"

Johnny explained that the plumber across the road thought he might be able to help.

The man stepped onto the veranda. "Did he now? If you ask me, that kid rules the roost. Carries on a treat every time he goes out."

Johnny followed and clarified the reason for his visit.

The old man eased himself into his chair and pulled reading glasses from the pocket of his shirt. He gestured for his visitor to sit—on the cat's chair.

Instead, Johnny squatted at his feet and handed over the woman's picture first. The old man breathed loudly as he moved his chin up and then down a little.

"I've seen a lot of people in my time but not that one."

Johnny passed him the man's image.

Frank repeated the chin dropping. This time he grunted on the exhale. A gnarled finger tapped on the page.

"This one. Reminds me of someone."

Johnny pulled out his notebook. "Who?"

"This one has more hair. Same beady eyes though." He lifted his finger and pointed. "Used to live on that old vacant block. Before the place got knocked down. Fella's been dead years though."

Johnny sighed. He could try the other houses but suspected they weren't going to give him answers. He thanked Frank and made a move towards the footpath.

"You young people. Always in a hurry. You miss all the good by rushing past it."

"Sorry, sir, but I have to keep door-knocking."

"I haven't finished. The bloke I mentioned. Well, he had two sons. Twins if I remember, born just after my wife died. 1970."

That would make them in their forties. Johnny stepped back up, this time sitting on the edge of the cat's chair.

"Do you remember their names?"

Frank smacked his lips. "Gough and Whit. Have you ever heard such nonsense? Bloody communists. If you ask me—"

It was pretty clear they were fans of the former prime minister, Gough Whitlam. If nothing else, they could have been registered members of the local Labor Party branch.

"And their surname?"

"Oh. Let me think."

The cat appeared and began to meow at Johnny's feet.

"Or where they ended up?" Johnny tried.

"Gough made a fortune out of paper cups of all things. The other one was pretty witless, from memory." He chuckled and coughed at the irony. "Became a gardener, I think, up Newcastle way."

"Do you remember anyone called Gus from the street? He'd be around the same age as the twins."

Frank rubbed his stubbled chin again. "Now that rings a bell. They had a cousin who hung around them like a bad smell in summer. My grandkids used to play with them. Don't know what it is with those people but this kid was named Alexandrus. Can you believe it? Alexandrus Wallace. No wonder everyone called him Gus."

Chapter 45

I ANSWERED JOHNNY'S call before the second ring.

It didn't take long for him to fill me in about the twins' house and Alexandrus Wallace. It was the breakthrough I was hoping for. I searched online. Alexandrus went by "Alex" now. His company, trading as Al Wallace, restored fine antiques. A further search on antique fairs and I hit pay dirt. It was a group shot but, second from the left, Gus Finch's bland face stared back at me. A few shots later, Jennifer's visage appeared.

And we had them.

I rang the business number. A recorded female voice said the office was closed for family reasons and would reopen on the second of next month. The business was located in Dural, forty minutes north of the CBD. A street search quickly showed it was a house on an acreage.

I couldn't make any of this right, but finding the baby was the best start.

Mary was working on Moss's background when I interrupted to tell her about the address for the man posing as Finch. I could use her help if things went sour. She didn't hesitate and suggested we could take her Jeep. I stopped to let Collette know where we'd be in case anything went wrong and we didn't check in within the hour. We'd call the police on the way to Dural. Collette crossed her fingers and wished us luck.

We headed north on the M2 and encountered surprisingly little traffic until Pennant Hills Road. I decided to wait until we could confirm Wallace was home before letting Brett Thorogood know. We couldn't afford any mistakes. If the Wallaces had already gone, Mark Talbot could accuse me of withholding information long enough for them to escape. The not-so-friendly Area Command could twist it any way he saw fit.

Mary was quiet, concentrating on the road. At a set of lights on Old Northern Road, she spoke.

"Lots of acreages, new and old money out here."

It was a part of Sydney I hadn't spent much time in. I knew it attracted some high-profile people who shunned publicity and attention on their private lives.

"This whole area used to be orchards." Mary glanced sideways and cleared her throat. "I was way out of line yesterday with what I said. About Cal."

I looked out at striking views of the Blue Mountains in the distance. "If anyone had the right, it was you. We've known each other long enough to be honest—"

"It wasn't true," she said.

I disagreed. "I let my guard down and got suckered."

"It isn't you I was angry with." She accelerated around a cement truck in an overtaking lane. "Surrogates in India are known to have borne kids to members of pedophile rings. Kids are bred for abuse and passed around the rings."

I knew Mary had survived a rough childhood and that thankfully things had changed once she was fostered by a loving family. She rarely spoke about it.

Opposite a school, cows grazed. Farther along, mangoes were being sold from the back of a truck. This area had rural advantages with city benefits. I let her speak in her own time.

"I was angry at a system that gives abusers rights just because they're biologically related," she finally said. "After everything they did to us, the courts gave our biological parents legal access. One weekend we were supposed to go for an unsupervised stay. Joanie refused and took off."

Her hands gripped the steering wheel tighter.

I hadn't known the full extent of the problems in her childhood, but I was aware that her younger sister had died at fourteen.

"The police found her in a neighbor's shed that night. She hanged herself." Her eyes were locked on the road. "We'd have been better off if we were dogs. No one would have tolerated that amount of cruelty to an animal."

Chapter 46

WE DROVE THE rest of the way in silence. There was nothing I could say to defuse her anger.

Mary pulled up about a hundred meters from the address, in the shade of a tree and out of range of the camera positioned on the electric gate.

The home was a single-level colonial style at the end of a gravel drive with pines planted on either side. Lawns looked recently mowed and the garden carefully manicured. To the side and behind the house sat a six-car shed. A stripped wooden chair had been left in the sun.

My pulse accelerated. The sliding access door was open. We had to play this right to get the baby out alive. I called Brett Thorogood using Mary's phone. Mine had zero reception.

I told him Johnny had managed to get a lead on an address in Dural. Our intel said the suspects may be inside. He warned me not to go near the house or approach Wallace. He'd take care of things from here. I wasn't in any mood to argue. It was the safest way of getting Zoe if she was, in fact, inside.

All we could do was watch the house and wait for the

posse. But I couldn't sit still. The more information the police had when they arrived, the better.

I stepped out of the vehicle to look for other ways in or out of the property. Fences on either side and at the rear were visible from our position. I clicked photos on my phone.

The sound of a helicopter in the distance made me stop. It was headed our way.

It would alert the Wallaces. Who the hell would compromise the scene with a helicopter? I dialed Brett Thorogood and told him to get rid of the chopper.

As I left a message, Mary reacted. The Wallaces had seen me at the office, but didn't know her. She drove the Jeep up to the gate, lurching the gears as she came to a halt. She slid out and lifted the bonnet before kicking the car.

The helicopter drew closer.

Mary held up her phone in full view of the surveillance camera, as if looking for reception. The chopper remained on course as Mary buzzed the gate.

I watched, out of sight, ready to sprint at the first sign of trouble.

The front door opened and a male figure appeared in a T-shirt and shorts. The cocky walk was impossible to miss. It was Alexandrus Wallace, aka Gus Finch.

He moved towards the electric gates and exchanged words with Mary. He had one hand in his pocket the whole time. He reached for something on the side and I tensed. Mary's body language remained relaxed but I knew she was alert.

The gates opened and Wallace casually strolled through. He stopped within arm's reach of her as he saw the helicopter closing in.

Chapter 47

THE WAIT WAS excruciating. I felt completely useless as Mary pointed to somewhere in the distance. Wallace shielded his eyes from the sun and nodded. I guessed
Mary had invented a reason the helicopter might be flying by. Whatever she said worked. He was now peering
over her engine.

The chopper buzzed closer. Mary moved swiftly and
deftly, pinning him against the vehicle with his legs
kicked wide apart and arms dragged behind him.

I dialed Brett's number again. This time, within seconds, police cars swarmed the address without sirens. If
the wife was inside with Zoe, she could still be unaware
of the ambush.

Tactical Response officers in full kit readied their
weapons. The scene was about to explode.

The officer in charge spoke into his cheek mike. I had
done training with Terry McMahon. He was outcome-
focused and fiercely protective of his team. The odds of
getting Zoe out just improved.

I sprinted towards Wallace as an armed officer tried
to block my way. I produced ID and explained the man

in custody was Alexandrus Wallace, the murder and kidnapping suspect. Terry gave instructions to allow me through.

Wallace was struggling against the cable ties Mary had applied.

"Thank God, you have to help me," he pleaded. "I came out to help and this crazy bitch attacked me."

"Clarkey, nice work." McMahon stood, legs wide, arms folded, smiling at her.

Wallace's head flicked from me to the special forces officer. "You know each other?"

I stepped in front of him. "Mary works with me. Where the hell is Zoe Ruffalo?"

Dust and wind picked up along with the noise from the helicopter. It dropped its nose and seemed to pause before accelerating rapidly down to roof level and making a low pass.

Terry McMahon gave orders into his mike. His manner was calm, but his message uncompromising. "Get that chopper out of here. Now! Shoot it down if you have to."

An officer waved it away. A weapon pointed in its direction seemed to deter the pilot from making another pass.

"You people are crazy." Wallace pleaded with Terry. "I swear to God, I just came out to help someone who had broken down."

"No," I said, "you played me with lies about a surrogate. All you wanted to do was kill her. Was the baby a bonus, or was she the target all along?"

"You are insane!" he shouted. "I haven't done anything wrong. I want this woman charged with assault."

"Who do you know this man to be?" McMahon asked me.

"Gus Finch," I said. "He presented to my office and I had no reason to doubt him."

Mary handed over the wallet she'd removed from his back pocket.

Terry McMahon leaned in. "Right now you're under citizen's arrest and I haven't confirmed your identity. For all I know you could have stolen this wallet."

"That's BS and you know it." He raised his head and called out, "I have rights. I want a lawyer. Can all of you hear me? I want a lawyer."

McMahon leaned in closer. "We'll be storming your house any minute. Our priority is getting the child out alive." He held the microphone, turned his head to the side, and spoke into it. "Get into positions and wait for my command."

As armed officers entered the property and spread out, I gave Wallace another chance.

"Tell us where your wife's got the baby. Once they go inside, if there's any resistance, they'll shoot."

Chapter 48

"YOU'RE CRAZY. WE don't have a child. That's the reason we went to you. To find out about Louise Simpson."

"You just admitted that in front of witnesses," I said.

Mary and I babysat Wallace while Terry rang the home number. A few seconds later, he hung up.

"She answered. She's inside."

"God Almighty." Wallace tried to free himself from the binds. "You've got it wrong. We don't have a baby. I'm trying to tell you. I swear that part was true."

"Then why did you lie to us?" Mary kept one hand on his shoulder.

"Friends we met on the surrogate site told us to. To protect ourselves." Wallace looked like he was about to cry. Gone was the arrogance. "Please don't hurt Jen. She didn't do anything wrong."

"Why would you need to lie if you were going through with an altruistic surrogacy?" Mary quizzed.

He lowered his head. "It was always about money. To start with, Louise wanted twenty-five thousand. Up front."

"Did she say she wanted more?" Mary demanded. "Is that why you hit her?"

"What? No! It was always twenty-five now, twenty-five after delivery. We met her and everything was fine."

"So what made you beat her? She change her mind? Is that why you rammed a knife into her?"

"I don't know what you're talking about. I didn't hit or stab anyone. Jennifer and I met Louise yesterday afternoon. At Queenscliff Beach. We worked out the arrangements and left. We've even got a medical appointment booked for next week."

"Louise isn't going to make that one," I said. "But you already knew that."

"I swear to God. Louise Simpson is fine."

Mary went to the Jeep and pulled out two crime scene photos. She slapped them on the engine in front of Wallace. "Do these jog your memory?"

He looked at them and turned his head away. "Why are you doing this?"

"Look closer. Ring any bells?"

"Please," he begged. "What does any of this have to do with us?"

"Louise Simpson is dead." I jabbed at the photos. "Because of you. Then you took Zoe Ruffalo, an innocent baby."

"Wait. Is that what you think?" He pleaded with both of us. "You've got it all wrong. I've never seen that woman before. I don't know who she is, but she definitely isn't Louise Simpson."

Chapter 49

THE TACTICAL RESPONSE team entered the house simultaneously through the front and back doors. Four more squad cars pulled up. Mark Talbot climbed out and headed towards us, as Terry McMahon checked in with his team.

The woman had surrendered and was in custody. No shots had been fired.

I pulled Mark aside.

"Wallace alleges our murder victim was not the same woman he met as Louise Simpson."

"Alleges? So now you're a defense lawyer?" Mark sneered.

"I'm just saying something doesn't add up. He had no reason to lie this time."

"It's called buying time by throwing in something from left field," he said curtly. "That's your specialty."

There wasn't time for agendas here. "What if there are two Louise Simpsons? Someone else is using her identity?"

He thought for a moment. "You could be onto something. Now ... you just have to prove the Illuminati are behind it."

Mark was reveling in the fact my credibility was at stake. I stayed calm, but stressed my point. "Wallace says he met someone claiming to be Louise Simpson, with two children, who lived in Killara."

"And he's an up-front kind of guy, that Wallace, or should I say Finch?"

Yes, Wallace had lied. But he was also a coward, full of bluff. The way he responded to the photos wasn't what I would have expected from a cold-blooded killer who took his time and made the victim suffer.

If the Wallaces hadn't taken the baby, someone else had. And they had diverted all our energies to looking in the wrong place.

Two officers came out with Jennifer Wallace. Her hands were cuffed behind her back. "Nothing so far," one said.

Sniffer dogs alighted from another car. The trainer held a flannel blanket, presumably belonging to Zoe Ruffalo, to their noses.

Mark instructed them to search the cars and boots, in every bush and cranny, and under every rock on the property.

Fifteen minutes later, the trainer came out. There was no trace of a baby.

Chapter 50

THE WOMAN THE Wallaces met had to be an impostor.

I phoned Johnny and asked him to go over all Louise Simpson's bills and debits again. We were looking for anything to suggest she was a victim of identity fraud.

He knew that meant the baby was still missing and agreed to get straight onto it.

Darlene's new machine was processing the DNA and would have an answer within minutes. I had to get clearance from Brett Thorogood to access the police's DNA database with the Gene-IE.

Mary and I decided to head back to the office. As we moved to the Jeep, someone called my name.

"Gisto. Hey, Craig! Congratulations on tracking down the killer."

The voice came from the sleaziest entertainment reporter, Marcel Peyroni. I tossed up whether to ignore or answer him.

"Where's the baby? Were you too late?"

"He's an idiot," Mary said. "Ignore him."

"Come on, Craig, you gotta have a comment," he called.

I couldn't pretend the guy wasn't an arsehole. But I needed to know how this fool had managed to get a TV crew here so quickly. Had someone from the police leaked the news about the Wallaces? His stupidity had compromised the entire operation. If it wasn't for him and his helicopter, Mary wouldn't have had to put herself at risk. And I wouldn't have to suffer the ire of Mark Talbot.

I walked towards him, hand blocking my face from the camera lens. Mary was one step behind. I asked if we could talk "off the record."

Peyroni faked a smile. "Of course."

His cameraman lowered his lens, but I knew it was still recording.

"You're a regular Johnny-on-the-spot," I said. "No one from the social pages here. You're in the wrong place."

"On the contrary. This story has it all. Murdered widow, the fashionable Craig Gisto, Investigator and Scandal Suppresser to the stars."

The microphone was suddenly beneath my chin. Peyroni had a blog, columns, and a TV show. Spiteful press coverage from him could harm the business.

But I had no intention of giving him a sound bite.

Peyroni tried again. "Do you have any response to the rumors that you provided the killer with all the details to find Louise Simpson?"

I turned away and Mary stepped in. "The police will be keen to know how you beat them here. Something about obstructing justice, interfering with an investigation."

Peyroni flashed an ultra-white smile. "Good old-fashioned investigative journalism. I've learned a lot studying the great Craig Gisto. Do you have anything to say, Miss Clarke, on his dramatic fall from grace?"

Chapter 51

PEYRONI'S STUNT COULD have put lives at risk. Zoe Ruffalo was still missing, and we were no closer to finding Louise's killer.

The one lead we had was the woman posing as Simpson. The Wallaces were our only hope of finding her.

I needed to get access to them during police questioning but didn't fancy my chances. I phoned Brett Thorogood, who, thankfully, picked up.

"Craig, what the hell went down? Mark Talbot is ropable. He says you leaked the address to the tabloid press."

"How many police knew? Maybe the leak's closer to home."

Recent raids on potential terrorists had been stage-managed for media. With state and federal elections looming, politicians and police ministers basked in megawatt coverage of high-profile arrests. PR stunts like this reminded the public police were "winning the war" against crime.

Brett paused. "It's possible it came from within our ranks but I was very specific. Only those directly involved were notified. Because of what was at stake and the intense media interest. It could have ended badly." His voice trailed off. "If it came from someone within the force, their career is over. No matter who they are."

Mark Talbot wasn't beyond suspicion either.

I described Wallace's reaction to the pictures of Louise Simpson's body. And how he seemed relieved that the dead woman was not the one he had met. Brett listened to my theory about someone impersonating Louise Simpson. With no other leads to finding Zoe Ruffalo, he agreed to see if he could get me in to question the Wallaces. With a warning. If I made any mistakes, the police relationship with Private would be terminated.

Mary and I headed back to the Jeep. She had been on the phone while I spoke to the deputy commissioner. She waited until we were alone inside the vehicle.

"I just spoke to the helicopter charter company. They've had a chopper on hold since yesterday. Booked by Craven Media."

I pulled the seatbelt across my chest. "That's Peyroni's employer."

"The pilot was on standby and took a call at eight-fifteen a.m. to fly to this address. Peyroni's team arrived twenty minutes later."

It was like a heavy blow. That was the time we were on our way to Dural. Before I phoned the police.

"We have to face it," Mary said. "The leak came from someone inside our office."

Chapter 52

MARY STOPPED AT a small shopping mall at the unusually named Round Corner.

"We can get a coffee. Looks like you need some sustenance."

News of the timing of the leak had rocked me. I still had to decide how to handle it. The day was proving to be worse than yesterday and we still had no idea if Zoe was alive or where she might be. Mary was the only person I could trust right now.

We found a quaint café, called Chat Time, and took a seat in the outside section. The clientele comprised elderly people, mothers with babies, and middle-aged women in exercise gear. They were all engaged in conversation at their respective tables. Not an electronic device in sight.

The atmosphere was homely, very different from city cafés. A middle-aged man dressed in a black shirt and trousers greeted us as I checked my phone for messages.

"We don't have wi-fi here," he said with a natural smile. "It encourages people to chat."

The strategy definitely worked. Mary ordered scrambled eggs on toast. I chose a zucchini, eggplant, and pesto melt. We both settled on lattes.

Before we addressed the office leak, I wanted to get an update on Eric Moss and his organization. He'd been missing for four days now.

"Where are you up to with the Moss case?"

Mary sat forward, elbows on the table. "This guy could be Roy Orbison. In the few photos he appears in, he's wearing darkened lenses. They completely hide his eyes and eyebrows. I couldn't locate one good facial image."

"What about when he was younger?"

"That's the thing. There are no photos of him before Contigo. I checked the enrollments for schools in the area his daughter said he grew up in. Nothing. This guy had no Internet presence."

The coffees and cutlery arrived.

"It's like he's hiding in plain sight. He gets national hero status, receives top business and citizenship awards, but doesn't appear in any press. He's the legs paddling under the water, out of sight."

"And Lang Gillies is the duck's head you see on the surface."

Our food appeared and I realized how little I'd consumed in the last two days. I ate like someone who didn't know when their next meal might be. In many ways that was true. This was going to be another long and draining day.

Mary devoured her eggs, pausing once to wipe her mouth with a serviette.

"I even checked for Throwback Thursday photos, brush-with-fame websites. No one's posted anything of Moss as an adult or child. And he doesn't appear on any politician's websites. Seems he avoided pics with them too. The man was definitely hiding in full view."

I began to wonder. If he had been hiding for that long, he could have had an exit strategy—in case he was ever exposed.

Chapter 53

BACK AT PRIVATE, a nervous Collette greeted us. We had a visitor who had already shown himself into my office. Two bodyguards waited in the foyer.

One scanned Mary first, with a handheld metal detector, then me.

"Standard procedure, for people Mr. Ambassador meets." He had a southern American twang.

Scanner Man stayed guarding our entrance, while the other guard walked us to my office and waited outside with Mary.

"Ambassador Jim Roden." A silver-haired man of around sixty greeted me. His suit was expensive, I guessed Italian. The tie was silk, with embossed blue flowers on a lighter background. A perfectly folded pocket handkerchief matched. An American flag badge was pinned to his lapel. We shook hands.

I asked if he would like something to drink before noticing the bottle of mineral water from my bar fridge.

"Hope you don't mind, I helped myself. Your receptionist said it was OK."

I suspected Collette was intimidated by the formality and accompanying muscle.

"What can I do for you, Mr. Ambassador?"

He unbuttoned his jacket and crossed a heel over one knee. "I'm concerned about Eric Moss."

I sat and leaned back. "Are you a friend?"

"Acquaintance. We've met on a couple of occasions. At a fund-raiser and again at the embassy. He was an impressive man."

I noted the use of the word "was." I wondered what he knew about the disappearance.

"Eric Moss only resigned four days ago."

"So I hear. My concern is not just personal. Mr. Moss has accessed a number of sensitive US facilities during his time with Contigo Valley."

"Are you worried he's sharing state secrets?"

"We'd like to know what his plans are from here. He has a vast body of knowledge and we'd like to make him a very tempting job offer."

I found that difficult to believe. He was fishing for information. Somehow he knew we were employed by Eliza. Then again, anyone could have seen us together last night and put two and two together. Word in the business world was leaching out about Moss's sudden departure from the company he'd been loyal to for decades.

I sat forward. "If I see him, I'll get him to give you a call."

"Mr. Gisto, I'm afraid you don't understand. There may be considerable embarrassment if Mr. Moss is not located quickly."

I decided to do some fishing myself. "Can you explain to me how someone without a passport or birth certificate gets access to your secure facilities? I'm guessing there are some red faces about that little oversight when a simple web search would have raised alarms." Unless, as I suspected, all information pertaining to Moss had been systematically removed from the Internet.

Roden sipped the mineral water from the bottle. "I hear you and Moss's daughter have developed a rapport."

I leaned in, uncomfortable about where this was heading. "I'm not at liberty to discuss clients or investigations."

"I'm just saying that relationship could be very useful." He stood. "International politics can be a minefield. My government would appreciate your sharing relevant information about Moss's whereabouts."

"Are you suggesting I break commercial confidence?"

"I'm suggesting you consider both our nations' security. I trust you'll keep our communication private."

I chose my words carefully. "For reasons of national interest."

He stared at me for a few seconds. "Precisely," he said, without a hint of irony.

Chapter 54

I SAT BACK. He'd caught me off guard. For him to mention my rapport with Eliza suggested someone *had* seen us last night, or she was under surveillance.

Mary saw the visitors out and returned to my office. "Secret Service. It's all I got."

Moss had to be in serious trouble if the US government wanted him found ASAP.

"They're desperate if they came to us for info," Mary said. "It's not easy to drop right off the grid. Especially theirs."

I agreed. Whatever Moss knew made him hot property. If he had planned his disappearance, it was years in the making. I thought of him in photos. The images I'd seen had him in half-profile, with the dark lenses. He was in the habit of hiding part of his face before the advent of facial recognition software. No passport or driver's license meant there were no documented facial images, front on, eyes captured. He had a strategy all along to avoid being identified. But why? The behavior dated back to his beginnings at Contigo, when they were a simple search-and-rescue group.

Mary wondered aloud, "Maybe he wasn't just working for Contigo."

From the amount of time he spent there, and the fact he lived on the premises, it was a stretch.

"Or…" I said, "Contigo is a front for something more." I thought again of the private contracts only Moss had access to. "Something the ambassador said bothers me. He specifically said they wanted Moss 'located.'"

Mary sank into the chair vacated by the ambassador. "No concern for his welfare."

Eliza was worried about foul play. Roden wasn't interested in finding out. He wanted us to locate Moss, dead or alive.

If he was alive, it couldn't be easy staying on the run from US security agencies.

And if Moss was CIA or an operative for another country, he'd broken a cardinal rule. No complications. Moss had blown that by adopting Eliza and having personal ties. A disabled child was more than a simple complication. Contigo Valley had to be supplying or developing something the US government wanted. Why else would US defense facilities give Moss access and then panic when he disappeared?

I wanted answers as to why the US government was suddenly on our back, and why they were using us to get to Moss.

I doodled on my notepad. It helped me think, piece together puzzles. "Roden mentioned sensitive facilities Moss visited."

"I know just the person to talk to," Mary said. "His personal pilot would have filed logs of times, dates of departures, and destinations."

"Good idea. We need to figure out what he was working on. Whatever contracts were in that locked desk."

Mary raised the other pressing issue. "How are you going to deal with the media leak?"

I rubbed my neck again. There was only one thing to do.

Chapter 55

I DOUBTED THE smashed office door was an accident now. We were the only business targeted in the attack and it provided access to plant listening devices. I wouldn't put it past Roden. The visit could have been an excuse to hide additional monitoring devices or modify ones already in place. Roden was unchaperoned in my office before we came back, and the crony with the metal detector kept Collette distracted. I thought back to the repairmen. They were from a company we hadn't used before. Collette had found the card under the door and they'd answered her call straightaway.

I suspected we'd been set up. I pulled out my phone and checked for their website. The company didn't exist in the Yellow Pages or online.

Whoever smashed the glass assumed a staff member would call the first available glazier. One thing concerned me: the timing. The door had been smashed *before* Jack Morgan rang me about Eric Moss.

Unless Jack's LA office was being monitored, a US agency wouldn't have known we would be involved. It was a stretch at best.

And how did Marcel Peyroni hear about the Dural raid if he wasn't tipped off by someone in our office? If we were being electronically monitored, there was no way a secret intelligence agency would be in cahoots with a tabloid gossipmonger, or risk exposure by leaking news of a raid. That left the question as to whether one of my team was on Peyroni's payroll.

I felt a deep knot in my gut.

I rang an old friend who specialized in technical security countermeasures sweeps. Without mentioning what I wanted, I asked if he'd like to come for a visit and see the offices. He agreed to be here within the hour. I trusted my staff and couldn't believe any one of them would risk lives by notifying a lowlife like Marcel Peyroni. I had no answer as to why a third party listening to us would, if only to discredit me and my team.

Mary and I headed to the lab. Darlene had just sent the DNA printout from the evidence beneath Louise's fingernails to the police. The new machine was beneficial but an arrest depended on other factors. We had to show motive and opportunity and compare the finding to a suspect's DNA.

Darlene was frustrated. "We won't know if Wallace is our killer unless he agrees to a DNA test."

His lawyer would no doubt advise him to avoid giving any samples that could be used against him until they had enough for a warrant.

Mary reached into her pocket. "Beg to differ."

She pulled out a bag containing the severed cable ties she'd used to bind Wallace's wrists.

Darlene's face beamed. "Give me an hour and a half and we'll know if it was Wallace at the murder scene."

Chapter 56

GIDEON MAHLER HAD always been slightly eccentric. We'd met in the US when I introduced him to an expat friend. The pair married and moved to Australia. The marriage didn't last but Gideon's services became more in demand. Politicians constantly used him to test their offices for listening devices. Rumor had it ADIA (the Australian Defense Intelligence Agency) had the country's one hundred wealthiest businesspeople under constant surveillance. With trade agreements including China, Japan, Indonesia, and Russia, it made some degree of sense—to ADIA.

Gideon was gaunt, sinewy, and had deep-set eyes that constantly scanned his surroundings. His first stop was the reception area. He looked under the desk for remnants of dust from holes drilled and checked for any pictures that were even slightly askew, anything out of its normal position. Gideon's assessment cost a premium but our business depended on confidentiality and that couldn't be compromised. I was not about to get Eric Moss killed if we tracked him down.

The smashed door and computer virus on Collette's

laptop, which meant the video cameras didn't record that night, had to be related. All I could do was wait. I tried Brett Thorogood and left another message. Once the DNA from the cable ties was back, we'd know if Wallace had lied about being at Louise Simpson's house. Instinct told me he hadn't. If Darlene could confirm that, I needed immediate access to quiz him about the woman he claimed to have met.

I rang Eric Moss's assistant, Oliver Driscoll, to see if he'd accessed the filing cabinet yet. He sounded as if he was in an echo chamber.

"Is Eric OK?" Apart from Eliza, the young assistant and accountant were the only ones who had asked about their former boss's welfare.

"We haven't found him yet, which is why I'm ringing."

There was an audible sigh.

"I don't know how I can help. I've been given until four p.m. to clean out my belongings and leave the building. We're not supposed to talk to you, but I'm worried. I can't get the diary copies out."

I asked him where he was at the moment and if anyone could hear him.

"I'm alone in the bathroom for now. I'm not the only one who's been told to leave. Renee Campbell, the lady you met with, was the first to go. Something is really wrong and I don't understand. I couldn't find the resignation e-mail."

"Did you manage to get into Eric's personal safe?"

"Sir Lang got a locksmith in but it was empty when he opened it."

If no one else had access, Eric could have cleaned it out before leaving. Something else was worrying the assistant.

"You think Gillies lied about the resignation?"

"I don't know. But it gets freakier. My flat was trashed. Police reckon it was druggies looking for cash because the flat-screen and Xbox One weren't touched. I thought it was my psycho ex, only he's in New Zealand."

It wasn't a usual break and enter, even for drug addicts. "Did you have work files there?"

"No. Only stuff on my laptop, and that stays with me. I think something happened to Eric."

The fear in his voice was clear.

"We're going to find him. In the meantime, can you stay with a friend for a few days? Just until we get to the bottom of whatever's going on?"

"My parents live on the north coast. I can go there."

I had one more question. "Have you ever seen or heard of a Jim Roden?"

"Sure, the ambassador's one of Lang Gillies's golf buddies. The old man likes to drop his name and how he used to advise President Bush on homeland security."

It may not have been Moss working for someone else. I began to suspect Lang Gillies of being more than he pretended.

Chapter 57

GIDEON ENTERED MY office and closed the door.

"I swept the entire place, toilets and bathrooms included. The building's clean."

That was a relief.

"There's a qualifier on that. I also looked at the computers and phones of all the employees, including yours, as you know."

Mine was the first I wanted checked. "And?"

"Good news is the computers are free of viruses and malware, as are your backups. No one called a reporter this morning from their phones or the office, no e-mails or texts either."

It was reassuring but didn't explain how Peyroni got the Wallaces' address as soon as we had it. Or why the computer was infected. Or the door was smashed. If that wasn't done to plant listening devices, what was the point? "What's the bad news?"

"There's spyware on one of your employees' phones."

I sat back. This was the moment I dreaded. "Spyware? What sort?"

"The sort that makes a phone a listening device,

whether it's on or off. And accesses computers when used as a hotspot."

Before I heard the name I needed to know. "Can anyone install it or does it require specialized knowledge? Can it be downloaded remotely?"

He shook his head. "The person installing it has to physically have the phone." He pulled a document from his case and handed it across. It was a detailed explanation of this particular phone spyware.

"Anything else?"

"Yeah, two of your employees are dating. Don't know if you have a policy on that, 'cause they're trying to keep it quiet."

"Did you go through all their texts as you scanned?"

"No," he smiled, "noticed them touching hands in the lab when they thought no one was looking. Otherwise, they're clean."

Johnny had been helping out more with evidence. It was because of Darlene.

"That's one headache we can sort out if the time comes." It left Mary and Collette. Mary had been livid about me taking on the background check but she always carried her phone and wallet on her. She never put them down. That left one person.

"Your receptionist's the leak," Gideon said. "Everything coming in and out of the office has been recorded for a third party."

I couldn't believe it. Collette? I had trusted her implicitly. "Any idea who's receiving?"

"Could take a while to find out. Everything's being rerouted."

"Can you tell how long it's been on there?"

"Again, I'll need some time. Oh, and one more thing. If she didn't actually load the software, it's possible she doesn't know it's there. You have to know what to look for."

So Collette either knew her phone was a listening device or her phone had been deliberately targeted. Either way, I couldn't afford to trust her from now on.

I thanked Gideon. I had a plan as to how to deal with Collette. We all needed to meet in the conference room.

Chapter 58

BEFORE THE MEETING, I handed each staff member a written note asking them to hand over their phone. All would be explained in the conference room in five minutes. In the meantime, I put the mobiles in my office for Gideon to work on. If the eavesdroppers weren't aware we'd found the software, we still had an advantage.

Once we were all seated around the table, Gideon did precisely what I'd asked. He announced that the phones had been infected with malware. At the moment he had no idea for how long. The software ensured that private discussions were recorded by an unidentified third party. Not just phone conversations, but in-person chats, in addition to texts and voice-mail messages. Anything previously thought private was now potentially in the public domain.

Johnny and Darlene exchanged the briefest of looks but said nothing.

Mary rocked back in her chair. "Hacks or pros?"

Gideon shrugged. "The software's readily available

online, which means a broad net. How they react from here will tell us a lot more. If there are any other 'incidents.'"

Collette's phone had been to every meeting and with her for every interaction with staff and clients. Like most twenty-somethings, the phone was permanently in her hands or within easy reach to check the latest message. I called it the fear of missing out that meant they were often engaged in social contact but experienced little meaningful interaction.

"Has anyone let their phone out of sight, or had someone ask to make a call, no matter how innocuous they could have seemed?"

I looked around the silent room. "When you exercise, do you leave it in a locker? When you shower, does anyone else have access? I don't care how close they are to you or how much you trust them."

Mary, Johnny, and Darlene all denied the possibility.

"Collette?" I asked.

She frowned. "I use mine for music in the bathroom, like when I'm getting ready or showering. And I have it strapped to my arm when I go walking."

"What about clients, visitors to the office? Maybe when you got them a coffee or tea."

"Always have it with me. Guess it's a habit."

I suspected Collette was unaware of the software. Now was the perfect time to lie if she knew the spyware would be found on her phone and wanted to divert suspicion.

I handed out brand-new burner replacements and asked if there was anything on anyone's phones they didn't want Gideon Mahler or me to see. No one responded.

"From now on, we use these to communicate for work and with each other."

Collette remained silent but her eyes darted from me to Gideon.

"Who do you think's behind it? Is it anything to do with the Moss case?" Mary queried.

"We're working on that," Gideon answered. "But we should have an answer later on."

I added, "Until further notice, everyone takes a phone, and make sure we have each other's new numbers. Until this is sorted, I want everyone to stay in constant touch, and give me the names of anyone who makes contact with you—socially or for work. I guarantee we're going to find out who's behind this."

Chapter 59

COLLETTE WAITED UNTIL the others had left.

Her face had become flushed and blotches extended to her neck. She was rubbing an index finger over her thumbnail repeatedly.

"How long do you think someone's been spying on us?"

I slid into the seat next to hers.

"We don't know yet, possibly a few days."

Her attention turned to rubbing her palms. "I don't know if this is important, but I just sort of met someone."

"How recently?"

"Couple of nights, but it feels like months. We just seemed to click."

It had to be the man I'd spotted her leaving with. That could have been their first date.

"Has he shown interest in your work?"

"No, but I met him here. In the office, the morning the door was broken."

The man I watched greet her that night wasn't one of the repairers. "Was he with the glass company?"

"No, he was headed to his office early when I arrived

and stopped to see if I was OK. He works in the next block. We got talking and he said he didn't normally ask someone out so fast, but he thought we had a—"

"Connection?" I doubted it was a coincidence. The timing of the computer virus, glass damage, and "accidental" meeting were too convenient. If the repairers didn't plant the devices, accessing Collette and gaining her trust could have been the purpose of the smashed door. "Let me guess. You're interested in the same things, he likes what you like, maybe even grew up near you?"

The blotches on her neck reddened. "He's from Tasmania. Devonport."

Collette's family came from Launceston. Like anywhere, a link to childhoods was a strong one. It was an easy "in" for a scammer to develop instant affinity with a target.

"What else do you have in common?"

"He learned to drive on a VW."

Collette owned one.

"And he listens to indie bands."

"Like the ones you have on your phone?"

She swallowed hard. "Is that how they knew about the raid at Dural? Has he been using me to get to…" Tears welled in her eyes.

I suspected they'd been intimate but it wasn't relevant. Whoever "he" was could have accessed her phone when they were together or when she slept.

"This is all my fault." She pushed the burner phone away. "I'm sorry I caused you all this trouble." Collette stood. "The keys to the office are in my bag. I'll go get them."

I rose and pushed the chair back into its place. I would bet money that Collette would never make the same mistake again. "You're not in trouble and you still have your job. In fact, you're our best chance of catching this character and finding out who he's working for."

She squinted, doubtful.

"He doesn't know we're onto him. When are you due to see him again?"

"Tonight. He is...I mean *was*...coming over for dinner."

"Everyone's got to eat. Looks like you have a date to keep."

Chapter 60

COLLETTE PASSED MARY on the way out.

"Eric Moss's personal pilot is headed to Contigo Valley later this afternoon." She raised her eyebrows.

"Where's he leaving from?"

"Bankstown airport."

"Any chance you can get us on the flight?"

"Hedge a bet?"

I laughed. "Not when you're on the job." If anyone could get us on the plane, Mary could. I was suddenly reminded how talented the team was. The office being bugged was a glitch. We still had work to do.

First, I needed to talk to Eliza Moss in person, without her phone. Ambassador Roden had implied she was being watched.

She agreed to meet in the foyer of her office building in twenty minutes.

I was there in ten.

A concierge sat behind a large marble desk answering queries from a constant stream of visitors. I watched from a black leather divan. The CIA would most likely have Eliza under surveillance. Once she arrived, from where I sat I could see who followed in the lifts and lingered even for a moment.

Eliza eventually appeared, wheeling herself out. She was dressed in a short-sleeved silk blouse and navy skirt. A silver filigree locket sat on a short chain. Her face was drawn with a touch of darkness under her eyes. She couldn't have managed much sleep.

The concierge looked up and called out to her. "Found your present." He held up a pack of gum. "Twenty-seven days today."

"You and your lungs are welcome," she called back before doing a half-circle to face me.

I kept my eyes on everyone exiting the lifts.

"Why the secrecy? Is Dad all right?"

I explained about the visit by Roden's crew and the fact that it was likely they were having her monitored and followed.

"Who'd want to follow me? It's pretty far-fetched, don't you think?"

"It isn't when the CIA could be involved. Someone planted spyware on my employee's phone and has been listening in to all conversations in the office. The break-in coincided with a virus on a computer as well."

"Why would the CIA care about Dad? He worked in safety and recovery, for Pete's sake."

People in suits, jeans, even a cyclist in Lycra and bike helmet filed out of the lifts. No one seemed to look twice at Eliza.

"He was obviously involved in defense contracts that were kept pretty quiet. Maybe he failed to deliver on time, or couldn't complete a contract for some reason. The US government definitely wants him found."

She sat back in her chair.

A woman hovered by the concierge desk, glancing at

her watch more often than necessary. She pulled out her phone and checked something.

"Well, why haven't they found him yet? People can't just hide from the CIA."

The woman with the phone knelt down and a toddler ran into her arms. They exited with a man pushing a stroller. For a moment the foyer was empty apart from us.

"Not unless they have some kind of training in how to avoid being caught," I explained. "It isn't just your father who has disappeared. So has almost all the evidence that he ever existed."

Chapter 61

ELIZA LISTENED INTENTLY. I'd noticed a man sit and start flicking through a four-wheel-drive magazine on an adjacent lounge.

"Could Dad have been arrested by these people?"

"Not yet. Otherwise they wouldn't have come to me, or need to watch you. It makes sense; you're his only family. He may try to pass something on to you, or send you a message." I looked directly into those intense green eyes. "Has he?"

"No. I would have told you." She dragged a piece of hair from her forehead and tucked it behind one ear. "He would have warned me if something was wrong. That's why I'm scared for him."

I instinctively reached out and took her hand. "Maybe it happened too fast." It occurred to me that Eric knew whatever he was involved in could endanger his daughter. Alternatively, he may have known she'd be under surveillance and was unable to get in touch safely. "I suspect he may have known a time would come when he had to disappear. He just didn't know exactly when until last week."

"Thank you for helping." Eliza gently squeezed my fingers. "What happens if the ambassador's people, or the CIA, or whoever, find my father? What will they do to him?"

"Honestly, I don't know. First I have to find out what they want from him."

The magazine reader got up and headed to the stairwell.

"Can you think of anything he could have said, hinted at, or something he maybe gave you that at the time you thought wasn't important?"

She stared at her lap, concentrating for a few moments. "Nothing stands out. We talked about going fishing again soon, or maybe a cruise. What if he did give me a sign and I missed it?"

"It's OK," I assured her. "Something might come back to you. For now, I want you to use this when we talk or meet." I pulled out a spare burner phone. "I'm the only one who has this but I've programmed in my staff's contacts as well as mine. Don't hesitate to call. What you may think is trivial could be vital in finding him."

She put the phone by her side so it was hidden from view. "You mean before anyone else gets to him." Her voice wavered.

"Your father may have ticked off some pretty important people. From what I know of him, he's good at hiding. We have the advantage because we have you."

She squeezed my hand again. "I'll go through what I have. Cards, gifts, photos, messages."

I felt a strange connection to this woman, one that I hadn't experienced in a long time. I put it down to her being a vulnerable client. Eliza Moss was no victim, but she could just be a target.

I stood and checked the foyer one more time. Apart from occasional glances, no one seemed particularly interested in us. "I'll come see you when I get back from interviewing the Contigo Valley pilot. Whatever your father is involved in is serious. You need to be careful."

Chapter 62

IN THE LAB, Johnny and Darlene sat on adjacent stools. He circled three recent billings on Louise Simpson's credit card, all for a radiology practice in Manly.

"Unless you know someone at a particular practice, why would you drive for what would be an hour-and-a-half round trip, with two small kids, just to get an X-ray?"

Darlene checked the billings. "My mum said her world shrank after kids. She stopped going to doctors, shops, and hairdressers who weren't near home or school."

"My point exactly. There are two other X-ray places within a five-minute drive."

Darlene flicked through a series of notes she'd taken. "The GP says Louise didn't have any medical problems apart from reflux and sciatica after the second child that settled in a couple of months. No tests either, nothing except the kids' vaccinations."

"Maybe she was a doctor shopper. It wouldn't be

unusual if she wanted sleeping tablets or painkillers and didn't want her regular doctor to know. Maybe they ordered the X-rays."

"That's easy to sort out then." Darlene winked. She clicked at the computer and then phoned Medicare, leaning across Johnny to read the credit card bill.

"I'm sorry to bother you, but I need to ask about one of my Medicare bills. Since my husband died, and the insurance company hasn't paid us, things are pretty tight for the kids and me."

She instantly had the operator's attention.

"I'm trying to go over my medical expenses, to see if we qualify for the safety net, but I can't remember all the tests I've had. I remember the last bill was for X-rays I had on the twentieth of last month. I paid $375." Her voice dropped away just a little. "My husband used to manage our finances."

Johnny watched as she read out Louise's name, date of birth, and Medicare number. It was enough to get the operator to answer her query. After a few nods and "uh-huhs," during which she took copious notes, she finished the conversation. "Thank you for this. You've been very kind."

Johnny admired Darlene's phone manner. She could charm a politician into giving away his dirtiest secrets.

"Well," Darlene turned to Johnny, "Louise had three ultrasounds in a month, and six in the last three months. All of them were abdominal. She must have paid for some in cash if they're not all on her credit cards."

"Don't suppose she said which doctor ordered them?"

"She did. The family GP—who has no record of them."

"And we know Louise *wasn't* pregnant." Johnny

flicked through his notes. "The Wallaces said they met the surrogate and paid a hefty deposit at Queenscliff. Which is…"

"Adjacent to Manly," Darlene added. "Chances are, the woman posing as Louise Simpson lives nearby."

Chapter 63

I PARKED AT Bankstown airport with Mary and entered the small gray building with the blue passenger terminal sign. It was smaller than that of many regional airports.

Inside, the sole check-in counter was unattended. A couple near the exit was uninhibited about displaying affection. The septuagenarian would have been twice, possibly three times the woman's age, with a wispy comb-over.

A man dressed all in white entered from the airfield side, greeted the couple, and collected their luggage. They headed to a Cessna on the tarmac outside. The woman struggled up the stairs in her six-inch heels.

"How long do you give it?" Mary asked.

"Not much longer than the trip," I guessed.

"Hard to believe cynics like us are single," she said as a thin gentleman in his fifties approached us.

"Ms. Clarke?" He reached out his hand, first to Mary then to me. "Geoff Andren."

"This is my boss, Craig Gisto," Mary said. "Thanks for seeing us."

The pilot's silver hair was cropped short, nothing

out of place. A white epaulet shirt bearing the Contigo logo was immaculately pressed, as were the navy belted trousers. Attention to detail was something I respected, especially in people who controlled the cockpit of a plane.

He escorted us through a security gate onto the tarmac. "Bankstown specializes in charters, cargo, and flight training," he said, as if taking a tourist group for the hundredth time.

A plane landed on a distant runway as we approached a hangar. Sitting outside was a scaled-down version of Howard Hughes's Spruce Goose.

Mary stopped to admire it. "Is that a Grumman Goose B49?"

Arms folded, Geoff paused and rocked on his heels. "Yep. She's a beauty. Been here since it was built, in 1944."

As we walked on, Johnny rang and I excused myself to answer. He said that Collette had agreed to meet the new boyfriend at her home tonight, with Darlene and Johnny outside monitoring the situation. I told him to keep me informed and get Collette out at the first hint of trouble. He also said he had a lead about the Simpson impostor he'd follow up first.

The pilot had become more animated.

"The hangars on this side are all original. They housed bombers in World War Two. In fact, when General MacArthur visited, this was the airport used by the US Army Air Forces."

The enormity of the airport became apparent. It was amazing all this existed in the middle of suburbia. "Did civilians object to having a military target so close to their homes in wartime?"

Geoff's eyes beamed. "They disguised this place to look like farmland. Fake houses, fake roads, dummy roofs to hide the hangars."

I thought it sounded a lot like Eric Moss. Something hidden in full sight.

A helicopter's rotor blades started up.

"Robinson R44?" Mary asked.

"You'd get on well with Eric. He loves military history and flying." Our host pointed to a helicopter that landed on a pad in front of another hangar. "Eric pilots the one we have at Contigo."

I knew Eliza hadn't mentioned that skill. Maybe she didn't know. She had said that her father didn't like flying that much.

If Moss had access to a helicopter, the odds of us locating him just got a whole lot worse.

Chapter 64

ANY INFORMATION GEOFF Andren could give us was critical. He had vital knowledge no one else at Contigo was willing or able to share.

"It would help us to know a little about Mr. Moss's routine, especially with traveling to and from Contigo," I said, pleased Mary had gained his confidence.

"I always had the plane at the terminal, ready for take-off as soon as Mr. Moss arrived."

At the four-seater Duchess, Geoff hesitated. "All staff were issued with advice from Sir Lang not to talk to private investigators."

"We don't want you getting into trouble, but we have real concerns for Eric's safety." Mary made the powerful point.

The pilot shoved both hands in his pockets and his eyes focused on the plane wheels. "He gave me a job when I was let go from a commercial airline. He's been good to me from the start."

Moss's intentions may have been noble, or he deliberately recruited people who were at a disadvantage and most likely to be compliant.

I asked why Moss chose the Duchess.

"His work was unpredictable. The Duchess is the most efficient way to get him around." He proudly touched the wing. "Extra instrumentation means she's more capable in rough conditions. We're over the Blue Mountains to and from Contigo, so he wanted something that could fly even in bad weather."

The pilot asked Mary which military bases she had worked on, which quickly segued into which installations he had flown Moss to. The list was extensive.

"I thought he spent most of his time in Contigo Valley," I ventured.

"True, but there are frequent short flights. Anything from one to four a week."

"To the bases?" Mary was almost drowned out by a plane taking off.

Geoff explained, "Often Mr. Moss is in transit at the bases. Sometimes I see the other plane he's meeting. Otherwise I leave him alone to wait on the runway."

The notion struck me as odd. "How do you mean alone? With the people he was meeting?"

"Funny thing, I never saw anyone else. Not even the other pilot. My instructions were to wait in the lounge if he was gone for a few hours. Otherwise, I'd fly home and then go back for him. The longest he was away was three days."

"Anyone return with him?"

"Not that I saw. He was always standing there alone when I arrived to pick him up."

"What did he take with him? Luggage? Did he bring anything back?" The whole thing seemed highly suspicious to me.

"He only ever had the same duffel bag. Khaki, about so big." He made a shape about 60 centimeters wide and 30 centimeters high.

The bag wasn't large enough to fit much of anything in it apart from a laptop and maybe a change of clothes. "Do you know what was in it?"

"Never saw. That thing didn't leave his side. He always insisted on carrying it himself."

I now understood how Moss had managed to leave the country without a passport. He was using military planes, which meant there was no available record of where he'd been.

Yet we still had no idea who Moss actually was, or who he was really working for.

Chapter 65

JOHNNY FELT THIS was the break they needed to find Louise's killer, and baby Zoe. He entered the radiology practice in Manly where a series of ultrasounds had been billed to Louise Simpson's Medicare number and credit card. She was a victim of identity *and* medical fraud. Paying her bills automatically meant it could have gone on indefinitely if the amounts weren't enough to raise suspicion and Louise didn't scrutinize every transaction. Like most people, she seemed to have just scheduled payments to avoid late fees.

Johnny suspected the fraudster was using other identities as well. This impostor knew not to be greedy and risk exposure. Otherwise, she could have cleaned out Louise Simpson's account, taken out loans, and financially ruined her for the sake of a quick payoff. This woman had other plans. Surrogacy was her way of leeching money from desperate couples. They could hardly report her to the police if things went sour, given their involvement was illegal.

A soap opera blared on a large TV screen to a waiting room full of children and elderly people.

Johnny joined the queue at the reception desk, wondering if he should have done medicine after all. The radiology business was booming.

"Request form?" A middle-aged woman held out her hand without looking up.

"I'm not here for an X-ray. I need to see whoever's in charge," Johnny began.

"I'm sorry. Doctors only see technicians and equipment reps with appointments. You'll have to wait until September." She tapped at a keyboard.

Johnny showed his ID, leaned over the countertop, and said quietly, "I'm investigating this practice's involvement in Medicare fraud in the case of a young mother who was brutally murdered."

That caught the receptionist's full attention. "I'll see what I can do."

She wheeled back her chair and rushed off behind the scenes.

Nothing like the mention of murder and scandal to get action, Johnny thought.

A small man in a shirt and tie appeared with the receptionist. She was flushed and tugged at the hem of her shirt.

"I'm Dr. Kwong," he said. "Please come this way."

Johnny followed him down a corridor and into a large X-ray viewing room. Multiple lit boxes held films of chests, limbs, and sections of a brain scan.

"How can I help you?" Dr. Kwong offered a seat.

"You may have seen on the news," Johnny said as he sat, "a woman was murdered in Killara. Louise Simpson?"

The doctor lowered himself into a chair. "My wife went to church this morning to pray for her and the baby. Do you know if she has been found?"

"Not yet. The woman who died supposedly had scans

performed here recently and I need to see documentation of who did them and why."

"With any patient and medical record, there are strict confidentiality issues. I have to check with the Medical Defense Association before we can speak about any cases, even a deceased patient."

"I respect legality and ethics." Johnny leaned forward. "There were a number of charges for ultrasounds billed to your practice. We believe Louise Simpson's Medicare number and credit card were used in those transactions. And because of that an innocent young mother is dead. A whole lot of trouble is about to rain down on this place."

"I'll make a quick call," Dr. Kwong said. "What do you need to know?"

Chapter 66

GEOFF ANDREN WAS taking replacement engine parts to Contigo Valley and agreed to take us there so we could see firsthand what Eric Moss had built. I wondered if it would give us any clues as to why the Americans were so desperate to find him. All things going well, Geoff estimated we'd complete his business and the three-hundred-kilometer round trip in four hours.

We climbed on board and were handed earphones with microphones. Geoff checked his flight plan and cleared us to taxi. Once the engines were on, my stomach felt unsettled. Lack of sleep, food, and a neck ache were adding up. I also hoped Collette would be safe. I had no idea who we had been targeted by. I disliked putting a team member at potential risk without knowing who we were up against.

The one positive was that we'd be back in time to monitor her house and provide backup for Johnny and Darlene.

We were soon cleared for takeoff. The engine hummed louder and we were seamlessly in the air.

Mary and Geoff chatted about the plane's technical

features and I closed my eyes for a few minutes. I could fly in helicopters and large planes. It was the small ones that unnerved me. I'd known at least two people killed in them, both due to pilot error.

And for some reason, I couldn't get Eliza Moss out of my head. The feel of her hands, the smell of her citrus perfume.

The hum and vibration of the engine hastened the need to doze.

I was startled by Mary tapping me on the leg. "You've got to see this," she said into her mike.

We were flying west over the Blue Mountains. I'd never seen them from this perspective.

"Gillies Falls." Our pilot pointed to the right side.

The site was spectacular even if clouds were moving in.

"We may be in for some turbulence," Geoff warned.

With the plane buffeting, we passed Lithgow and came on a spectacular green valley, like something from a lost world.

"That's Contigovale, known locally as CTV. It isn't part of the organization but is dependent on our staff to stay afloat."

There were a small number of buildings on the ground, more like a village than a town, I thought. It had what appeared to be its own runway.

Mary asked, "How much land does Contigo own?"

"Thirty-three acres surrounded by grazing land and national parks. The actual base sits above the valley, by the Casta River."

This had to be the wealthiest nonprofit organization in the country. It made me more than curious to find out where Moss really got all the money.

Chapter 67

WE FLEW OVER a series of shipping containers, one of which was located next to a helipad.

"Did Eric ever invite guests out here with him?" I asked.

"Bankers, potential donors, celebrities, politicians. We've brought people who begged to come out and be photographed here."

The engine buzzed and the aircraft dropped a couple of times.

"We fly everyone over this spot to show them what we're developing."

"What's in those?" Mary pointed to the containers with helicopter access. There was nowhere else to land.

"Collateral, resources. Each is filled with millions of dollars' worth of high-tech equipment and can be opened if bankers need to see them before they approve loans. They view a couple at the base first, but they're free to see the others if they wish."

I was curious about the funding. "Did the GFC affect the organization and make it more dependent on loans?"

Geoff checked the instruments and adjusted something I couldn't make out. "The tours increased for sure, when donations slowed. Banks were banging on Mr. Moss's door, throwing million-dollar loans at him. Mr. Moss is good with people. A hands-on guy. He was on every tour, answered every question. Equipment sales and contracts repay the loans and all profits go straight back into research and development."

Mary prompted, "Were international businessmen interested in investing or donating?"

"Sure. Everyone from the Chinese, Russians, Indonesians, and Americans wanted to invest, even a Bollywood actor. Not that I knew who he was, although Mr. Moss said he was a superstar."

"Do you know which ones shook on deals?" she pushed.

"Couldn't say. That was all done back at the base."

I tried to elicit more on the secret trips. "Did you ever wonder who he met on those other bases, or where he went?"

The plane shuddered a little. "Wasn't my place."

We were no wiser about the contracts missing from Moss's office safe.

I had to know what the pilot thought. "Do you think Eric chose to resign?"

"I can't believe he would, and by e-mail? This is a man who does deals with a handshake. He doesn't text or e-mail you. He phones. It's all personal."

"Do you have any idea where he might have gone?"

"Wish I knew," Geoff admitted. "This place was his life. He would never have given it up without a fight."

We took in the near-vertical sandstone cliffs below; adjacent fields merged into dense forests. If Eric Moss hadn't absconded and instead met with foul play there were infinite places to dispose of a body out here.

Chapter 68

JOHNNY AND DR. KWONG reviewed the scans and billings. The first was performed at eighteen weeks' gestation. The report by Dr. Kwong's colleague described a fetus with significant abnormalities of the lungs, heart, and brain. Dr. Tan concluded that the developmental abnormalities were incompatible with life. The baby was unlikely to survive beyond twenty-four weeks. The second scan described an eighteen-week pregnancy. The irregularities were identical. Only this scan was performed three weeks later.

Dr. Kwong pulled up the dates on the films and viewed the first. He then located the second on the computer and placed the video recordings on dual screens. The angles and close-ups were identical.

"If this is the same pregnancy," Johnny asked, "could the dates have been wrongly typed in?"

Dr. Kwong's brow furrowed. "Different ultrasonographers, different days should produce unique scans no matter the condition. Each ultrasound is like an original piece of art, dependent on pressure, position of the baby and mother, and depth of abdominal tissue, among a host of other variable factors."

He searched computer records for another few minutes. Johnny checked his watch. All he wanted to know was who had access to the billings and who fraudulently presented Louise's details.

Dr. Kwong used the phone and spoke in what sounded like Cantonese. "My colleague will join us shortly," he said and viewed the third scan. It looked exactly the same as the others.

An older gentleman wearing a green surgical gown and protective glasses entered the room. Dr. Kwong introduced Dr. Tan, describing him as their most experienced interventional radiologist.

Dr. Tan took a seat at the screen as the videos were replayed.

He moved closer and craned his neck.

"I remember this patient. From a couple of years back. She had already suffered a number of miscarriages. The baby died from a rare congenital condition not long after that scan."

"Do you know the name of the syndrome? I mean, is there a database of cases like it, carriers, for example?"

He shook his head. "I can tell you their name wasn't Simpson though. They were first cousins from a small village in Lebanon. I remember because the mother spoke English but the father needed an interpreter. She was too distraught to tell him."

"Are you certain the scans are all identical?" Johnny needed to be sure.

"There is no doubt," Dr. Kwong answered.

So the doctors had just confirmed what they'd suspected—that the woman claiming to be a surrogate was using the same scan, with altered dates, to con couples.

The question was, how had she managed to pull it off?

Chapter 69

JOHNNY POINTED OUT that the unknown surrogate using Louise Simpson's identity was their only link to finding the missing baby. Dr. Tan was keen to cooperate.

He explained that the only way to date the scans and patient details was within house. The machines themselves embedded the names and dates into the scan. Either someone reentered details onto a copy of the scan, or had somehow managed to copy the videos and alter them on the main computer system.

Johnny wanted to know every other possible means. "What about obscuring details for teaching purposes? If you send them to someone else, can they alter the information and print out images?"

"In theory, that's possible. However, most doctors obscure the patient details with a sticker or leave them blank."

It still meant other doctors or ultrasound technicians theoretically could alter patient information.

As expected, the reports were even easier to change. The practice logo and wording could be done by anyone with a computer and printer.

The realization seemed to hit both of the radiologists hard.

Because the original scan with the Lebanese couple had been performed in their practice, they had to consider that one of their employees was involved in a murder and baby kidnapping. They both wanted the source found and punished. Johnny doubted either of them was personally involved in the scam.

Dr. Kwong provided a list of employees with accompanying photos that had been taken for ID badges. A total of forty-four full- and part-time staff. Nearly half were male, which left twenty-three potential female suspects. Johnny knew that the Wallaces could identify the surrogate they had met. If the woman had a male accomplice, he'd have to consider investigating the men and their partners. At least the photos were tangible.

What kept him positive was the fact that the other scans had been billed to the same practice. In case anyone checked, there would be a paper trail to suggest the scans had all been performed in Manly.

Johnny needed to be sure the location was significant. Given the Wallaces had met the supposed surrogate at the nearby Queenscliff Beach, he reasoned this was the most likely source of the fraudulent scanner. He knew that if he was wrong, the time wasted investigating the staff could cost baby Zoe her life.

Chapter 70

GEOFF ANDREN TAXIED to a hangar at the north end of Contigo's base. A security guard met us but didn't check our IDs or ask us to sign in, something I found surprising. We weren't provided with visitor badges either. That meant we were free to wander unmonitored.

The guard, Arnie Pymble, offered to show us around while our pilot disappeared to meet with the maintenance crew. From the air the place had resembled a university campus, with summer camp touches. Buildings were separate, connected by concrete paths. The corporate office was dwarfed by a research and development section. A basketball court, indoor swimming pool, and gymnasium were featured on our brief tour.

Arnie informed us that Eric Moss may have worked 24/7, but he was adamant that employees stay healthy and fit in order to avoid work injuries and maintain efficiency. Eric believed that by coming out for a game of basketball, they could get together and exchange ideas while getting fit. It was the same reason they had weekly barbecues for staff. There was no alcohol consumed on the premises, so employees visited the Contigovale pub, which maintained good relations with the residents as well.

"Did Eric attend the social functions?"

Arnie hoisted his trousers up. "He does barbecues but rarely visits the pub, unless it's someone's birthday. He's usually working."

As we walked around, Mary asked if the staff lived on the grounds.

"No, all hundred or so of us live in temporary housing in town. In fact, some of the staff were born and bred in the area."

"Do you work in shifts?"

Arnie stared at his shoes and rubbed a scuff mark on the back of one leg. "Most are gone by seven at night. Eric discourages hours longer than that. We pool cars and come back to get an early start."

It meant the base was minimally staffed through the evening and night. "How many guards do you work with?" Mary inquired.

"Four in the daytime—sometimes we act as tour guides to officials—and a couple at night."

That seemed like minimal security for such a large organization, particularly one with private government and defense contracts.

It also meant that flights could come and go without scrutiny or knowledge of staff. And so could Eric Moss.

Mary bent down and picked up a dead wasp. It was the only other form of life they'd seen, apart from Geoff and the security guard.

Arnie continued to sing Moss's praises. "One of the first things he did was build a public pool in Contigovale. The local council gave us all these awards for service to the community. You see, the young kids were leaving town, businesses were closing. That changed when we came here. With all the training crews we get through, thousands of people bring money into the local economy every month."

Clearly, Eric had ingratiated himself and Contigo Valley with local officials.

For a nonprofit organization, it seemed Moss was more than generous with borrowed or donated money.

Chapter 71

MARY AND I returned to the plane, ready to head back to Sydney. Geoff wasn't there so we looked around the hangar.

I turned to Mary. "Did you notice any security cameras?"

"None."

It was alarmingly lax for an organization with international interests and million-dollar equipment stored in shipping containers in the open.

The hangar next door contained a helicopter, a Robinson R44.

Geoff wandered in as I was checking inside the cabin. "Is this the one Eric Moss flew?"

"Sure is. She's on standby for search and rescue now."

Mary stepped back. "How often would Mr. Moss take the chopper up? If she'd been mine, I'd have been in her at every opportunity."

"Come to think of it, not for a few months. We fly guests over the property in the Duchess." He became serious, almost morose. "Do you think Mr. Moss is alive?"

The question took me a little by surprise. "Are you worried he may not be?"

"Just that this all seems out of character for him. I can't shake this feeling something bad has happened. I saw him on Thursday and he seemed off. It was as if he was distracted. He didn't say anything, but I knew something was wrong."

"We're going to find him," I reassured the pilot.

He took a deep breath. "You and Ms. Clarke might as well grab a bite to eat at the canteen. I'll come and get you once I've refueled and done the safety check."

I mentioned again that I had to be back in Sydney as early as possible. I'd agreed to meet Eliza Moss and to be there in case the sting to catch Collette's boyfriend went awry.

Mary was waiting outside the hangar. We found our way to the canteen building, which was a large wooden log cabin, with tables on a veranda. Over freshly cooked burgers, we discussed what we'd seen.

It bothered me that Moss could fly a helicopter and there was a landing pad by the shipping containers they flew over. Geoff had said that he had flown all visitors over the area in the last six months in the Duchess. Moss obviously didn't want them landing.

"Or he developed something that stopped him from flying," Mary suggested.

One thing was clear. The CEO hadn't disappeared in his helicopter.

"Maybe he was hiding something in those containers," I suggested. "He didn't want potential investors finding out."

Mary wiped her hands on a napkin. "The only way to know for sure is to look ourselves before they're moved or emptied."

The problem was, we were about to fly back to Sydney.

Chapter 72

WE WERE FINISHING our coffees when Geoff Andren walked into the canteen and grabbed himself a teabag and hot water from the urn near the ordering station. He slid into the chair next to Mary.

"We have to delay takeoff until morning. I'm sorry to do this to you, folks, but safety is my prime concern."

"Why?" I didn't understand. "We just flew here without any trouble."

"I found an insect lodged in the pitot-static tube."

"One insect. How?" I wasn't convinced it was serious enough to ground the plane.

He sighed. "It can affect instrument readings. Have to be sure there isn't a hive down behind it."

"He's right, Craig." Mary seemed unfazed. "Better to make sure it's cleaned out. That's why they have such rigid safety checks."

"Is there any other way of getting back to Sydney?" My first concern was Collette, meeting the man who bugged our offices without extra backup.

Geoff blew across the top of his drink. "Someone might be able to give you a lift into Lithgow, and there's the train, but no guarantees you'd get there any quicker. All nonessential crew here have been given leave until Sir Lang replaces Mr. Moss."

"Explains why the place is so quiet." Mary looked over the rim of her white mug.

"What about a hire car?" I had to try to get back. Somehow.

"No services around here."

"We're better off staying." Mary reached over and patted my hand, then raised an eyebrow at Geoff. "Anywhere we can sleep?"

"Trainees' accommodation. It's where the police and army troops sleep during survival training. Each one's equipped with gear and supplies."

"Let me guess," I said, "Gillies canceled all courses too."

"No," Geoff answered. "From what I hear, trainees are the ones pulling out. In droves. Moss is the backbone of this place." He glanced around. "Hate to think what will happen to us all without him."

He took his cup with him and walked out, shoulders a little more rounded than before.

As Mary finished her coffee, it became clearer.

"Any chance the insect blocking that tube was a dead wasp?"

She shrugged. "Johnny and Darlene have Collette's boyfriend under control." There was a mischievous glint in her eyes. "And it'll be a long night for us if we're to get to that helipad site and back without being noticed."

Chapter 73

I RANG JOHNNY and explained why we wouldn't be back. He filled me in on the ultrasound billings from the Manly radiology practice. I agreed there was a good chance Louise Simpson's impersonator had access to the facility or someone on staff. He assured me Collette was in good hands. They planned to see if the boyfriend tampered with her new phone, then track who he was working for. We should know then who had been bugging our offices.

Next I texted Eliza to let her know I wouldn't be back until the morning. I found myself looking forward to seeing her. I knew it had little to do with her disability. She was intelligent, resilient, high-achieving, but down-to-earth with no pretenses. I liked her quirky sense of humor. In my world of obscenely wealthy men, trophy wives, celebrities, models, pop stars, and movie stars, she was intriguing.

I knew she was a client but it didn't mean we couldn't enjoy each other's company while it lasted. The thing that bothered me most was the feeling that the news about her father was unlikely to be good. The pilot's concerns echoed mine. If he was dead, chances were the body would never be found. Especially if he was somewhere remote on Contigo's base or the parkland surrounding it.

Mary searched Internet maps and discovered the containers were approximately five kilometers directly southwest of our location. Most of the terrain we had seen from the plane was manageable. She collected dark overalls, night-vision goggles, water, and other essential supplies.

Geoff Andren was right. The cabins were equipped for any bush expedition.

We dressed and waited until dark to head out. Mary had gone for a light jog around the perimeter and noticed a guard who looked military. His walk and build suggested he was in charge. It wasn't unusual to have one professional and others to make up the numbers. Arnie was polite but hardly a threat if he challenged someone. He hadn't even checked our IDs. Without that attention to detail, the chances were we could leave the main compound without being seen.

Chapter 74

OUTSIDE COLLETTE'S HOME, Johnny and Darlene sat in his black V8 Commodore. Collette had asked to have the place to herself tonight, so her flatmates were headed to the movies. On cue, the pair wandered out the front door and drove off in a compact Mazda.

The target, who Collette knew as Callum Byrne, arrived early, carrying wine, flowers, and a large gift bag.

"Our boy's a player," Darlene declared. "It isn't only information he's after. In my book that makes him a prostitute." She raised her can of diet cola. "Here's to locating his pimp."

Johnny made a mental note to hide the chocolates he'd bought for Darlene from the convenience store. He had ducked off for snacks while Darlene planted listening devices in the bedroom, bathroom, and kitchen area in the hope Callum would give something away. It was more, though, for Collette's safety. First hint of a problem, they would enter the house and get her out.

Right now, the couple were in the kitchen. Callum was asking if she'd had any "brushes with fame" in her work. She turned the question on him. "You first."

He started by telling her he'd met a few famous people. Jon Bon Jovi in New York once, Katy Perry down at Bondi, and he'd taken a selfie with Russell Crowe when up near Byron Bay.

Collette gushed that Callum was more handsome than the actor.

He responded by wanting to know all about the famous people she'd met in her job.

Collette said she'd signed a confidentiality agreement when she joined the agency and couldn't possibly tell, but there were some *major celebrities*—she emphasized the words—who came to them for help.

"She's doing well," Darlene said. "Knowing how nervous she is, you can't pick it in her voice."

Johnny hoped so. He opened a bag of crisps and offered some to Darlene, who declined.

As the sun set, they heard a pop and both went for their car doors.

Collette giggled. "The cork almost hit the glass cabinet."

Johnny and Darlene relaxed, knowing Collette was commentating for their benefit.

"That bottle's been opened pretty fast," Johnny said. "Maybe he thinks if she's drunk, she'll talk more or not notice him checking her phone."

"I sent you a song today but it didn't go through," Callum said as glasses clinked.

"My phone battery died," Collette replied. "Was thinking of getting it checked 'cause it's been running down really quickly."

"No need for that—I can check on it. Why don't you heat up the butter chicken? I'm starving."

Darlene grabbed a crisp from the pack. "Didn't take him long. He's definitely the one who put the software on it."

But Johnny's attention had turned to a dark Ford

sedan that was pulling up a block down the road. No one left the vehicle. When a car turned into the street, its lights silhouetted two large figures inside.

He and Darlene slunk down, out of view. "What do you think they're doing?" she asked.

"Not sure. Three of them makes serious muscle. Things just got a lot more complicated," Johnny said.

Chapter 75

THE CAR'S INHABITANTS hadn't moved by the time Collette was ready to serve dinner. Alcohol flowed.

Collette pressed Callum about his work. "How about we have lunch tomorrow? I can come to your office this time. Where is it exactly?"

"Sorry, babe. I'm outside on jobs tomorrow. All week, actually."

The clang of forks on plates filled the silence.

"You've never said what it is you do. I'm betting human relations." Collette sounded coquettish.

"It's pretty dull, really. I run a team of auditors. Your work sounds way more interesting."

"Hold that thought while I get the cheesecake."

"Indian food and cheesecake?" Darlene groaned. "You did that, didn't you?"

Johnny shrugged. "Protein and carbs, it's a good combo."

"Mind if I step outside to return a call?" they heard Callum ask.

"No problem," Collette answered.

Callum emerged from the front door, phone to his ear

and one in his hand. He bent down and deposited something on the front step, seemed to finish his conversation, then returned inside.

"We shouldn't talk politics or religion," he began as glasses clinked again. "What about that poor baby who got taken? My aunt lives right near there."

Johnny sat a little higher, still watching the dark sedan. "Here we go."

The conversation inside continued. "It's terrible. That poor mother. My aunt's really shaken up about some maniac randomly killing women and babies."

"Maybe it wasn't random," Collette said. A chair moved.

"Tell me your theory," Callum said, "...on the lounge."

"Hang on." Johnny saw a man step out of the Ford. "I don't have a good feeling about this."

The pair waited as the man approached. Darlene dialed Collette's phone, which went straight to voice mail.

Then the man crossed over to Collette's side of the street.

Johnny grabbed a hoodie from the backseat and quickly pulled it over his head, with the hood up. He collected the crisps and slipped out of the car without closing the door properly. He punched Darlene's number into his phone so she could hear everything that transpired. Johnny loped along, hunched, stopping short of Collette's house.

The other man was holding Collette's gate when Johnny sauntered into the yard next door.

"Hey," he said loudly, pulling a crisp from the bag. "They went to the movies. I can give them a message if you want."

The man paused for a moment before saying, "My mistake. I was looking for number 28."

"That would be the next block down," Johnny said and watched the man leave. The stranger headed straight back to his car.

Johnny had already memorized the number plate when the car started up, did a U-turn, and left at speed.

"That was close. Didn't like the look of him." Johnny spoke into his phone now.

"And the bastard was after Collette's phone. Lover-boy left it on the step for his partner-in-crime. My guess is, the software was beyond him, which is why he had backup."

Chapter 76

THE MAN SUPPORTED his injured arm by resting it inside his half-zipped jacket. After making a call with a burner phone, he walked slowly along Roseby Street. In the day, the historic Birkenhead Point shopping center buzzed with activity. At midnight, Drummoyne resembled a ghost town. In many ways, the former rubber factory built in the 1800s belonged to the past.

He pulled in behind a tree when he saw movement in a doorway across the street. A car approached and the figure sat up. Headlights illuminated a small-framed male hugging a bag to his chest. The boy couldn't have been older than seventeen, dossing on the doorstep.

The man pulled his cap lower and donned dark glasses before crossing the road. His thoughts ran to the people he'd left behind. The family and friends he'd never see again. It was the only way to protect those he cared most about.

"Someone will appreciate knowing you're OK," he said, bending forward to hand the teen his phone. The pain in his shoulder and wrist clipped his breath. He cradled the arm tighter. "There's enough credit to call home. Maybe a shelter for the night."

The boy wrapped filthy fingers around the offering. "Hey—"

The man didn't stop and continued on his way.

He used his good hand to pull the jacket collar up to his ears. Avoiding the marina's security cameras, he levered himself over the fence to the locked facility. With nearly two hundred boats moored, this was the largest privately owned floating marina on Sydney Harbour. Every berth had its own water access and power. Exactly what he needed.

The trawler-style hull made it easy to spot the boat he was after. A Riviera Clipper 34 motor cruiser. Water slapped between the boats and the pier. Ropes banged rhythmically on masts. The boats were covered in a cloak of darkness once clouds obscured the crescent moon.

If everything went to plan, he'd be cruising through Sydney Heads in the next hour or so. Away from the city and everyone in it.

Chapter 77

WITH HER FATHER still missing, Eliza Moss couldn't face people tonight. Relieved she could postpone a client dinner, she hoped to take advantage of the quiet to think and focus on where Eric could have gone. Using forearm crutches, she eased onto the lounge and sank into the large cushions, exhausted. Her shoulders and hips ached.

The question played on a loop in her mind. Why hadn't her father called?

The only answer was the one she didn't want to face.

He wasn't able to.

The thought made her heart beat faster and her breathing accelerate. Her father meant everything to her. He'd been the one to save her from an institution, made sure she was educated, cared for, and loved. More than that, he taught her that she wasn't defined by her disabilities. They presented specific challenges, but everyone had some disadvantage to overcome. How she faced difficult times, like this, defined her.

Part of her wanted to scream at him for leaving. Abandoning her. If Craig was right, somehow he had managed to live without any proof of who he was. How? The question haunted her.

He drove cars but managed to do it without a license? She couldn't face the possibility that he had lied to her and everyone else for all these years. The alternative was that his identity had been erased. Someone wanted every trace of him gone. Which meant something terrible had happened.

Hot tears dripped onto her shirt.

She consciously slowed each breath in, aware her lungs were already functioning well under capacity. Stress affected her physical resilience more than infection. She had to remain in control. Her father needed her to be strong now more than ever.

Felix was soon on her lap sleeping, as Eliza stroked his white fur. "Everything's going to be OK. It has to be." For the first time in years, she prayed before falling asleep where she sat.

A bumping sound in the bedroom roused her. She immediately thought of Felix, but the cat was still asleep on her lap.

Craig had warned her to be careful. Someone was monitoring her movements and contacts. It had to be something falling in the laundry. The clothes hanger wasn't that stable.

She lifted Felix off her lap and onto his own cushion and hauled herself onto her bare feet. Holding on to the lounge, then the wall, she listened from the corridor. Another soft thud followed.

Someone was inside. Heart hammering in her chest, she tried to stay calm. Maybe it was just a young kid looking for wallets, cash, and jewelry. Her purse was in her bag on the kitchen table.

Her phone was in its charger, next to a marble Buddha statue on the hall table. She silently braced herself

against the wall and reached for the phone to dial 000.
Before she was connected, a large man in a dark jacket
and black jeans appeared.

When Eliza saw the balaclava, she knew she was in
trouble.

Chapter 78

ELIZA REACTED QUICKLY and grabbed the Buddha statue. Her best chance was on the floor. She was too unstable on her feet. Sliding down the wall, she flicked off the light switch and pulled the hall table over just as the man lunged. He tripped, hitting the wooden floor hard.

Eliza clambered backwards. A hand gripped her right ankle. With all her strength, she flexed her knee and lashed out. Her glutes may have been useless, but her quads were her strongest muscles. Her shoe connected with something solid, possibly a face. The intruder growled and released his grip.

She rolled over and commando-crawled to the kitchen in the dark.

The man was quickly above and flipped her onto her back. "You'll save us all trouble if you tell me where you hid it."

"I don't know what you're talking about!" She began to scream "Fire" loudly, in the hope a neighbor might hear and at the least call for help.

He bent down and covered her mouth with his hand.

He whispered, "Tell me where you hid it and this will all go away."

She could smell his sweat and garlic breath. What frightened her most was how controlled he sounded. She had to fight.

She bit hard on his hand and swung at his head. The Buddha made heavy contact as she let go. The intruder moaned and fell back. She rolled over and dragged herself on her stomach to the kitchen, heading straight for the cupboard under the sink. She opened the door and reached inside for something, anything.

He grabbed her shoulders. "Tell me where it is or—"

She fired a prolonged blast of flyspray from one hand and oven cleaner with the other.

The man wailed. She kept spraying as he stumbled backwards. She felt his footsteps on the boards. He was headed to the front door. It opened and slammed. She tightened her grip on both triggers. What if he let someone else in to finish the job?

After straining to listen for what seemed like hours, she heard no noises or footsteps. Eliza sat back against the cupboards and realized she'd been panting the whole time. Her fingers had cramped clutching the chemical bottles at the ready. Finally, she carried the oven cleaner with her as she crawled to the front door, pulled herself up, and locked it.

With the lights now on, she held on to the wall and crept back to where she'd hit the man with the statue. There was blood spattered on the tiled floor.

"I'd call that karma, Felix," she murmured and dropped the spray. Hands shaking, she called one of the numbers on the phone Craig had given her.

Chapter 79

AS MARY AND I trekked through dense bush, my burner phone vibrated. Not surprised that Moss had made sure there was reception out here, I answered but continued walking.

Before I could ask about Collette, Darlene told me there had been a break-in at Eliza Moss's home. I assumed she was out at the work dinner she'd mentioned.

"Anything stolen?"

"No," Darlene said. "The guy was after something specific. Tore her bedroom apart, then wanted to know where she'd hidden it. Whatever 'it' is."

My adrenaline surged. "Wait. She was home at the time?"

"She canceled plans at the last minute. My guess is this guy wasn't expecting to see anyone, though he was wearing a balaclava."

I stood still. "Is she hurt?"

Mary stopped in her tracks and looked at me.

"She's shaken, but fine. Turns out she packs a mean punch with marble and is a demon with kitchen chemicals."

I wasn't sure what that meant but was filled with relief. Eliza was safe.

Darlene elaborated, "Eliza says she has no idea what he was talking about but he was prepared to hurt her to get what he came for. She was lucky this time."

The police were on their way but Darlene said she wanted to fingerprint the place before they arrived.

Heart pounding, I asked to speak to Eliza. The phone crackled and I heard her voice.

"I'm OK. Honestly. Darlene came straightaway."

Mary tapped her watch. We needed to keep moving.

"To be on the safe side, can you pack an overnight bag, and take whatever is most valuable to you? There's a top-level security system at my place Darlene knows how to access."

"I'd rather go to a hotel room. They have those locks—"

"They're too easy to override. It's how housekeeping gets in when someone's inside."

There was a moment's pause. "Then I'll stay here. After what I did to that guy, he isn't coming back tonight."

"That's a bad idea," I stressed. The intruder would most likely return. Maybe with backup next time.

"Eliza, please trust me. You'll be safest at my place, even if you're being followed. Darlene can let the deputy commissioner of police know you're there. The police can watch your place, just in case."

The wider implications of the attack seemed to stun Eliza. Suddenly her world would never be an entirely safe place again.

"This is insane. What was Dad really involved in?"

"I'm trying to get to that now." The phone crackled. Reception deteriorated the farther away from the compound we got.

Mary signaled we were almost there.

"You'll be safe tonight. Just stay there until I get home."

"Hurry back," she pleaded.

While I had Darlene on the line, I needed to know about Collette. She filled me in on the car with two inhabitants, one of whom was on his way to grab Collette's phone from the step when Johnny intercepted him. After that, the boyfriend took a call, excused himself, and left.

I was relieved we at least had a lead on who'd put the malware on her phone. "Can you trace the plates?"

Darlene was ahead of me. "Sure did. It belongs to Craven Media, owners of *The Sydney Post.*"

Chapter 80

RANSACKING A HOUSE with the owner inside sounded amateur, or desperate. The CIA or ADIA should have known better. Unless they knew Eliza's schedule and expected her to be out. I wouldn't put it past some of the agents I'd met to be that incompetent. The physical risk to Eliza bothered me most.

What if her intruder was from the media group? If Craven Media was bugging our offices, it was a new low, even for them. There'd been phone hacking incidents in the UK, but nothing as overt in this country. Obviously, things had changed. It explained how Marcel Peyroni managed to get to the Wallaces' house in Dural before the Tactical Response unit.

Craven Media fed their scandal appetite via stunts like the one they pulled on Private. We looked after clients who wanted to hide scandal. They wanted to capitalize on that. Now we had a source for the malware, Gideon Mahler could trace it right back to Peyroni and Craven and prove the illegal bugging. Once we were back I'd let the police and federal agencies sort him out, along with his media magnate boss. A mere suggestion they were *suspected* of breaking, entering, and threatening a disabled woman would be enough to irrevocably damage their business. Like the rot they printed, there didn't need to be truth in the accusation.

This late, the bush around Contigo Valley was eerily quiet. The only sounds were our feet crunching on twigs and rocks. I was perspiring heavily and stopped for a long drink.

Eliza's break-in preyed on my mind. I doubted even Peyroni and his team would have risked being caught in there.

For anyone chasing Eric Moss, Eliza was an easy target, given she was the only family Eric Moss had as far as anyone knew. Instinct told me it had to be someone from ADIA or the CIA in her home. Whoever broke in had to believe Eliza knew more about her father than she let on, or that he'd given her whatever it was they wanted.

That meant something tangible existed. Not just what Eric Moss kept to himself. A file, an object, papers? A code?

Farther ahead, Mary checked her bearings.

"The containers should be just up here." A hundred meters later, she unstrapped the bolt cutters from her backpack. Mary was the fittest person I knew, but her endurance was exceptional. She seemed to function without sleep or rest until a crisis was averted. Even then she'd be back at work a few hours later.

We pushed through to the clearing. Searching with night-vision goggles, there was no suggestion of surveillance out here. No wires, no cameras, and no power source.

We checked the helipad first. Small cracks had formed in the concrete. I wouldn't have wanted to land anything on a helipad that hadn't been maintained. It seemed odd, given Eric Moss's obsession with detail, cleanliness, and presentation. I suspected nothing had landed on this for quite a while. It could have partly explained why Geoff Andren flew prospective lenders right over it. The question remained, *why* would Moss neglect this site?

The locks to both containers were rusted and didn't appear to have been recently disturbed.

Mary got to work with the bolt cutters and the first padlock snapped with a loud crack. With a fair amount of effort we managed to creak open the door.

I shone the light inside.

Mary and I stood back in stunned silence.

Both containers were empty.

Chapter 81

PICKING THE LOCK on the boat would have been child's play, if not for his injuries. Just as the man thought he'd have to break in, the lock clicked and the hatch doors opened.

Down in the galley he went straight for the cupboard under the sink. He removed a tin marked "herbal tea" and a bottle of gin strategically hidden behind it. Buried under the peppermint tea leaves was a set of keys wrapped in plastic. He peeled them free with his good hand.

Next he unscrewed the cap from the gin and placed it on the small dining table before descending the aft stairs and lifting out a spare set of clothes from the storage area under one of the bunks.

Above and to the left of the sink was a latched cupboard containing a first-aid kit. He placed it on the saloon table. He unzipped his jacket and examined the still painful wrist. The shoulder ached but would heal. The spider bite still gave him grief. Sweats and nausea slowed him down more than he would have imagined. On the positive side, the lymph nodes under his arm were reducing in size. His body was slowly clearing the toxin.

He popped a pill from the kit to counteract nausea, washing it down with a sip of gin. He carefully washed his wrist with liquid soap, dried it, and applied antiseptic cream before covering it with a bandage.

Thirty-six hours without sleep. He needed to rest so he slid into the bench seat, closed his eyes, and lay his head on the table while he waited.

Moments later a noise above deck disturbed the quiet.

He stayed silent and still. He was no longer alone. A light shone through the window, then a pause. Footsteps slowly descended the companionway. Fifth step, fourth.

He splashed the bottle's contents down his front and on the table.

Third.

He slid on the dark glasses.

A light moved through the crack above the hatch. The handle on the hatch moved.

The man gripped the flick-knife in his pocket with his left hand.

When the door opened, he was sprawled face sideways on the saloon table.

Chapter 82

FROM WHERE HE lay, he could make out the image reflected in the window. The intruder had a mouthpiece wired to a radio on his epaulet. Marina Security.

He moaned.

"Hey." The guard stepped closer and poked the stranger's arm. "You all right?"

The man snorted and sluggishly lifted his head off the table.

The guard recoiled. "Jeez, you reek."

The man licked his lips and slurred, "Officer, I didn't do it."

The guard lifted the half-empty bottle. "How can you even drink this stuff? I need to see some ID."

The man fumbled for his wallet, then pointed to a shelf. The guard turned his light to a framed photo of two men on a fishing trip. One currently stank of alcohol. The other was the boat's real owner.

"That was before my wife left with...our bastard of a lawyer."

The guard hesitated and swung his torch around inside.

"I got a report someone broke in." He kept the light on the boat's keys. "Next time let us know you're coming. Save us all a lot of hassle. And, mate, I've been there. Alcohol is never the answer."

The man folded himself down on the table.

The guard reported to base that the owner was sleeping off a binge, and was informed two kids had been spray-painting on the other side of the marina. The police were on their way. He sighed, took one look back, and left.

The man quickly set to work.

Chapter 83

ELIZA GAVE HER statement to the police. Meanwhile, Darlene fingerprinted all drawers and door handles in the apartment. Eliza watched her use a swab to sample the bloodstain from the floor and store it in a clear plastic tube.

A female constable was asking Eliza if the assailant had made any physical threats. Eliza shook her head.

"No. It all happened so fast."

"We can take you to hospital," the female constable spoke softly, "and have any injuries looked at privately?"

Eliza shook her head once more. Minor bruises on her elbows, wrists, and knees would heal. Thankfully, nothing was broken so she still had her mobility.

"Is there anywhere you can stay for the night? With friends, in case…?" a senior officer inquired hesitantly.

Eliza's heart raced again. "You really think he's coming back?"

"Only if he fancies another dose of flyspray and caustic burns," Darlene said from the far side of the room. "It's OK—she's coming with me."

Eliza smiled weakly and wheeled herself to the

bedroom to pack some things while the police took photographs of the mess in the hallway.

Felix rubbed against his owner's feet.

"It's just for one night," she said. Before more loudly adding, "I'll leave you plenty of food; don't worry."

While Darlene saw the police out, Eliza wheeled herself towards the back door, stopping short in the laundry. She reached down into a sack of kitty litter and extracted a small sandwich bag containing a mini USB device. She quickly shoved it into her jacket pocket then leveled the pellets with a wooden spoon she kept next to the litter box.

"No one needs to know it was ever here," she said to herself, and wheeled back out to the corridor.

Chapter 84

THE MAN REMOVED a panel from beneath the sink and pulled out a computer and cord. He tore the lining of his jacket and removed a USB from inside the hem.

So far he was still on schedule to meet his contact. He plugged in a series of passwords and broke through a firewall.

He tapped his fingers on the laminate, urging the program to open. The spinning wheel on-screen set his pulse rocketing. The computer couldn't freeze now. It should have been near-impossible to hack.

He forced quit and held his breath as the program restarted. His wrist had begun to throb again. All these years of planning his escape had almost been derailed by a spider. The icon finally appeared.

Two more clicks.

The waiting was more distressing than any pain. All these years distilled into this moment.

Attaching the USB, his finger hovered slightly over the enter button to transfer the program to the USB, then delete itself.

His other mobile phone jolted him out of the moment. He retrieved it from his trouser pocket and took a deep breath before answering.

This was the most important meeting he would ever have. At stake was his life.

Chapter 85

THE CALL DIDN'T go exactly as hoped. The contact wanted to meet in a cove only accessible by boat. The offer expired in twenty minutes. That left barely enough time to make it, and no chance of assessing the meeting place for signs of an ambush.

But if things went well, he'd be on a plane out of the country tonight.

He started the engine from the internal helm. As soon as the key turned, he could smell something burning. Plastic.

He scanned the gauges overhead. Water temperature, oil pressure, rpm on the tachometer were all in the normal range. The amp meter was erratic and read low but the engine was running. There was more than enough fuel to get there.

The smell dissipated as quickly as it came on.

His eyes darted back to the computer. The download was still in progress.

Seventy percent.

Seventy-three.

There was no time to waste. He stepped out and

around the deck to the fore and untied the mooring rope with his good arm. The boat butted against buffers on the pontoon as he hurriedly released the aft.

Back at the helm, he pushed the throttle forward and steered free. The hairs on his neck prickled. Something was wrong.

The laptop read eighty percent downloaded.

Then he smelled smoke.

Eighty-four.

Beyond the laptop, a flash of light caught his eye. A fire had started in the aft.

If it took hold, the fuel tanks could ignite. In a split-second decision he grabbed the fire extinguisher from the galley and rushed to the source. He pulled the pin and doused foam on the flames but the fire seemed to rear. Sweat pouring from his face and chest, he made one more choice.

He raced back to the computer.

Ninety-eight...

A loud whoosh sounded behind the cabin. Flames were out of control. And he was out of time.

Yanking the USB, he took off to the deck and levered himself over the safety rail. He leapt outwards. Midair, the explosion thrust him higher and farther.

Intense pain as his shoulder hit the surface caused him to gasp. Water filled his burning lungs. Disoriented in the blackness, he struggled to find air. The surface had to be close. Fingertips broke through.

The next explosion propelled him backwards.

Deeper.

Into an abyss.

Chapter 86

I WALKED IN the door of my apartment clutching pastries and coffees from the local bakery. The sun had risen and streamed in the ocean-side windows. A wheel-chair was parked behind the front door.

I wanted sleep after an exhausting night trekking through the bush but there were greater priorities. I heard the shower running and a quick check showed Eliza had spent the night in the spare room.

As I put breakfast on the kitchen bench, the bathroom door opened and Eliza appeared, dressed, hobbling on forearm crutches. Her legs swung wide from the hips as she moved forward. Her hair was wet and fell in soft waves around her face. She stopped when she saw me.

I'd never seen her stand, let alone walk. It struck me how tall she was.

"Good morning," I said. "Hope you were comfortable."

"You were kind to let me stay."

She looked drawn, as if she hadn't slept much.

"You should see the expression on your face. Surprised I can walk?"

I *was* a little taken aback, but didn't want to say something clumsy or insensitive. "Maybe a little."

"Don't get excited, I can't go far. The legs run out of oomph pretty quickly."

Eliza deflected conversation, something I suspected she was very good at. There was no hint of the trauma she'd experienced last night.

I wouldn't normally open my home to a client but this case was bigger and more threatening than I'd imagined. And there was something special about Eliza.

"Hungry?" I nodded at the food.

"I am now." She pulled herself onto one of the stools by the kitchen bench and placed her crutches in the corner.

I tore open the bags to expose cheese and bacon rolls, croissants, and fresh bread. Plates from the cupboard went on the bench along with the two takeaway coffees.

Eliza asked if I had sugar. I rummaged through the cupboard but came up empty. Living alone, I tended to cook the essentials—meat and veggies, salads, sometimes roast a chicken.

"Sorry."

"No problem. It's all about the caffeine."

I thought about moving outside to the balcony, with the ocean view, but the chairs out there were low set. I joined Eliza, facing the ocean.

"We learned some things last night."

"Go on." Her back straightened and she picked small pieces from the cheese and bacon roll and popped them into her mouth.

"With the visit from the US ambassador, you being followed and then broken into, we have to think your father was involved in some kind of government organization, overt or covert."

"You mean like the CIA? You're kidding, right?"

I'd expected at best denial, at worst an argument. But Eliza had to believe last night was a targeted attack, irrespective of what the police may have said.

"I'm serious. It isn't unusual for government agencies to set up in other countries. These organizations sometimes use legitimate businesses as shopfronts. They call it 'mutual advantage.'"

Eliza listened intently.

"Operatives are paid by the business, or organizations, pay tax, and really believe they're contributing. It's an ideology as much as a job."

"You think Contigo Valley is one of these fronts?"

"Honestly, I don't know. It could be that government agencies became interested because of the defense contracts and research and development projects your father initiated."

"He is against war, of any kind. Everything he's done, with the surgical inventions, rehydration techniques, has been to save lives." She became absorbed in a tiny piece of bacon. "There's no way he is involved in warmongering." She looked directly at me. "If you believe that, you're crazier than that guy who attacked me."

Chapter 87

I KNEW ELIZA wouldn't take the theory well. Still, it had to be said.

"We have to consider the possibility your father was an agency operative. He didn't have any form of documentation. If it did exist before he disappeared, it has to have been wiped from every government database. No one else has that sort of power."

Eliza stared out the window. "We often talked about how the CIA overthrew dictators and replaced them with even worse despots. It was like a hydra—every time they intervened, the situation was made worse. Then there's South America, the Russians in the Ukraine; the list is endless. Those interventions never once ended well or made people safer." She flicked her hair, almost defiantly, and the scent of coconut from her shampoo reached me.

"There's more," I said. "Your father was courting bankers for loans. He used containers that supposedly held high-tech equipment that could theoretically be inspected as proof of the organization's value."

Her eyes narrowed. "Supposedly?"

"There were two shipping containers next to a

helipad. Your father could have taken investors there and shown them, as collateral for the loans. He could fly them there anytime. He could pilot helicopters too."

From the shocked expression, it was clear she didn't know that.

"Mary and I trekked out to them last night. The containers were empty."

"Sir Lang must have had them emptied as soon as Dad left."

I bit into a roll and shook my head. "They hadn't been opened recently and were pretty much rusted closed. Contigo was on the fraud squad's radar."

"Wait! Fraud? My father would never—"

I put a hand on hers. "Just hear me out, please, and it may make more sense. We think he showed prospective lenders one container at the base, then flew them over others, which were supposed to house expensive equipment."

"What was the point?"

"That's what I wondered. By then the bankers trusted him. Eric was accepting hundreds of millions of loans based on government contracts, which we can't confirm, and I can't see how he could have paid the loans back with interest. When the finance officer asked about some missing charity dinner tickets, I suspect your dad panicked." I sipped my coffee. "Once the in-house accounts team started auditing, they would have found evidence of much more substantial fraud. It's the only explanation as to why a missing receipt for ten thousand dollars triggered his disappearance."

"But the organization was financially sound."

"If your dad was lying to bankers about nonexistent technology and equipment, something was very wrong. I suspect your father had built a house of cards that was about to collapse. It would explain why he disappeared in such a hurry, without telling you."

Chapter 88

A KNOCK ON the door broke a long, tense silence.

It was Mark Talbot. He was alone and didn't apologize for the interruption. I wondered what bombshell he was about to drop by turning up at my home uninvited. I knew there was still no word on baby Zoe.

He wasn't forthcoming with the reason for his visit so I let him know about the phone hacking by Craven Media and how Collette's mobile was evidence. If they tracked the car that Johnny saw last night, the police would no doubt find illegal listening and surveillance devices.

"For what it's worth," Mark said, "I didn't think you'd risk a child's life for publicity or kickbacks. I know you better than that."

Was that actually an apology? Maybe my cousin had been upset about his breakup and taken it out on me. I decided to let it go and offered to make him a coffee, but all I had was instant. He looked at the takeaway cups.

"I'll pass. I need to talk to Miss Moss. Alone."

"I want him to stay," Eliza said, reaching for my hand.

It didn't go unnoticed by Mark.

"Your prerogative." He shrugged.

I offered him a seat but he preferred to stand. This wasn't just about the Zoe Ruffalo case or information leaks. Mark hadn't come to apologize or make peace. This visit was serious, and official.

"I've been asked by the commissioner to liaise with the Federal Police on Eric Moss's disappearance. He's asked me to personally update you on the case. And before you say anything, Craig, I'm as surprised as you. It's my area of command, but the investigation is being run by other agencies. My team has no official involvement."

Eliza bit her top lip and I could see the pulse in her neck. We were both anticipating the worst news.

"We believe Eric Moss was using a false identity." Mark let his words hang but there was no reaction from either of us. "Evidence suggests he was a Swiss con man by the name of Hans Erikson Gudgast, born February 11, 1956. He was a mathematical genius who completed university by the age of sixteen and was recruited by a Swiss bank. He took bribes to set up bank accounts in false names for foreign nationals and was due to face trial for embezzlement and fraud. Something about skimming point zero, zero, zero, zero something cents from every account transaction. Made millions before anyone could notice."

"Did he skip bail?" I asked.

"He was thought to have died in a kayaking accident on Lake Lucerne, at the ripe old age of twenty. A shoe and safety vest were all that washed up and they were positively identified as his." He crossed his arms and leaned back against the stove. "A few months later, in June 1976, a man with a French passport entered Australia with the name Hans Gudgast. His mother was purportedly French so he had dual citizenship. Documents confirm he was six foot one and a hundred and sixty pounds. This of course preceded the European Union and digital records."

I quickly did the maths. Gudgast would have been fifty-eight years old, the same age as Eric Moss. "You think Gudgast flew here to avoid prosecution?"

"He was on the passenger manifest for a flight to New Zealand a week after arriving in Sydney and there were no further entries to Australia."

"Then that can't be Dad," Eliza said. "Once you're confirmed on the passenger list, you have to board or they take your luggage off and stop the plane."

"Not back then," I remembered. "You could get your boarding pass and leave the airport. If he didn't have luggage, no one would have noticed or recorded his absence."

"We believe," Mark said firmly, "that Hans Erikson Gudgast and Eric Moss are one and the same person."

Chapter 89

ELIZA SAT STARING out at the ocean as I escorted Mark out. I sat with her in silence for a few minutes.

"I don't believe any of it," she said finally.

"It would explain why he didn't have a passport, or any documents about where he was born, went to school, why he didn't have a bank account. That wasn't lost on the police either."

"That isn't true. Contigo paid him. You can't get a salary without a bank account. Nonprofit organizations don't pay cash wages."

Obviously, Eliza didn't know about the payout awaiting her. "Actually, he didn't take the money. He negotiated a low salary and put it in a trust."

She looked up, confused.

"The trust was for you. So you were always taken care of."

Eliza's shock turned to anger. "Are you falling for all the crap the police are spouting?"

"Think about it," I tried. "It hasn't made sense from the start."

She reached for her crutches, slipped her forearms into the open cuffs, and stood, shakily at first.

"And you think that my father was defrauding Contigo Valley, the very company he built from nothing and which saved countless people's lives? You have *no idea* what my father is like. You just said he took no money, no salary." She hobbled towards the spare room. "Someone has set him up and you don't want to see it."

I couldn't blame her for reacting this way.

"Where are you going?"

"Getting my things. Then I'll find Dad so he can clear his name."

I paced, hands on hips. It wasn't safe for her to go out, especially if she was still being followed. But this was a determined, stubborn woman who needed to defend her father's honor. She couldn't go out alone.

"If you wait, I'll drive you," I called out.

Through the open door I saw her crumple on the bed and the crutches drop to the floor. At first she began to cry quietly, then her body gave way to heavy sobs. I went in and sat next to her. I wanted to stop her pain but for now all I could do was hold her gently.

"Wait." She sat up, eyes swollen. "Someone wanted him out of Contigo Valley. It has to be Lang Gillies. He's the one capable of fraud. And he's rolling in cash."

It was possible, but the police seemed pretty sure Moss was the Swiss man.

Eliza wiped her face. "How tall did he say Gudgast was?"

"My height. Six foot one. 185 centimeters."

"Well, that proves he isn't my father." She composed herself enough to make complete sense. "You can make yourself look taller, but it's hard to cut inches off. I used to measure him to see how tall I was getting in comparison. My dad is 180 centimeters. A whole *five* centimeters shorter."

Chapter 90

I WONDERED IF the police genuinely believed Moss was Gudgast, or whether that's what they wanted us to think. I left Eliza to gather her things and headed for a quick shower. No sooner had I turned on the taps then I heard a scream. Towel hastily wrapped around, I ran out to find Eliza holding a hand over her mouth, staring at the TV in the lounge.

A badly damaged body had been pulled from Sydney Harbour. Sources believed it to be Eric Moss, missing CEO of the world-renowned Contigo Valley. The banner continued to scroll across the screen informing viewers that Moss had disappeared four days earlier.

I quickly dialed Mark Talbot and couldn't hide my contempt.

"Do you know what's blazoned across the TV right now?"

My cousin sighed heavily. "As far as I know the body's still in the water and hasn't been identified. An anonymous caller told the Water Police they'd find Moss in the harbor. I needed confirmation it wasn't a hoax before

I could tell Miss Moss. That's why I'm headed to the scene now."

I watched Eliza.

"Craig?" Mark was still on the phone. "I'm sorry she had to find out like that. If it isn't him, I'll let you know ASAP."

I hung up, believing the media had found out before the local area command. The news report was on Craven's channel. I suspected we weren't the only office Craven Media had bugged.

Not wanting to leave Eliza alone, I dressed quickly and took her to the office, where Johnny promised to look after her. She hadn't spoken in the car and was still in shock when we arrived.

Darlene and I headed out straightaway to where the body had been discovered.

Police and media vans were already there and the scene had been cordoned off. Uniformed police and bystanders tried to block public view with rugs and space blankets. We bobbed under the police tape as the corpse was being placed in a body bag.

Darlene pushed through with her kit and began taking photos as I fended off challenges from officers who didn't know her.

The body was bloated. The face was darkish blue, swollen, unrecognizable. There was a foul stench, like rotting fish. Rex King was already on his haunches, examining the wounds.

His assistant instantly recognized Darlene. "Fish have been at him," he said enthusiastically. "Nothing like fresh meat for a frenzy."

Rex concentrated on a head wound. "The state of the body is consistent with six to twelve hours in the water, which fits the time frame for the explosion reported back at the marina."

A jet skier zoomed past about fifty meters from shore. "This is a well-used stretch of water." I wondered if the body had been dumped from another location. "Is it surprising the body wasn't found earlier?"

"Not really. It would have sunk to start with. Decomposition produces putrefactive gases that make the body float. That, of course, depends on the water and temperature conditions."

"Identifying the remains could prove difficult," I said out loud.

Rex looked up. "Police tell me they believe the victim didn't have medical or dental records."

"And the only family member we know was adopted," I added.

Under the circumstances the extensive facial trauma seemed a little too convenient.

Chapter 91

FARTHER UP THE bank, Mark was questioning a security guard from the local marina. I moved over to listen and Mark filled me in. "Giorgio Kalafedes was on duty last night at Birkenhead Marina and says he saw the victim on one of the secured boats. He identified the man as Moss from a photo. Says he was drunk and stank of alcohol." Mark turned to the witness.

"You're certain they're the same clothes he was wearing before the explosion?"

"Absolutely sure. He said his wife left him for someone else." He looked to me then Mark. "If I ever thought he'd take off drunk like that, I'd have grabbed his keys and called you guys."

Something struck me. Geoff Andren and Eliza had said that Eric Moss never touched alcohol.

"Did he say if he was planning to head off the next day?" I asked.

"No. Just wanted to sleep it off. I thought it was his boat because of the photo."

"What photo?" I asked.

"The one with the other man holding a fish."

"Did the man you saw have sunglasses on in the picture?"

"Yeah. He had the same pair on inside the boat. I thought it was weird at night. And the beard was the same. That's why I thought he was the owner." The guard looked over his shoulder at the scene, and the body. "Can I go now? I don't feel so good."

"Sure, have a seat in one of our cars. Someone will be with you soon," Mark said, before gesturing for me to walk with him.

We stepped away from the action. "Early indications would suggest an electrical short triggered the boat explosion."

It had to be sabotage, I thought. "You think it was a freak accident?"

"If it was, this character Moss, or Gudgast, must be pretty unlucky." Mark raised his eyebrows. "He resigns, goes away for a few days, and happens to pick the only boat with an electrical defect."

"Are you thinking he rigged it to blow and somehow stuffed up?"

"No, but I am suggesting you may not be the only one looking for him. Someone else got to him first."

"Until you told us, Eliza had never heard of anyone called Hans Gudgast. Neither had I." I didn't want to let on what Eliza had said about Eric's height. "All we knew was that Eric Moss had no official documentation and wasn't big on having his photo taken without sunglasses. He kept a very low profile for all his public works."

"I did some checking too, on the fire at Moss's friend's cabin. The local boys tell me magnesium was used to ignite it. Water only made it worse. So whoever lit it knew more than a bit about chemistry."

"Or specifically fires," I suggested.

Mark nodded, studying my face. "And I suppose it

was a coincidence that his daughter was assaulted in an attempted robbery and hid out at your place."

I didn't want Mark setting off alarms with government agencies until I knew more.

"Is there anything else I need to know to get to the bottom of this?" he pressured.

"The less you know for now, the safer a lot of people will be."

He clenched his jaw. "I can't help if you keep me in the dark."

"I guarantee I'll fill you in as soon as I work out what Moss was up to."

"You're on extremely thin ice right now and can't afford to piss anyone else off. Me included." He lowered his voice. "I hear some pretty heavy hitters will be relieved Moss is dead. You expose what Moss was up to, you'll need to watch your back."

Chapter 92

MARCEL PEYRONI CALLED my name. "Hey, Gisto. Remember me?"

I felt the anger rise in me as I saw him behind the police lines. This time I didn't hold back and stormed over. "You crooked scumbag!"

"Unusual metaphor, coming from an ex-lawyer who takes obscene amounts of money to make scandals…"— he made a *pfff* sound—"disappear."

It took all my self-restraint not to hit him square in the face.

Peyroni made a rolling hand gesture at the cameraman who'd been slow to start recording. "This is the second time in a week you've been involved in a death. The police have suggested you are implicated in Louise Simpson's death. I'm informed you were working on finding Eric Moss as well. Will you still be paid now he's dead?"

I clenched both fists and tensed my shoulders. The camera ensured there was irrefutable evidence if I thumped the pompous little git. The bastard had caused a lot of trouble and compromised at least one police operation. *And* he'd violated the privacy of my firm and clients. He deserved to be publicly exposed. I held back because footage of his eventual arrest would do far more damage than any punch I could deliver.

"What? No quips, no retorts?" He shoved the microphone close to my chin. I noticed an investigative reporter from an independent newspaper approaching.

I spoke loudly enough for the more respected journalist to hear. "Who did you illegally bug this time, to get here faster than your rivals?"

It did more than pique her interest. I smiled as Peyroni refused to comment on the accusation I'd made.

Mark tapped my shoulder. "You may want to intervene," he said, pointing to a commotion near the body bag.

Darlene's arms were raised as two men in dark suits blocked her from the corpse.

"Who are they?" I leapt across a pine log and hurried over.

"No idea." Mark followed me. "But they look like Feds or spooks."

Federal police or ADIA agents. They certainly had the arrogance to go with the jobs.

Darlene was assuring them she was here to help with the forensics investigation but they were physically pushing her from the scene.

"IDs," Mark demanded, showing his own.

The dark suits retreated but said something I couldn't hear and Mark stood down to make a call. When he hung up, he turned to us.

"They override our jurisdiction. Only their authorized personnel are permitted near the body."

"I'm not some ghoul off the street," Darlene argued. "This is my job, and Rex King can vouch for me."

"I know," Mark said, "but they have their orders and

I have mine. They'll formally identify the deceased. There's nothing more you can do here."

I wondered how they could confirm whether it was Moss in the body bag without dental records or DNA. We needed to get some of Eric's DNA to compare to the body's. In exchange they could answer some of Eliza's and my questions about her father and his activities.

"Darlene, grab your gear. There's somewhere we need to be."

Chapter 93

I GOT LUCKY with a parking spot in Hunter Street, close to Martin Place. If Moss used his workplace as a bedsit when he was in Sydney, Darlene should easily find DNA in his office or on toiletries to identify who he truly was, and if the body in the water was in fact him.

"Craig Gisto, private investigator," I announced to the man standing guard outside the offices. "I'm here on behalf of Eliza Moss to collect the personal possessions Eric left behind."

"I'm not supposed to let anyone in," said the tubby man with a face scarred by past acne. "Sir Lang has to approve visitors now."

Darlene waited beside with her bag as I stepped forward and lowered my voice. "Look, I don't know if you knew Eric Moss well but a body's just been found in the harbor and the police think it's him."

I let the news sink in. The guard turned an ashen hue. "The poor man. And Eliza. He adored her."

Darlene lowered her head. "You can imagine how devastated she is."

"They're having trouble identifying the body because

it's been in an explosion," I explained as he slumped back against the wall.

"He asked me about my holidays. Just last Thursday. He was never too busy to chat."

We didn't have much time before Lang Gillies sniffed us out. "We just need to get into his office and collect some things for Eliza. Things that he would have wanted her to have."

"Of course," the man said. "It's only right. Go on in."

"Thanks. We know the way. Your name is...?"

"Barry. Please tell Eliza I'm real sorry. Eric was a good man."

"I will." I shook his hand as Darlene and I quickly slipped past Gillies's closed office door.

Inside Moss's office I had to look twice. The area had been gutted of furniture. The carpet had been ripped up and the walls freshly painted. Darlene entered the bathroom. "Smells like it's been scrubbed with ammonia," she said.

Lang Gillies had made damn sure there were no physical traces of Eric Moss in the building.

It was as if he never existed.

Chapter 94

"YOU PEOPLE ARE trespassing!" Lang Gillies was standing behind us, a mobile in his hand.

"We came on behalf of Eliza." I turned to him. "To collect her father's personal possessions."

"Tell that to the police."

"Or I could tell it to the media. Marcel Peyroni is particularly interested in this case." I'd done my homework on the old man. "Craven Media and I have a special relationship. He'd love to know about your penchant for visiting"—I made quotation marks with my fingers—"a certain exclusive men's club." I turned to Darlene. "They have casual Fridays. And by casual, I mean butt naked."

Darlene feigned shock. "And what about this for a quote... 'I was horrified to think he could have used the hard-earned donations of struggling families like mine who wanted to help make a difference'?"

"Don't forget the pensioners," I urged.

Darlene ran with it. "My grandmother is going to be devastated. She sacrificed so much to help people in disasters, through Contigo Valley. People who had lost everything."

"Shut the hell up!" Gillies's face was ruddy and veins distended on his forehead and throat. He banged his walking stick against the wall.

"Why don't we take this to your office?" I said. When Lang didn't move, I led the way with Darlene.

Once inside, Sir Lang slammed the door. He looked on the verge of a stroke but he was obviously the master of temper tantrums.

I pulled up a chair, sat defiantly, and placed both hands behind my head. The action irritated him even more. The power had shifted and he didn't like it one bit.

His entire face was engorged with blood. "What do you want?" he spat.

"Simple. Eric Moss's personal possessions."

Darlene offered him a chair as if it was her office.

He waved her away. "The man walked out of here, abandoned everything. I had every right to dispose of them."

"He was missing," Darlene corrected, "and those things could have helped find him."

"There was no proof he was missing apart from the paranoia of his needy, unbalanced daughter."

Darlene flashed me a warning look and I consciously relaxed both fists.

"If the press got wind of her erratic behavior, she'd be humiliated. Just when her father's been dragged from the harbor."

"You already heard?" Darlene sounded shocked.

"It pays me to know." He sat now, facing me, walking stick held between his spindly legs. "My job is to distance this organization from that traitor."

I wanted to see what else he knew. "Your grief is choking us up. Can we count on you for a eulogy?"

"There'll be no one at the service once word gets out."

I sat forward. "About?"

"His lies, deceit, schemes to commit fraud."

Crimes I suspected Gillies had known about all along. He could even have been behind them.

"You mean the containers scam."

The color in his face faded. He'd underestimated me.

"As chairman of the board, you are as guilty as sin. You'll be going down too. No more casual Fridays for you, old boy."

"That's where you're wrong. Eric Moss was a con man. Or should I say Hans Gudgast? Or whatever the hell his name really was. Everything about him was a *lie*."

Word traveled fast in police and business circles. Lang Gillies wasn't the complete fool I'd taken him for. Then again cockroaches were the ultimate survivors.

"You think the mighty Craig Gisto is the only one who was investigating Eric? The man was convincing. Look at Eliza. She thinks he's a saint. I can testify we had no idea who he really was or what he was capable of."

That was it. Any responsibility Lang Gillies had in the fraud scheme would be buried with Eric Moss. He would be made the scapegoat for the entire organization's corruption and ineptitude. Gillies was absolving himself of all responsibility.

Chapter 95

JOHNNY ARRIVED AT the Wallaces' home in Dural. A news team and station van hovered nearby.

The couple had been interviewed and released without Private being allowed to question them further about the woman posing as Louise Simpson. Johnny hoped the pair might recognize one of the women in the radiology staff photos as the woman they paid the twenty-five-thousand-dollar deposit.

Understandably, after the media coverage they were loath to leave the house and spoke through an intercom on the gate.

"Go through our lawyer," the husband said coldly.

Johnny tried the soft approach. "I'm so sorry about what you've been through. I know this is difficult but you are still the best chance of finding Zoe Ruffalo. All I'm asking is that you look at these photos and tell me if the woman you met claiming to be Louise is among them." There was no reply, but the crackle on the line told Johnny Mr. Wallace was still listening.

"You understand loss. We can only imagine what Zoe's parents are going through. But *you* know." Johnny placed his forehead on the brick above the intercom and appealed one last time. "All any of us want is to bring her home safe."

There was silence, then a buzz and the gates separated. Johnny made the sign of the cross and thanked God.

"Five minutes. That's all," Wallace said. "My wife can't take any more stress."

"Thank you, sir." Johnny walked briskly up the drive. The couple had been embarrassed, harassed, and arrested in full public view. Johnny could understand they would be reluctant to talk to anyone without a lawyer present. And, despite a police statement saying the Wallaces had helped in the investigation but were *not* suspects in the homicide or in the kidnapping of baby Zoe, they were still being hounded by journalists.

Alexandrus Wallace opened the door in tracksuit pants and a ragged T-shirt. Unkempt hair and a day's worth of stubble were indicators of a nightmare twenty-four hours.

"Thank you for your time." Johnny pulled out the photos of the female staff.

Mr. Wallace stood just inside the door, out of view from the road, keeping his visitor on the step.

He looked carefully at each image, shaking his head, then arrived at the final photo. "She isn't here."

"Are you certain?" Johnny was sure the woman worked at the radiology center. He produced the photos of the male employees, including the two doctors he'd spoken to. "Do you remember seeing any of these men on the beach when you met with that woman, or any other time?"

Wallace exhaled but took the next set of pictures. "I'm sorry. I don't recognize anyone."

"OK. Well, I appreciate your time," Johnny said.

"People say time heals. Nothing can heal the pain of

losing a child." He part-closed the door. "For everyone's sake, we hope you find the baby."

Johnny trudged back up the drive, painfully aware that without any other leads Zoe Ruffalo might never be found.

Chapter 96

JOHNNY WASN'T ABOUT to give up, however. He headed back to Manly. This time he wanted to know about any practice employees who had left in the last year. Ones who could have printed out X-rays in advance.

One had married and moved to Glasgow with her new husband. A radiography student, Felicity Wenham, had begun a rotation with them but failed to return after the fourth week. No one had heard from her since. Dr. Kwong explained that wasn't unusual. Sometimes students didn't fit in, or wanted to work closer to home. According to the practice manager, the student was a fast learner and was eager to know how the business worked. If Felicity had finished her rotation, she might have been given a job after graduation.

Johnny found her name on the electoral roll and was pleasantly surprised to see she was living in Balgowlah, close by. He drove straight to the address and parked a short distance from a blue weatherboard home set back from the street. A separate garage down the drive looked like it had been converted into a studio or office.

A woman in her forties answered the door. He asked if it was possible to see Felicity Wenham.

The woman inquired, hesitantly, "Are you a friend from college?"

"No. I'm investigating the disappearance of a young baby and a possible link to the radiology practice Felicity spent time at. We're interviewing current and former staff members in case they came into contact with the kidnapper."

Mrs. Wenham was shocked. "I saw that on the news. My daughter may have met the kidnapper? The person who killed that poor woman too?" She grabbed Johnny's arm. "Is Felicity in danger?"

Johnny patted her hand. "No. I just need to talk to her. She may know something she doesn't realize is significant. Is she home?"

After a few moments, seemingly deep in thought, Mrs. Wenham looked up. "Our daughter has always been a hard worker, good at everything she ever tried. Out of the blue, she developed anorexia at fourteen." She swallowed. "We thought it was all behind us. Then she found out her boyfriend was seeing someone else. Our daughter is just so hard on herself."

"I understand and I'll be very sensitive to that, but a child's life is at stake."

A man appeared behind Mrs. Wenham. "The answer is no. We're sorry for the child's family, but we can't risk you upsetting Felicity. She's all we have."

The door slammed in Johnny's face.

Chapter 97

DESPITE BEING STONEWALLED by her parents, it wasn't difficult to find Felicity Wenham. There were a limited number of treatment options—psych, acute medical, or a facility for anorexia. Twenty minutes and three phone calls later, Johnny entered the cardiac ward at the Royal Balgowlah Hospital. A slim young woman with short layered hair sat by the window of her private room. Leads extended beneath her pajama top to a monitor on the wall above the bed.

He knocked on the open door and she continued gazing into the distance. "Felicity? My name is Johnny Ishmah."

"I'm done with shrinks." She curled her lip in disgust.

"Don't blame you," Johnny grinned. "I'm a private investigator. Psych is my major. The criminal kind."

This time she made eye contact. "Has my father sent you to see how crazy I really am?"

Johnny mentally noted "father issues" but quickly moved on. "I wanted to ask you about your Manly radiology rotation."

"Yeah, well, flunked that." She opened her buttoned

pajama top just enough to reveal a well-defined, square lump under her collarbone. The wound looked fresh.

Johnny looked at the pulse rate monitor. "Is that a pacemaker?"

She stared at the implant, as if still in disbelief. "Attractive, don't you think?"

"Sounds serious." Johnny knew how much damage anorexia could do to vital organs.

"When the defib kicks in and you're awake, it's a blast. The ultimate accessory." Felicity's sarcasm couldn't hide her anger.

She looked back out the window overlooking a patch of garden. "What are you investigating the radiology practice for?"

Johnny pulled up a visitor's chair.

"There were some X-rays that had false dates and names on them. I'm trying to work out who could have got into the system and changed them, before printing them out."

He watched for a reaction. Her heart rate on the monitor remained consistent at sixty beats per minute.

"Theoretically anyone with a code to the system could."

"Who has access to the X-ray codes at Manly?"

"The doctors. The radiographers. Receptionists can't normally enter patient data on the machines."

"Were any of the staff interested in the machines who maybe shouldn't have been?"

She thought for a moment then looked up. "Only Sigrid."

Johnny flicked through his notes. "I don't have that name on my employee list."

"She works at night. Sometimes I'd stay back so she could teach me."

Johnny thought office hours were eight a.m. to five p.m. "Is she a doctor?"

Felicity wrapped a lock of hair into a small curl. "Only in Norway. Sigrid researched radiation exposure in people with chronic bone disease. Then married a boy from the northern beaches and followed him here. It didn't last. She was left with no money and no job." She seemed to soften. "It's tough. The government doesn't recognize her qualifications and she couldn't afford to sit the medical exams all over again."

"Do you know her last name?"

"Hale? Holt? No. Hall. That's it. Sigrid *Hall*. She said her ex had a used-car business."

"If she couldn't work as a doctor, what was she doing at the practice?"

"She's in charge of the contract cleaners. It was either that or drive a taxi."

Chapter 98

I GOT THE call from Johnny. He was at Balgowlah and had a strong lead this time. Sigrid Hall. A woman who was medically trained and knew her way around X-ray machines. *And* who worked nights cleaning at the Manly radiology practice.

While he was on the line, I searched for her business. All I could locate was a post office box for her contracting company along with a phone number. I dialed the landline but was sent straight to voice mail.

There was no one with the name Sigrid Hall listed in the White Pages. All the usual databases came up short.

Johnny mentioned an ex-husband with a used-car business.

"That's something. We can call them all if we have to, to find him."

There were multiple entries with the surname Hall in that postcode area.

"Bingo," I said aloud. "Hall's Honda is on Military Road."

Johnny wasn't far and I told him I could be there in minutes. We pulled up at the same time and entered the office.

A friendly receptionist said Tony Hall was with a client. "We'll wait, thanks," I said.

Johnny phoned Mary and told her where we were. She wanted to be kept in the loop the second he got an address for the radiologist-cum-cleaner.

A toned man in his thirties in a red polo shirt and black trousers greeted us.

"I was told to ask for Tony," I said.

"At your service," he grinned. "What are you after today? It's a great time to buy. We do fantastic deals on trade-ins." He glanced at Johnny. "And can provide instant finance at competitive rates."

The white toothy smile and spiel were well practiced.

"Actually, this is about your wife."

"Ex." The friendly persona instantly vanished. "Piss off," he said, storming back towards the showroom. "Tell her the goddamn well is dry. I don't care if she can't make bail. She can rot in hell."

Johnny followed. "We're not here for money. A baby is missing and Sigrid could be at risk."

"Boo hoo," he mocked. "Let me guess. One of you screwed around with her; she got knocked up. You did the right thing and paid all her expenses. Well, wake up and smell the bullshit. She never was pregnant."

A female staff member in heels, black dress, and red scarf came through the sliding glass doors and asked if everything was all right. Her badge said "Marianne."

"This guy wants to know about Sigrid. He was just leaving." Tony turned to go inside. The employee rested her hand on his upper arm.

"Isn't it enough she almost bankrupted him?" She threw her hands up. "You people are unbelievable. They are divorced and Tony isn't legally responsible for her debts."

I interrupted. "Sigrid could be in serious trouble.

Right now. We need to find her before someone else gets killed."

Marianne rolled her eyes. "You really bought into the whole drama, didn't you? Poor little Sigrid? What about the people she's hurt?"

"We're private investigators, working on a police investigation," Johnny tried.

"Then why don't you talk to your police colleague? I gave him Sigrid's address to get rid of him."

Someone else was after her. Before us. "Who else was here?"

She folded her arms. "The detective. He said Sigrid had ripped off the wrong person. I figured the police had finally caught up with her."

"How long ago was this?" I pressured.

"About an hour."

"Can you give me the address? This is important!"

The ex-husband didn't hesitate. "Gladly. 17/22 Rolfe Street in Manly. I can't wait to see that bitch finally pay."

Chapter 99

JOHNNY AND I raced to the address Tony Hall had given us. In the car I phoned Mary to fill her in.

"Don't spook her yet," she suggested. "We don't know if she has the baby, and can't afford for her to do a runner. Wait," Mary said, "Darlene just came in. I'll put you on speakerphone."

"Where's Eliza?" I asked.

"Working from your office. She can't hear us."

I sped through an orange light as Johnny gave details. "Sigrid Hall is Norwegian. Blonde. Scammer, pretends to be pregnant to get money, according to her very angry ex. She's familiar with X-ray equipment and had the contract for cleaning at the Manly radiologist."

"I'm on my way," Mary said. "Where are you now?"

"Turning into the street. We'll wait for you." Mary was invaluable in a confrontational situation. If there was time, she was worth waiting for. There were no cars parked near the home.

"Be careful," Darlene warned.

"We will be. Martyrdom never ended well," Johnny replied.

I asked Darlene where we were at with the IP address used for the e-mails our impostor sent to the Wallaces.

"We've narrowed it down to Manly. It's the closest I could get for now."

"So far we've only got circumstantial evidence. Anything specific I can use for leverage will help."

"I'll try to get the account name, but it may take time," she said.

"Do what you can from there and keep an eye on Eliza."

As I hung up, Johnny frowned. "Do you think it was a detective ahead of us?"

That's what bothered me. Neither Hall nor the receptionist asked to see our IDs and had merely assumed we were police.

"We need to be careful how we play this." I referred to the GPS for directions. "If the police arrest her, she'll lawyer up and is likely to use what she knows to bargain with the prosecutors." I was talking to myself as much as to Johnny. "That could take days. And we don't have time to mess around."

We finally had the chance to find Zoe and Louise Simpson's killer. If the man claiming to be a detective hadn't beaten us there.

Chapter 100

I PARKED A good two blocks from the house and didn't have to wait long for Mary. A caravan and trees along the curbside obscured the view of my car from Sigrid Hall's house.

I told Johnny to sit tight and call the police if there was trouble. Mary and I walked towards the gate.

So far it was quiet apart from cockatoos squealing in the trees.

Mary scouted around the side of the house. I did up my suit coat and knocked three times on the front door.

A small woman opened the chained door, revealing only half her face in the gap. She was blonde, as Johnny had described.

"Sorry to bother you, ma'am; I work for Reed Armstrong Real Estate and we have buyers keen to move into this area."

"I'm not interested in selling." She tried to close the door but my foot was already blocking it.

"I could give you an obligation-free quote on the spot. I think you'd be surprised what homes like yours are selling for in the current market."

She part-turned at something behind her. I glimpsed marks on the side of her face.

"I'm not interested," she said. This time she slammed the door. I only just got my foot out in time.

She had looked scared. Someone else had to be inside.

I headed back down the drive and into the street before doubling back via the neighbor's yard. All the curtains and blinds were closed.

I signaled for Mary to find a way in. She climbed on the rubbish bin and managed to lift the screen of the open bathroom window.

I kicked off my shoes and pulled myself up through the window while Mary took off around the back. I had just climbed through when something crashed inside.

From the bathroom door I caught a glimpse of the living room. The woman was now tied to a chair, crying.

And a man a lot larger than me was standing over her.

"You destroyed my daughter!" He wrenched hard on her ankle ties.

Sigrid Hall winced. "I never hurt anyone, I swear."

I pulled out my phone and quickly hit record.

"You're a liar! My son-in-law was tested. He has *no* genetic defects. He doesn't carry the condition you say the baby had." His tone suddenly calmed as he bent down, right in his captive's face. "At first I thought it was you who had it and knew you could pass on the defect."

"No!"

"Then I got to thinking..." He gave her a long, calculating look. "I saw a specialist who said the gene was dominant. Do you know what that means?"

She closed her eyes, tears spilling down her cheeks.

"You claimed to have two healthy children but we both know that's not possible with a dominant gene." He paced in front of her. "The specialist thought it was odd my daughter didn't get to see the body. That all we had was your word."

She flicked hair from her doe-like eyes. "If you untie me, I'll tell you everything."

The man gave her a hateful smile. "No need. I *know* the baby didn't die. There was never anything wrong with her."

He cocked his head and raised his hand.

Sigrid blurted, "Wait! The scan could have been confused with someone else's. It happens sometimes."

"Wrong answer." He landed a slap to her left cheek. She slumped to the right and he pulled her up. "Try again."

"All right!" Her breathing became shallow. "I lied about that."

"So you admit it. You and that other woman planned the whole thing. You kept my grandchild." He raged. "Is there a standard fee for a white baby girl? Or is there some kind of bidding war?" He stormed into the kitchen and I could hear drawers slamming.

Sigrid's eyes widened with panic.

Chapter 101

I TEXTED MARY: escalating. stand by. tall male 120 kg.

"There is no baby," Sigrid Hall screamed. "You've got it all wrong."

The man returned; this time his expression was even more menacing. "You would have sold my grandchild like a piece of meat." He raised a hand and struck her across the face again. Not hard enough to knock her over, but solid enough to cause pain.

I tensed, ready to intervene at any second.

"I wasn't pregnant!" she shouted. "I'm infertile!"

He stepped back, looking at the woman. "You're doing exactly what the other bitch did. She acted all shocked and innocent. Until I heard the baby cry. Then it became clear. You kept my grandchild so I took her back."

"Oh my God. You killed Louise Simpson!" Sigrid tried to scream but he clamped one hand over her mouth.

"That's when I realized that Simpson woman must have faked the scans. She would have needed an accomplice. Someone at that X-ray place. I watched all day yesterday. I was ready to leave when I saw something through the windows. What sort of cleaner uses the computers and leaves with envelopes?"

Sigrid couldn't talk back. His hand gripped her reddened face even tighter.

"I lost you in traffic when you left but your car has a yard sticker on it, same last name as your cleaning company."

She spluttered and tried to writhe free.

"Letting parents think their baby died and allowing them to grieve. You two are evil." His rage was building with every word. "You *both* deserve to die."

I searched again for something to use as a weapon. There was a hot curling iron on the bathroom bench. I flicked its power point on.

Sigrid was sobbing. He took his hand away.

"I'll tell the police everything. You can call them now."

"And see you just get a slap on the wrist? I don't think so. What you did to my daughter, to my grandchild... You need to be punished."

I looked through the gap in the doorway again and saw the flash of a carving knife in the man's hand.

Chapter 102

SIGRID HALL BEGGED for her life.

"I didn't sell a baby," she cried. "There never was a baby. It was a scam. That's all it was. I didn't even *know* Louise Simpson. I just used her name. The ultrasound your daughter saw was fake." She sniffed. "I swear to God, there never was a surrogate pregnancy. Your grandchild never existed!"

The man straightened to his full height.

"I found an abnormal scan in the X-ray archives," Sigrid continued, tears streaming down her battered face. "I changed the name and date. If you let me go, I'll give you back the twenty-five thousand. Every cent. *Please* just let me go."

He ran a hand through his hair. "You expect me to believe my daughter lost everything because of a baby that *never existed?*" He was mumbling to himself and pacing.

I knew as soon as he realized he'd killed an innocent woman and taken someone else's child, Sigrid was dead. I grabbed a towel and wrapped it around my left arm, then I texted Mary.

NOW.

I snatched up the curling iron and rushed down the corridor.

The man swung around, slashing at me. I deflected the knife with the hot iron and clamped it onto his hand. He screamed in pain as his flesh burned.

At that moment, Mary kicked in the back door and knocked the woman and the chair out of the way.

The man, distracted, didn't see her right cross coming. As he staggered back, she kicked him hard in the chest. He landed heavily and she trapped him, straddling him and pinning both arms with her knees.

He struggled to breathe.

I held the hot iron to his face. "Where's the baby?"

"I want a lawyer!" he yelled, face engorging.

Mary put more weight on his biceps. "What did you do with the baby?"

He refused to answer.

"Sigrid is telling the truth," I said. "She never was pregnant. The baby you took isn't your grandchild."

As realization hit, the man looked winded. He'd murdered Louise Simpson for nothing.

"My daughter, Majella, has her. Oh God. She thinks that's her child."

Chapter 103

MARY SECURED THE man with cable ties while I scoured his pockets and extracted a wallet. Evan Piper was his name. The baby was at his daughter's Mosman home.

I phoned Mark Talbot. "We've got Louise Simpson's murderer, and the woman who took her identity," I told him. "I'll explain the specifics later, but we have detained them and have a recorded confession. They're at 17/22 Rolfe Street, Manly. I'm going for the baby." I gave him the Mosman address. He was sending a team here and heading to the daughter's house.

I moved over and sat Sigrid Hall up but I refused to release her ties. She was a liar, a con woman, and had committed the cruelest act, letting couples think their unborn children had died of an incurable condition. She'd also stolen an innocent woman's identity, and money. She may not have foreseen the danger she was putting Louise in, but she still had blood on her hands.

I phoned Johnny and told him to back Mary up. No one was to leave. The police were minutes away.

Then I sped all the way to Mosman. Majella Piper

believed the baby was hers. She wouldn't just give Zoe up.

I pulled up outside the house just as Detective Sergeant Kristen Massey, in plain clothes, was climbing out of her unmarked car. She let her hair out of its ponytail, stripped down to a singlet, and unself-consciously slipped off her skirt. She grabbed some khaki shorts from inside the car and stepped into brown Blundstone boots. A sweat-stained cap finished the look.

"We don't know how suspicious the woman will be."

"So what's your plan?" I deferred to her.

"She may open the door to me like this. You're my husband in case you're wondering."

"Good to know."

Kristen knocked and a young woman answered.

I took the detective's hand.

"Hi there. We live down the street and have been admiring your roses. Can we ask what you feed them with? Ours keep dying."

The sound of a baby crying came from inside. The woman looked around, then back again. "I'd love to help you but I'm sorry, I have to go."

"Wow," Kristen said. "How old's your little one?"

"Eight weeks." The woman didn't seem at all suspicious. If anything, she was bursting with pride.

"That is so exciting. We're expecting ourselves. Ten weeks."

I touched her belly as if confirming the fact.

Majella seemed to hover for a second, then said with a grin, "She's due for a feed. Wait there."

Kristen moved her leg forward even though the door was ajar. Majella was soon back, with the baby clasped tightly at her chest.

She exposed its face.

"She is so tiny," I said. "What's her name?"

"Elspeth. It was my grandmother's name."

"You are a cutie," Kristen cooed. "Can I hold her?" She reached over and took Zoe before Majella had the chance to object. I admired the baby, placing myself between the two women.

Within seconds, two squad cars pulled up and six officers ran towards the house, weapons drawn.

It all happened so fast Majella Piper didn't appear to react. Until Kristen turned back and said to her gently, "My name's Detective Massey," and flashed her police badge. "I'm sorry, but this child is not yours."

Chapter 104

"LEAVE MY BABY alone!" Majella thrashed to break free from my grasp.

The child began to cry.

"These people are stealing my daughter!" Majella Piper was panic-stricken.

I had the woman in a vise-like grip and locked eyes with her. "Listen. That baby isn't yours. The police are here because your father took someone else's child."

The fight went out of her at the mention of her father.

"You're wrong. She's mine. The surrogate is the one who should be arrested. She was going to sell Elspeth."

Mark was now at my side. "I think we'd better go inside," he said softly, "where we can talk. Paramedics are checking the baby. She's safe and they're not going anywhere unless I say."

His soothing, rational tone seemed to calm her down, at least enough to walk into the lounge room and sit.

Only her hands, clasped tightly together, betrayed the emotions she was battling to keep in check. She focused her attention on the portacot that had been set up next to a rocking chair.

Mark offered, "A simple DNA test will clear all this up. For now, your father's talking to us about Louise Simpson."

"Have you arrested her? All this time we thought she'd been stillborn." Her face became animated. "I couldn't believe my baby was alive."

Mark cleared his throat. "Have you seen the news in the last two days?"

"No. Elspeth and I have been getting to know each other." She began to fold a crocheted rug from the lounge. "Did you know she loves classical music?"

Mark rubbed his hands on his trouser legs.

Majella Piper was in denial. She needed to hear the full truth.

It was up to me. "I just left your father with the surrogate you met with. Her real name is Sigrid Hall. She stole Louise Simpson's identity, feigned being a surrogate, and took money from couples like you and your husband. She faked a pregnancy then pretended she'd miscarried."

"No." Majella was adamant. "The pregnancy was real. I saw our baby's heart beating on the video of the scan."

"That was part of her scam. She used the scan of a child who died two years ago, with the names and dates changed to look like she was a surrogate mother."

Majella's eyes narrowed as the truth began to sink in.

"But Dad said she admitted it was my baby."

I pieced the story together for her, and the police. "He went to the house of the real Louise Simpson, whose identity had been stolen. She was innocent and didn't know anything about the fake surrogate. She was baby-sitting an eight-week-old girl, Zoe Ruffalo, for a friend."

Majella's eyes flashed from Mark to me, confused.

"Your father admitted to murdering the real Louise

Simpson and taking Zoe Ruffalo. If it's any consolation, he really believed she was yours."

"*Murdered* ...? No. That can't be," Majella pleaded, as the truth slowly sank in.

This poor woman had already grieved for a child that never existed. Now she'd lost a child who was never hers.

Mark stood. "You'll need to come with us to the station for a formal statement," he said, with a hint of regret.

Kristen Massey came in and took Majella Piper formally into custody. It was up to the Director of Public Prosecutions as to whether or not she'd be charged with conspiracy after the homicide.

"Don't answer any more questions," I advised, "without a lawyer present."

I handed Mark my phone with the recorded confessions. There was nothing more I could do here.

"I'll make my statement later."

Mark nodded. "Give you the heads-up. There'll be a press conference shortly on the Moss case."

It was his way of thanking me for today. And letting me know Eliza would need all the support I could offer.

Chapter 105

I DROVE BACK to the office. Exhaustion was hitting me hard. Any relief at finding baby Zoe safe and well was countered by knowing the pain and grief Eliza was going through.

We still had no DNA to compare with the body from the water, even if we could extract a tissue specimen. Darlene was denied access to the autopsy even as an observer.

Mark Talbot texted my usual phone number.

Televised press conference 4 p.m. Family NOT briefed.

That was barely enough time for the autopsy to be performed. Toxicology results and microscopic examination of the body were impossible to complete by then. This reeked of a cover-up. Relatives should be told before information was made public. Eric Moss's only family member was being frozen out. The instructions had to be coming from the highest level. But from whom?

I decided to leave Eliza in my office. She had only just

fallen asleep. According to Darlene, she hadn't received any calls from the police.

The rest of us gathered around the TV in the conference room. The police commissioner was confirming the death of Eric Moss in a boat explosion.

"We are satisfied there were no suspicious circumstances surrounding Mr. Moss's death. The coroner has released Mr. Moss's body for burial. There will not, at this point, be an inquest. I'd like to take this opportunity to offer my condolences to his family and friends." He looked up from the podium. "Any questions?"

"Can you confirm an investigation is under way into fraud at Contigo Valley?" a reporter asked.

He cleared his throat. "An investigation was conducted into alleged fraud at Contigo Valley. I believe Mr. Moss was aware he would face charges. As a result of that investigation I can confirm the name Eric Moss was in fact an alias for a Hans Gudgast, a Swiss national who fled Switzerland before being tried on embezzlement charges. At this stage I would like to stress that Contigo Valley is in no way implicated in the fraud perpetrated by the man we now know to be the fugitive, Hans Gudgast."

That was news to my team and me. The investigation into Contigo's finances was still pending. This had to be a stitch-up, with Eric Moss being tainted with guilt when he could no longer defend himself.

"Now we know why Eliza wasn't briefed," Mary said coldly. "She was blindsided so she couldn't refute any of it."

"Did Moss commit suicide?" a TV broadcaster queried.

The commissioner sighed, and became more somber. "We never know what was going on in someone's mind in the moments before death. Mr. Moss resigned from the organization on Friday afternoon and was reported missing by a family member. It appears Mr. Moss was intoxicated when he started the boat and may or may not have intentionally set the fire that caused the explosion. Only he and God know what he was thinking that fateful night when the police were closing in on him." He went on to add further insult. "The coroner has released Mr. Moss's body for burial. As I said, there will not, at this point, be an inquest." He abruptly ended the press conference.

I sat in complete disbelief. The commissioner had implied that the investigations into fraud and Moss's death were both closed, exonerating Contigo Valley and Lang Gillies from any wrongdoing.

I stood up, replaying in my mind what we had just witnessed.

"Eliza's going to be devastated when she finds out," Darlene said quietly.

I turned to see Eliza in the doorway.

Chapter 106

I DROVE ELIZA back to my place. She didn't speak at all on the way and her withdrawn state concerned me. Once back home, I tried to get her to open up. Even a little.

She used her crutches to step out onto the balcony. Hair gusted across her face as she stared at the waves pounding on the sand. I placed two hot mugs of tea on the table.

"If you like, I can organize a funeral home. The coroner's releasing—"

"Dad didn't drink. Why was he on that boat?" She seemed bewildered. "And how could he be Hans Gudgast? I thought they were different heights."

I suspected we'd never get to the truth behind who Eric Moss really was but he'd officially been declared dead. Everything had happened so fast, even for a high-level cover-up. Perhaps Moss did go to the boat that night to get drunk. Whether it was suicide or an accident, the result was the same.

"Maybe he was so tired from running and pretending to be someone he wasn't."

"This can't be happening." Eliza covered her mouth with her hands. "He can't be gone."

With that, her emotions erupted and she buried her face in my chest. I held her, and felt every ounce of her pain.

The doorbell rang and I ignored it. It rang again. Next thing, Mark Talbot was calling out from below.

I waved for him to come up and eased away from Eliza to answer the door.

"This is an official visit, I'm afraid." He fidgeted on the spot. "You saw the press conference?"

"Someone could have warned Eliza."

Mark paused. "I had no say in that. I need to speak to her if she's here." He lowered his voice. "How's she doing?"

"How do you think?"

Mark headed to the balcony. Eliza looked up, soulfully, as if hoping he had good news.

"I'm sorry for your loss," my cousin began. "But there are some questions about the trust fund your father established on your behalf."

"Seriously, Mark, this can wait. Eliza didn't even know about the trust."

Her eyes didn't leave his face.

"Well, she needs to know the account has been frozen, as it may contain the profits from crime," he said to me. "I'm sorry, but Lang Gillies and some pretty high-flyers are rapidly trying to distance themselves from anything your father was involved in."

"You mean his *alleged* criminal activity." Eliza was curt.

Mark looked out towards the sea. "I met your father and believe he was a good man. If there's anything I can do to help, please don't hesitate to let me know." He placed his card under the mug closest to Eliza.

Outside, I challenged him. "What the hell was all that about? What were you fishing for?"

"Craig, you need to bury the guy and move on. It's *over.*"

All my frustrations came to the boil and I shoved him against the wall.

"What are you going to do now? Burn me with a curling wand?" he snapped.

"Cut the crap, Mark. This is a cover-up and you're part of it."

He raised both hands in surrender. "I'm telling you this as a favor. To you and Eliza. You're in way over your head. This is bigger than any of us and some serious players are pulling the strings."

I stood back. "Who exactly?"

"All investigations into Moss's activities are being dropped. He made idiots out of people who can't afford to be embarrassed. Not when national security is such a vote-winner."

"Doesn't anyone want to know how a guy with zero credentials or documentation got access to restricted military bases?"

Mark pushed back. "Think with your head, not your dick for a change. A contact in the prime minister's office told me the US secretary of state had Moss on speed dial. *Do you hear what I'm saying?* For your sake and Eliza's you need to drop it. You had a win today finding Zoe Ruffalo. You'll never get lucky with this. Trust me. Bury the guy and let it go."

Chapter 107

ELIZA WAS FINALLY accepting the fact her father was no longer with her. She said he would want to be cremated and his ashes released over Contigo's forest valley.

Thankfully, the grisly task of choosing a coffin was one she didn't have to perform. She had just taken a call from Lang Gillies. He'd already made the arrangements, to "save her the pain at such a time."

The service would take place the next morning at the Northern Suburbs Memorial Gardens on Delhi Road, North Ryde. Ten a.m. It smacked of a rush job. Moss being dead clearly wasn't good enough for some. They wanted him cremated as soon as physically possible.

I thought about what Mark had said. Was he trying to warn me, or protect me? Or both? He didn't agree with what was happening but he had become more of a pragmatist lately. Every fiber in me sensed a cover-up by authorities and it had to do with his supposedly secret contracts.

I stood in the lounge, watching Eliza for a moment. She had already been through so much, and I didn't want anything to compromise her safety.

Time was running out to discover who, if anyone, had murdered her father. There were too many unanswered questions. Ambassador Roden's determination to find Moss, the US secretary of state's close ties with Moss, who was really behind any fraud at Contigo and what the secret contracts involved.

First, I wanted to call Rex King and ask about the blood alcohol level in his system. It was a quick blood test and would confirm whether or not Moss had been drinking or was just acting drunk for the security guard.

Rex didn't answer his phone. I left a message.

The best way to delay the service was to call the coroner and request a second, independent autopsy. As a family member, Eliza had that right. That way we could access any report on the cause of the boat explosion. Any physical evidence and test results would have to be kept until then. Eliza could make a public statement saying that if there was a fault with the boat the manufacturer needed to be aware and safety measures put in place to prevent another death. It sounded reasonable and focused on the mechanics of the boat, not the politics of the death.

I talked to her about making the calls. She agreed. It was our only chance to buy time and maybe get some answers.

Chapter 108

I COULDN'T REMEMBER the last time I'd slept in a bed. I dozed for short periods until morning, unable to shake the feeling Lang Gillies wasn't doing Eliza any favors by rushing to put Moss to rest. Eliza had remained holed up in the spare bedroom since sending e-mails to the coroner's office and the department of forensic science at the morgue. She was now leaving voice-mail messages, stressing the urgency.

Time was running out for a response.

Darlene had kindly collected clothes from Eliza's home for the funeral. Not knowing what she'd need, she brought multiple changes of outfit, some dark, with bright accessories.

By six a.m. I had the desperate need to get out and clear my head. I changed into running clothes and left a note saying when I'd be back. Closing the door, I noticed dark gray clouds blanketing the sky. A cold front had hit and storms were brewing from the east.

I didn't bother stretching, just began jogging. Soon I was sprinting along the beach. Waves pounded and sprayed me as my leg muscles contracted and extended against the sand's resistance. Trying to make sense of the past few days, I pushed harder, until my body ached with fatigue and lactic acid. Short of breath, I stopped and bent over, hands on knees. My chest heaved trying to get air.

I had to face facts. Someone had attacked Eliza in her own home. She defended herself then, but opening up the mystery of Eric Moss to public scrutiny could get her hurt, or worse. Maybe Mark was right. I hadn't been thinking clearly. What good was truth if it got people you cared about killed? Nothing would change who Eric Moss was to his daughter. Or how much he cared for her.

One thing I did know. I had feelings for Eliza and wanted to protect her from any more hurt. The cost of exposing any cover-up could be too great. And would it really do any good? Her father was still gone.

Chest still heaving, and shirt soaked with sweat, I headed back home, knowing what I had to do today.

Chapter 109

WE ARRIVED EARLY at the crematorium, hoping to avoid the media. Eliza met the minister who would conduct the brief service. As far as we knew, his would be the only eulogy, with a small group paying their respects.

As Eliza sat, one hand on the coffin, in a private moment, a man with a wreath asked to say good-bye to his old boss. Within seconds he'd pulled out a camera from inside the wreath and was photographing Eliza in her wheelchair beside the coffin.

I didn't waste time evicting the man who, coincidentally, resembled a poorly fed vulture.

Eliza turned to me, barely holding it together. "Is this ever going to stop?" I'd reluctantly talked her out of an inquest for that very reason. It would raise more questions than it answered and what was left of Eric and Eliza's reputations would be destroyed by Gillies and his cronies.

I stood guard next to her from then on. A handful of people filtered through. Lang Gillies wasn't one of them. Moss's assistant, Oliver Driscoll, and the former financial officer, Renee Campbell, came forward and hugged Eliza. The pilot, Geoff Andren, took a seat without fuss.

Mary quietly let me know there was a horde of press outside, like red fire ants at a barbecue. I told her to remind them this was a private service, for family and close friends only.

I moved forward to take my seat next to Eliza and felt my phone buzz in my jacket pocket. I checked caller ID. It was Darlene. I walked towards the back of the church and answered.

"Craig, we don't have much time. I need to access the body."

"What?" I couldn't believe her timing. "The minister is about to start."

"I'm five minutes away. Trust me. You have got to stop the service!"

"I need specifics, and they'd better be good," I told her.

"Jack Morgan can explain. He's calling in a minute. I'm almost there." The phone cut out.

As if on cue, my mobile rang again. I recognized the caller ID.

"Jack, what the hell is going on?"

"When you told me about Eric Moss, something didn't sit right. I did some digging and a CIA contact came through. A US air base has been extracting a number of undercover operatives from the Asia-Pacific region, code-named Eagle-watch. There is supposed to be one rogue agent."

"You think it was Moss?"

"Looks like he went off the grid, vanished. My contact just sent through a photo of Moss. CIA had him as deceased in a boat accident until a surveillance camera snapped him at a car rental place in Mascot. Time and date stamp registered six a.m. today."

"After he was supposedly killed." I knew there was

little picture documentation of Moss. "How can you be sure it's him? We haven't been able to establish facial recognition in anything we have."

"Beard's shaved, glasses are gone. Craig, I've met the guy. It's him."

"Then we're about to cremate the wrong body."

"Sorry about the timing. The image just came through."

There was one thing I needed to know, unequivocally. "How sure are you about the timing of the photo and your source?"

Jack didn't miss a beat. "I'd trust him with my life."

I closed my eyes.

Somehow I had to stop the funeral. I watched Eliza as she nodded for the minister to begin.

"I'd like to welcome everyone on this sad day, to celebrate the life of a man few people knew as well as you who are gathered here."

It was now or never. I took a deep breath, then shouted: "Stop! There's been a bomb threat and we need to evacuate the building."

Chapter 110

THE MINISTER AND the dozen or so mourners turned around. I ran forward, arms outwards.

"We need to clear the building. Bomb squad is on the way."

I didn't look directly at the mourners. I couldn't bear to see the distress on Eliza's face.

The minister urged people to grab their bags and move quickly and quietly towards the back doors, which Mary held open. Darlene and Johnny slipped in via a side entrance.

We had to move fast. With the media outside, someone was bound to call the police. This could turn nasty.

Eliza had refused to budge.

"A bomb threat?" she demanded. "Is this some perverted joke?"

"I'm sorry, Eliza. There is no threat. I just needed to buy some time. There's reason to believe the body in that coffin isn't your father's."

"What?" She appeared hopeful at the news until Johnny approached the coffin clutching a handheld drill and crowbar.

"You're insane!" she shouted. "Get away from there."

Johnny began removing screws on the lid while Darlene set up her mobile kit.

Eliza was yelling at them to stop. She flinched with every whir of the drill. I could hear sirens outside. Time was running out so I grabbed the crowbar. Together Johnny and I began to lever off the lid.

Eliza wheeled herself back in horror.

I knew she would never forgive us for what we were doing.

The lid gave way and a putrid smell seeped out.

Darlene was wearing surgical gloves and a surgical mask and handed me the same as I looked down at the body. The face was badly bloated, more decomposed. A section of cheek was missing.

The body was shrouded in a white sheet. No one had bothered to dress it. Darlene cut through the sheet with scissors before ripping it apart. She was looking for anything to suggest another cause of death.

In his left side, irregular chunks of flesh were missing in small sections. On the upper left arm was a straight-edged mark.

"See this wound?" Darlene said. "The others look like they were caused by fish or trauma. This one's a surgical excision."

Johnny snapped images with his phone.

Loud banging on the wooden doors stopped us momentarily.

Mary was still on guard at the back doors. "Craig, what do you want to do?"

The police had arrived and over a loudspeaker we could hear them demanding we evacuate immediately.

Darlene scraped a small piece of skin and dropped it into a half-sized tube. She quickly shoved it under her shirt at the back.

I closed the coffin lid and we all stepped back.

"We need to do what they say," I instructed.

Mary opened the doors and Eliza wheeled through first. I quickly followed to explain about Jack's call.

"Why?" Eliza said to me through clenched teeth.

Two police in protective gear were feet away. I had to explain later. There was one thing I needed to know.

"I know what you're thinking. But did your father have a tattoo or skin lesion removed from his left arm? Any kind of minor operation?"

She wheeled herself away, Mary close behind. I waited until they were clear.

"There was no bomb scare," I shouted, hands raised in the air. "I made it up and acted alone."

Darlene and Johnny followed, passing Eliza in her chair.

"Craig, you were right," Darlene whispered.

Right now that wasn't much consolation. We'd unleashed a shitstorm I had no way of controlling.

Chapter 111

ELIZA TRIED TO fathom what had just taken place. Had Craig completely lost his mind? Lying about a bomb to break into the coffin at the service attended by the few people who still had any respect for her father.

Numb, she watched bulbs flash as police handcuffed Craig and ushered him into the back of a marked car.

A team of heavily padded police entered the building.

Johnny was clearly shaken by what they had done. He squatted on his ankles as police questioned him. Darlene stood defiantly, casting sympathetic looks towards Eliza.

None of this made sense. These people had been so kind until now. The last thing she could do for her father was to make sure the service was dignified. He had died alone, in a violent explosion. Everything he'd worked for, his innovations and dedication to helping others, was instantly erased. More than that, he had been publicly vilified, now physically desecrated.

A man who never drank would be remembered for dying in a drunken stupor trying to avoid charges for stealing from the charity organization he'd dedicated his life to.

"All clear," the police announced and left the crematorium.

Eliza wheeled herself inside right up to the casket.

She placed a hand on the polished wood and tried to connect with the man she thought she knew better than herself.

Had his life been one giant lie? Part of her wanted to hate him for leaving her without an explanation, or even the chance to say good-bye. If he had met her one last time, how could she have believed anything he had to say, knowing everything up until now was a lie?

Anger surged through Eliza's veins and her heart accelerated. Her breathing became shallow and rapid. Air. She needed to get outside and get some air.

She moved and felt something dig into her thigh. A plastic specimen tube had dropped into her chair. She picked it up and thought of what Craig had asked her.

Did her father have any tattoos or skin lesions removed?

The last time she'd seen him was in the city office. He'd spilled tea on his shirt and changed before a meeting. He always wore a white Bonds singlet underneath. She thought back. His skin was pale to the elbows and tanned below the level of his sleeves. There were definitely no lesions, marks, or scars on his upper arms.

Eliza took a series of slow, deep breaths, counting to four with every exhalation. The heart flutter slowed and she was finally able to speak.

She glared at Johnny, who was blessing himself in the entrance. He opened his eyes and met her gaze. "I am so sorry, but we had good—"

"Tell me what Darlene saw. Inside the…"

He took a step towards her. "A mark that didn't appear natural. I mean it didn't look like a fish—"

She wheeled closer. "Tell me exactly what it was."

He seemed to hesitate.

"I'm sick of being protected. Lied to. Tell me the *truth*, Johnny."

"It looked like a wide section of skin had been excised." He pointed to the outer, upper part of his left arm. "About here."

"Why did Darlene sample it?"

"To see if it was done before death. Microscopy would show if it had healed."

Eliza spun around and raced out the doors. When she realized Johnny was still behind, she held up the specimen.

"Are we going to get this to Private or not?"

Chapter 112

MARY PICKED ME up from the police station. I was escorted out the front of the building to run the media gauntlet. Public humiliation was part of the punishment for trying to stop a cover-up, it seemed. I just hadn't figured out who was directly involved.

My lawyer had hoped to label me a whistleblower who would be legally protected from prosecution. The problem was, we were only protected if we actually worked for the government institution we were trying to expose. Laws recently passed under the guise of antiterrorist measures were more likely to bury whistleblowers. It also gave secret agencies unprecedented powers without scrutiny or recourse.

That worried me more than charges pending for interfering with a body. If Eric Moss's corpse had been substituted—either while still in the water or while in the morgue—someone had wanted him cremated quickly and with few questions asked. The ambassador's cronies could have murdered Moss with impunity, if he'd offended or compromised the US government. The question was whether the Australian government was involved as well. What was Lang Gillies's involvement? It would explain the rush to funeral service and cremation.

The other possibility was that Moss was still alive and managed to somehow fake his death. But that meant he needed access to a body, or killed a man to take his place.

With police and authorities satisfied the case was closed and would remain that way, there was little chance of getting to the truth.

On top of that, I'd just put a giant target on Private Sydney's back.

Mary brought the car around and I climbed into the passenger seat, unable to forget the horror on Eliza's face as we broke into the coffin. Jack Morgan's intel had to be accurate. But I'd never be able to prove it.

Mark Talbot had realized this was far bigger than any of us knew.

Mary dropped me outside Private's building and I headed inside. Collette greeted me with a long hug.

"I'm so proud of you." She wrestled back a tear but didn't elaborate. "You better get to the lab."

I was confused when Johnny appeared in the corridor outside, face beaming.

"Lucky we have a Gene-IE to grant us wishes," he said.

Darlene brushed past in her white coat.

To my surprise, Eliza was at the computer desk behind the lab door and looked up at me.

"You took your time," she said with a glint in her green eyes. "Leaving us to do all the work."

I had an overwhelming urge to hug her, which I didn't fight. She responded very tightly, then slowly broke away.

"What are you doing standing around? I'm still paying you to find my father."

Her smile made the morning's events worth it. "All

right then." I stepped back, fully realizing Eliza was the reason I cared so much about the case.

"First, though," she added, "there's something I need to tell you." Her tone was suddenly grave. "And I don't think you're going to like it."

Chapter 113

I SUGGESTED WE talk outside. My paranoia about surveillance meant Eliza and I left our phones at reception. This time, I didn't want to take any chances.

"Keep all the doors locked," I advised Collette. "Don't let anyone in we don't already know and trust, and don't accept any deliveries."

"I won't let you down," she said, locking the doors behind us.

Whatever it was Eliza wanted to reveal had me concerned. I opted for a café we hadn't been to before.

I had no idea what this morning could have triggered. If ADIA or the CIA had murdered Moss and had switched his body in the coffin for some reason, they'd be mighty pissed off with this morning's events. And if they had nothing to do with the death, they'd be back on Eric's tail now they knew he wasn't dead. Which meant on Eliza's tail too.

The hissing of the machines and grinding beans made eavesdropping almost impossible. We found a seat in the corner and ordered two lattes, and a chicken salad on sourdough to share.

As soon as the waiter left, Eliza began.

"A couple of days ago, flowers arrived for the accountant in the office next to mine. Inside the envelope that came with them was something addressed to me, asking him to hand-deliver a micro USB."

Whoever sent it had to know all mail and deliveries to Eliza would be monitored. "Is it from your dad?"

"It has to be. It contains a file with the text of a kid's story he used to read to me, word for word. I knew it by heart, so Dad didn't need to remind me."

"Was there anything else on it? Maybe some encrypted files?"

"I asked my neighbor, who's an IT whiz. He said there was nothing else on it."

"Who else knew you read that book together?"

She moved the salt and pepper to the side of the table to make way for the coffees. "No one."

It was also plausible there were encoded or encrypted files that couldn't be readily deciphered. Whoever sent the USB didn't want it seen by the authorities.

"What's the book?" I asked.

"It was part of a series. *Oh, The Things You Can See.* This one was about Asia and highlighted exotic animals, costumes, and landmarks. You know the sort of thing, orangutans and rainforests, panda bears, warriors, and the Great Wall of China. I loved the intricacy of the pictures. They were works of art in their own right."

If Eric Moss wasn't Hans Gudgast, maybe this was a clue to where he had been, or where he intended to go. Even so, Asia encompassed a broad range of countries.

"Did anywhere seem to mean something special to him? Or did he talk about any of those places?"

"Dad insisted I learn about the world, not just our backyard."

I swallowed a mouthful of coffee. "Why didn't you tell me this before?"

She poured sugar into hers. "I was going to, only that guy broke into my house. Then I saw the TV news." She looked around the café. "If this is how Dad wanted me to remember him, I didn't want anyone taking or—"

"Dissecting it like a piece of forensic evidence."

"I know, it sounds stupid now to have kept quiet."

I understood completely the need to keep a part of someone to one's self, especially when they were gone.

"Where is it now?"

"I'll have to go to the bathroom to retrieve it. And before you raise an eyebrow..." She reached into her oversized handbag and removed, of all things, a sewing kit with a fine-tipped pair of embroidery scissors. "I had to hide it somewhere no one would think to look."

Chapter 114

I SUGGESTED WE go straight to Eliza's and pick up the book. Maybe there was a subtle message pointing to something in the text. And she could also extract the USB from her clothing in private.

My car was parked in the underground garage. I opened the passenger door and pain immediately exploded in the back of my skull. I hit the roof forehead first. Dazed, I felt my head suddenly in an arm lock.

"You need to stay out of things that don't concern you," a gravelly voice ordered, his grip tightening.

"Like hell." I managed to pull more upright and jammed the heel of my shoe down his inside leg. The second he loosened his grip, I thrust my elbow hard into his solar plexus. He lost contact, staggered back. Using momentum, I spun around and struck. The crack echoed as my right fist made contact with his jaw.

He stiffened and dropped backwards onto the ground. He wasn't getting up soon so I turned to Eliza. She was still in her chair, stunned.

"Are you all right?" She wheeled closer.

"Better than him right now." A lump on my forehead

throbbed. At least we were both alive. Bending down to check the pulse in his neck, I noticed red marks around his eyes. They looked like chemical burns. "I think this is the guy who attacked you the other night." I rifled through his pockets and found the wallet. Inside he had an Australian Department of Defense pass with his photo and name on it. Graydon Knight. I'd seen IDs like this before, different from ones carried by defense force members or public servants. "He's Defense Intelligence," I said, as tires squealed somewhere on a floor below.

"ADIA was in my house?"

"This time he didn't mention handing anything over from your father."

I suspected the Australian government wanted Eric Moss to stay dead as much for their own reasons as the CIA's.

"Craig?" Eliza said. "Don't move."

I felt the sting of cold metal on the back of my neck.

Chapter 115

THE VOICE BEHIND me instructed, "Get him up."

Knight had begun to rouse. I glanced sideways at Eliza, who nodded for me to do it. I wasn't about to argue with the barrel of a gun at such close range.

A black van pulled up alongside us. The man with the gun aimed it now at Eliza. "Put him inside."

It took what strength I had left to drag the semiconscious lug to the van. The man with the gun used his spare hand to open the van's sliding door without his weapon losing its focus. I levered the dead weight of the agent in.

"I've done what you wanted so let her go."

"Not so fast," he said. "I want Ms. Moss to get in. We'd like to ask her some questions. Off the record, of course."

He turned his back on Eliza for a moment and trained the gun on my chest.

"Don't hurt him," she pleaded. "I'll go with you." She wheeled towards us.

Then I saw a silver glint in her hand. With one swift action, she lurched at the back of the man's knee. He instantly buckled and I seized the gun.

Face contorted, he reached behind, yanked out the weapon and held up a bloodied pair of embroidery scissors.

Now that I had the gun, I wanted answers. "What does Moss have that you need so badly?"

The man winced as blood gushed from his wound. "We thought he died in that blast, just like you."

"Who was behind the explosion? Moss can't have acted alone."

"Ask her." He gestured with his head at Eliza. "She knows more than she's letting on. That's why we need to question her."

I tightened my grip, aware the van had a driver I hadn't seen yet, who could be armed. No one was taking Eliza. "Is ADIA acting alone or is the CIA pulling the strings?"

"You already know Moss was privy to defense contracts." He tried to stem the bleeding with his hand. "Disabled or not, she's dangerous. Next time it could be you she stabs."

He wasn't going to give me anything useful and his color was fading. He needed medical attention.

I kept the gun steady. "Slowly get in the van and leave us alone, or we'll go public with what we know. Ambassador Roden's friends won't be impressed at your cock-up."

He limped to the open door and slid in, nursing his leg. The driver gunned the engine and sped off towards the exit. If they wanted Eliza, they had to be desperate. I dropped the gun to my side and moved to her.

"Is there anything you can't do?" I asked in amazement.

"The 'YMCA' dance is out of the question. Can't lift my arms above my head, remember?"

She was shaken but hadn't lost her sense of humor. I

pulled her to standing position, arm around her waist, and eased her into the passenger seat. She drew the seat belt across with her left hand.

I grabbed a packet of cleaning wipes from the side door and wiped blood from her hands.

"Did I just commit grievous bodily harm?" she asked.

I bent down so our eyes were level. "You stopped yourself from being kidnapped. They would have used you as a bargaining chip to get to your father." Or worse. They could have held her as a terrorist because of her father and his defense contracts. From what the agent had said, it sounded like ADIA really *did* think Moss had died in the explosion. So they weren't part of any cover-up. They'd been duped like the rest of us. Maybe that was true of the US too. And if ADIA and the CIA didn't switch the bodies, who did?

I closed the car door and folded her wheelchair into my boot, senses heightened for other potential threats.

We needed to find out what message Eric sent Eliza before anyone else tried to stop us.

Chapter 116

I PULLED OUT of the garage at top speed and called Mary on the hands-free about the ambush and threat. I warned them all to be alert and go to their cars in pairs for safety right now.

Darlene came on the line.

"Craig, our little Gene-IE came through. The data from the DNA sample of the body was compatible with one on record."

I flicked a glance at Eliza, who held her breath.

"All I got was a name, Bobby Sim, but he left a trail of media reports and public records. Fifty-nine years old, multiple convictions for drug possession, one for trafficking, and a couple for aggravated sexual assault. This guy drugged and assaulted his victims."

Eliza looked relieved it wasn't her father.

"How and when did he die?" I asked.

"Two weeks ago from lung cancer."

"Did he have any identifying features?" I was thinking particularly about the arm lesion.

"A press shot showed him in a T-shirt with a jacket

over his face. He had a tattoo of what looked like an angel on his left upper arm."

"Great work, Darlene. Remember, we all need to be careful. This isn't over. In fact, it just got a whole lot worse."

As soon as we arrived at Eliza's house, she collected her spare set of crutches and headed to the bedroom. I followed. A double bed was raised higher than normal, easier to get down from, I assumed. A bookshelf in the corner only had books on the middle shelves, at a functional height for Eliza. The top and lower shelves were filled with photos, vases, and trophies. I couldn't help noticing the multitude of swimming awards, including a gold medal in one corner. There was so much I didn't know about this woman.

"Wait a minute. This is gold from the 2008 Paralympics!"

"For breaststroke. As you know, butterfly wasn't an option."

I had done a quick background search on Eliza and this wasn't something she promoted in her company or online.

"You won this and never think to mention it?"

"It doesn't make me any better than anyone else. It was a personal goal I set and got to achieve it. It doesn't define me. That blue ribbon"—she pointed to a small, wide ribbon with faded writing—"for running twenty-five meters in first grade means far more. Doctors said I'd never walk, and it took me longer than anyone else, but it was my proudest moment. Dad's too. It showed me life was about potential, not limitations."

She leaned across and removed an old, faded picture book. "Here it is."

We sat on the bed and she lovingly stroked the cover. I noticed there was minimal dust on it.

"When was the last time you looked at it?"

"Couple of years, maybe."

Someone else had touched it since.

She opened it and flicked through the pages. "Every page is here."

"May I?" I ran my hands over the cover and binding. "We need to pull it apart."

Eliza hesitated then agreed. "Do whatever you need to."

I used a knife from the kitchen. The lining inside the back cover came away more easily than expected. I opened the binding and separated the cover, exposing a thin piece of paper.

Chapter 117

ELIZA READ THE letter slowly, then handed it to me.

My dearest Eliza,

These words are my legacy to you. I see you rolling your eyes because you have heard all of this before, many times, in various forms over the years. These are my firm beliefs. If we are separated, this is what I pray you remember.

I have always been the best person I could be. I beg you never forget that.

It isn't who you are in life that matters. It is what you do and WHY that counts. Intentions are paramount. I have always believed that inaction is more harmful than well-intentioned actions that fail.

Life is a series of illusions. Things aren't always what they seem.

Each of us is the hero in your own story (and you in mine). However, we may equally be viewed as a villain in others' stories, for genuine or per-

ceived crimes. Despite holding different views, looking or sounding different, originating from another place, one truth is certain:

We all strive to live in a just world, and to see that our loved ones are safe and cared for.

If events occur beyond your control, accept them. You were neither complicit, nor responsible. You should never be shamed by them. Hold your head high for the woman you are. Innuendo, supposition, and accusations of others have no role in your life.

Anger, hatred, and bitterness are lethal poisons. They cause a slow, painful emotional death that only you suffer. Self-destruction will never defeat an enemy or create justice.

Be prepared to live with the consequences of your actions. If you will not be proud of an act, don't commit it.

In times of struggle, always remember that when the pupil is ready, the teacher will appear. You will always have help should you need it.

Words can start wars, so be careful what you say and whom you say it to. Again, if you are afraid to own those words in a public forum, they are best never said.

Remember these things and you will have a safe, fulfilling, and satisfying life.

Be true to yourself, my darling Eliza. Let each step bring you closer to your ultimate destination.

You are the greatest inspiration a man could have, and the dearest child. I love you forever, in this life and the next, from Questacon to Timbuktu and beyond.

This was a farewell note. Wherever he was, he was sure he would not be back.

Eliza slid off the bed and rested herself against the tallboy. She held a photo in a frame and handed it to me. In the faded image, a toddler grinned with pure joy at being held high in the air. The back of a man's head was in the frame, as the child looked down adoringly.

"I thought I could fly when I was in his arms." She wiped a tear from her cheek.

The letter referred to wars, crimes, and self-destruction but I had to ask if Eliza had picked up anything else from his words. I reread the final sentence.

"Is there any significance to the phrase 'from Questacon to Timbuktu and beyond'?"

"Timbuktu was the silliest word I'd ever heard." She smiled. "It made me laugh every time Dad said it."

"Could he be letting you know he's going to Africa?"

Eliza studied the photo again. "He'd ask me where it was, tickle me every time I got the answer wrong." She half-smiled. "I knew exactly where it was, so I mentioned every other city I knew, just to make the game last."

Maybe the letter was a confession of sorts. Jack Morgan said CIA intelligence believed one of their operatives had turned. But who was he turning to?

There had to be something vital in the message. Questacon was a hands-on science center in Canberra, the home of parliament.

As we headed back to Private so Darlene could examine the USB, I began to quiz Eliza, hoping to prompt a memory or association.

"Did you ever visit Questacon with your dad?"

"A few times. I loved that things were at wheelchair height and I could use almost every exhibit. But that was years ago."

I thought about the buildings around that site on Lake Burley Griffin. The High Court, Old Parliament House, the National Gallery, government departments.

"Did you visit any other places when you were there?"

"We went to the zoo, the Australian Museum, the War Memorial. I always wanted to go in those paddling bikes, but Dad didn't think it was safe for me."

"She who became a Paralympian swimmer."

"He was just protecting me." She looked out the window.

"Did he ever go to meetings or stop for business when you were there?"

"When we were together, he left work behind. It was just him and me. Unless there was a massive bushfire or floods or something he needed to be involved in, which was rare when we were on a road trip."

"Where did you stay?"

"Close enough for us to get to Questacon without a car. He got a good deal, I think, at the Hyatt, the one on Commonwealth Avenue."

I knew the hotel. It was a favorite for visiting politicians and dignitaries.

Eliza reflected, "I remember the first time he took me around the embassies. I loved the different types of architecture but one was my absolute favorite."

Eliza's eyes widened. She reached out and gripped my left arm tightly.

"Oh my God, Craig. I know where my father is."

Chapter 118

"DAD'S AT THE Chinese embassy. He has to be."

I didn't need proof. Eliza's revelation made complete sense now. So much so, we were quickly back at the Private office. I stopped Eliza from mentioning our destination in the car or in the office. We had no idea who could be listening in. First, we needed to know if Darlene could extract any useful data. She put it straight in her computer.

"I can't see anything else on here apart from the kids' book," she admitted, defeated. "Not even encrypted or corrupt files."

I had been sure there was something else on the USB. Otherwise, Eric Moss could have sent his daughter a card or note making reference to the text. I hid the USB in a zippered compartment in my belt, something Becky had bought me for when we traveled. At the time I'd humored her by wearing it. Now it might just come in handy.

We needed to get to Canberra ASAP. If Eliza's hunch was right, her father could be preparing to leave the country with the help of the Chinese. And after the fiasco with his supposed funeral, he couldn't afford to wait much longer. Thanks to us, the police, ADIA, and CIA now knew he hadn't died in that boat explosion. He could have already gone, but I believed the only reason he'd left the letter and USB was to give Eliza a chance to find him.

There were two major operative rules, both of which Moss had broken. Adopting Eliza was a complication he was supposed to avoid. He'd also failed to walk away and not look back when he had the opportunity.

But how to get to Canberra? Three hours on the road was too dangerous. We'd be followed for certain. I contacted Geoff Andren and explained the situation. Within half an hour Eliza and I were seated behind Geoff, in one of his friend's private planes.

"I just wanted to thank you for everything." Eliza leaned over towards me. "I couldn't have had this chance to find Dad without you."

"We haven't found him yet, and we may be too late. Not to mention the trouble we could be in if we try to get into a foreign embassy."

The engine started and I placed my palms flat on the armrest. Not knowing what we'd face, Eliza seemed keen to talk.

"I loved seeing the variety of architecture among the embassies. Weird, for a child, but hey, I've always been different."

I smiled. "I see you more as a standout. For all the right reasons."

She looked down and pulled a section of hair behind her ear. I had to admit, from someone so confident and accomplished, the action was more than a little endearing.

"We've got about forty-five minutes," I said. "We should rest while we can."

Within minutes she was dozing. I watched her, wondering what the next few hours had in store. Eliza had made it clear that no matter the consequences, she'd seize any chance to see her father again. I consciously hadn't asked what she would do if Eric wanted her to join him.

When the wheels finally hit the tarmac Eliza opened her eyes and stretched her neck. "Are we here already?"

"Better grab your things. We don't know when we'll be back."

The keys to a rental car awaited us at the terminal and we were soon headed northwest towards the city. Extensive roadwork slowed us. I obeyed every speed zone to avoid unwanted attention.

Within a few kilometers, it became apparent—two cars were tailing us. One was a marked police car. I accelerated, it accelerated. I slowed, it slowed. The Feds already knew we were here, and had to be still after Eric Moss.

We passed the Royal Military College on our right. Neither car turned off.

I had two choices. One was to drive somewhere else and throw them off the scent. But that might cost Eliza the only chance to see her father.

I took the second option.

Chapter 119

"HOLD ON," I warned Eliza as we approached the Kings Avenue exit ramp.

Seizing the opportunity, I slammed the accelerator to the floor. The Commodore engine screamed to life, letting us overtake an elderly couple in a Mazda.

The police kept pace as we sped across the bridge. Without sirens, they were likely to follow us all the way. Traffic ahead pulled to the left. I capitalized on the extra lane space and wove between lanes, gaining some distance.

The Chinese embassy was only minutes away. Once we were inside its walls, we would be safe—temporarily. The problem was, Eliza couldn't make it out of the car quickly and the Chinese didn't know who we were, or that we were coming.

"Call the embassy, tell them who you are, and see if they'll open the gates," I urged.

She used her smartphone to find the number.

We were fast approaching the Parliamentary Triangle, an area rife with tourists, workers, and the highest concentration of police. And the biggest security response to potential terrorist threats. I needed to put time between us and our pursuers. We had no chance of losing them.

The traffic lights onto King George Terrace remained green. I tapped the brake, then accelerated on the orange and swung right, barely missing an ACTION bus. The police lost time slowing at the red. But not enough.

Clinging to the left verge, the rear wheels barely hung on. A furniture truck loomed just ahead and indicated right. I took it on the inside, thumping up the curb, then swung hard right.

Tires squealed as the back wheels slipped. I took my foot off the pedal and steered out. The truck stopped mid-turn, buying me precious seconds.

I crossed two more sets of traffic lights and found myself behind the Hyatt Hotel. The police were gaining.

I looped around to the embassy but the gates were closed.

On the phone, Eliza continued to plead for someone to open them. We needed more time. I passed the embassy and swung left onto Commonwealth Avenue then whipped into the Hyatt entrance, barely missing a row of parked cars. Accelerating out of the bend, I turned hard left as the police car entered the drive, close behind, carefully steering past a Lamborghini and Porsche. Our pursuers weren't so lucky. Eliza spun her head around at the crash.

In the rearview mirror, I saw the mess. The marked car clipped the Lambo and pushed it into the Porsche.

I flinched at the carnage, cornered left, and floored it to the embassy, meters away. "We're outside now!" Eliza shouted, and the gate began to open.

I braked and spun hard. The car slid into the driveway as an unmarked car jumped the curb and cut off my path, blocking our access to the gate. I put my left arm out to protect Eliza.

Our car squealed to a sudden stop, just short of the vehicle that had swung in to block us. Eliza's seatbelt locked but her head was thrown forward and back against the headrest.

I unchecked my belt and saw a gun pointed in at me through the window.

Chapter 120

THE POLICE OFFICER yelled at me to raise my hands, as he opened my door.

"Slowly exit the car!" he ordered.

As I stepped out, hands raised, I saw the Glock aimed at Eliza.

"Get out, ma'am, with your hands up."

"She can't physically lift her arms," I shouted. "And she needs a wheelchair. It's in the boot."

Two plainclothes men assisted her and she stood, propped against the car.

There were sudden shouts in Chinese, and three armed guards appeared in the drive from within the embassy.

Guns were pointed at the police now, who diverted their attention to the new threat.

"Stand down!" a voice behind me shouted.

A well-groomed gentleman gave an order in Mandarin. His men lowered their weapons as he stepped through the gate.

"Sir, this is Federal Police business." The officer who still had his gun trained on us did the talking. "I ask you and your guards to step back and away."

"This has just become official business of the People's Republic of China," the other man answered, now switching to perfect English.

I noticed cameras on the brick fence, recording every minute. A fleet of police vehicles began filling the street.

"Sir, you don't understand. These two are wanted for aiding a fugitive, and are suspected of illegally selling classified information. Their crimes are covered by the Terrorist Act."

"What?" Eliza demanded. "This has to be a sick joke."

The senior officer announced, "You two are under arrest." He gestured for us to be taken away.

The Chinese official put himself between the gun and Eliza. "I'm afraid you will not be taking anyone from this embassy." He handed the officer a card.

I lowered my hands a little. Eric Moss had to be inside.

"Mr. Chin, is it? They are on Australian, not Chinese, soil." The officer stood firm.

"Technically, yes. Your laws allow you to arrest suspects, even on embassy grounds. However, it is customary to do so with the permission from the relevant ambassador. That would be Ambassador Xing. He is currently in Beijing but will return next week." He pulled out a notebook. "May I have your name, please?"

"Detective Sergeant Scott Wilson."

Chin wrote it down.

"With respect, Mr. Chin, we don't need your boss's permission. We are on a public street, outside your gates. Federally owned land."

"I am afraid you are mistaken. You are standing on our paved drive, which is very much part of our embassy."

The police looked at each other. We were at a standoff.

Wilson tried again. "Sir, we don't want to concern you

or your staff. We just need these two to come with us and we'll be out of your way." -

Chin stepped forward. "Forcibly removing anyone from within this perimeter will create—how do you say?—an international incident. Is that something you have authority to do?"

The detective sergeant looked furious. He ordered his men to make sure no one moved then stepped away to make a phone call.

Eliza and I were trapped. If we did manage to get inside the embassy, the Feds would be waiting for us the second we showed our faces.

We were trapped with no way out.

Chapter 121

WE WERE IN limbo. No longer on "Australian soil" yet outside the protection of the embassy, on a small patch of asphalt, meters from the Federal Police. Without so much as Eliza's chair.

Eliza leaned heavily against the car. Her legs were fatiguing quickly.

Tense minutes passed before the senior detective returned. The other officers still had their guns drawn on us.

And all this time, the Chinese guards hadn't altered their positions.

"Mr. Chin, I have been instructed to comply with your request." The Fed looked like he'd choke on his words as he directed his team to pull back, out onto the road.

"I'm glad we could come to an arrangement," the embassy official said.

I moved around to support Eliza and she wrapped her arm around my waist as I took some of her weight.

"The wheelchair's in the boot," I said. "Can someone get it?"

Wilson clenched his jaw. "No. The car comes with us," he said. "And everything in it."

I looked at Chin, who shrugged.

"My bag," Eliza said.

"If it's in the car, we're taking it." Wilson stood ram-rod straight.

"But the car and its contents are on embassy grounds," I argued.

Mr. Chin walked over, reached into the car, removed Eliza's bag, and dumped it at my feet.

"Thank you," Eliza said. "I need my wheelchair."

"You will not require it," Chin said, matter-of-factly.

"We'll be here when you get hungry or thirsty," Wilson declared before reversing the hire car onto the road.

Mr. Chin called his guards inside and the metal gate began to slide closed in his wake. With us on the outside.

Chin raised a hand and the gate stopped, before he turned to us.

"Miss Moss, Mr. Gisto, you are very welcome to come in."

Chapter 122

"ARE THEY ARRESTING us?" Eliza whispered as I helped her walk. Two more military guards had appeared.

I wasn't sure. They knew who we were so they had to have been monitoring us. We were ushered through a door, down a corridor, and into a lift. We were underground, no windows and no natural light. They searched us both at gunpoint. Our phones, watches, and personal effects were immediately confiscated. A handheld metal detector beeped at my belt. I had to remove it, with the USB still inside. It was then handed back, thankfully without being searched. I quickly replaced it around my waist.

Next we were each photographed against a wall and moved to what looked like an interrogation room. A scratched wooden table sat in the center, with two sealed bottles of water. Two metal chairs on one side, one on the other.

I helped Eliza into the first chair and she almost flopped into it with exhaustion.

"Dad must be here. Why else would they let us in?"

"They need to confirm our ID. Maybe they want to know why the Federal Police were on their territory." The thought occurred to me: the only possible reason for the Chinese government to harbor Eric was that he worked for them.

I walked around the small room. Reflective glass inside, viewing room behind it. I was convinced we were being watched and possibly filmed. None of this felt right. I hoped we hadn't walked into something far more dangerous than Detective Sergeant Wilson and his mates.

"I'm sorry I got you into this," was all I could say.

"I'm the one who got you into this . . . I just couldn't let it go. Let Dad go."

I kept thinking of the Federal Police in the street. Even if there was a secret exit to this place, and we managed to evade them, we would be arrested as soon as we were recognized, anywhere in the country. There was no way to let Mary or the others know where we were.

"Eliza, they may know of your dad but it isn't clear if he's with the Chinese or against them."

She unscrewed the lid on a bottle and stared at the label. "He kept so many secrets. What sort of person can be that deceitful? I didn't know him at all."

I sat beside her and held her hand, aware we were being monitored. "Not his birth name, maybe. Or what he was involved in, but the man loved you, read to you, cared for you. That was him. That wasn't an act."

"Thank you, Craig. For everything." She squeezed my hand. "No matter what happens, I'm glad we met."

A bang on the door interrupted us and an armed soldier marched through. He was shouting in Chinese and English. "Where is USB?"

Chapter 123

THE DOOR OPENED farther and a man appeared dressed in a navy jumper, gray tracksuit pants, and ill-fitting slippers. He had a sling that positioned his hand over his heart. He looked thinner but, at five foot eleven, was still stocky. This time there were no reflective glasses, no dark lenses. Even in humble clothing, it was easy to appreciate the charisma he exuded to staff and politicians.

Eric Moss spoke softly to the soldier, in Mandarin. He lowered the gun and the unlikely pair exchanged further words before the soldier left the room, closing the door with a bang.

Wide round eyes glistened when he saw us.

Eliza slowly lifted her face and wiped her eyes. "Daddy?" She saw the sling.

I slipped out of my chair and stood in front of the glass, to give them some modicum of privacy.

"You're hurt," she said.

"Not as much as I've hurt you." He reached forward to touch her face.

A thud on the glass made it clear. Contact was forbidden.

"This is Craig—" she tried.

"I know who he is. I figured you'd contact Jack Morgan again, who would refer you to Private Sydney. Months ago I put a small tracking device on your chair so I could monitor your whereabouts on computer. I'm sorry, but I had to know you were safe."

That was why the Chinese embassy hadn't seemed that surprised we were on our way. I couldn't hide my frustration that he'd put his daughter at risk. "Did you know Eliza was attacked at home? And ADIA tried to detain her earlier today? She could have been killed."

"I was informed by my contact here. I'm sorry. If I could have stopped them from hurting you, Eliza, I would have."

Somehow "sorry" didn't seem to make up for all the lies and deception. If it were my child threatened, I would have been beyond angry. He didn't show any emotion or remorse for what she'd suffered.

I watched Eliza, studying her father's face as if meeting him for the first time.

"Do you know what they wanted with me? And that USB?" she eventually asked.

"I couldn't just abandon you after things changed at Contigo. Unfortunately, my selfishness made you a target."

I felt protective of Eliza and didn't want her being deceived anymore. Selfishness? "You mean when your illegal account keeping and secret contracts were about to be exposed?"

He slipped into the chair I'd vacated. "All these years of work compromised by a few missing event tickets. The internal audit would have found more discrepancies. I'd managed to keep the fraud squad at bay. Time ran out."

He wasn't going to worm his way out of what he'd

done. "You're not just talking about a routine audit," I interjected. "I had a visit from Jim Roden, who was eager to find you, dead or alive."

He sighed. "I broke their rules with what I did to keep Contigo afloat. There was no going back once I became an embarrassment to the US and Australian governments. The simplest solution was the one they chose."

"Are you saying the Australian government tried to assassinate you twice?"

"The assassination attempts were CIA. The Americans had a mole in with the Chinese who warned them I was meeting at a bay only reachable by boat. The exact location was secret even from me, until twenty minutes before time. Obviously, the boat was the best way to make sure I didn't make it to that meeting. Only I got lucky."

I couldn't let Eliza be taken in by him again. I stepped forward and slapped the table hard.

"You're a liar! You've been playing us all right from the start."

Chapter 124

ACCORDING TO JACK Morgan, the CIA had suspected a rogue agent, which is why they were pulling operatives out of the country. Moss was that rogue agent. I guessed the missing tickets were incidental, and didn't set off the series of events.

"That isn't true," he pleaded with Eliza. "You know me. Better than anyone."

"The fire at the cabin," Eliza concluded. "I knew you'd been there."

"You just happened to have magnesium on you, and get into an escape hatch which happened to be beneath a friend's cabin?"

He didn't blink at the accusation.

I leaned forward. "You set a trap for them, didn't you?"

He sighed and looked up towards the glass. "I did what I had to to survive."

"You're a regular MacGyver," I mocked.

"Craig," Eliza warned. "Stop it."

"And the boat," I said. "Did they get lucky assuming you'd go there and rigged it to blow?"

He pulled the chair close to his daughter, without touching her. His sole focus became Eliza. "I need to know where the USB I sent you is."

"Oh my God, it's the only thing you care about." She covered her mouth. "You used me to get it here?"

"I know you can't understand. But it is our ticket to safety. Without it..." His voice trailed away.

"I can't believe you worked in secret for the Americans, then made a deal with the Chinese."

"It isn't that simple. It was only through sheer luck I survived that explosion." He moved the fingers on his right hand in the sling. "The Americans and the Australians wanted me dead. They still want me dead. By running, I confirmed their suspicions that one of their agents had turned rogue. That put you at risk. It made sense to have people think I was dead and it ended the attacks on you. The man who took my place was part of a Chinese drug syndicate. His relatives couldn't afford the burial. Chinese agents witnessed the explosion and pulled me from the water. They came up with the idea of substituting and the family signed over the body. I had to protect you, Eliza, and this was the only way."

Eliza shook her head, suddenly defiant. "Don't make this about me. You've been lying my entire life. Hans Gudgast? Is that your real name?"

He shrugged. "Gudgast was an embezzler, but in death he gave me a chance to do good."

I understood. He couldn't fake the height difference, so wasn't Gudgast at all. "You took his identity to enter Australia with the help of the CIA."

He lowered his gaze. "I came here from Europe, where doesn't matter, after being recruited as a university student interested in biomedical engineering. I had no family and was idealistic back then. I saw it as an opportunity to do good. And the CIA offered to fund lifesaving research in exchange for information about foreign defense force bases and technologies. That's why I developed training programs." He rubbed darkened eyes. "I never agreed to hurt anyone."

"Except the people who lent or gave you money," I said. "They won't be seeing it again, after you conned them out of it." This man was either phenomenally naive or extremely manipulative.

He flashed me a quizzical look as if the answer were obvious. "I did that for the staff. The CIA was starting to funnel their funds elsewhere, to their latest projects, and sucking the business dry. If I didn't borrow more, the staff and Contigo would have lost their jobs. We had sold so many of our assets, I had to be creative in presenting to the banks. The employees were like family after all those years. I couldn't let them suffer for something I started."

I couldn't work Moss out. "You must have known it would eventually unravel."

"I had to buy time. Until the last series of secret projects was complete. Now, Eliza, I need that USB."

"I'm sorry, Dad. I can't give it to you."

Chapter 125

MOSS'S EXPRESSION HARDENED. "Eliza, how is your breathing?"

His daughter made no comment.

"You know it's seventy percent normal. There is a clinic in Zurich that specializes in degenerative neurological diseases like yours."

The word "degenerative" was like a blow to my chest. I had no idea Eliza's condition would deteriorate. I moved and sat at the desk opposite her. She would not make eye contact with me.

"Why didn't you say anything?" I tried to process what that meant.

She bowed her head. "I couldn't."

"You're already at seventy percent lung function," her father continued, "and stress speeds the disease process. Who knows what the last few days have done to your immune system. Again, I'm truly sorry for that."

He placed his hand on the table, next to hers. "You just book in for an assessment when you're ready. They do stem cell therapy." He lifted his hand, revealing a card. "It's all been taken care of."

A long silence hung in the room.

Eliza then spoke, a quiver in her voice. "Is that part of the deal you brokered with the Chinese?"

"I had two conditions. In exchange for my research they get me out of Australia safely, and you get the very best medical care. The genetic testing has been paid for in advance. Eliza, this clinic could have the answers no one else does."

Eliza began to tremble.

I wasn't buying it. "So what's on the USB that makes it so valuable? Our computers couldn't detect anything."

"The USB is half of a complex series of systems that will change the face of warfare. That means limiting civilian deaths and carnage." He looked at both of us. "I developed an advanced encryption code, which is why you couldn't decipher it. It needs to be paired with the other USB to be read." He took a deep breath. "Contigo Valley started out as an altruistic, forward-thinking company but in the last ten years it became overrun with agendas I could no longer influence, or stomach. War is a powerful industry and makes certain interests extremely wealthy. Resources and politics are the endgame. Power of the worst kind."

"All this because you're disillusioned with American foreign policy?" I was incredulous.

"The West continues to prop up militants who overthrow those who would keep the US, UK, and Australia away from oil and other resources. Inevitably, the underdog rises to fill the power vacuum and, morally corrupted, becomes the monster it fought. Look at Iraq, Iran, Afghanistan, the list is endless."

"The proverbs we used to talk about," Eliza argued, "like the one about the teacher coming to the pupil. They're fiction. Buddha never said those things. China is no different from anyone else. It's a superpower and equally prone to corruption."

"I disagree. China is looking to the future to break old habits. They are leading the world in commercialization of renewable energy, and are proving giants in the manufacture of those technologies."

Eliza shook her head. "This can't be about solar energy, Dad. It's too far-fetched. And you're going to sell your life's research to another superpower. How can you be sure you can trust them with it? How do you know you're not selling your soul to another devil?"

"Think about it. The Middle East is a debacle, in many ways trapped in the Middle Ages, still obsessing about crusades and infidels. China is on the rise and will have the economy, trained workforce, political influence, and autonomy to orchestrate a better way. We're not talking about a larger version of North Korea, like propagandists would have you believe. Without the West dependent on oil, Middle Eastern wars won't have to be fought. If oil isn't in demand, the power of Saudi Arabia will dissolve."

For the first time, he made a reasonable point. The industry behind wars would need to look for new sources of income.

"Finally, armies can save lives, not take them." He sounded like a politician campaigning for election.

Eliza paused, then spoke firmly. "I'm lucky, happy, and prepared to let fate take its course. I won't accept you doing this for me." She pushed the card back at him.

"The old ways aren't working. The spy game doesn't work. This is my way to make a positive difference."

Despite his motives, I was concerned what would happen to us all if the USB wasn't located. After all, it was the reason the Chinese were helping him escape. I reached into the zipper on my belt and pulled out the tiny device, still mulling over what to do. I eventually slid it across the table.

"Thank you, Craig." He stood. "I have a clear conscience for what happens from here on. Eliza, you've made me a far better person. I will always love you."

Eliza and I both realized that this was the last time we'd ever see the man known as Eric Moss.

Chapter 126

A KNOCK ON the door broke the tearful silence. "Time is up. I have to go," Moss said.

"Please ask for more time, *ask them*." Eliza grabbed her father's hands.

He looked at her with eyes full of love.

"You couldn't make me happier, or more proud."

"What about Lang Gillies?" I asked. "How is he involved?"

"Lang likes to think he's involved in secret work. Truth is, Jim Roden has him in his pocket, for his own reasons. He would have let the ambassador know the second I sent him the resignation e-mail."

I wanted to know one more thing. "Was he complicit in the fraud?" Seeing him pursued by the fraud squad would give me a certain satisfaction.

"He can't tell his left from his right. Subterfuge is beyond his minimal talents." Moss smiled to himself, then looked again at Eliza.

"When will I see you again?" she asked. "How will I contact you?" She reached for his arm and he bent down, tenderly kissing her forehead.

"I have to go somewhere no one will find me. While we've been talking, a deal has been brokered with the Australian and US governments. You will be free once you leave here. Fortunately, Ambassador Roden and his friends at the CIA won't want it getting around that a man with no records and no passport conned the CIA, defense forces, even the Secretary of State into providing intimate knowledge of highly classified defense contracts and bases. The Australian government wouldn't be proud of it either. The only price you pay is silence."

"Please, Daddy, don't do this. We can work something out."

An official entered the room with the guard.

"It's time."

Eliza's hands gripped him tightly and she cried softly in his arms. "I love you. Please don't go."

After a couple of minutes of silence, the guard moved to separate the pair.

I blocked him and took Eliza's hands. Her father walked slowly towards the door. He turned and blew a kiss. "I hope you'll see me one day as a hero in your story, not a villain."

He didn't look back.

Chapter 127

AS ERIC MOSS predicted, we exited the embassy via the front gates. The police were nowhere to be seen and Eliza's wheelchair had been returned. We sat in the back of a diplomatic car, with a Chinese driver separated by an electric screen. I had no doubt he was listening to everything we said on the way to the airport.

She gripped my hand tightly in the backseat, all but emotionally spent.

I ran over what Moss had told us. Eliza would never know his true identity, for his own reasons. The lack of documentation was deliberate. He was a CIA operative and didn't leave a paper or digital trail. Anything else could have been wiped by the CIA once he went rogue.

Eliza placed her head on my shoulder. "Do you think he was lying?"

I watched the view from my window.

"I think he honestly believes he's doing the right thing. It sounds as if he's been disillusioned with his work for a long time. Maybe it was time for him to stop lying."

She lifted her head and turned her face to mine. "He's

still trying to look after me. Swiss treatments? Wasn't stopping wars enough?"

I smiled at her resilience. "Maybe that's how he justified it to himself—his last act to make sure you're taken care of."

"Craig, he's a traitor, isn't he?"

To be honest, I wasn't sure. "It depends on which side you're on. Julian Assange, Edward Snowden polarize opinion all the time. If he does change the face of warfare, he'll be a hero in a lot of people's stories." Although I suspected it was more likely the regime he was defecting to would be just as disillusioning. "One thing is clear," I added. "He loves you more than anything and wants you to get the best possible treatment."

"About that. I didn't know how to tell you. There never seemed to be a right time."

I kept painful secrets myself and couldn't blame Eliza for shielding her privacy. If disability didn't define her, a progressive condition wouldn't either. I looked into her eyes and our faces touched. I kissed her softly at first, then with increasing intensity. For a few minutes, the world went silent.

Chapter 128

WE'D ARRIVED AT the international airport early and were outside the departures gate. I couldn't believe the day had come so quickly.

"I can always tag along if you change your mind, carry your bags?"

Eliza held my hand and smiled. "Kiss me like Peyroni and the paparazzi are watching," she joked.

"Think he's a little busy preparing for that court case of his. Now talking of cases..."

"We've been over this. I have to go alone. If they think I'm suitable for the trial and there's a chance of improvement, I'm going through with the treatment no matter the risks. I don't need Mr. Logic here muddling my thinking, or kissing me to cloud my senses."

I bent down and kissed her again. These months had been memorable. My apartment would be lonely without her. That incredible smile, the raucous laugh, and her zest for life, in spite of the loss and heartache.

"The genetic testing should be able to—I mean,

before things go any further between us, I need to know."

Eliza had no idea if her condition could be passed on to children. Before committing to any long-term relationship, she deserved the chance to find out.

I kissed her button nose.

"Well," she held up her passport, "love you and leave you."

She wheeled away, then spun around. "Hey, you'd better get practicing the 'YMCA' dance. It's the first thing we're doing when I get back."

I raised both arms in a Y-shape and she laughed before disappearing through the departure gate.

Books by James Patterson

FEATURING ALEX CROSS

Cross the Line • *Cross Justice* • *Hope to Die* • *Cross My Heart* • *Alex Cross, Run* • *Merry Christmas, Alex Cross* • *Kill Alex Cross* • *Cross Fire* • *I, Alex Cross* • *Alex Cross's* Trial (with Richard DiLallo) • *Cross Country* • *Double Cross* • *Cross* (also published as *Alex Cross*) • *Mary, Mary* • *London Bridges* • *The Big Bad Wolf* • *Four Blind Mice* • *Violets Are Blue* • *Roses Are Red* • *Pop Goes the Weasel* • *Cat & Mouse* • *Jack & Jill* • *Kiss the Girls* • *Along Came a Spider*

THE WOMEN'S MURDER CLUB

16th Seduction (with Maxine Paetro) • *15th Affair* (with Maxine Paetro) • *14th Deadly Sin* (with Maxine Paetro) • *Unlucky 13* (with Maxine Paetro) • *12th of Never* (with Maxine Paetro) • *11th Hour* (with Maxine Paetro) • *10th Anniversary* (with Maxine Paetro) • *The 9th Judgment* (with Maxine Paetro) • *The 8th Confession* (with Maxine Paetro) • *7th Heaven* (with Maxine Paetro) • *The 6th Target* (with Maxine Paetro) • *The 5th Horseman* (with Maxine Paetro) • *4th of July* (with Maxine Paetro) • *3rd Degree* (with Andrew Gross) • *2nd Chance* (with Andrew Gross) • *1st to Die*

FEATURING MICHAEL BENNETT

Bullseye (with Michael Ledwidge) • *Alert* (with Michael Ledwidge) • *Burn* (with Michael Ledwidge) • *Gone* (with Michael Ledwidge) • *I, Michael Bennett* (with Michael Ledwidge) • *Tick Tock* (with Michael

Ledwidge) • *Worst Case* (with Michael
Ledwidge) • *Run for Your Life* (with Michael
Ledwidge) • *Step on a Crack* (with
Michael Ledwidge)

THE PRIVATE NOVELS

Missing (with Kathryn Fox) • *The Games*
(with Mark Sullivan) • *Private Paris* (with
Mark Sullivan) • *Private Vegas* (with Maxine
Paetro) • *Private India: City on Fire* (with Ashwin
Sanghi) • *Private Down Under* (with Michael
White) • *Private L.A.* (with Mark Sullivan) • *Private
Berlin* (with Mark Sullivan) • *Private London*
(with Mark Pearson) • *Private Games* (with Mark
Sullivan) • *Private: #1 Suspect* (with Maxine
Paetro) • *Private* (with Maxine Paetro)

NYPD RED NOVELS

NYPD Red 4 (with Marshall Karp) • *NYPD
Red 3* (with Marshall Karp) • *NYPD Red 2*
(with Marshall Karp) • *NYPD Red* (with
Marshall Karp)

SUMMER NOVELS

Second Honeymoon (with Howard Roughan) • *Now
You See Her* (with Michael Ledwidge) • *Swimsuit*
(with Maxine Paetro) • *Sail* (with Howard
Roughan) • *Beach Road* (with Peter de
Jonge) • *Lifeguard* (with Andrew
Gross) • *Honeymoon* (with Howard
Roughan) • *The Beach House*
(with Peter de Jonge)

STAND-ALONE BOOKS

Dr. Death (with Howard Roughan) • *Penguins of America* (with Jack Patterson with Florence Yue) • *Two from the Heart* (with Frank Constantini, Emily Raymond, Brian Sitts) • *The Black Book* (with David Ellis) • *Humans, Bow Down* (with Emily Raymond) • *Never Never* (with Candice Fox) • *Woman of God* (with Maxine Paetro) • *Filthy Rich* (with John Connolly and Timothy Malloy) • *The Murder House* (with David Ellis) • *Truth or Die* (with Howard Roughan) • *Miracle at Augusta* (with Peter de Jonge) • *Invisible* (with David Ellis) • *First Love* (with Emily Raymond) • *Mistress* (with David Ellis) • *Zoo* (with Michael Ledwidge) • *Guilty Wives* (with David Ellis) • *The Christmas Wedding* (with Richard DiLallo) • *Kill Me If You Can* (with Marshall Karp) • *Toys* (with Neil McMahon) • *Don't Blink* (with Howard Roughan) • *The Postcard Killers* (with Liza Marklund) • *The Murder of King Tut* (with Martin Dugard) • *Against Medical Advice* (with Hal Friedman) • *Sundays at Tiffany's* (with Gabrielle Charbonnet) • *You've Been Warned* (with Howard Roughan) • *The Quickie* (with Michael Ledwidge) • *Judge & Jury* (with Andrew Gross) • *Sam's Letters to Jennifer* • *The Lake House* • *The Jester* (with Andrew Gross) • *Suzanne's Diary for Nicholas* • *Cradle and All* • *When the Wind Blows* • *Miracle on the 17th Green* (with Peter de Jonge) • *Hide & Seek* • *The Midnight Club* • *Black Friday* (originally published as *Black Market*) • *See How They Run* • *Season of the Machete* • *The Thomas Berryman Number*

BOOK**SHOTS**

James Patterson's
BOOK**SH✷TS**
Flames

Horowitz • *Bedding the Highlander* by Sabrina
York • *The Wedding Florist* by T. J. Kline • *A
Wedding in Maine* by Jen McLaughlin • *Radiant*
by Elizabeth Hayley • *Hot Winter Nights* by Codi
Gray • *Bodyguard* by Jessica Linden • *Dazzling* by
Elizabeth Hayley • *The Mating Season* by
Laurie Horowitz • *Sacking the Quarterback* by
Samantha Towle • *Learning to Ride* by Erin
Knightley • *The McCullagh Inn in Maine*
by Jen McLaughlin

For Readers of All Ages

MAXIMUM RIDE

Maximum Ride Forever • *Nevermore: The Final
Maximum Ride Adventure* • *Angel: A Maximum Ride
Novel* • *Fang: A Maximum Ride Novel* • *Max: A
Maximum Ride Novel* • *The Final Warning:
A Maximum Ride Novel* • *Saving the World and
Other Extreme Sports: A Maximum Ride
Novel* • *School's Out—Forever: A Maximum
Ride Novel* • *The Angel Experiment:
A Maximum Ride Novel*

DANIEL X

Daniel X: Lights Out (with Chris
Grabenstein) • *Daniel X: Armageddon* (with Chris
Grabenstein) • *Daniel X: Game Over* (with
Ned Rust) • *Daniel X: Demons and Druids*
(with Adam Sadler) • *Daniel X: Watch the Skies*
(with Ned Rust) • *The Dangerous Days of
Daniel X* (with Michael Ledwidge)

WITCH & WIZARD

Witch & Wizard: The Lost (with Emily Raymond) • *Witch & Wizard: The Kiss* (with Jill Dembowski) • *Witch & Wizard: The Fire* (with Jill Dembowski) • *Witch & Wizard: The Gift* (with Ned Rust) • *Witch & Wizard* (with Gabrielle Charbonnet)

CONFESSIONS

Confessions: The Murder of an Angel (with Maxine Paetro) • *Confessions: The Paris Mysteries* (with Maxine Paetro) • *Confessions: The Private School Murders* (with Maxine Paetro) • *Confessions of a Murder Suspect* (with Maxine Paetro)

MIDDLE SCHOOL

Middle School: Escape to Australia (with Martin Chatterton, illustrated by Daniel Griffo) • *Middle School: Dog's Best Friend* (with Chris Tebbetts, illustrated by Jomike Tejido) • *Middle School: Just My Rotten Luck* (with Chris Tebbetts, illustrated by Laura Park) • *Middle School: Save Rafe!* (with Chris Tebbetts, illustrated by Laura Park) • *Middle School: Ultimate Showdown* (with Julia Bergen, illustrated by Alec Longstreth) • *Middle School: How I Survived Bullies, Broccoli, and Snake Hill* (with Chris Tebbetts, illustrated by Laura Park) • *Middle School: My Brother Is a Big, Fat Liar* (with Lisa Papademetriou, illustrated by Neil Swaab) • *Middle School: Get Me Out of Here!* (with Chris Tebbetts, illustrated by Laura Park) • *Middle School, The Worst Years of My Life* (with Chris Tebbetts, illustrated by Laura Park)

Cory Thomas) • *House of Robots* (with Chris Grabenstein, illustrated by Juliana Neufeld) • *Homeroom Diaries* (with Lisa Papademetriou, illustrated by Keino) • *Med Head* (with Hal Friedman) • *santaKid* (illustrated by Michael Garland)

For previews and information about the author, visit JamesPatterson.com or find him on Facebook or at your app store.

About the Authors

JAMES PATTERSON received the Literarian Award for Outstanding Service to the American Literary Community at the 2015 National Book Awards. He holds the Guinness World Record for the most #1 *New York Times* bestsellers, and his books have sold more than 325 million copies worldwide. He has donated more than one million books to students and soldiers and funds over four hundred Teacher Education Scholarships at twenty-four colleges and universities. He has also donated millions to independent bookstores and school libraries.

KATHRYN FOX is a medical practitioner with a special interest in forensic medicine. She is the author of seven internationally bestselling novels, most recently *Death Mask, Cold Grave*, and *Fatal Impact*. Her debut, *Malicious Intent*, won the 2005 Davitt award for adult fiction. She has twice been shortlisted for the prestigious Ned Kelly award. Her books have also been selected in the "50 Books You Can't Put Down" Australian reading initiative and are published in over a dozen languages. Kathryn lives in Sydney and combines her passion for books and medicine by actively promoting the links between literacy and health, particularly in disadvantaged communities.

JAMES
PATTERSON
RECOMMENDS

INTRODUCING THE MOST SUCCESSFUL
AND SEXIEST PRIVATE INVESTIGATION
FIRM IN THE WORLD

#1 *NEW YORK TIMES* BESTSELLER

JAMES PATTERSON

PRIVATE

NEW YORK · LOS ANGELES · LONDON · PARIS

& MAXINE PAETRO

PRIVATE

I've always been a curious person. It's one of the many reasons why I'm a writer. Something I always asked myself was: "What happens if a 'one percenter' gets into trouble?" The answer: Jack Morgan and PRIVATE. On Jack Morgan's agenda in his debut outing is investigating a multimillion-dollar NFL gambling scandal and solving a series of schoolgirl slayings. Then, the unthinkable—his former lover turned best friend's wife is murdered. One thing you should know about Jack is that beneath his Lamborghini-driving, red-carpet-event-attending surface, he's a very smart guy. And he takes no prisoners. Just wait till you get to the end of PRIVATE. You'll see what I mean.

JACK MORGAN
IS WANTED
FOR MURDER

THE WORLD'S #1 BESTSELLING WRITER

JAMES PATTERSON

PRIVATE

#1 Suspect

& MAXINE PAETRO

PRIVATE: # 1 SUSPECT

Over the years, I've learned that reputation is everything when it comes to business. While Private's Jack Morgan has a reputation for being effective and discreet, he's also known for being quite the lady killer. But when an ex-lover shows up dead in his bed and all evidence points to him, Jack realizes someone wants to kill more than just his good name. To make things worse, another event threatens Private's stability, and Jack suddenly finds himself with his back against the wall. Characters will do the most shocking things when they have no other options, especially characters like Jack who are used to being in control. I won't tell you what happens, but I will say it'll blow your mind.

JAMES PATTERSON

Was Hollywood's most
famous couple kidnapped?
Or murdered?

PRIVATE

L.A.

MARK SULLIVAN

PRIVATE LA

If you've ever wondered what celebrity power couples do behind closed doors, you can stop all of your conjecturing—the answers are all in PRIVATE LA. America's most popular celebrity couple has made an exit…from their lives. No one knows where they went or why, and it's up to Jack and his Private team to breach the walls of security and hordes of paparazzi to find the power couple. But when has anything good ever come from a pile of secrets buried under miles of genius PR? Jack's about to find that out, up close and personal, and he's in for the shock of his life. Because in the city of big dreams, nothing is what it seems. Especially if I'm involved.

PRIVATE BERLIN

Every now and then, I find myself wanting a big change in scenery. Don't get me wrong. Jack Morgan and the Private team are great fun, but sometimes a little taste of the foreign makes life a bit more exciting. And by "exciting," I really mean dangerous. At Private's German headquarters, Chris Schneider—superstar agent—has gone rogue. He's the keeper of quite a few pieces of sensitive information, but one in particular could have earth-shattering consequences. Hang on tight and don't blink. This one is a rollercoaster of tension that'll leave you reeling.

BOOK**SHOTS**

THERE'S A REVOLUTION IN READING—IT'S CALLED BOOKSHOTS.

BookShots are a whole new kind of book—100% story-driven, no fluff, always under $5, and written and co-written by James Patterson himself.

At 150 pages or fewer, BookShots can be read in a night, on a commute, even on your cell phone during breaks at work.

THE ODDS

Of meeting an attractive man at a casino:
1:1

Of having one impulsive night with said
attractive man: 5:1

Of falling for your brand-new lover: 10:1

Of becoming pregnant from your one-night
stand: 100:1

Of his tracking you down clear across the
country: 10,000:1

Of his turning out to be a millionaire:
500,000:1

Of his offering to marry you: 1,000,000:1

Of his actually falling in love: ?????????:1

Dear Reader,

This book was born out of serendipity. While attending a national romance writers' conference, I was having coffee with an old and dear friend, and suddenly we we were talking about gathering some other friends and writing a series together. We got together in one of the hotel rooms, brainstormed, laughed, got giddy and put a story together. In the end, that story didn't fly, but another did, conceived over the Internet, with e-mails flying back and forth.

Working on a continuity is always fun. Working with authors you already love and respect is phenomenal. We had an incredible time creating our guys, and I hope you'll give all six stories a try.

Susan

SUSAN CROSBY

BOUND BY THE BABY

Published by Silhouette Books
America's Publisher of Contemporary Romance

SILHOUETTE BOOKS
®

ISBN-13: 978-0-373-76797-7
ISBN-10:   0-373-76797-8

BOUND BY THE BABY

Recent Books by Susan Crosby

SUSAN CROSBY

believes in the value of setting goals, but also in the magic of making wishes. A long-time reader of romance novels, Susan earned a B.A. in English while raising her sons. She lives in the central valley of California, the land of wine grapes, asparagus and almonds. Her checkered past includes jobs as a synchronized swimming instructor, personnel interviewer at a toy factory and trucking company manager, but her current occupation as a writer is her all-time favorite.

Susan enjoys writing about people who take a chance on love, sometimes against all odds. She loves warm, strong heroes; good-hearted, self-reliant heroines…and happy endings.

Susan loves to hear from readers. You can visit her at her Web site, www.susancrosby.com.

For the Gilroy connection—
a great place to write a book. Thanks so much.

For Elizabeth Bevarly, Maureen Child,
Anna DePalo, Susan Mallery and Christie Ridgway—
five talented and generous women.

Prologue

January 2, Sterling Palace Hotel and Casino,
Atlantic City, New Jersey

Devlin Campbell had been taking up space at a blackjack table for two hours. By rights he should be down thousands of dollars, since his head wasn't in the game but on a letter he'd jammed into his inside coat pocket that morning. It took a lot to shake Dev up, but the one-page document typed on a California law firm's letterhead had shaken him to the core, the repercussions still resonating. It was impossible to forget the letter, so he'd settled instead on ignoring it as best he could.

He swigged his fourth Scotch and water, then glanced at the woman standing at his shoulder, observing him silently. Even before he'd gotten himself semidrunk, she'd been easy on the eyes. Her hair was long, light brown and shiny, her

body curvy and tempting, but her smile didn't reach her beautiful blue eyes. Oddly, her sadness drew him as much as the physical attraction. He didn't know her name, only that she'd brought him luck since he'd first laid eyes on her more than an hour ago.

He'd been in the hole a few hundred dollars when he'd spotted her walking toward his table. He had gone on full alert, everything about her appealing to him, calling to him. She'd stopped to talk to a passing employee, who had pointed toward someplace in the distance. She'd glanced in that direction then straight at him and seemed to freeze in place. Her eyes widened. For long, increasingly fascinating seconds, neither looked away. The dealer drew him back into the game, and he won the hand.

When he looked toward her again, she was gone, only to pass by him at that very moment, within reach.

"Wait," he said, his hand on her arm, the contact sizzling. "You're my good luck charm."

Amazingly, she waited. When she tried to walk away several times over the next hour, he implored her to stay, although more with his eyes than his words. He dubbed her Ms. Fortune, hoping to make her laugh, but the sadness in her eyes only deepened.

And yet she stayed, even as a small crowd gathered, curious, as his winning streak continued and his bets became more daring. A pit boss watched. Security people milled.

They scrutinized Dev's every move, but he wasn't cheating. Wasn't counting cards, either, although he was proficient at it. He and numbers had a remarkable affinity. However, no one could count cards at the big casinos anymore, their systems too refined for cheaters to prosper. But this time he didn't care whether he won or lost, didn't have the mental wherewithal to do anything more than play the game.

Yet all he did was win.

Dev jiggled the ice cubes in his otherwise empty glass, then set it down as the next hand was dealt. He lifted the corners—a jack and a five—the kind of hand any sensible person would've stayed on, letting the dealer's hand determine the outcome, but Dev took a hit. Odds were he would be dealt a face card, putting him well over twenty-one.

He drew a six. Twenty-one. It was that kind of night.

As conversation buzzed around him, Ms. Fortune leaned close. "I really have to go," she said. "Congratulations."

He turned his head. Their noses almost touched. "Have dinner with me."

She pulled back. "I can't," she said quietly.

She left. He would've had to stop her by force, something he was tempted to do, but instead he watched her disappear into the crowd, wondering what her story was, wishing he could get his hands on that incredible body.

The thrill of the game gone for him, he scooped up his winnings, was accompanied to the cashier and cashed out. Now what? He couldn't drive home to Philadelphia, not with four Scotch and waters in him.

He could get a room, order room service and face the contents of the letter, and the memories….

He hesitated, a rarity for him. He usually dealt with situations head-on and quickly. But this was going to require some soul searching, and he wasn't comfortable with that. *Damn you, Hunter.*

Dev found the front desk, got himself a room on the twenty-fifth floor and headed to the elevator banks. When a bell pinged he moved to stand in front of the arriving elevator. The doors opened. Ms. Fortune stood there.

More than a coincidence, he thought. *Fate.*

She didn't make a move to exit. He entered, pushed the button for his floor. The doors closed behind him.

A tight, hot ball formed inside his chest at the pain he saw in her eyes. "Who broke your heart?" he asked.

Her eyes filled instantly with tears.

"Let me fix it," he said softly.

Wordlessly he moved closer, put his arms around her and gently pulled her close. She resisted, then she pressed her face into his shoulder and slid her arms around him, squeezing tight, a small sob escaping. He brushed his lips to her temple.

All too soon the doors opened.

"Come with me," he said into her ear. "Stay with me tonight."

After a moment she nodded then stepped away.

He reached for her hand. "What's your name?" he asked, holding the door, preventing it from closing.

"Nicole."

"I'm Devlin."

Hand in hand, they walked down the hall.

One

Where was Ms. Fortune when he needed her?

Devlin Campbell studied his surroundings, his equilibrium challenged by the garish neon lights and incessant slot-machine noise. This time he couldn't win at the blackjack table, not one hand. He wasn't superstitious, wasn't blaming his losses on his former lucky charm not being at his side. He knew it was, instead, that sly culprit, jet lag.

And so instead of focusing on the cards, he found himself watching the people milling around, even though there was no reason to continually search the casino for *her*...Ms. Fortune. Nicole. After all, he'd met her on the other side of the country, ships passing in the night—or more appropriately

in this case, ports in a storm, finding comfort and refuge in each other's arms for reasons neither of them had confided. He hadn't experienced another night like it, before or since, although he'd gone back twice, hoping…

Yeah, jet lag. With the three-hour time difference in Philadelphia, he'd already put in a full day. Not to mention the fourteen-hour days he'd been working the past month in preparation for this trip.

Dev watched the dealer dispense the cards, then turn up a king for himself. Dev looked at his hand—seven and five.

He didn't know why he'd come to the casino in the first place. The refrigerator at the lodge where he was supposed to stay had been stocked by an attractive, efficient young woman named Mary, who'd met him with a key dangling off an ornate keychain. He could've heated up one of the meals from a local restaurant she'd thoughtfully provided, then gone to bed. Instead he hadn't even unpacked, hadn't taken time to tour the spectacular log house.

"Hit or stay, sir?" the dealer asked, awaiting Dev's decision.

He signaled for a hit. A queen landed on his cards. Twenty-two. *Loser.* It wasn't a word associated with the name Devlin Campbell. Ever.

Dev scooped up his few remaining chips and left the table, in need of food. He'd spotted a sports bar earlier where he could order from the bar. He would eat something quick and simple, then go back to the lodge and sleep for at least twelve hours.

The televisions were tuned to a baseball game between his beloved Phillies and the San Francisco Giants. He ordered a beer and checked out the menu, deciding on a burger and fries. He lifted the frosty glass set before him and scanned

the room. A woman walked past the entrance. A woman wearing a Sterling Palace uniform. A woman who reminded him of—

Beer sloshed over his hand as he thumped his glass onto the bar, then rushed out. He could see her maybe twenty feet ahead, moving at a quick, steady pace. The same long, shiny, light-brown hair, this time braided neatly. Killer body. Sexy legs that had wrapped around him and held tight.

"Nicole!" he called.

She turned, looked straight at him, hesitated, then picked up speed. What the hell? She was trying to get away? Why? He posed no threat. He hadn't even learned her last name. Not that it mattered, since he hadn't been on a second date or spent a second night with a woman in the past couple of years, no matter how beautiful or sexy.

Except…he'd wanted to have a second night with Nicole, who had been one passionate handful, as intense as he, assertive and demanding in a way that had made him forget everything else that night.

Even the letter.

He caught up with her, cupped her elbow. She had no choice but to stop.

"Are you in training for a marathon?" he asked. His gaze slid to her name badge: Nicole, Sacramento, California. He'd had no idea she was an employee of the Palace. She hadn't been wearing a uniform when they met, but jeans, a dark sweater and boots with heels high enough to bring her close to his height. He'd tugged them off her, then her jeans, exposing knock-out legs…

"Oh, hi," she said. "Um…"

"Devlin," he supplied, surprised. She'd *forgotten?* "January? Atlantic City?"

She tugged her jacket together, freeing herself of his grip at the same time. She was even more voluptuous than he recalled. His memory hadn't failed him. And he definitely wanted a repeat of their night in Atlantic City.

"I remember," she said, finally smiling a little but, like the first time they'd met, the smile not reaching her eyes.

"You work here," he said, looking again at her name badge.

"I'm an assistant manager for the hotel."

"Were you employed by the Palace in when we met in January?"

"Yes, for the hotel, as head reservations clerk. I wasn't on duty when we…that night. I transferred here to Tahoe…two months ago."

She gave the information reluctantly and barely made eye contact.

Both intrigued and irritated, he said, "Have dinner with me."

"I'm working." She glanced around, as if seeking someone to come to her rescue, a bit of panic in her eyes.

Surely she wasn't afraid of him, not after the night they'd shared. "When do you get off?"

She finally looked him in the eyes, perhaps concluding he wouldn't back down, although nothing in her demeanor indicated she was backing down, either. "At nine."

Less than an hour. His jet lag vanished at the anticipation. "I'll wait for you."

"Please, don't." She took a step back. "Please. I have to go."

Dev let her leave. He returned to the bar just as his food was being set on the counter.

There was something to be said for timing. Food first, then Nicole.

She wouldn't get far.

He knew where to find her.

Nicole didn't know for sure that Devlin hadn't trailed her until she slipped behind the front desk and turned around. Holding her breath, she scanned the crowd. He hadn't followed.

She slipped into an empty office and shut the door, leaning against the wall beside it, one hand pressed to her mouth, one to her stomach. Light-headed, she made her way to a chair and dropped into it.

What was *he* doing here?

What was she going to do?

Nicole stared into space until the room came into focus. After a minute she typed his name into the computer on the desk, accessing the reservations data base. No Devlin Campbell. So…he wasn't a guest. Not yet, anyway. Why was he here? Where was he staying?

For how long?

One of the front-desk clerks, Ann-Marie, came up to the window and made a face. Nicole tried to smile. The clerk opened the door and leaned in.

"Are you okay, Nic?"

I am far from okay. I am worried. And I am scared. "I'm fine, thanks."

"You look like you've seen a ghost."

Devlin Campbell was a vision, all right, but completely earthbound. Tall, dark and handsome. High-society born and old-money rich—things she'd learned about him after their night together.

"Did you need something, Ann-Marie?" Nicole saw her recoil. She moved toward the twenty-three-year-old trainee.

"I didn't mean to be so abrupt. I guess I don't really feel well, after all."

"Maybe you should just go home."

Nicole was proud that she hadn't missed even an hour of work and had no intention of starting now. Anyway, she couldn't. She was filling in for someone who'd needed to come to work an hour late. She could manage another forty-five minutes.

Under normal circumstances, she would've been gone by now, would not have run into Devlin. Once again the hands of fate had grabbed hold of her and not let go. It was too soon. She wasn't ready—

"Nic?"

She smiled at Ann-Marie. "I'll be okay until the end of the shift."

The bubbly blonde smiled back and returned to the desk. Nicole followed. It was Tuesday night. The chances of there being a rush on rooms was slim, although the possibility that Devlin might want one kept her milling around the desk, waiting.

A few minutes before nine, he approached, pointing toward a place where they could talk without being overheard. "If not dinner, then a drink?" he asked.

She shook her head, made herself smile.

"I'll be here every night until you say yes."

Every night? Just how long— "Are you here on business?"

"I'm not sure how to answer that. It's supposed to be pleasure, but it's someone else's definition of pleasure. I'll be here for a month."

A month! She gripped the counter. Everything would be different in a month. Now what? What should she tell him? And when? She needed to figure out what to say.

But not tonight. Not tonight. Tomorrow would be soon enough. Nothing would change in that time.

"Do you need a ride home?" he asked.

"I have my own car, thanks."

"I'll walk you to it." His tone was more order than offer.

She'd never responded well to orders. "I have something to do first. I'm sure we'll cross paths another time." Take a hint, Mr. Campbell. You are dismissed. She turned away, took a few steps.

"What are you afraid of, Nicole?" he asked, his voice carrying enough that Ann-Marie looked in their direction.

She stalked back to him. "Why are you pressuring me?" she whispered harshly.

"That was a helluva night we spent together."

So. He was looking for an encore. What had she expected? Love at first sight? "That was then. Good night." She walked away, taking refuge in the office again and watching the lobby through the window. Seconds later she saw him head toward the parking lot exit.

Someone waved a hand up and down in front of the window then stepped into view. She focused abruptly on the man standing on the other side of the door, grinning.

She grinned back. Who could resist? Juan Torres was the sweetest man on the face of the earth. She opened the door.

"Thanks so much for staying the extra hour," Juan said as he pinned his assistant manager badge onto his jacket. "I owe you."

"I'm sure I'll be calling in the marker." She handed him a sheet listing the problems that had arisen during her shift, then pointed to one in particular. "The guest in 1015 has changed rooms three times since he got here at six o'clock."

"What's his problem?"

"Room's too close to the elevators. View's lousy. Noisy neighbors."

"Ah. The usual. Trying to get us to comp him."

She started to answer, then saw Mr. Room 1015 approaching the desk, his stare steely, his stride determined, obviously back for round four. "Saved by the time clock," Nicole murmured with relief. "See you tomorrow, Juan."

Nicole grabbed her purse and called a good-night to the front-desk personnel, glad to be on her way home. She needed to be alone, to think. To come up with the right words to say to Devlin Campbell.

"Wait," Ann-Marie said, hurrying to catch up, then matching her stride. "I want to make sure you get to your car okay."

Nicole couldn't help but smile. Ann-Marie was five years younger, yet she was mothering Nicole. "I'm fine." She set a hand on her belly, emphasizing her point. "*We're* fine."

"Humor me. I'm headed your way, anyway."

A few seconds later they reached the exit door to the parking lot. Devlin stepped in front of her, startling her, blocking the exit. His green eyes cold and hard, he stared into hers, then dropped his gaze to her belly.

"Um, you…go ahead," she said to Ann-Marie, who looked back and forth between Nicole and Devlin.

"Are you sure? I mean—"

"It's fine. I'll see you tomorrow." Nicole motioned Ann-Marie toward the door, then waited for Devlin to speak, aiming for calm, but failing. Fate. She couldn't seem to escape this man.

He moved closer. "Is it mine?"

Two

Dev waited for her response, then waited some more. If her answer was yes, it should've come instantly. He took a longer look at her, surprised that he hadn't noticed right away. But a minute ago when she'd curved her hand over a bump that hadn't been there when they'd made love in January, he'd calculated the time gap. Four months. His older sister was five months pregnant, her condition a little more visible. Still, every pregnancy was different—and every woman—or so Dev'd heard his sister say.

Maybe it wasn't his. Maybe his assumption was wrong. Had she turned down his invitation for dinner or a drink because she carried another man's baby? Had she cheated on that man in January? She'd never told him her last name. Maybe because—

"Were you spying on me?" she asked, shock, or maybe anger, coating her words.

"I was looking out for you. Making sure you made it to your car safely."

"I get myself safely to my car five nights a week."

"You're avoiding the question."

She crossed her arms. "Of course it's yours."

Of course? The casino sights and sounds faded as the shock of her acknowledgment ripped through him. Could he believe her?

"You took a long time to answer. Too long," he said, mimicking her posture.

"Not because I was lying."

"It's not looking like that to me, Nicole."

She finally softened a bit, losing a little of her defensive posture. "I didn't want to tell you here, among all these people and the noise."

"You should have told me months ago."

"I know. Devlin, please. This is where I work. Several coworkers have already walked by and stared."

"Fine. Let's go." He cupped her elbow, propelling her forward, but she broke away.

"I'm not going anywhere with you."

No surprise there. "We apparently have a lot to talk about."

"I agree. But not tonight. I'll meet you tomorrow."

He didn't want to give her time to fine-tune her story. He wanted the raw, uncut version. Otherwise, how could be believe her? "Why didn't you tell me? You had access to the guest data. I'm sure you found out my name and address."

"I'll give you all the details…tomorrow."

Short of kidnapping her, he couldn't make her come with him. Security would be all over him. "You won't skip town?"

"I promise."

"Like that's supposed to mean something?"

"You know where I work. How can I avoid you?"

"What's your last name?"

"Price."

Ah, the irony. There was going to be a Price to pay for falling into bed with a stranger, and then, like an idiot, not using protection. He pulled out a business card and pen, wrote down the address and phone number of the lodge, then passed it to her. "Here's where I'm staying. Do you need directions?"

She shook her head. "Every local knows about that lodge. Is it yours?"

"No. What time should I expect you?"

"I have to be at work at noon, so how about eleven o'clock?"

"Ten-thirty."

"All right. I'll see you then."

He opened the door for her, then followed her out.

"I don't need an escort." The words came through gritted teeth.

"Tough."

She stayed silent until they reached her car, a Subaru that looked to be a few years old.

"Four-wheel drive?" he asked.

"Of course. I live in snow country." She unlocked the door and climbed in.

He waited until she started the engine, then he signaled for her to roll down her window. Her expression reflected her annoyance at being delayed even longer. "Are you seeing someone?" he asked.

Her brows rose. "You mean, dating?"

He nodded.

"No."

"*Were* you seeing someone?"

"In January?"

Was she being deliberately obtuse? Probably. She probably wanted to irritate him. She'd succeeded. If he was the father of her child, and she'd known his name and where he lived, and then had decided not to tell him about the pregnancy, he had reason to be irritated. And furious. He could see no justification for her keeping it a secret from him.

He didn't answer her question about the month but gave her a look he figured she could interpret.

"I was not dating anyone then," she said, looking straight out the windshield, a white-knuckled grip on the steering wheel. "And no one since, either."

Again, no eye contact. He didn't trust someone who wouldn't look him in the eyes. In the banking business you learned to trust your instincts about people. Body language spoke loudly. He didn't like what hers was saying.

He took a step back. "See you tomorrow."

She didn't even roll up her window against the chill but backed out of the parking space and sped off.

He watched her go. He'd come to Lake Tahoe as part of a deal he'd made ten years ago. He'd come with a plan to change his life, giving himself the month to work it out, since he was stuck here, anyway.

Now his life was being changed for him.

It wasn't a good start.

At midnight Nicole wrapped herself in a quilt and stepped onto her porch. She glanced at the thermometer tacked to the porch post—thirty-eight degrees. The roads would probably be icy by morning.

Her breath puffed white in front of her, but the fresh air felt good. Since she'd moved to the area two months ago, she'd

come to crave the crisp coldness of Lake Tahoe the way some people yearned for the heat of her hometown, Sacramento. She wouldn't miss the hundred-degree summers a bit, nor the humidity of Atlantic City, which she'd called home for ten years.

Nicole sat on her porch swing and eased it back and forth, the chains groaning quietly against the overhead hooks, the motion calming.

It wasn't as if she hadn't known this day would come. She'd planned to tell Devlin—just probably not until the baby was born and DNA testing could be done, because she knew he would require that.

She couldn't blame him for not trusting her. They'd been strangers, without reasons to trust each other. All he knew of her was that she'd fallen into bed with him without knowing him, without any prelude at all. The sex had been like nothing she'd thought herself capable of—anonymous, all-consuming and with little tenderness—exactly what she'd needed that night. And even without the reminder growing inside her, she would've remembered everything about those hours with Devlin. She'd cried in his arms more than once. He'd never asked her why but had simply held her, then made love to her—*with* her—again. And again. And again.

In the morning, she hadn't sneaked out, but woke him up to tell him thank you, kissing him goodbye. That was supposed to be the end of it. No regrets.

Surprise!

Nicole closed her eyes, keeping the swing moving, remembering the exact moment two months after that incredible night when she'd realized that it wasn't lingering grief making her feel so miserable, but pregnancy. Now in her second trimester, the morning sickness gone, she felt healthy and strong and capable of dealing with Devlin.

She shivered, but whether from the cold or the anticipation of contending with Devlin, she wasn't sure. She needed sleep, would try again and hope for better results than the past hour of tossing and turning.

As she stood she saw headlights coming up the road. The vehicle slowed at her driveway, stopped for a few seconds, then turned in and eased up the twenty feet to her house. Not recognizing the big black SUV, she sat again, grateful she'd turned off the porch light.

The car door opened and a man got out. Devlin. She held her breath. What was he doing? How had he found her? Did he plan to bang on the door and wake her from what should've been a sound sleep?

Apparently not. He just stood there looking around. After a minute he walked around the side of the house, out of sight, then reappeared shortly.

She wondered about his reaction. She loved her little cabin. It was only seven hundred square feet, but cozy and comfortable and hers—or in twenty-nine years and eleven months it would be hers. She'd always rented before.

Dead leaves and pine needles crunched under Devlin's shoes as he came close again, this time veering toward the porch. His hands tucked into his jacket pockets, he put a foot on the lowest step but went no farther.

"Looking for someone?" she asked, figuring he would spot her soon enough.

He swore, which made her smile. She liked that she'd been the one to do the startling this time.

"What are you doing out here?" he asked, coming up the remaining stairs. "It's freezing."

Vanity had her wishing she wasn't in a robe, flannel pajamas and fuzzy slippers, and free of makeup. "How'd you find me?"

"Typed your name into the White Pages on the Internet. I wasn't going to knock. I just wanted to see where you live." Without invitation he sat next to her on the swing. His breath billowed in front of him, as hers did. "You couldn't sleep, either?"

She shook her head. She was cold to the bone now, but she wasn't about to let him know that. And her entire body reacted to being so close to his. Memories invaded, warming her, arousing—

"Invite me in," he said, leaning toward her slightly.

Apparently the word *please* wasn't in his vocabulary. "We'll talk tomorrow, as scheduled," she said.

"You're not sleeping. I'm not sleeping. Why not talk now?"

"Because we're both overtired. One of us is bound to misspeak."

"I don't misspeak."

"Then you must be immortalized in some comic book with those other superhumans."

"You're shivering," he said, ignoring her remark. "It can't be good for the baby."

"I don't do anything to put this child at risk." What was she doing? Acting like an idiot just to prove a point—that she was doing fine without him and would continue? She'd already been headed into the house when he'd shown up. She was twenty-eight years old and acting like a teenager. "Want some hot chocolate?" she asked.

To his credit he didn't look smug but stood and held out a hand to her. He'd kept his in his pockets, so they were warm compared to hers. She let go as soon as she was standing, then led the way into the house.

Nicole had almost finished decorating. She had combined

yard-sale finds with consignment-shop treasures, had reuphol-
stered, painted and sewed, with only the baby's room to go.

The living room, dining nook and kitchen were visible
from the front entry. She laid her quilt over a chair, tightened
the sash on her robe and headed into the kitchen. She pulled
out a saucepan, milk and cocoa mix.

"Mind if I look around?" Devlin asked, tossing his jacket
atop her quilt.

"Go ahead." She was glad to have him wander off for a
minute. Her bedding was jumbled, but what did it matter?
She'd gone to bed, tried to sleep. He would know that. On
the other hand, the place was so small he would be back
before the milk had even gotten warm.

"Do you own or rent?" he asked, returning and leaning
against the refrigerator, watching her.

"Own."

"It's small…to raise a child."

"How much room does a child need?" she countered.

"More than this."

"I disagree."

He seemed about to argue but didn't. "It's rustic," he
offered after a moment.

She shook her head, amused. He was skirting around saying
what he really wanted to, apparently trying to keep the peace
between them for the moment. Obviously he wanted something.

"What do you expect, Devlin? It's a cabin in the woods.
Rustic fits the environment," she said, getting down two
mugs. "The roads are plowed in the winter, and I've got the
fireplace and a generator if the power goes out. It's perfect."
It's mine. She poured the hot chocolate into the mugs and
passed him one, then cupped hers in both hands, treasuring

the warmth. She was sorry she'd let him come in, was too tired to deal with him, just as she'd said.

"Did you know who I was?" he asked.

"I looked you up in the database." She watched him over the rim of her mug as she took a tentative sip, testing its heat.

"When?"

"In the morning, after I left your suite."

"Not before?"

She frowned. "Before, I was standing at the blackjack table with you. Before that I was passing through the casino on my way to my boss's office when I stopped to talk to a friend, a fellow employee. You caught my attention, and I stayed to watch for a minute. Then you wouldn't let me leave."

"You were my good luck charm."

"So you said." She gestured toward her sofa, which faced the unlit fireplace. "Are you asking if I recognized you or something? Stalked you?"

"Did you?" he asked as they sat at opposite ends.

"The answer is no, to both questions. How could I know who you are? You're not a celebrity, are you? And even if I'd recognized your name from the reservations—which I wouldn't have—you didn't get a room until after I left the table." She was working up a little righteous anger at his ego. "And how could I accidentally run into you in the elevator? There were twelve banks of elevators. What were the chances the one I was in would stop on the right floor at the right time to run into you again?"

"I—"

"I understand you don't want to believe this baby is yours," she said, "but you seem to be an intelligent man, a

logical one. Nothing was preconceived," she added, trying to lighten the mood.

He didn't smile even a little bit at her joke, hadn't smiled once since he'd asked if it was his. "It wouldn't be the first time a woman falsely claimed a child's paternity."

Nicole's attempt at patience evaporated. "DNA testing has taken care of that problem. It makes it impossible to lie."

"So why didn't you tell me?" He set his untouched mug on the coffee table. "If you knew you could prove it, why keep it from me?"

"I did try to tell you. I even went to your house."

"When?"

"The day after I found out. The day before I was set to move here."

"I wasn't at home?"

"You pulled up to your house moments after I got there." She'd parked in front of his Society Hill town house, the beautiful building confirming her fears—that he came from wealth and status. "But you weren't alone."

The woman on his arm had worn a short, sexy black dress and very high heels. He'd slipped his coat jacket around her, then kissed her before they'd climbed the stairs arm in arm and disappeared into the house. Soon after, a light had gone on upstairs. He'd stood silhouetted in the shade-drawn window for a long moment and undone his tie, then he'd moved out of sight.

"I waited for hours," she said. "Eventually I decided it was fate that you weren't available, because as I sat there I came to the conclusion that you would think I was shaking you down for money. I figured I should wait until… Well, I thought you had a girlfriend. It sure looked like it. I decided to wait until I was settled in here."

"You've been here for two months."

She nodded. What could she say? She'd been stalling. Who wouldn't?

He leaned forward, his arms resting on his thighs, his gaze on the fireplace, even though it wasn't lit. "What do you want from me?"

She sat back. He hadn't disputed having a girlfriend. "Nothing."

"I don't believe that."

"To quote you from earlier—tough." Annoyed, she stood. She was too tired to argue with him. "You need to leave now."

He hadn't taken even one sip of his drink, but he headed to the door, grabbing his coat along the way. He hesitated, his hand on the doorknob. "Why'd you do it, Nicole?"

"Be specific."

"Go to my room with me that night. You were upset about something, enough to cry."

She closed her eyes for a moment, memories slamming into her, then made eye contact. "Yes, I was hurting, and you offered a kind of comfort. But you were upset about something that night, too."

He nodded slightly. "I'm usually scrupulous about using condoms. And I assumed you were on the Pill. I should've asked."

"I can't tolerate the Pill, and I should've said so. I don't know why I didn't, except that I was a mess that night. But you need to know that I'm not sorry." She curved her hands over the child she already loved and wanted. Not that she'd accepted her situation instantly, but it had taken a surprisingly short amount of time to do so. "I really don't expect anything from you."

Hope was another matter altogether, however. She'd felt something powerful that night, a connection she couldn't even describe. Yes, she *hoped*.

"A decent man doesn't abandon a woman pregnant with his child," he said.

"We'll come to some agreement, Devlin. But not tonight, please. I'm exhausted."

He nodded. "I'll see you at ten-thirty." He shut the door behind him.

As his car pulled away she poured his cocoa down the drain then leaned against the sink to sip hers. He was a cool one—unemotional and practical—so different from their night at the hotel, when he'd bombarded her with emotion in the form of incredible sex, intense and challenging and satisfying. Tonight she'd seen the businessman. She'd looked him up on the Internet and learned his family's business was banking, with several branches in the Philadelphia area.

Old money. Old values, too, she guessed. The privileged son of such a family wouldn't get involved with a strictly middle-class someone like her—except for a night of anonymous sex.

She wondered how he was going to explain it to his family. *If* he was going to, that is. Maybe he'd offer her a payoff to keep quiet about the child's paternity. Wasn't that the usual way of things in *his* world?

Just how much was her uncomplicated world about to change?

Three

At exactly ten-thirty the next morning, Nicole pulled into the driveway leading to the grand entrance of the lodge where Devlin was staying. She'd fallen asleep easily after he left and slept well, not waking until almost nine. She felt ready to face him.

Like everyone else in the community, she'd been dying to see inside the lodge, situated outside the small community called Hunter's Landing. The locals had been abuzz about the house—a 9,000-square-foot, multilevel, log-and-stone structure that had taken almost a year to complete. She'd climbed the path to peer inside at the end of construction, amazed by the number of fireplaces and the majestic staircases. Building permits had been issued to a nonprofit corporation in Los Angeles, the Hunter Palmer Foundation, information deemed newsworthy enough for the local paper. But beyond that, details had been stingy. Curiosity had died when the house

was completed and nothing happened, except that a man had stayed there in March, then a different one in April.

And now Devlin, who said he would also be staying there for a month.

What had he called his trip? Not business, but someone else's idea of pleasure? What could that possibly mean? It must somehow tie in with the other solo occupants who'd lived there for only a month. She wondered what the connection was.

Nicole approached the tall oak entry doors flanked by stone columns. She reached to ring the bell but the doors opened and Devlin stood framed there, looking very much like the lord of the manor in his jeans, boots and plaid shirt, the sleeves rolled up. It wasn't his clothing that labeled him, but his posture and inborn confidence.

She wanted to walk into his arms, as she had in the elevator that night. "Good morning," she said instead.

"Did you sleep okay?" he asked, stepping aside, giving her room to enter.

"Yes, fine." She faced an enormous staircase that split into two different directions at the top. "Did you?"

"No." They moved side by side up the stairs, then up another flight. "Have you eaten?" he asked when they reached the top of the staircase. "Would you like some coffee?"

"I've eaten, thanks, and I stopped drinking coffee."

"Then we'll go into the great room instead of the kitchen."

Could she ask for a tour? Maybe she should ask now, in case she never got another chance. But then she saw the view from the great room and stopped to stare. The sight of Lake Tahoe rimmed by trees never got tired, and this particular view was stunning. Boats were already cruising, specks on the lake, including the paddle-wheeler sightseeing boats that

ran year-round. She kept promising herself she would take one of the tours but hadn't gotten around to it.

"Have a seat," he said.

He'd lit a fire in the immense stone fireplace. She sat in a burgundy leather chair next to it. He didn't sit but stood, his arms crossed, staring at the fire. She waited, getting more nervous by the second. Which was the real Devlin? Was it the caring, perceptive, sexy man she'd known in Atlantic City or this stern-faced one who seemed to have a steel backbone?

"I'm sorry you didn't sleep well," she said into the long silence. She locked her fingers together in her lap. Her waistband cut into her. If she could just unbutton her skirt…. She slipped her hands under her jacket, behind her back, trying to unobtrusively unfasten—

"What's wrong?" he asked, looking at her intently.

"Nothing."

He raised his brows.

She stopped short of sighing. "My skirt is too tight. I'm trying to unbutton it. Okay? Satisfied?"

"You're cutting off your circulation, which is bad for the baby."

"Oh, for heaven's sake. I'm not endangering the baby. And I'm getting some maternity uniforms today. I seemed to expand all of a sudden."

His gaze slid down her body. She automatically folded her arms in front of her.

"I'll be right back," he said, then left the room.

She let out a long, slow breath, not realizing she hadn't been breathing normally until she did. Why was she letting him intimidate her? It wasn't like her at all. He was just a man, flesh and blood.

And what great flesh…

She'd dreamed about him for weeks after their night together, had hunted for him among the blackjack players, hoping he would return. She remembered every detail. How he'd looked naked. The feel and scent of his skin. His amazing hands. The incredible way he used his mouth—everywhere. He'd bombarded her senses, and she'd become someone she'd never known she could be. The night had been all about pleasing—and forgetting. She'd gotten the sense that it had been the same for him.

Nicole decided not to be sitting when he returned. If he was going to stand, so would she. The small, internal rebellion giving her a bit of satisfaction, she wandered closer to the floor-to-ceiling windows. Snow still frosted the mountain peaks but had melted from the ground. The lake was too cold for swimming, but from where she stood, the blue depths looked inviting.

Devlin came up beside her and passed her a piece of paper. "I need you to fill this out."

There was no heading, just a questionnaire with spaces for her answers: name, address, birth date, social security number and other personal information. Like a credit application or something.

"What's this for?" she asked.

"My lawyer wants to run a background check."

"On me?"

"Yes."

"Oh, your *lawyer* wants it." She almost laughed at the absurdity. While she had no doubt his lawyer had provided the form, Devlin wanted it. Wanted her to sign on the bottom line giving him permission to delve into her private life—which he would undoubtedly do with or without her permission. It was just tidier with her permission.

"If we're going to be married," he said, "I need to know who you are."

The words on the page blurred. She lifted her head. His jaw flexed, his eyes bored into her. She wished she knew him well enough to interpret his expression. Accusation? Anger? She wasn't sure.

"Who said *anything* about marriage?"

"No child of mine will be born out of wedlock."

"So you believe the child is yours?"

He barely hesitated. "Yes."

"Why?"

"For the same reason I slept with you that night."

"What reason was that?" she asked, intent.

"Damned if I know. Instinct." He paused. "Look, Nicole, DNA testing will prove paternity. Anyway, I'm laying the groundwork for our union so there will be no delays later."

How romantic. The thought stung. Just the kind of marriage proposal every woman hopes for. "This isn't the Dark Ages."

He smiled slightly, coolly. "Feels like it to me."

Well, she hadn't expected him to be thrilled, after all. "I expect you to fill out one of these forms, too," she said just as coolly. "For *my* lawyer."

His mouth quirked. In appreciation? Admiration? Irritation? She didn't know, couldn't tell if he was laughing or mocking.

"That's fair," he said.

"I'll bring your form back to you tomorrow. I expect yours to be ready then, too."

"I'll stop by the hotel when you get off work, and we can exchange papers."

"Mine won't be ready by then. I'll do it at home tonight, after work."

"You have a lunch break, don't you?"

"I eat on my lunch break. And put up my feet. And relax. It's good for the baby." Ha! He couldn't argue that point.

He crossed his arms. "I also want your doctor's name and number. When is your next appointment?"

"In three weeks. I was just there last week."

"Make an appointment for us to see him together this week."

"Her. My obstetrician is a she." No wonder she hadn't told him yet about the baby. Subconsciously she'd known he was sexist and paternal and accustomed to having someone jump at the snap of his fingers. Well, not *this* someone. "When things are more settled with us, I'll make that appointment."

"Then I'll go without you. I have questions."

"Which she won't answer without my permission."

"A reasonable person wouldn't have any problem sharing the information I need as the father of this child."

What was left of her patience went up in smoke. So now she was witless? She'd tried to be understanding, she really had. "I'll drop off the paperwork tomorrow on my way to work," she said, then walked past him a few feet before stopping and turning back.

"Here's a hint to getting to know me, Devlin. Try talking to me. *With* me." She went down the stairs and out of the house. It would take thirty minutes to drive to the Sterling. Time enough to calm down before starting work.

He just needed time, too. She'd been able to come to terms with the baby and all the changes it would entail. So would he.

She hoped.

Dev watched her drive off. She didn't burn rubber to get away, didn't even speed, but he knew she was angry. He didn't blame her.

While no one would accuse him of being easygoing, he wasn't usually a jerk. He'd also never been responsible for a pregnancy before. But he was now—to a woman he knew only sexually.

He shoved his fingers through his hair, clasped his hands at his nape and blew out a slow breath. Exhaustion was too mild a word for what he was feeling. He hadn't slept a minute last night.

He'd made this trip—this forced trip—with the intention of firming up a plan to redirect his career. He'd reached a point where he could afford to take some risks, was willing to risk what he'd earned. He planned to get out of the family business, where he'd been stagnating, a realization brought home to him when he received the letter in January that would send him to Lake Tahoe for the month of May.

He needed to be his own boss. He had achieved huge success for the bank, beyond what his father or grandfather had done before him. Now he wanted individual success, not just financially but personally. He'd been aiming toward it all his adult life. But how could he take that risk now, with a child to provide for?

And a wife.

That much he'd decided during the night. Nicole would marry him, period—even though his lawyer had tried to talk him into waiting until the child was born.

Maybe he was being a fool. Maybe it was old-fashioned and inflexible, but some values were ingrained too deeply to be ignored, like not wanting his child born out of wedlock.

Sometimes Dev felt constrained by the conservative label he lived with, personally and professionally. But when people entrusted you with their money, they expected someone who

might take a few risks, but only calculated ones. Losing someone else's money was a direct path to career suicide.

His expertise was in commercial real estate investments, and he had a reputation for having the Midas touch, even with his hands tied by the bank's board of directors some of the time. Another reason for him to go off on his own.

Dev climbed two flights of stairs to the loft. When he'd wandered through the house during his sleepless night, he'd come upon the well-equipped office on the top floor. He'd also discovered a corkboard on the wall onto which photographs were tacked, all reminders of a time when his life had been carefree. During college he'd been required to have good grades and establish lifelong contacts. Beyond that, his parents asked little. Until he graduated. Then everything changed.

Dev hadn't looked too closely at the photos last night, having too much on his mind to clutter it with the past. But as he glanced at them now, he realized he didn't know much about any of the men portrayed anymore. He remembered a remarkable camaraderie, but he couldn't pick out one as a best friend at the time, except Hunter. Maybe Ryan…

He turned his back on the past and put himself squarely in the present again by sending an e-mail to his lawyer asking him to fill out the form for Nicole and fax it back, then he grabbed a cup of coffee and headed onto one of the decks overlooking the lake. The direct heat of the sun turned the chilly air bearable. He sat on a lounge chair and watched the boats make their way across the expanse of water.

As exiles went, Lake Tahoe was more than palatable. He'd intended to spend some of his time setting up his career move and some exploring the region, maybe throw in a little gambling now and then.

He hadn't counted on…Nicole. In the past few months he'd wished for more information to go on to find her, but she had seemed to be a tourist, like him. A couple of times during their night together he could've sneaked a look at her wallet and learned more about her, but he'd resisted. They'd had a tacit agreement that they would share that night only, each of them easing an unspoken need.

But she had dropped into his mind since then, memories of her lush body tantalizing, her lips soft and hungry. She hadn't hesitated, hadn't just taken, but had given in ways he'd dreamed about since. A true partner, physically.

He'd wondered why she cried but figured she would tell him if she wanted to. She didn't. Nor had she yet.

What could have been so horrific that she would forget she should've insisted on using birth control? She was obviously intelligent.

He could say the same thing about himself, of course. It was stupid not to have taken care of the protection. Stupid. Which only proved how much Hunter's letter had affected him that day.

He should've just stayed home and gotten drunk instead.

Four

A couple of minutes before eight that evening, Nicole glanced across the lobby and saw Devlin leaning against a column, watching her. Although seeing him so suddenly startled her, she wasn't really surprised, having anticipated his showing up at some point.

When she clocked out she didn't try to avoid him but walked over to where he stood. "Did you get some sleep?" she asked.

"Yes. How are you feeling?"

"I'm fine. I guess you're here to walk me to my car again."

"You guessed right."

"And follow me home." She didn't know why that comforted her, but it did. She'd calmed down significantly since she'd left him earlier in the day. They were both stuck in the same pool of quicksand. It was up to them to help each other out of it.

Plus she'd decided it was kind of nice not to be figuring things out alone anymore.

"I want to pick you up and drive you to work and back from now on."

Temptation reared its hopeful little head. They could spend time together.... "There's no need," she said.

"I know. But I think you'd like it, too."

How did he see inside her like that? He'd done so from the beginning, from that moment in the elevator. "We'll talk about it later."

"How about dessert somewhere?" he asked, switching gears easily.

"I'm not hungry, thanks."

"Then keep me company while I eat."

"What's this about, Devlin?"

"Conversation. Getting to know you."

She studied his bland expression, catching the barest twinkle in his eyes. Since she was the one to suggest it, she couldn't very well turn him down—and he knew it. "Okay. But not here."

"Name the place."

"There's a coffee bar in another casino where they also serve dessert."

"We'll take my car and come back for yours later."

"Actually, we can walk. It's less than a block away."

He took her down jacket and held it for her, lifting her braid out of the way then letting it fall against her back. She felt his nearness all the way down her back as if he'd spooned with her, just like in Atlantic City during the brief time they'd slept. Back then she'd felt safe in his arms. Comforted.

It wasn't what she felt this time.

He made small talk as they walked, asking about her

day, listening to her stories. Something unusual happened most days.

"Do you gamble?" he asked.

"Nope."

"Not allowed to?"

"It's an unspoken rule. It wouldn't be good, whether we won *or* lost."

"How did you end up in Atlantic City?"

They both had their hands stuffed into their pockets against the cold. She was grateful he wasn't pushing a physical connection.

Liar. You want that more than anything.

She ignored the honest voice in her head. "My best friend from high school and I decided to take the summer after graduation to see the country. We ran out of money in Atlantic City, found jobs, then stayed. I stayed, that is. She saved enough to get herself home and off to college. I had no college plans."

"Wouldn't your parents have sent you the money to get home?" he asked.

The surprise in his voice told her a lot about him. "I was being independent."

"I see."

"Anyway, I liked the city. My job was okay, and I found an apartment to share with two other girls. After a couple of years, the Sterling hired me. They've been good to me. And good *for* me. I'd been very sheltered at home."

"Were your parents disappointed you didn't go to college?"

"I imagine so. They never said so, not directly. How about you? Where did you go?"

"Harvard."

Harvard. Of course. The divide between them cracked wider. The only thing they had in common was the child they'd created.

Don't forget sexual compatibility. The words didn't whisper but yelled in her head. Since they'd bumped into each other last night she'd been remembering even more of the details of that night in Atlantic City. But sexual compatibility wasn't enough to make a relationship work beyond the short term.

"Why did you come to Tahoe?" she asked, as he held the casino door open. She pointed in the direction of the coffee bar.

"To honor a pact I made during college."

The casino noise prevented easy conversation. They reached the coffee bar and examined the desserts in the display case. A mile-high decadent chocolate cake called her name, but she resisted, determined to keep her pregnancy weight under control. "I'd like a hot chocolate," she said to the clerk.

"Coffee and a piece of that," he said when it was his turn, pointing to the slice of heaven Nicole had been coveting.

Great. Now she was going to have to sit across from him while he indulged himself. It blackened her mood.

They sat at a table tucked in a corner. As soon as they were settled he produced two forks, giving one to her. He smiled slightly as if daring her to argue that she didn't want any.

She supposed she could manage a bite or two. After all, how bad could it be if they shared? A quarter of a piece wouldn't hurt anything.

Well, maybe half, she amended after one bite.

She glanced at Devlin. His expression was just short of smug.

"It's good," he said, toasting her with his cake-laden fork. "Reminds me of the cake we had in Atlantic City."

She'd forgotten about it. During the middle of the night he'd called room service and ordered a couple of sandwiches and a piece of chocolate cake, her absolute favorite dessert. She'd devoured most of it, making orgasmic sounds of appreciation, which he'd commented on. He'd scooped frosting onto his finger and dragged it between her breasts and down her abdomen, then licked it off....

She met his gaze—direct and bold. He remembered, too, and had no doubt ordered the cake to make her remember.

She picked up her mug. "What kind of pact did you make?"

His eyes sparkled at her change of subject. "During my freshman year I met a fellow freshman named Hunter Palmer. He was charismatic, the kind of guy who could get you to break rules and take adventure to a whole new level. He accumulated friends, of which I was one. Because of that association I also made friends with five other freshmen he'd brought into his circle."

He sipped his coffee, his eyes unfocused, as if living that time again.

"He sounds special," Nicole said.

"Yeah. I'd had good friends before, but nothing like that—a group of guys I could count on. Eventually we called ourselves the Seven Samurai. One night we'd been partying enough to have covered our dining table with empty beer bottles, and we pledged to build a lodge on the shores of Lake Tahoe ten years after graduation. Each of us promised to spend a month there, then we would all gather after the last month for a get-together, to celebrate our friendship and successes. Hunter probably chose Hunter's Landing as his idea of a joke."

"Why spend a whole month?"

"We thought that a decade later would be a good time to examine where we'd been and where we should be going. A month seemed like the right amount of time. We were twenty-two. What did we know?"

"So you're supposed to be assessing your life while you're here?"

"Pretty much."

"And you all own the lodge?"

"No. In fact I'd forgotten about it. I've had very little contact with the guys since graduation."

"There's a story there."

"Hunter died."

He said it matter-of-factly, but his grip tightened on his mug and his jaw hardened. "Suddenly?" she asked.

"He had melanoma, but it wasn't caught until it was too late. He died right before graduation."

"It devastated you."

He nodded.

"So how did the lodge come about?"

"Hunter left instructions in his will. He created a foundation to have the lodge built in time for our pact to be carried out, then at the end of the six months, the lodge will become a respite house for cancer survivors and patients, plus twenty million dollars will be disbursed to charity. The only requirement is that the six remaining Samurai each stay here a month, as we all promised."

Amazing. Twenty million dollars given away, just like that. And the lodge must have cost millions. "That's a lot of money."

"Hunter's family is in pharmaceuticals and personal-care products. You'd recognize the brands."

It felt nice having a regular conversation with him, Nicole

thought, leaning back, sated with cake and cocoa. "Why didn't you all remain friends? I would think that would bind you even further."

"I don't think we knew how to deal with it. No one expects a twenty-two-year-old to die like that. Plus we all graduated immediately after and went our separate ways, onto lives and careers. We exchanged Christmas cards for a few years, but even those stopped."

"Are you looking forward to seeing them again?"

"In some ways. It seems like taking a step back instead of forward."

"So, you don't know if they're married or have children or how their careers have gone?"

"After I got my letter from Hunter's estate lawyer in January I checked them out on the Internet. Everyone is successful."

Awareness clicked on a light of understanding in her head. "You got your letter in January?"

"Yeah."

"I'll take a wild guess and say it was the day we met."

He laid a hand on top of hers. "About that night...I think—"

"Hi!"

Intent on Devlin, Nicole hadn't noticed Ann-Marie come up to the table.

The young woman stuck out a hand toward Devlin. "I'm Ann-Marie. Nicole and I work together."

He released Nicole's hand to stand and shake Ann-Marie's. "I remember seeing you last night."

Nicole noticed he didn't introduce himself. She glanced at her watch. "Oh, look at the time. We need to get going," she said to Devlin, standing up. "See you tomorrow, Ann-Marie."

"Are you embarrassed to be seen with me?" Devlin asked as they exited the casino.

The temperature had dropped a few degrees more and the wind had picked up. Nicole tugged her collar up around her neck. "I'm not embarrassed, just…private. Ann-Marie probably assumes you're the father of my baby. Nobody knows much about me here."

"Why not?"

She tucked her chin inside her collar and wished she'd brought the woolen cap she kept in her car. Her ears were freezing. "I've lived here for only two months, and I spend most of my days off with my father. Which hasn't left me much time to develop any friendships, just work associations, and that's not easy, either, unless you work in different departments. I'm only an assistant manager, but it does mean I have to maintain a different relationship with the people who work under my supervision." She really missed her girlfriends in Atlantic City.

"Where does your father live?"

"In Sacramento. It's where I grew up." A gust of icy wind blasted her.

"Think it'll snow?" Devlin asked after a while, looking at the sky.

"I didn't hear the forecast today. I gather it's not unheard of in May."

"I checked it out on the Internet. An average of four inches. Are you a skier?"

"No. Are you?"

"Snowboarder."

Nicole found herself tensing, waiting for the other shoe to drop. He was being too nice. Too conversational. Was he lulling her into complacency before he dropped a bomb she

wasn't going to like? It made her hesitate, even as she wanted to get to know him better. He was the father of her child. They would be connected forever. But that didn't make him the boss.

"Where'd you go?" he asked as they reached her car in the Sterling parking lot.

"What do you mean?" But she knew what he meant. Everything about him set her on edge, even when he was being nice. Especially then.

"You checked out of the conversation as soon as Ann-Marie showed up."

"Did I?" She unlocked her car, anxious to get inside and fire up the heater. "I'm just cold."

Which was a stupid thing to say, since they'd been indoors when Ann-Marie had come over.

He didn't call her on her glaring error in logic, which probably meant he had more to say on the subject but knew he shouldn't keep her standing in the cold. Stuck between a rock and a hard place. She almost smiled.

"Don't leave until I pull up behind you," he said.

"I want to let the car warm up, anyway." She shut the car door, silencing the discussion.

Less than fifteen minutes later they pulled into her driveway. She parked in front of the garage. By the time she walked to her front door, he was there waiting for her.

"Safe and sound," she said. "Good night."

"Invite me in."

"We just had a really nice…" She hesitated, not knowing what to call it.

"Date. We had a date."

"Did we? Okay. Anyway, it was nice. Why ruin it?" She stuck her key in the lock.

"Do you really want to have this conversation out here?" He pointed to her thermometer. "It's thirty-three degrees."

"No, I don't want to have this conversation out here—or anywhere. I want you to go."

"Invite me in."

"Why?"

He reached in front of her and turned the key, then opened the door.

She didn't move. "Intimidation is a real turnoff for me."

"You're shivering."

Truthfully, she wanted him to come in, because she wanted to know what he'd been about to say when Ann-Marie showed up. *About that night,* he'd said. What about that night?

But she also didn't want to back down after she'd said no.

From behind her he set his hands at her waist and propelled her gently into the house. She could barely feel his hands through her thick jacket, but she remembered how his palms had felt against her skin, and the way his fingers had explored and coaxed and teased. She wondered how many other women he'd been with since then....

"I'll light a fire," he said, "while you change into something more comfortable."

She'd been about to do that. She had fleece pants and a top that were cozy but not pajamaish. Because he'd suggested it, however, she would stay dressed as she was. She took off her jacket and hung it on a hook by the front door, then reached for his to hang next to hers. "I'm comfortable, thank you. I'm wearing my new maternity skirt."

He eyed her with the barest of smiles. She was getting to know that look well, one that seemed indulgent and paternal at the same time.

Nicole bumped up her thermostat so that the rest of the house would get up to a comfortable temperature, then sat on the sofa while he got a fire going. She rarely lit one herself, because it meant a lot of ash in the house, plus having to buy wood and clean out the fireplace. Devlin's lighting of it seemed to imply he would be staying a while.

She didn't mind sitting and watching him work, however, all hunkered down, the lean lines of his body a pleasure to observe.

"Your answering machine is blinking," he said.

"I noticed. It can wait."

"Hiding something, Nicole?"

Startled, she focused on the back of his head instead of his body. "You think I'm hiding something because I don't want to listen to my messages in front of you? That's a leap, don't you think?"

"If the hurdle fits…"

Nicole couldn't decide if he was joking or serious, since he hadn't yet joked with her. She *didn't* have anything to hide, but should she prove it?

The debate went on in her head, then she finally decided it was more important that he learn to take her at her word, and for that, she needed to prove herself. For a while, anyway.

She went to the kitchen counter and punched the message button.

"Hi, Nicki. Thought you'd be home by now. Give me a call when you get in, okay? You know how I worry. Bye."

The call had come in at 8:30 p.m., a time when she was almost always home from work. "There," she said to Devlin. "Satisfied?"

"Who is he?"

None of your damn business. "Mark. An old friend."

"Boyfriend?"

"When we were teenagers. The boy next door, but just friends now. Just friends since I moved away ten years ago." She sat on the couch again and watched him baby the flame to get it going.

"How did you hook up again?"

"What does it matter? And before you ask, no, he doesn't have feelings for me, either, except as a friend."

Devlin was quiet for a few seconds. "In a pocket inside my jacket," he said finally, glancing over his shoulder, "you'll find the form you wanted me to fill out. Why don't you have a look."

She heaved herself up with a sigh and retrieved the form. Devlin Gilmore Campbell. "Gilmore?" she queried.

"Mother's maiden name."

He would be thirty-two on his next birthday, which was September twenty-third. She looked up, her breath catching a little. "The baby is due on your birthday."

"I figured it would be close." The tinder had caught. He added a few larger sticks. "Poor kid. I hope he's either early or late. It's no fun to share a birthday."

"He?"

He grinned at her—finally. She'd begun to wonder if he remembered how to smile.

"Speaking in general terms," he said. "I've learned we can find out the gender for sure when you have an ultrasound, which I gather can be sometime in the next few weeks."

"I don't want to know the gender."

"Why not?"

"I want to be surprised. Besides, ultrasounds aren't always accurate. I don't want to be prepared for one sex then have it be the other."

He got quiet again, which probably meant it was something they would discuss later. She went back to reading the form. His medical history pronounced him in good health, as was his financial condition. He owned a town house valued at two million dollars and other property totaling more. A whole lot more. She swallowed. She'd known he had to be well-off, but she hadn't expected the staggering amount. It made her very, very uncomfortable. Everything she discovered about him widened the gap between them.

"Why do you own so much property?" she asked finally.

"As a hedge against inflation. It's a quick way to build a portfolio. I have good instincts for choosing the right property."

"A quick way if you have the money," she said.

"Or are willing to take the risk."

Flames licked at the small log he added, enough that he could set the screen in front of it and join her on the couch.

"Tell your lawyer he can contact mine, if he has questions," he said.

"She."

He smiled. "Figures."

"Does it?" She smiled back, wanting to keep things as tension free as possible.

"You'll need to sign a prenup. The lawyers can hash out the details."

The other shoe had finally dropped. "I want you to be involved in your child's life, and I will accept some financial assistance, because I know it will make life easier. I like knowing that I wouldn't have to take a second job. But we both know that marriage is out of the question."

"Marriage is the only answer."

She could remind him forever that there was little stigma

attached to a child being born out of wedlock these days, but he would just counter it again with something about how things were done in *his* world.

"You have nothing to say about that?" he asked.

"I've said it already. And you've said your piece, as well. We're at a stalemate."

Silence echoed in the room, not one of those comfortable moments between people who liked being together, but a now-what? uncomfortable tension. She sensed he had a lot more to say but was holding back.

"Before Ann-Marie came up to the table," she said, "you started to say something about that night."

His hesitation created a heaviness in the room. "I don't remember what I was going to say."

She didn't believe him for a second. He'd been in the right frame of mind then to confide something, but that mood was gone. Disappointment weighed on her.

"Have you lined up a nanny yet?" he asked.

Laughter rose at the very thought. He *really* needed a reality check. While she hadn't grown up in poverty, it was nothing like how Devlin was raised, in a world where children had nannies, not babysitters or day care centers.

"Why is that funny, Nicole?"

"There's plenty of time for lining up child care," she said. "I'd like to show you where I grew up, if you're interested. I have Sundays and Mondays off and I usually go see my dad on Sundays. How would you like to come along?" It was time she told her father about the baby, anyway. And maybe her father's reaction would be tempered some by Devlin being there. She could hope, anyway.

"What about your mother?"

Nicole's throat tightened instantly. "She passed away.

Two days before Christmas." She watched him digest that information.

"So, when we met…"

"I had just returned from her funeral."

"We were quite a pair that night," he said quietly.

She nodded. She hadn't been herself at all but a shell of her normal self, hurting deeply, desperate for anything to assuage the pain. Devlin had done so.

She couldn't sit still with the memories bombarding her. She walked to a low table to check the soil of her houseplants, hoping they needed water. None of them did.

After a few seconds he joined her. "You have a green thumb."

"Not usually. Most of these are too new for me to know whether they'll live or die. I generally kill plants just by looking at them—except this one." She fingered a blooming African violet. "My mom brought it with her the first time she visited me in Atlantic City. A reminder of home. Of her. It needs repotting, and I'm scared to disturb it. She always did it for me when she came to visit."

"You're afraid it will die."

"Yes. It's fragile."

"And a reminder of her in a different way now."

She nodded.

After a long silence he said, "So, you'll fill out the form and have it ready tomorrow?"

"I said I would."

"Have you made that appointment with your doctor for me yet?"

"No."

He stared at her for a long moment, long enough that she wanted to squirm, so she moved away instead, intending to see him to the door.

Wordlessly he left the room, heading toward her bedroom. After a few seconds he walked past the doorway and into the nursery.

"What are you doing?" she asked.

"Checking that the windows are locked."

"I'm not an imbecile."

"Humor me."

"Trust me," she said.

"Can't happen overnight. I doubt you trust me yet, either."

He was wrong. She did trust him. Completely. That kind of blind faith was probably unknown to him. The word *trustworthy* was probably encoded into his DNA, it was so apparent.

When he seemed satisfied that her cabin was locked as tight as Fort Knox, he came to the front door, where she was waiting impatiently for him to leave so that she could finally let down.

He snagged his jacket and slipped into it, his eyes searching hers the whole time, then he moved close to her.

"Pregnancy becomes you," he said.

Flustered by the compliment and his nearness, she said nothing.

He brushed his fingers across her cheek. "You do have that glow that I've always heard about. And your breasts—" his gaze never left hers "—are even fuller. Do you plan to breastfeed?"

She nodded. He finally looked down, easing even closer as he did. She could barely breathe. Memories assaulted her. She jumped as he laid a hand on her abdomen, then dragged his wide palm and long fingers over and down the taut, rounded flesh.

"Have you felt him move yet?"

"Her."

He smiled. "Have you felt *the baby* move yet?"

"No."

He explored her belly with feather-light touches. "Have you been well?"

"I had some morning sickness. It's gone—" Her breath caught as his fingertips grazed low. She grabbed his wrist. "What are you doing?" She barely got the words out.

"I want to know what it feels like. What you feel like. I didn't even notice when I first saw you… Was it only last night?"

Heat and longing coursed through her at his touch. She hated that he could do that to her so easily. "Good night."

He didn't smirk. She almost wished he had, so that she could be even more ticked off. But instead he just seemed reluctant to go. His gaze landed on her answering machine, then returned to her.

"He's a friend," she said. "Honest."

She shut the door behind him and leaned against it, waiting until the car was gone before curving her hands over her belly, as he had.

She didn't want to let herself hope. Like most girls, she'd dreamed of marrying her Prince Charming and living happily ever after. And Devlin Campbell seemed to be some kind of American prince.

Which meant he and his family had power.

Nicole went still as the implications sank in. Power and money knocked out roadblocks standing in the way of goals—and she could be considered a roadblock.

She shook her head. No. There wasn't any reason to worry. He couldn't take the baby from her.

No amount of money could make that happen.

She decided to return Mark's call, since he would probably

panic if he didn't hear from her, maybe even alert her father and get him all upset for nothing.

She dialed his home number and got his answering machine. "Hi, it's me, checking in. Don't call me back, because I'm going to bed. I hope everything's going okay with you. Talk to you later."

Nicole could've called his cell phone, which he always had with him, but she really didn't want to talk to him. She needed to think about Devlin and his family and his place in the world.

And where she fit in.

Five

Dev glanced toward the passenger seat in his rented Lincoln Navigator as he drove from Tahoe to Sacramento four days later. The SUV rode so smoothly that Nicole had fallen asleep, her head bobbing gently, her hand resting on her abdomen. It was the first time he'd seen her out of uniform; she was wearing black pants and a loose, long-sleeved pink blouse. She hadn't braided her hair, and it flowed around her face and over her shoulders, shiny and tempting. He lifted a strand carefully and rubbed it with his fingers, was tempted to draw it to his nose to take in the fresh floral scent he remembered from their night in Atlantic City.

She stirred slightly, so he dropped the silky strand and glanced at the map he'd printed before they'd headed out, glad he wouldn't have to disturb her sleep to ask for directions.

They'd left Tahoe at 10:00 a.m., had been on the road for

two hours. The next exit was her father's. As Dev let the car slow on the off ramp, Nicole opened her eyes. He'd hoped to ask questions during the drive, but she'd fallen asleep not long after they got on the road. On purpose, to avoid talking to him? He didn't know. They'd spent a couple of hours together each night after she got off work, making tentative progress in getting to know each other, but he'd been frustrated by how little she revealed and how much she kept him at bay.

She hadn't allowed him physically close since the night he'd touched her belly. Any time he moved toward her, she stepped back or aside.

He should be trusting her more by now. Instead he found himself questioning everything about her.

"We're already here?" she asked, sitting up and readjusting her seat belt. "I've been sleeping all this time? I'm so sorry!"

"Why?"

"I didn't keep you company."

"It's not important."

"Turn left at the signal." She pulled a brush from her purse and ran it through her hair, then put on a little shiny lip stuff.

"Did you tell your father you were bringing me today?"

"No."

"Why not?"

"The surprise element seems to work best with him."

"Does he know you're pregnant?"

"No. Turn right at the stop sign."

Dev wondered what he was walking into. A father who would point a shotgun at him? Although that would solve Dev's problems if her father would force her to marry him. "So, we're telling him together today?" he asked.

"Yes." She pointed ahead. "There's the house. The one with the big blue pickup... Shoot."

"What's wrong?"

"That's Mark's truck."

Dev didn't pull up in front of her father's house but the next-door neighbor's, out of direct sight. A sign on the truck advertised Moore's Tire and Brake.

He turned off the ignition and angled toward Nicole. "Why would he be here?"

She shrugged, but Dev figured she knew the answer. Mark was more than a friend—or wanted to be, anyway. Maybe Nicole felt the same way, but felt stuck because of the pregnancy. Dev wouldn't know until he saw for himself.

"Are you afraid of your father, Nicole?" he asked instead.

"Just of what his reaction will be."

"Why? What do you think he will do?"

"Yell. Show his disappointment."

A parent yelling was beyond Dev's experience. His parents never even raised their voices. Civility was the norm, and also was expected of him and his two sisters. Not that the siblings hadn't argued out of range of their parents, but never in front of them. Emotion was heard of, not seen.

"Won't he support you?" Dev asked.

"After he calms down."

"If he causes you any stress, we're leaving." He opened his car door.

"Wait." She touched his arm. "I don't want to tell Dad while Mark is there."

"I couldn't agree more." He strode around the car to help her out. She'd initially protested what he considered good manners by opening her car door for her, but she'd learned to wait for him.

"Do you think Dad will notice on his own?" she asked as they walked up to the front door.

He glanced to where she rested a hand on her abdomen, then raised his gaze to her breasts. Images of those breasts had been waking him up at night. She had nipples that seemed to stay hard—like now. A memory flashed of her on top of him, leaning forward and grabbing the headboard so that he could fill his hands with her firm flesh and draw her nipples into his mouth.

"It's obvious to me, now that I know," he said, forcing himself to look away. "I doubt your father looks at you in the same way that I do. Your friend, on the other hand, could notice."

Nicole opened the door without knocking, something Dev hadn't done at his parents' house since he'd left for college.

"I'm here, Dad," she called out.

"In the kitchen, honey."

Dev looked around the tidy living room they'd entered. The decor was probably called country, the furnishings comfortable and unpretentious. Homey. He pictured Nicole playing there as a child, or in the backyard, visible through sliding glass doors, another well-tended spot. Several pots of African violets sat on a kind of plant ladder, each of them in full bloom.

A man who couldn't possibly be her father stepped into the kitchen doorway. The smile on his face faded when he spotted Dev, who sized him up in an instant. *Just friends, my ass.* The black-haired man was competition. He was a couple inches shorter than Dev and probably twenty pounds heavier, all brawn. He couldn't hide the green monster of jealousy fast enough for Dev not to see how he felt.

"Hi, Mark," Nicole said, an edge to her voice.

He stepped back, letting Nicole and Dev into the kitchen, where her father was piling deli meats onto a tray. He was tall, slight and almost bald. Nicole had inherited his bright-blue eyes.

"You're early," he said to Nicole, then shifted his gaze to Dev.

"No traffic," Dev said, deciding it wouldn't be wise to admit he'd been testing the speed limits while Nicole slept. "I'm Devlin Campbell." He extended his hand toward the man, who quickly wiped his off on a towel before shaking hands.

"Rob Price," he replied, looking curiously between Nicole and Dev. "You're a friend of Nicki's?"

You might say that. Dev discarded the flippant remark. "Yes."

"And this is my old friend, Mark Moore," Nicole said.

Mark's handshake was brief and hard.

"No hug?" Mark said to Nicole.

Dev watched the man bury his face into her hair and tighten his arms around her for longer than was usual for "just friends." Dev also saw Nicole try to free herself several seconds before the guy actually let go.

"You didn't say you were bringing someone along," Rob said to his daughter.

"It was last minute." She had the grace not to look at Dev as she lied. "I didn't know Mark was going to be here, either. What can I do to help, Dad?"

"Mark brought everything—sandwich fixings and salads."

"And chocolate cake," Mark added. "Your favorite."

How many more of her "favorite" things did Mark know? Dev wondered, annoyed that Mark had that kind of intimacy with her.

"Table's set. Let's sit down," Rob said abruptly, carrying the tray to the kitchen table, where the rest of the food was already in place.

"So, Devlin, is it?" he asked heartily. "Do you live in Tahoe?"

"Philadelphia."

"We met when I was working in Atlantic City, Dad."

"You never mentioned him. What are you doing out here?" Rob asked.

"Mixing business and pleasure." He smiled at Nicole, who gave him a nervous smile in return.

"Nicki and I went steady in high school," Mark said, out of the blue.

Dev had never dealt with a jealous man before. It would be a simple task to get a rise out of the man. All Dev had to do was touch Nicole in a way that implied intimacy. Although the fact that she'd brought him home to meet her father spoke loudly enough. "Nicole told me," Dev replied.

"Did she tell you we had our first kiss together?"

"Yes." Dev sensed Nicole's reaction to his lie, but she didn't contradict him. "I was amused by her story of puppy love."

"How are you doing, Dad?" Nicole inserted. She didn't exactly elbow Dev, but her tone said it all. She wanted the conversation between him and Mark over.

"Oh, you know. Okay."

"Are you sleeping better?"

"A little, I think. So, what do you do for a living?" he asked, shifting the conversation back to Devlin, who sensed Nicole's deep sigh even though she didn't make a sound.

"I'm in banking."

"I own my own tire-and-brake business," Mark said. "Been in business for five years."

And so the one-upmanship had begun. "I'm vice president of Campbell Bank. We've been in business for two hundred years."

The silence was like the aftermath of cannon fire.

"What could you two possibly have in common?" Mark asked, not hiding his disdain.

"A baby, for one thing."

Nicole groaned.

Her father paled. "Is that true, Nicki? You're pregnant?"

"Yes." She'd turned as bright as he was pale.

"When?"

"I'm due late September."

"Are you married?"

"Not yet," Dev replied, sliding his arm around Nicole's shoulder.

"Do you have a date set?"

"Not yet."

"Why not?" Mark asked, fury in his voice.

Dev looked at Mark. "This discussion doesn't concern you."

"This is my home," Rob said, tossing down his fork. "I decide that."

"Then we're leaving." Dev set down his napkin. "Nicole—"

"Stop it!" she shouted. "Just stop it. All of you. What a bunch of Neanderthals you are. Especially you," she threw out at Dev, then pushed back her chair and fled the room, leaving the men alone.

Nicole looked at her watch. She'd been hiding in her old bedroom for fifteen minutes. She hadn't heard any shouting or gunshots, so it was probably okay to go back out there, but she was so angry at Devlin for announcing her pregnancy like that, especially since he'd agreed they would wait until they were alone with her father.

At least Mark was gone. She'd heard his truck pull away less than a minute after she'd locked herself in her room to escape the explosion of testosterone that had made it hard to breathe, much less think.

She sat up on her bed and looked around the familiar space—the lace curtains and handmade wedding-ring quilt, the maple dresser and oval mirror. There were photos on the wall from proms and sporting events, where she'd been a cheerleader.

She wished her mother was there to give her a hug and tell her everything would be okay. Her mom would've been disappointed, too, but she would've tried to help find solutions.

All Nicole wanted was the same unequivocal love and devotion her parents had shared. She didn't want to marry someone who didn't absolutely adore her, who wouldn't willingly abide by the vows spoken in the marriage ceremony.

Well, she had to face the music sometime. She left her bedroom and walked down the hallway. Devlin and her father had moved from the kitchen to the living room. Devlin stood in front of the fireplace looking at a photo he'd taken down from the mantel. Her father sat in his recliner, his fingers gripping the arms.

"That's Sherry, my wife," her father said.

"Nicole looks very much like her."

"Peas in a pod. Opposite in personality, though."

"In what way?"

"Sherry was as quiet and gentle as they come—" Rob stopped, as if he'd started something he realized he shouldn't finish.

"Nicole isn't?"

"I'm not what?" Nicole asked, making her presence known.

Both men looked at her but said nothing. Devlin's gaze drilled her.

"I'm fine," she said, hoping it would answer all unasked questions.

He replaced the photograph, then took her hand and made her sit on the sofa.

"I imagine you have questions," Dev said to her father.

He leaned toward them. "I expect you're going to make an honest woman out of my daughter."

"Yes."

"Hold on," Nicole said. "I'm pregnant, not dishonest."

"In my day, Nicki, people who were expecting got married."

She rolled her eyes. "Your day was the sixties, Dad. In San Francisco, no less. Your generation defined free love and women's liberation and all those free-choice kinds of things."

Rob smiled for the first time, although crookedly, a little sheepish. "So, when did you say my grandchild is due?"

"The end of September."

"And what exactly is your problem with marrying the father of your child?"

Before Nicole could answer him honestly, Dev wrapped a hand around one of hers. "Nicole and I are making decisions together. We will keep you in the loop."

Rob's brows rose at being put in his place. "What about your family? Have you told them?"

"No."

"Why not?"

"Because I haven't had the chance yet. Be assured I am looking out for Nicole and the baby."

"And apparently you can support my daughter just fine."

"No dowry is necessary."

Silence settled between them.

"Did you need help with your bills or anything?" Nicole asked her father.

"I've finally got them figured out," he said. "I appreciate all you did to help, but everything's under control now."

Nicole was sorry she'd asked. He seemed embarrassed at Devlin's knowing he'd been leaning on her. The lack of conversation allowed for the sound of children playing in the street outside, and traffic noise and a siren that stopped nearby.

"Is it against the rules to ask how you met?" Rob asked. "You said it was in Atlantic City, but how? It doesn't seem like your paths would cross."

"At the casino," Nicole said.

"She was my good luck charm," Dev added.

"In what way?"

"I'd been losing at blackjack until she came along, then I wouldn't let her leave. Won a lot of money that night, too."

"You're a gambler?"

"Occasionally. Recreationally." He squeezed Nicole's hand. "You need to finish your lunch."

"I'll wrap it up and take it with me. Did you eat?"

He nodded. She guessed his appetite wasn't bothered by emotional upheaval the way hers was.

"We should be going," she said to Dev, who knew how to take a cue. He stood.

"So soon?" her father asked, although he also looked relieved. "I'll get your lunch."

Nicole tugged her hand free of Devlin's. "Please wait here for a minute." She followed her father into the kitchen.

"Are you disappointed in me, Dad?" she asked as he tucked her lunch into a paper bag.

"Only if you don't do the right thing."

"The right thing isn't necessarily marriage." She held up a hand when he started to protest. "I don't want a marriage that will end in divorce. I need to know it will last. Surely you understand that. You were married to the love of your life. You don't want anything less for me, do you?"

"Of course not. But you slept with the man. Made a baby together. You cared about him enough to do that."

Since she would never share the details of how she and Devlin had gotten together, there wasn't much she could say in answer. "Give us time to get things figured out." She hugged him. Tears sprang to her eyes at how familiar and comforting he felt. "I love you, Dad."

"Love you, too, honey."

They walked together to the living room. He held out a hand to Dev. "Take care of my baby."

"Count on it."

"You never told me what happened to your mother," Dev said to Nicole as they got on the freeway headed back to Tahoe.

"She had a stroke the day before Christmas. I caught the first flight out, but I didn't get to the hospital before— I never got to say goodbye."

"I'm sorry."

She nodded. "It was just so unexpected. She'd always been in such good health and had taken care of herself. And I hadn't talked to her for a couple of weeks. I don't know why. I'd just been…busy. I was supposed to fly home the day after Christmas and was going to stay until New Year's, so I hadn't worried about…talking to her or anything."

"Guilt is useless, Nicole."

It took her a moment to react. "I suppose you have no regrets about anything?"

"I examine where and how something went wrong, but then I put it out of my head."

"How nice for you."

"It doesn't mean I don't feel anything."

"You seem part robot."

If that was true, his father would be one proud man. Dev had been trained by the best. Particularly in banking, one had to be rational. Money and emotion didn't belong in the same sentence.

Nicole wasn't the first to allude to his inability to fill a woman's emotional needs, complicated as they were. His familial duty had been made clear, however—find an acceptable wife who could provide the next generation of Campbells. Ever since that edict had come down two years ago from his father, he'd taken to dating perfectly suitable young women, but his interest never lasted beyond the first date. Since it wasn't something he was in a hurry to do, it hadn't mattered. Nicole had been the only woman he'd wanted to see again.

And look how that turned out.

Dev merged into the middle lane. Hunter had to be laughing. Years ago, he had called Dev a rebel in conformist's clothing, had challenged him not to go directly from college to the bank but to set off on his own, saying that the confines of that business and his family would turn Dev into an old man before his time.

Dev had even been considering it. Then Hunter died, and Dev had no interest in causing a rift with his family. He'd graduated on a Thursday and reported to work on Monday.

The recent events were strikingly similar. Thanks to the letter from Hunter's estate, Dev had come to Lake Tahoe with a plan in mind for his future, one where he would take the big step away from his family—then, wham, he found out Nicole was pregnant and he would have to put her and the baby's needs ahead of his own.

He could write a book about his life: *The Dutiful Man.*

"I'm sorry," Nicole said, breaking into his thoughts. "I shouldn't have said you are part robot. I barely know you."

"Yeah. Let's change that."

"What do you mean?"

"Move into the lodge with me. Today."

"No," she answered, just as unequivocally.

"You would have your own bedroom."

"I already have my own bedroom. It's comfortable. I like it. All my stuff is there."

"How much stuff do you need? We're talking a few weeks, and you can swing by and pick up anything you need, anytime." He glanced at her. "It's my right to be involved, Nicole."

"In the pregnancy?"

"More than that. This is a lifelong connection."

She took a long while to answer. "I'll agree to stay with you," she said finally, "if you agree to one thing. That you don't pressure me about marriage. We get to know each other, period."

"Agreed." A wise man knew which battles to choose.

She settled back again. "Have you ever been married?"

"If I had gotten married, I would still be married."

"Meaning what?"

"I will marry once, and only once."

"Have you ever lived with a woman before?"

Was that tightness in her voice jealousy? He eyed her, but she looked straight out the windshield. "No, I've never lived with a woman."

"Why not?"

"My father and grandfather wouldn't have approved, for one. As a bank officer I have to uphold certain moral and ethical standards, which may seem strange in this day and time, but it's a fact of my life."

"So you're going to be in trouble because of me…and the baby?"

He smiled slightly. "It's not something that matters to me. Anyway, the most important reason is that I never met a woman I wanted to live with. If I had, I would've married her. How about you?"

"I've lived with women, lots of women." She grinned when he raised his brows at her. "No, I haven't been married or shacked up, either. These past couple of months have been the first time I've lived alone. I love my cabin and my privacy."

"I understand that. The last three years of college I rented a house with my six friends. It was great, but I was ready to be on my own."

"I'm guessing that Hunter was one of those friends?"

"The ringleader. He found the house in Cambridge, signed the lease, then took us all there. No one had a choice."

"Was there something else you wanted to do? Live in a fraternity house or something?"

"No. We just became a kind of fraternity ourselves. We initially came together as a group when Hunter convinced us to nail the Hall's rec-room furniture to the ceiling."

The way he smiled at the memory said a lot to Nicole. She'd missed out on that kind of experience, since she'd never gone to college. She'd had a series of roommates, some good, some not, but since she'd left Atlantic City, even the good friendships were fading. "Did you get in trouble?"

"Yeah, but Hunter got us get-out-of-expulsion-free cards with an oratory defending the action as an engineering experiment. You'd have to know Hunter to understand his charisma. If he'd lived, he would've been president some day. I'm sure of that."

Devlin made a quick lane change to avoid a huge pickup about to move into the same lane without enough clearance.

Devlin didn't swear, didn't exhibit any impatience at the un-observant driver. Nicole probably would've been shaking her fist.

"Do you like to cook or should we stop to eat before we get to the lodge?" he asked, deftly changing the subject.

Nicole had dated a lot, having had several steady boy-friends over the years, so she was accustomed to men not wanting to discuss anything remotely emotional. She also wanted not only to keep the peace with him but to find a way for them to learn about each other without a lot of friction. She wondered if that was going to be possible.

"I like to cook *and* I like to go out," she answered, allowing the change of subject.

He nodded. She would be glad to get home and out of the car, the intimacy of the confined space getting to her. She had closed her eyes on the trip to Sacramento to avoid talking to him, but had fallen asleep almost instantly. She'd slept so long that she wasn't tired now. What safe topics could she bring up for the rest of the trip?

"You mentioned once that you had sisters," she said.

"I do. Older sister, Joan, younger sister, Isabel. Joan's thirty-four. She's five months pregnant with her third. Izzy's twenty-four and finishing at Wharton next week."

"Finishing?"

"She'll have her MBA."

"Will she join the bank?"

"She's been politicking for that."

"Why does she have to campaign for a job in her own family's business?"

"She's female."

"Women aren't employed by your bank?"

"Not Campbell women."

"How sexist."

"Izzy's the first Campbell woman to express an interest in joining the bank. She's been talking to my mother and our grandmother, trying to get them to campaign for her."

"Do you get along with your sisters?"

"Joan and I are close. Izzy's eight years younger and very...strong willed."

She pictured him as a brother, wondered if they'd fought like most siblings. He was always so polite. Did he ever let loose? And how?

"Did you work while you were in college?"

"At the bank, during the summers. It was my internship, so that when I graduated, I went into management right away."

"You told my dad you are the vice president." Which was utterly intimidating to her. Being his wife would require social skills she didn't have.

"I've held that position for the past four years."

She thought about his beautiful town house she'd seen that one time from the street, a public symbol of his success. She never would have met him in his normal life. And now they'd not only met but had a lifelong connection ahead of them, as he'd termed it.

But she needed to be honest with herself, too, about the fact she was hopeful that the relationship could become something more than being the parents of the same child. Girlhood dreams didn't die easily. She wanted the happy-ever-after ending.

What was wrong with loving the father of your child, anyway? She knew it was probably just a fantasy that they could be a real family. Could she risk falling in love with him in hopes that he would fall for her, too? In hopes that he

would be proud enough of her to take her home to meet his family?

It was just that she kept remembering that night in January, and how emotional he'd been and yet attuned to her needs and desires, how he hadn't asked questions but had recognized she was hurting about something, too. There'd been nothing robotic about him then.

Of course *then* he hadn't been stuck with an unplanned pregnancy, either. That changed everything.

The question again was, who was the real Devlin Campbell?

She wanted to know more of the Devlin she'd met in January. The Devlin she'd met since was more difficult. More dictatorial. Less flexible.

She wanted to *know* him. That's what it came down to. There wouldn't be a better time to discover each other and make decisions about the future.

Now, how would they do that without falling into bed together? Because she was just as attracted to him now as she'd been that night. And from the looks she caught him sending her way, he felt the same.

It seemed that they'd just lit a long fuse on a powerful stick of dynamite.

Six

Nicole surveyed the kitchen, cupboard by cupboard, getting the lay of the land. Night was upon them.

"This is quite a kitchen," she said, admiring the interesting combination of contemporary stainless-steel appliances and Tuscan-look antiqued walls and decor. "I think my whole house could fit in here."

The space easily accommodated fifteen for eating, suiting the huge expanse of the lodge well.

"I put your things in the guest room," Devlin said. "I'll show you to the room so you can unpack."

"Okay, thanks."

They hadn't spoken much in the past hour or two. In the car he'd finally put in a Coldplay CD to cover the silence, and she'd sung along now and then. He'd tapped his fingers against the steering wheel. It hadn't been completely awkward, just strange and new being with him.

Now they headed upstairs. They hadn't gone halfway when she turned around, catching him lifting his gaze in a hurry.

"These stairs are wide enough for three, maybe four people, side-by-side," she said, challenging him to deny he'd been following her to stare at her rear.

"But the view from here is spectacular," he said, then climbed two stairs to meet her. "Attraction isn't an issue between us, Nicole, I think you'll agree. The only question is what we do about it."

"I'm as aware of that as you are," she said. "What would you like to do?"

"Are you sure you want an honest answer to that?"

"We can't afford less than honesty."

"Okay." He held her gaze as he moved closer, then put his hands on the banister behind her, trapping her. "I'd like to know if your ass is as firm as I remember."

Very little space separated their bodies. He held her gaze, his expression intent, his breath a whisper of warmth on her face.

Nicole didn't want to be known as a tease, but she also craved his touch. A slow roll of arousal made its way through her. Her body felt heavy and hot.

"No response?" he asked. "Honesty, Nicole."

"I guess I don't know how firm you remember it to be."

"Very."

It wasn't the word but the way he said it. She moved his hands to her rear. He took it from there, cupping her flesh with his long fingers and broad palms and squeezing.

"Yeah," he whispered. "Exactly." He inched closer, tucking her close against his abdomen.

Nicole felt him, hard and thick. She'd wondered at the accuracy of her own memories. They were true. All true.

"You don't have to stay in the guest room," he said, his mouth close enough that they were almost kissing.

She touched her tongue to her lips, nervous and excited. "It would confuse the issue," she replied.

"I think it would help settle it."

"As you said, sex is easy for us. It's the rest that's going to take time."

He pressed her into the banister and moved against her. "Remember how good it was?" he whispered, his lips grazing hers.

How could she forget the most memorable night of her life? Her best sexual experience ever? His body was perfect—lean but well muscled, with barely any chest hair, but still a line that had tapered down his abdomen, inviting fingers and tongue to follow it. He'd filled her hands, her mouth, her very core. Once they'd undressed, she hadn't felt any shyness. Nothing but appreciation and satisfaction in a long night of exploration.

She wanted that again. Now. She wanted him. Now.

"Come to my room," he urged. "Be mine again."

His words stunned her into awareness. Be his? She wasn't his. Sex *would* only confuse things, distort problems that they needed to deal with.

"We need to have our own rooms, Devlin."

He pulled back slowly, then slipped his hands in his pockets, his expression blank. "The offer will remain on the table," he said, then he started up the stairs, leaving her to follow.

Nicole realized she could make a big deal of his attitude—or not. She decided to ignore it, determined to find a connection with him beyond the baby.

She didn't rush to catch up but followed at her own pace. She saw a door open to what must be the master suite, dominated by another stone fireplace and an enormous sleigh bed.

She entered the guest room—suite, she amended, a large space with views and its own bathroom. "What, no fireplace?" she asked, smiling.

His shoulders relaxed. "Guests should be accommodated but not made so comfortable they won't leave."

"Oh, is that the way your people treat company?" She opened her suitcase and began to pull out items. He'd hung up the clothes she'd brought that were already on hangers.

He laughed, a very nice sound. "My people?"

"If the label fits." She grabbed a handful of lingerie and slipped it into a drawer as casually as possible, although she noted his interest in the stack of silk and lace.

"You dropped something," he said, then dangled a purple lace thong in front of her face.

She snatched it out of his hand and shoved it among the rest of her things.

"So, you haven't switched to granny panties yet."

"Never." She planned to be sexy at nine months. "This is another beautiful room," she commented as he sat in a chair, apparently in no hurry to leave. "I've never seen paneling like this. It's more like planks, isn't it? Are all the other bedrooms decorated like this one?"

"There are six suites, but only two are decorated, although the walls are like these, yes. I'm assuming the others will be furnished by the time it's turned over to the foundation."

She carried her toiletries into the roomy bathroom.

"Are you hungry?" he called out.

"A little. Are you?"

"Yeah." He came up to the open bathroom door. "I'll fix a tray of something for us."

"Would you mind if I peeked into the master suite?"

"Go ahead." He left.

After a moment she wandered down the hall and into his room, enormous and elegantly rustic. She went into the bathroom, which showcased a huge whirlpool tub with a fireplace in the wall beside it and a large separate shower. She still couldn't imagine having the money to build such a place.

Nicole could hear him in the kitchen. She started downstairs then changed her mind and went up a different flight instead, encountering an office space with a balcony overlooking the room below. The desk had a full-size computer that was shoved to the back and turned off, a laptop in its place in front. All the other necessary equipment was there—fax, printer, scanner. A bulletin board covered with photographs drew her. It didn't take long to determine that these were the Seven Samurai from his college days. She singled out Devlin. His hair was slightly longer, and in all the pictures he was smiling, even grinning broadly. He was ten years younger then, of course, and more carefree than now.

Now he was going to be a father—and not by choice.

"Quite a crew," he said from behind her.

She jumped. His hand came down on her shoulder, steadying her.

"Not a mediocre one in the bunch," she agreed. Indeed, they were all very good-looking men. "And twins," she said, angling closer to one photo.

"Luke and Matt Barton. Luke was here last month. He left me a note."

"What'd it say?"

"It was cryptic. I haven't figured it out yet. Requires digging into my memory."

"Who put up the photos?"

"I don't have a clue. Maybe it was part of Hunter's plan. I can't picture either Nathan—who was the first of us to

come here—or Luke having kept all those photos, much less bringing them along."

"Why?"

"I think only Hunter would've been called sentimental. Plus everyone's busy with their careers. Luke owns a wireless technology firm, and Nathan's president of the Barrister Hotel."

"Just your ordinary working men," she said, with a grin.

He tugged on a hank of hair.

"Who were you closest to, aside from Hunter?"

"Ryan, probably." He pointed to the picture of the brown-haired, brown-eyed man, as tall and handsome as the rest of the group. "We didn't have so much in common as we just… clicked. Both of us were pretty serious. Hunter changed that. Ryan's scheduled to come here next."

"For the month of June?"

"Yes. Food's ready."

"Peanut butter and jelly?"

"I did a little better than that, I think."

He'd done a lot better, having prepared a tray of antipasto items—three kinds of olives, artichoke hearts, salami, two cheeses and pepper crackers. He'd poured her some apple cider in a wineglass that matched his. The fire he'd started in the great room made the huge space seem cozy. Only one lamp was on, and that on low. Light jazz came from the many speakers. Outside, the sky was inky black, except for the infinite expanse of stars.

They sat side by side on the sofa so that they could share the plate of food. She had an urge to feed him, and smiled at the thought.

"What?" he asked.

"I'm just relaxed. It feels good."

"It wasn't an easy day for you, with your father finding out about the baby."

"I'm glad that's over." She lifted her glass, then stopped. "I really miss my mom."

Devlin eyed her steadily. "You were close?"

"She was my best friend, as well as my mother."

"I can't imagine that. A parent being a friend." He popped a large green olive in his mouth and chewed, his expression thoughtful. "I respect my parents, but I don't confide in them."

"Who do you confide in?"

He frowned, not answering right away. "I talk to my sister Joan the most about non-work-related issues. I can't say I've felt much need to confide. Not my style."

"It's been hard for me since I moved here and didn't know anyone and with my mom gone. And being pregnant." She set down her glass and faced him, folding her hands in her lap. "I need to know if you have a girlfriend."

His brows rose slightly. She tried not to squirm at his direct look. She had a right to know if some woman was going to come after her for stealing Devlin away with a surprise pregnancy.

"No."

That was it. *No.* Short, simple, definite.

"Have you ever been in love?" she asked.

"No. Have you?"

"If you can call what I felt for Mark as a teenager love."

"*Is* that what you call it?"

"At the time I would've said so."

"Yet you took off for the summer then never returned. No regrets for leaving him behind?"

She tried to remember. "We'd been next-door neighbors

since we were kids. Friends who started dating. It seemed easy and natural."

"Too easy?"

"What do you mean?"

"No passion?"

"There was passion."

"Did you sleep together?"

"That's none of your business, Devlin."

"You won't answer the question?"

"I don't see how knowing whether Mark and I slept together is important."

"He's still in your life. It affects me."

"No."

"No, you didn't sleep together?"

"No, it really doesn't affect you, too." Nicole decided he seemed a little jealous, which she found interesting. Or maybe just possessive, not quite the same thing as jealousy.

He swigged the remainder of his wine. "I'm going to assume you did."

"Assume away."

"So much for getting to know each other." He poured himself another glass of wine, then moved to look out the windows at the night sky.

"Some things are going to take time and trust." Nicole joined him, sorry he was upset, but unwilling to give him everything he wanted when she knew he wouldn't be opening up and sharing with her in return. She wanted a partner in this relationship, a balance. She would meet him halfway, if and when he decided to do that, too.

"You asked me if I had a girlfriend," he said. "I answered."

She figured he was used to having control, and this was outside his control in many ways. She had a certain sympathy

for him in that sense. "Mark isn't my boyfriend. He hasn't been for ten years. I did already tell you that I wasn't seeing anyone when we met, nor have I been since."

He angled toward her and met her gaze. "Tell me honestly how you feel about having a baby."

She didn't hesitate. "It's not about having *a* baby. It's about having *this* baby, which I consider a gift sent to fill the emptiness of my mother being gone. I'm grateful. It wasn't anything I sought, but I'm happy about it. I know you're not."

He said nothing. She didn't know how to react to his silence. Her throat burned. She was afraid she would cry.

"It's been a long day, Devlin. I'll say good-night now."

He didn't stop her. Normally she would've put the food away and washed the dishes, but she walked past them, leaving them for him, not caring.

In her room she sat on the bed and fought tears. Her dreams of marriage to a man who loved her passionately and infinitely weren't going to come true. If he resented her, or resented the baby that was changing his life, it didn't bode well for his being a good father. He didn't seem to have had much of a role model, either, which made it doubly hard.

After a while Nicole heard the music shut off. She had no idea whether he stayed up late or was an early riser, and didn't hear him climb the stairs if and when he did.

She changed into a pink-flowered cotton nightgown, which clung to her in ways it hadn't before she was pregnant. She loved the changes in her body, except that she was warm all the time, a byproduct of pregnancy, and Devlin seemed to like a warm house.

Nicole climbed into bed and turned out the bedside light. She'd left the curtains open so that she would see the sunrise in the morning.

Morning. A fresh start. A new beginning. She always looked forward to the new day. Maybe tomorrow would be a better day.

She rubbed a soft woolen blanket between her fingers as sleep eluded her. Refusing to let him take the joy out of her pregnancy, she vowed to be more patient, to understand what a shock it was to him, and to lower her expectations.

It was good to have a plan.

Dev glanced at Nicole's bedroom door as he headed to his room. While he'd enjoyed the beauty of the surrounding country, he hadn't enjoyed the vast spaciousness of the lodge itself—one person living in 9,000 square feet seemed ridiculous—yet having Nicole there made it all seem…too small. Closed in. As if there wasn't enough space at all. Everything seemed more personal now. Intimate.

Intimate.

He didn't even like the word. Sex, yes. That was easy. Intimacy? Nothing he aspired to.

Neither, apparently, did Nicole. She didn't want to answer personal questions? Okay. No big deal.

Dev peeled his shirt over his head and tossed it on the closet floor, his designated hamper. He sat on a chair and yanked off his boots, lobbing them toward the open closet door, as well. Socks. Jeans. Those he wadded up and heaved. Stripped down to his boxer-briefs, he shoved his fingers through his hair then slumped in the chair.

Why wouldn't she answer his question about Mark? She denied having feelings for him beyond friendship. And what the hell kind of thing was that, anyway? Everyone knew that men and women couldn't be friends. Did she not see that her faithful Fido, Mark, was her self-appointed sentry? Her love

slave? Hell, all she would have to do was crook a finger and he'd be kneeling in front of her, awaiting any command.

Dev had no respect for a man who gave himself up to a woman like that.

However, Mark wasn't someone to dismiss easily. He had an inside track with Nicole—longevity and first love. Dev didn't want Nicole confiding in him. No man wanted his woman confiding in another man. He knew how that game was played—be a little sympathetic and she fell right into your arms. Worked every time.

Dev shoved the quilt off the foot of the bed and slid under the covers. It was early for him to try to sleep. He'd been up late every night since he'd arrived, working on his plan to break away from the bank—his family, really. The early numbers he'd put together seemed to indicate he could pull it off—enter the world of venture capitalism through real-estate investment. His father and grandfather would be furious, especially since he'd brought more to the bank's coffers—and therefore to the Campbell family bank accounts—in the past ten years than had been made in the previous twenty. And family was loyal to family. In some ways he would become their competitor, except that they would turn down deals he would take.

There was a lot more money to be made, but not within the bank's conservative constraints. He was ready to take more risks, *had* taken more risks with his personal wealth, and was about to take even more.

He tucked his hands behind his head and stared at the ceiling. He figured he needed about five years before he would feel financially secure. He hadn't expected to marry for another few years, would've put off having children for a few more….

Had Nicole and Mark slept together?

Dev snapped off the bedside lamp, socked a fist into his pillow and laid his head in the indentation. Like he could sleep. Right.

He sat up on the side of the bed. Restless, he left the room. He would work for a while, until he was tired enough to close his eyes without visions of Nicole kissing the lumbering old boyfriend.

In the kitchen he found Nicole standing at the sink drinking a glass of water. She wore a sleeveless midthigh-length nightgown made out of T-shirt fabric that conformed to her body.

"I was…thirsty," she said, crossing her arms, her gaze slipping down his body. "All that…salty food."

"Yeah. Me, too."

He walked toward the refrigerator, aware of her watching him. He should've put on his robe, but the house was warm. Anyway, she'd seen him in less.

The only light in the room came from a small pendant lamp above the sink. "I didn't know you were up," he said after the ice cubes had landed in his glass, which he then pressed against the water lever. "Not sleepy?"

"I'm tired, but my mind doesn't want to slow down."

He nodded.

"You, too?" she asked.

"It's early for me. Thought I'd do some work. Aren't you cold?"

She shook her head. "Pregnancy stokes up the internal temperature." She gestured toward him. "What's your excuse?"

"I didn't expect your…presence. And I upped the heat intentionally so that you wouldn't get cold. I'll turn it down a little." He put the counter between them, leaning his elbows on the granite.

"I've got a couple of books on pregnancy you might like to read," she said.

He'd done some research online already, had even seen pictures of how large the baby would be at this point. Five inches long and weighing seven ounces. He'd held out his hand, trying to picture it. "I'll ask questions as we go along."

"Okay." She set her empty glass in the sink. "Good night again."

"Nicole?"

She stopped next to him, her eyes wary. "What?"

"I don't want you having any contact with Mark."

Her lips stretched thin. "Dictating to me doesn't win you any points, Devlin."

"You're carrying my child. I don't need any more points than that." He talked over her sputtering reaction, saying, "If you want to give us a chance to figure out where we're going, we'll need as few outside influences as possible."

"We don't need to make changes for each other. We need to adjust to each other's lives as they are."

She had a point. When it came down to it, the only thing Dev wanted different was Mark gone from her life. And for her to quit her job. And for her to marry him.

He decided not to bring up those other issues yet.

Nicole patted his arm and smiled sweetly as she continued on. He didn't like her having the upper hand, so he wrapped his fingers around her arm, stopping her. He hadn't kissed her on the stairs earlier—close, but no real contact. He'd been trying not to upset her, but he couldn't keep the peace at the cost of losing control. He would do what he needed to do to get what he wanted.

He cupped the back of her head and drew her close, not

letting her have a say in the matter. He'd let her earlier, on the staircase. Not now. Maybe not ever again. She was his now.

He captured her lips with his, pressed them open, slipped his tongue into her mouth. When she tried to pull back, he didn't let her. She stopped resisting. Started responding. Came at him.

Her belly was hard against him, a reminder. He gentled the kiss then, enjoyed her soft, throaty moans and the feel of her tongue tangling with his, exploring. She dragged her hands down his chest, his abdomen, and stopped at the elastic waistband. He sucked in a breath as just her fingertips slipped under the band.

His turn to moan, to attack her mouth with a new frenzy of need. He moved his hands to her breasts, full and firm. Her fingertips pressed into his flesh, but she didn't move her hands lower, just that tantalizing nearness. He remembered how wet and hot her mouth had been on him there….

Dev thumbed her nipples, circled them, brushed them back and forth. He fisted her nightgown, dragged it up—

"Stop," she said, pulling back. "We have to stop."

He slid his mouth along her jaw. "Why?"

"We just do." She moved farther back.

He lifted his head, her nightgown still crushed in his hands. It wouldn't take anything to peel it up and off her, to toss it aside, to lay his hands and mouth on her naked body. He knew he could convince her after that.

Then he looked into her eyes, bright with desire and… fear? Of him?

He released her. Without a word she left. He heard her jog up the staircase, then close her bedroom door with a ring of finality echoing through the house.

Seven

The following Sunday Nicole stood at the stove, making breakfast—eggs over easy, ham and English muffins, a simple meal. Since the previous Sunday when she'd moved in with him, they'd established a routine, avoided talking about the future and never got below the surface of each other's thoughts. Nicole wanted to share more, but she was afraid to give him ammunition—for lack of a better word—since he never opened up to her emotionally. She felt as if she was a business deal he was waiting to close.

Except he also wanted to sleep with the client.

She knew enough about business to know that was a big mistake. So she resisted as much as she could and hadn't let things get out of hand as they had that first night in the kitchen. But he'd asserted his rights as the father of the baby to touch her belly, to leave his hand there as they talked in the evening in front of the fire or watched television.

Did he know how much that simple gesture aroused her? Not just the contact, but the possessiveness of it, which she liked a lot more than she probably should. He said he was waiting for the baby to move, wanted to feel it the first time when she did, even though she'd read to him from a book that stated that she would feel movement internally before anyone could feel it externally.

"First time for everything," he'd said.

She'd learned he liked his coffee strong and black, and that he didn't talk much until he'd downed the first cup while also watching the business news on television. He took short showers and long hikes. He could work at his computer for hours straight, forgetting the time. His phone calls were all business—succinct and numbers oriented. He wrote notes on yellow legal pads and never doodled. If he made contact with anyone other than for business, she never heard it.

What an insular life he led, she decided, one dedicated to financial pursuit and gain, driven by a need she didn't understand. He shared little of his work, only that he was in the process of making a big change. How it affected *her* she didn't know.

All she knew for sure was that they had about two and a half weeks until his month was up.

Nicole dished up their meal, then called up the stairs toward his bedroom that breakfast was ready. They should get on the road soon to go to her father's house for the day. She hadn't heard from Mark, but then she hadn't given him Devlin's phone number, either, and the only time she turned her cell phone on was when she wanted to make a call. She knew she should have called him from work sometime to try to patch things up, but she'd been dragging her heels about it.

She missed having a close girlfriend now more than ever. There was no one to confide in, to help her sort out her

feelings. She was so afraid she would fall in love with Devlin and that love wouldn't be returned.

He strode into the kitchen. "Morning." He took the plates from her and set them on the table, then held out her chair for her. "How'd you sleep?"

"Good." She had a full eight hours. "How about you? What time did you go to bed?"

"Couple hours after you." He sliced into the ham. "Need a shot of whiskey before facing your father again?"

She caught the twinkle in his eyes. "I think the worst is over. What more can he say?"

"He's your father. He probably has plenty to say, now that he's had a week to think about it."

"You may be right. So. What are you working on that's keeping you up so late at night?"

"I've got six deals in the works. Takes a lot of research and analysis."

"Real-estate deals?"

"Commercial ones."

"Big deals?"

"About eighty million."

She held her fork midair. "Dollars?"

"Poker chips."

She didn't know if she was more surprised by the eighty million or the fact that he'd made a little joke. "How big a gamble are you taking?"

"Big. But I won't do all six deals. Three of them, maybe. I haven't decided which ones for sure—*if* I'm doing any of them. Some other things have to fall into place first." He got up to fill his mug. "I'm going to fly home tomorrow for my sister's graduation, so I'll meet with a few people while I'm there. Get some answers in person. I need the face time."

Nicole was stuck on the fact that he was leaving tomorrow but hadn't told her until now.

"I just decided this morning," he said, sitting down again.

She smiled. "Was I that transparent?"

He smiled back.

"What about Hunter's will? How will you get around the rule that says you have to stay put for a month?"

"I'll be gone less than twenty-four hours. I chartered a jet." He cocked his head. "Will you miss me?"

The phone rang.

"Saved by the bell," he murmured, humor in his voice as he picked up the portable from the counter and said hello. "Yes, sir. How are you?" He listened for a second. "Sure. Hold on, please."

He covered the mouthpiece as he held the phone out to Nicole. "Your father."

She sat up a little straighter. "Hi, Dad."

"Hi, honey. How're you feeling?"

"Fine. No problems. We'll be heading down to Sacramento in about fifteen minutes."

"Um, that's why I'm calling. I just got an invitation to do something I'd like to. Can we skip today?"

Was that all there was to it—another invitation? Or was he avoiding her? "Sure we can skip today. What's happening?" She noted Devlin's curiosity and shrugged at him.

"A picnic with some people I know. Next week, okay?"

"I guess—"

"Bye, honey."

At the immediate click, Nicole lowered the phone and stared at it, then finally hit the off button. "We're uninvited for the day. He's going on a picnic."

"That's unusual, I gather?"

She set the phone on the table. "Unheard of."

"So, what would you like to do instead today? Go to a movie or something?"

It seemed like such a normal, mundane thing to do—go to a movie. And their week had been filled with a kind of manufactured normalcy. It could've been an exciting time, filled with sex and revelations.

"A movie would be good," she said finally.

"That was a long, tough decision for you?"

"Well, I—"

He laid a hand over hers, stopping her words. "We're doing a lot of tiptoeing, aren't we? Trying to guess the motivations behind everything. It's just a movie and dinner."

Which was all it did turn out to be, except that he held her hand, as if they were on a real date, and at dinner was attentive in a new way, a more focused way, instead of seeming as if most of his thoughts were on crunching numbers, calculating risk and profit.

And instead of kissing her good-night at her bedroom door, he held her for a long time.

"I'll be up and out of here by four," he said, stepping back, his hands still cupping her shoulders.

"Come tell me goodbye before you go."

"I think you should just sleep."

"Either you come say goodbye or I'll get up to tell you goodbye."

"When you put it that way…"

"Good."

"How're you going to spend your day off tomorrow?"

"I'm going to my cabin to work on the nursery."

A tense silence settled, then he released her. "Why?"

"There's nothing for me to do here."

"Read a book."

"Why does it bother you?"

"The task is unnecessary."

She didn't want him to leave with an argument between them, but she also didn't want him to think everything was resolved. "Nothing's been decided."

"*Everything* was decided on January second, Nicole."

It struck her how much she wished everything was different. Wished that they'd fallen in love first, courted, got married, *then* made a baby. Establishing a relationship backward was hard, especially when trust was involved.

"I don't want to argue with you," he said.

"I can't just blindly do whatever you want me to, Devlin. How much respect for me would you have if I did? Do you want someone that easy?"

After a moment he smiled. The smile grew broader.

"Okay, okay, okay," she said, fighting a smile in return. "I was pretty easy in January. But so were you."

"Not arguing the point. Extenuating circumstances on both our parts, however. I'm assuming you don't routinely pick up men in the casino and take them to bed."

"I didn't pick you up. You picked *me* up."

"Murky point."

"Crystal-clear point, Mr. Campbell. Do you have a lot of one-night stands?"

"Yeah."

She didn't know what to say to that.

"Not women I pick up," he clarified. "I've dated a lot of women one time."

"Why?"

"Just the way things worked out."

She frowned at the vague answer.

"Mostly I've been married to my work. I knew I had a responsibility—a duty—to continue the Campbell name, but I wasn't going to worry about it for a few years, until I was successful enough to satisfy myself about the future."

"And now here I am. Someone not of your acceptable breeding."

"And pregnant, besides," he added, although not with any heat.

"Your parents aren't going to be happy." In fact, they would probably resent her. "Will you tell them while you're back there?"

"No, not until you and I have finalized our plans."

A reprieve, then. "Remember to wake me before you leave."

He nodded and slipped his hands in his pockets.

She shut her bedroom door, then waited there until she heard him walk away a few long seconds later. What was he thinking? About telling his parents he'd disappointed them? About how to introduce her to them? To his friends?

Would he thumb his nose at them? Throw caution to the wind and tell them he'd fallen madly, hopelessly in love with a strictly middle-class woman, and to hell with them all?

Well, maybe it wouldn't go that far, but every girl had a right to the dream.

Eight

Just back from Philadelphia the next night, Dev pulled into
the casino parking lot. He relaxed at the sight of Nicole's car
and parked next to it. He'd called the lodge on his way from
the airport but hadn't gotten any answer, which worried him
as it was pretty late. She'd left a message on his cell phone
that said she'd traded days with Juan Torres and was working
instead of having the day off.

Why was she working so late?

After a few hours with his family and a few more traips-
ing around properties with men and women fawningly
anxious for his investment dollars, he wanted Nicole's quiet,
steady company.

He'd almost confided in his sister Joan about Nicole and
the baby after Joan commented on how relaxed he looked.
Relaxed? That surprised him. He felt stressed almost to the
breaking point. Too much was up in the air. He was task

driven and accomplishment-minded, and there were too many incomplete items on his agenda at the moment. Anyway, the opportunity to talk to Joan slipped away when her three-year-old daughter fell and needed her attention.

In the end, he'd been grateful for the interruption. He needed to make his own decisions. He also didn't want his family to know all the circumstances of his personal life.

The casino noise bombarded him as he stepped inside the building. He'd read that fetuses could hear some outside sound. Could the clinks and clanks and other odd clamor imprint before birth? It was a far cry from Mozart, the recommended music of prenatal stimulation.

He headed across the gaming area toward the hotel's front desk, where only a drift of casino noise could be heard, which made him feel better about it all. Nicole didn't spend much time in the casino itself. After a couple more weeks she wouldn't be spending any time there at all....

"Hi! You're Nic's friend, right?"

The bouncy blonde with the hyphenated name—Ann something—blocked his path.

"Yes. Is she working late?"

"She's downstairs in the coffee shop."

"Thanks." He walked past her.

"Um. She's not alone."

He turned around and waited for her to continue.

"She's with some guy. Cute. Buff." A slight questioning inflection ended her words, as if asking if Dev knew who she was talking about.

Dev showed no outward reaction. "Okay." He didn't pick up speed, but everything inside him raced as he made his way down the escalator and to the coffee shop, where he'd met Nicole for lunch several times during the week, satisfying his

need for her to take a real break from work. He didn't like how much she was on her feet all day.

"I'm meeting someone," Dev told the hostess as he breezed by. He spotted Nicole tucked in a quiet booth with a man whose back was to Dev, his head down, as if looking at the table. There was no doubt who it was.

Nicole's hand rested on Mark's on the table. She was speaking, her expression earnest. He finally lifted his head.

Something poker-hot twisted into Dev's gut. He didn't stop until he reached the booth, then he slid in next to Nicole, startling her. He cupped the back of her head and pulled her close. "Hi, honey, I'm home," he said evenly, then he kissed her, not thoroughly enough to embarrass her but long enough to establish possession.

"You're early," she said, her cheeks pinkening.

"Surprise." He turned to Mark, extended his hand. "How are you?"

Mark couldn't politely ignore the gesture.

"Passing through town?" Dev asked, sliding his arm along the top of the booth behind Nicole. He fingered her hair.

"I came to see my friend. You got a problem with that?"

"Maybe."

"Devlin," Nicole said low. "Please."

"The man asked a question. I answered."

"Nicki doesn't seem all that happy to see you, Campbell."

Dev studied her face, which took on a deeper, allover pink hue. "She looks happy to me. Are you unhappy, Nicole?" He was counting on her to keep their public image a united one.

"I'm glad you're back," she said, not truly an answer to his question, which upped his admiration for her a notch. There were reasons why he'd dated all those other women

only once, and why he'd gone searching for Nicole again—reasons he'd just begun to understand.

He wanted to know who'd set up this meeting. Had Mark called and asked if he could come? Had *she* called and invited him, thinking Dev wouldn't be home yet? Or had Mark ambushed her? Questions with critical answers.

"Why haven't you set a wedding date?" Mark asked, challenge in his voice, as if he knew something Dev didn't. "A decent man would've married her long before now."

"Decent men don't pursue another man's woman," Dev countered easily.

The thought of Nicole confiding in the hulk annoyed Dev. He understood that women needed to talk about their issues more than men did, but she should be talking to a girlfriend, or him, not to an ex-boyfriend who so obviously still carried a torch.

Dev didn't like that Mark remained an option for her. She should've figured out by now that no other man would raise his child.

He turned to Nicole. "Shall we go?"

Her irritation was barely restrained but obvious in the way she set her tightly clasped hands on the table. "I'll catch up with you by the escalator."

Again he was surprised by—and he admired—how she didn't let him dictate to her. He nodded, ignored Mark and left the table. The escalator was out of sight of the dining room. Dev wouldn't see what transpired in the farewells. Would they hug? Kiss? Look longingly at each other? Had Nicole confided in Mark how she'd come to be pregnant because of a one-night stand? Or perhaps just hinted at the circumstances enough for Mark to jump to his own conclusions?

The fury that rose in Dev as he reached the escalator was something he'd never experienced before over a woman. The only thing comparable was how angry he'd been at the world when Hunter had died, a twenty-two-year-old young man of such huge potential. Without him the Samurai would've never come together, never found that bond they'd had, as evidenced by how easily the ties had broken after his death. Had Hunter lived, Dev was sure they all would've remained close friends. Hunter wouldn't have settled for less.

Dev hadn't known how much he missed that camaraderie until now, with his life in upheaval. He'd rarely doubted himself before, but where did self-confidence leave off and arrogance begin? The answer was in the eye of the beholder, he decided.

His father was arrogant. His grandfather, too. Dev hadn't recognized the trait in himself until Hunter had bluntly told Dev once to lighten up, that he was being an arrogant son of a bitch. And for the next few years, Dev had been different, more open to change and adventure.

Where had that Dev gone? He must have died along with Hunter.

Nicole caught up with him. She was alone. There wasn't happiness in her eyes, as he'd hoped for upon his return, but hurt and distance. In *her* mind he probably should've handled that situation differently, but he didn't regret anything. She was his.

"Don't," she said when he started to talk. "We'll discuss this at…the lodge."

Had she started to say *home?*

He stood a step below her on the escalator, his gaze trailing her back. He admitted to himself that he'd wanted her to be at home when he got there. Had wanted her to greet him with a hug and a warm welcome, like the sweet, sleepy goodbye she'd given him the morning when he left.

If he could just get her into bed again, everything would be different. All their problems would be solved.

In the parking lot she climbed into her car, started the engine and took off.

Oh, yeah. Furious.

It was going to be a long night.

Nicole saw Devlin pull into the driveway right behind her. She got out of her car and headed toward the door, key in hand, ignoring him, refusing to feel any kind of guilt, which he seemed to want to put on her. He didn't follow immediately, giving her time to start up the second flight of stairs before she heard the front door shut.

"I'm going to change," she said, not wanting him to follow.

"I'll start a fire."

"Whatever." Nicole loved that word, one nuanced by the tone of voice that accompanied it. *Whatever* could be an expression of disdain, annoyance, dismissal, even acceptance. Let him wonder.

That morning she'd gone defiantly to her cabin to work on the nursery, then hadn't even cut out the curtain fabric, going shopping instead for maternity clothes before going to work, her purchases including a couple of comfortable, casual long gowns to wear for times like this, sitting in front of the fire. She changed and went downstairs.

"Are you hungry?" she asked, stalling their conversation.

He glanced over his shoulder from where he was hunkered in front of the fire. She didn't know why he insisted on starting fires from kindling when there was also a gas line that made the process simple. Some latent Boy Scout genes in him, she guessed.

"I wouldn't mind a sandwich," he said.

She fixed him a ham-and-Swiss on rye, added a dill pickle and some chips, and poured a glass of beer. He was closing the fire screen when she placed the tray on the wood-plank coffee table in front of the sofa.

"You're not eating?" he asked.

"No."

"You look nice. Is that new?"

"Yes."

He didn't sigh audibly but she saw its equivalent in his body language. She didn't want to be annoyed with him. She had anticipated his return with more pleasure than she'd expected, then he'd ruined it all with his me-Tarzan, you-Jane routine. If he wanted information, he was going to have to ask the questions. She wouldn't offer anything voluntarily. He still didn't trust her. She got that. And she didn't like him much at the moment. That gave them an even playing field, as far as she was concerned.

"You're not going to make this easy, are you?" he asked, lifting his sandwich from the plate.

"No."

He sort of smiled, examined his ham-and-Swiss a moment, then took a bite. The crackle of the fire was the only sound in the room.

"I don't like Mark," he said.

"I got that, loud and clear. Is it Mark or any man?"

"I haven't seen you with another man, so I can't answer that question. Did you invite him up here?"

"He showed up right before the end of my shift."

"Uninvited?"

"Yes. He was worried. I hadn't called him since he found out about…us. The baby. I hadn't given him the number here."

"Why not?"

She shrugged.

"Why not, Nicole?"

"Avoidance, I guess."

"Shame?"

"Maybe a little. Although more embarrassment than shame, I think."

"At what?"

"Getting pregnant," she said in a tone she figured he should understand. It was stupid in this day and age to get pregnant accidentally.

"You're embarrassed about me."

She had to think that through for a minute, then finally said, "I don't know what to make of you. You say you won't tell my father about the baby in front of Mark, then you do. You barely know me, yet you claim public ownership. I spend a lot of time trying to figure you out."

"Me, too."

"Figuring yourself out or me?"

"Myself. I'm going to be a father. That's amazing. I'm not the man I was before because of that."

Since he'd given her that much, she decided to tell him everything that had happened with Mark. "Mark came because he was worried and a little irritated, too. He blames you for keeping me from him, which wasn't true, since I'd done that on my own."

"But would've been true if I'd known about it," he offered, surprising her with his honesty.

"I think he'd been hoping he and I might get back together."

Devlin laughed, short and unamused. "You think?"

"He offered to marry me if you didn't." Nicole hadn't

intended on telling Devlin that. Maybe she liked his jealousy some. What did that say about her?

He stared at the fire a few seconds, then said, "You told him that wouldn't be necessary, right?"

"You showed up at that precise moment."

"And when I left you alone later to say your goodbyes?"

"He didn't bring it up again. Neither did I."

"You don't seem like the type to tease a man, Nicole. Or give him false hopes. Maybe you're keeping him on a leash, just in case."

Maybe she was. She didn't like that about herself, but there it was. "I think he could see where things stand between us," she said toward the fireplace.

He turned her face to his. "There's never going to be another man in your life but me."

"Even if we don't love each other?"

His hesitation was brief but intense. "There's more to life than love. More to a partnership, too."

"Do your parents love each other?"

"I have no idea."

How sad. How very sad. "My parents adored each other. Their love was strong and solid and infinite. I want the same thing for myself. I don't want to settle for less."

"We don't always get what we want, Nicole. There are consequences for our actions that must be faced, must take priority. In this case, an innocent child."

"Which is why I'm here." Although that wasn't exactly the truth. She was also there because he intrigued her, as he had from the first night. There was so much more to him than he shared. What would it be like to open those floodgates?

"I have something for you." He pulled out a box from under the coffee table and presented it.

It wasn't wrapped like a present, didn't have a bow, yet from the look of expectation on his face he was presenting her with something special. A gift. His first gift.

She peeled off the tape, folded back the flaps. Bubble wrap surrounded the contents. Safe inside the protective wrapping was a beautiful white ceramic plant pot. Her throat and eyes stung as she looked at him. "Thank you. Thank you so much."

"I noticed you like white pots," he said, running a finger along the scalloped edge.

Was he nervous, waiting for her reaction? She hugged the pot to her chest. He'd remembered about her African violet, her special, important plant.

"I know you're nervous about repotting your violet. I'll help," he said.

"You garden?" The thought made her grin.

He smiled, too. "No. But I think I can manage that much. I talked to the garden expert at the nursery that my sister Joan uses."

"You got this in Philadelphia?" He'd carried it on the plane? Across country?

"Yeah."

"This is one of the nicest gifts anyone has ever given me. Thank you."

He looked pleased. It was a good moment between them, a simple, normal, everyday kind of moment. But she didn't know what to do next. She was tired, not having gone back to sleep after he'd left that morning. She'd heard every sound the lodge made, every creak of wood, every whistle of wind outdoors, every brush of tree branch against the log siding. She was tired, yes, but she didn't want to leave him yet.

"Let's enjoy the fire together for a little while before bed." He patted the sofa cushion next to him, once again discerning exactly what she wanted.

How could she turn down that invitation? He put his arms around her and pulled her close, so that her back nestled against his chest. His hands settled on her belly.

"Relax," he murmured. "Close your eyes."

"I might fall asleep."

"Sleep is good."

She didn't know what to do with him when he was gentle, but she gave in to the moment. It had been a very long time since she'd just been held, taken care of. Independence always had a price.

He massaged her belly with sweeping circles. After a minute he angled her differently, giving himself room to rub her back. She moved catlike against him, almost purring. His chin rested on her head. She loved the smell of him, the sturdy feel of his chest, the steady rhythm of his breathing. She matched her breaths to his, slowing hers until she felt a lack of oxygen and let her breathing return to normal. She drifted along, loving his touch, wishing it never had to end.

Her body started to object to the position, cramping a little, stirring up sensations of…not numbness, but something different and hard to describe.

She opened her eyes, pressed her hand to the spot.

"What's wrong?" he asked.

"I think I feel movement." She angled her head back. "I'm not sure."

"Where?"

She grabbed his hand and moved it where the fluttering was. "It's like little ripples," she said.

"I can't feel anything. Has it gone away?"

"No." She pressed his hand harder against the spot. "Oh. It stopped." Disappointment washed over her. She wouldn't know if it was the baby until it happened again. "I'm sorry you didn't feel it."

"Yeah. Me, too."

They lay still then. The anticipation of a repeat sensation took the tiredness from her for another ten minutes or so, then her eyes closed again.

"Want to go to bed?" he asked.

She nodded.

"Want me to carry you?"

She nodded again, then adamantly shook her head.

He laughed. "Should I just grab a pillow and blankets and let you sleep here?"

"On you?" she asked, sleepily, rubbing her cheek against his chest.

"If you like. Or you can just come to bed with me."

He moved her hand down him, until she blanketed the placket of his jeans, finding him aroused.

She curved her hand over him, remembered how his skin had felt, how hot and hard he'd gotten. She'd made him shudder. She remembered that distinctly, because she'd never made a man shudder before.

And he'd given her three orgasms in a row just with his mouth....

She sat up, intending to sit on his lap, wanting him, but before she made a move, his cell phone rang, jarring her out of her fantasy.

Wake-up call. She pulled back. He squeezed her shoulder, keeping her close as he dug the phone out of his pocket and glanced at the screen.

"My sister Izzy," he said, surprise in his voice. He flipped it

open. "How's the graduate?" He looked quickly at Nicole. "This really isn't a good time, Iz…. What? Now? Here? Hold on a sec."

He covered the mouthpiece. "My sister decided to pay me a surprise visit. She's about fifteen minutes away."

"Do you want me to leave?" *Please say no. Please say no.*

"No. You okay with her coming here?"

"It's up to you. Is she staying overnight?"

"I assume so."

"Where? There's only one guest room with furniture, and all my stuff is in there."

He stared at her a few seconds more then spoke into the phone again. "I'll leave the lights on…. You've got directions?… Yeah, the Internet is amazing. See you soon."

He snapped the phone shut, then stood. "I'll transfer your stuff into my room. You might want to change into something less comfortable."

"I can't sleep with you." She said the words with panicked conviction.

"Do you want my sister to know we don't share a room?"

She hated that he was being logical. She accepted his help to stand. "Good thing I changed the sheets this morning," she muttered, then headed toward the stairs. "Is she going to like me?"

"I don't have a clue."

"Great."

"Nicole?" He caught up with her. "It doesn't matter."

"It doesn't matter if your sister likes me? What planet do you live on?"

"We also need to look like we're…together. A couple. It's important, Nicole. If she notices that things aren't quite right with us—"

"I got it," she interrupted. And she did. He wouldn't like losing control.

After ten minutes of frenzied activity, they headed down the stairs just as the beam of car headlights swept across the great room.

Nicole straightened her shoulders. *Showtime*.

Nine

Nicole stood at the top of the stairs, just out of view of the staircase, her hands clasped, her heart pounding. She could hear the conversation between brother and sister but couldn't see them.

"What are you doing here?" Devlin asked.

"I'm meeting Ashley in San Francisco day after tomorrow for a few days. I've never seen Lake Tahoe. One plus one equals—"

"Why didn't you tell me you were coming?"

The volume of their voices rose as they climbed the stairs.

"I was going to surprise you on the plane. I figured you were on the company jet, but you didn't show, so I asked Father if I could take it. How'd you get here?"

"I'd hired my own plane. You should've talked to me about it, Iz."

"I didn't think you'd mind. I mean, you don't have a woman stashed or—"

She came to a quick halt as she spotted Nicole.

"Actually," Devlin said, humor lacing the word. "Nicole Price, this is my impulsive sister, Isabel."

Nicole had changed into one of her new maternity outfits, a deep-purple, washable-wool pants and top. She'd added a chunky necklace, hoping to draw Isabel's gaze upward, but she fixated on Nicole's slightly rounded belly right away.

"It's nice to meet you," Nicole said. Isabel had the same green eyes as Devlin, but auburn hair in a straight, shaggy, chin-length cut, stark and contemporary. She was maybe an inch taller than Nicole's five-seven, but probably thirty pounds lighter, her facial features angular but attractive. She wore pencil-leg jeans, a forest-green pullover and boots that probably cost more than Nicole made in a week. An air of sophistication surrounded her, for all that she was only twenty-four.

"You're… She's…" Isabel turned to her brother, her brows arched high. "Apparently you neglected to tell the family something important at my graduation."

"Which is the point—it was *your* graduation. But, yes, Nicole and I are having a baby in September. I'm asking you not to tell Mother and Father."

"Why didn't *you?*"

"When I'm ready I will."

Sensing a rising tension between the siblings, Nicole interrupted. "Would you like something to eat or drink, Isabel?"

"A glass of Merlot, thanks."

Devlin set her suitcase at the bottom of the next staircase. Thank goodness he didn't take it on up to the guest room and leave Nicole alone with his sister.

Nicole escaped to the kitchen. She hadn't missed the up-and-down look Isabel had given her. It was important not to alienate Devlin's sister, but Nicole had a bad feeling about

her. According to Devlin, Isabel wanted to join the bank, a first among the Campbell women—which meant she was ambitious. And that assessing once-over she'd given Nicole hadn't been a friendly one, not by a long stretch, rather one that seemed…calculating?

Nicole returned to the great room with the wine and also a tray of grapes, cheese and crackers, even though Devlin had already eaten. She wondered if Isabel ate such high-calorie foods.

Devlin moved to help Nicole with the tray. She smiled her thanks, then caught Isabel looking back and forth between them intently.

Nicole had no appetite, so she sat in a chair by the fireplace, leaving the sofa for the siblings to share the tray on the coffee table.

"Congratulations on your graduation," Nicole said. "I imagine it feels really good to be done."

"Like the prison doors just opened up."

"Are you going to take some time off?"

"That depends on Devvie."

"Devvie?" Nicole repeated, fighting a smile.

Devlin eyed his sister. "Payback for 'Izzy.' Which is actually short for Dizzy. When she was little, she would spin around and around until she got dizzy and fell." He grabbed a stem of red grapes. "Why does your time off depend on me?"

"I'm counting on you to convince Father and Grandfather to hire me. You'd think an MBA in finance from Wharton would have earned me the right for at least a trial run. I have exactly the same credentials as that Brett Allen they hired last year. I'm even more qualified than *you* were, brother dearest."

Devlin had told Nicole that he hadn't gone on for an MBA

because his job was already secure for life, so what was the need for more? And after his friend Hunter had died, more college was the last thing Devlin was interested in.

"Why would they listen to me, sister dearest?"

"Because you're the golden child, and you know it. I could be, too, if they'd give me a chance."

"You didn't apply anywhere else?"

"Why should I? I belong at Campbell Bank." She clasped her hands. "We had a bit of an argument about it."

"Ah. So *that's* why you left town in such a hurry. I'm surprised he let you use the jet."

"He wanted me gone as much as I wanted to *be* gone."

Their discussion went on until Nicole couldn't keep her eyes open any longer. She stifled a yawn. "I'm sorry to duck out on you, but I really need to get to bed." She stood, as did Devlin. "You don't mind, do you?" she asked him. "It'll give you two a chance to catch up."

"We'll have tomorrow while you're at work. I'll come with you."

"Where do you work?" Isabel asked.

"At the Sterling Palace."

"The casino?"

"I'm an assistant manager at the hotel. Really, Devlin, stay and talk with Isabel."

"It's been a very long day for me. I'm ready for bed." He slid an arm around Nicole's waist, then looked at his sister. "You're welcome to stay down here and enjoy the fire, but let me show you your room first."

"I'll go to bed, too."

Nicole moved to pick up the tray. "I'll take care of this."

"I'll come back down and do it," Devlin said. He urged her along, and Isabel followed. She'd gone quiet, and

Nicole wondered what she was thinking. She must have a ton of questions.

"Good night," Nicole said when they reached the top of the stairs, then she headed into the master suite. She shut the doors quietly and slumped against them. She would make a friend of Isabel, Nicole vowed. Devlin had thought about Nicole while he was gone. Had bought her the pot. Had said he would help her transplant her precious flower.

For his sake, for her own sake, she would find a way to be friends with his sister.

Nicole wasn't anywhere near sleep when Devlin slipped under the covers beside her fifteen minutes later. "Are you awake?" he asked.

She was being cowardly, not answering, afraid to start something she wasn't ready for, at least not with his sister there.

He went silent and still. She didn't move from her spot on the far edge of the bed, wondering if he would continue to talk to her in the dark.

The bed was enormous. Several feet of empty space stretched between them. She thought it would feel strange sleeping in the same bed, but it didn't. Of course, they'd shared a bed before, but the circumstances were so different that she couldn't compare them to this time.

At midnight she still hadn't relaxed enough to sleep and needed to go to the bathroom. She crept out of bed and returned just as quietly. While she was gone, he'd moved to the middle of the bed. Suspicious, she brooded over what to do. If he'd fallen asleep, he was the most silent, least fidgety person she'd ever known, because he hadn't made a sound, hadn't even rolled over—until she'd left.

Which led her to believe he was still awake, since she'd

done exactly the same thing. She glanced around the room, searching for an alternative, but although the overstuffed chairs looked comfortable to sit in, sleeping wouldn't be easy. Plus there was the issue of his ridiculing her....

She got in bed and rolled onto her side, facing away from him, and closed her eyes. The ripples she'd felt earlier returned, in exactly the same spot. So it *was* baby movement, she decided, happy about it, wanting to tell Devlin that it hadn't been some fluke.

"You're thinking too much," he said from behind her, sleep in his voice.

"I feel the ripples again."

"Yeah?"

She backed up until she was right next to him. He tucked his legs behind hers and wrapped an arm around her. She pressed his hand to the spot. "I think we have a night owl," she said.

"I don't feel anything."

Nicole relaxed, enjoying the feel of his body against hers. His heat soaked into her, more than she needed with her internal temperature already high, but she didn't want him to move away, either.

"Maybe the fabric gets in the way," he said, not waiting for her to agree but tugging her nightgown up high enough that he could easily touch her belly. "Do you still feel it?"

"Yes." Her voice came out a little breathless. "It just shifted more toward the middle." She moved his hand, holding hers over his and pressing down. "Feel that?"

"No." Frustration layered the word.

"It'll happen soon, I'm sure."

After a while he said, "You haven't slept."

"No. Have you?"

"With you finally where I've wanted you? No."

Her heart fluttered at his words, but she had to ignore them. "Do you think your sister will keep quiet about us? The baby?"

"Yeah."

"What makes you so sure?"

"I asked her to."

Since Nicole didn't have siblings, she didn't understand his conviction, but she hoped he was right. Nicole got the impression that Isabel would do whatever was necessary to get what she wanted—which was a job at Campbell Bank. If she could discredit Devlin somehow, maybe her loyalty would somehow be rewarded. Nicole didn't know exactly how that kind of thing worked in their world. Her only experience with their social level had come from television and movies, hardly accurate sources. But didn't art imitate life? Of course, it also exaggerated life.

Fitting into Devlin's world wouldn't be easy.

Sleep finally wouldn't wait any longer. As she drifted, she wriggled against him, getting more comfortable. His hand went lax against her belly, indicating he was fading, too.

The little ache that had throbbed between her legs settled now that his hand wasn't making the same kind of contact—until he adjusted his position a little. His hand flattened against her stomach then slid up and curved around her breast.

"Nice," he murmured.

"Big," she said, smiling.

"Yeah."

His tone of voice told her everything. He liked the changes in her body. "I've gone up two cup sizes."

"I noticed."

"I guess you're a breast man."

"And legs. Yours are exceptional."

She loved listening to him talk, his voice low and sexy.

"Every part of you is exceptional, though," he added.

"I can say the same about *you*."

"Yeah? What's your favorite?" He tucked himself closer, until she could feel he was aroused—and naked.

"That part's high on my list," she said.

He made a low, growly sound. "You feel very warm."

She was more than warm. She was on fire. "Your heat added to mine creates a furnace."

"Why don't you take off the nightgown? That'd help." At her hesitation he said, "Nothing will happen unless you want it to, Nicole."

Nothing had changed. She didn't want to be intimate with him again while they had company. He probably wouldn't understand that, but it kept her from allowing things to get out of hand.

"What are you afraid of?" he asked.

Giving in. Giving up any semblance of control over my own life. Falling in love with someone who won't love me in return. So many things....

Although sex would be nice. Very nice.

"We have a lot to work out first," she said, staying stronger than she thought she could.

"You'll let me know when we've reached that point?" he asked drily.

She grinned. "You'll be the first."

She thought she felt his lips brush against her hair, then he said good-night.

She finally let herself sleep.

Dev heard the shower come on. He opened his eyes and glanced at the clock—8:43. They'd slept in.

The shower in the master bathroom was enclosed by crystal-clear glass. He had a choice—invade her privacy or leave her alone. He'd bet anything she was trying to take the fastest shower of her life.

He tucked his hands behind his head and contemplated his situation. Things were happening one step at a time. He'd gotten her in his bed, thanks to Izzy. A natural progression would follow.

Izzy had peppered him with questions. He'd put her off. The hardest question to fend off was why they weren't married. No one in his family would understand that. He didn't know how much longer he could wait for Nicole to come around to the fact they had to get married as soon as possible. It was an issue not open to debate. He'd been more tolerant with her than with anyone in his life, but he couldn't let her dictate their relationship, not when appearances mattered so much.

He felt as if he was losing control of this relationship. He needed to rethink how he was handling it.

To hell with it. He got out of bed and walked straight into the bathroom. She was rinsing her hair in the shower, her eyes closed, head tipped back. Shampoo bubbles trailed down her magnificent breasts and rounded abdomen.

He didn't hesitate, but opened the door and stepped inside with her. She reacted in the most female way, trying to cover herself with her arms.

"Don't," he said quietly. "You're beautiful." *And you're mine.*

He watched her gaze drift down his body, too, his need for her evident. "How'd you sleep?" he asked.

"Like a baby." She smiled hesitantly. "How about you?"

"Incredibly well. I like having you in my bed."

She swallowed, obviously nervous.

"Need soap?" he asked, reaching for it.

He lathered his hands then placed them on her shoulders. He worked his way down her body, slowly, teasingly. Whenever he looked at her face, her eyes were closed, her head angled back slightly. He slid his hand lower, felt her body jerk in reaction, then teased her, taking her to the brink, then leaving her there. He handed her the bar of soap and turned his back to her.

She didn't curse him out loud, but he figured she was reading him the riot act in her head. Maybe she wouldn't return the favor? But after a long moment he felt her hands glide slickly along his back, over his rear, down his legs. He turned around. She started at his shoulders, made her way down his abdomen, then skipped to his legs, her face level with his hips. She stood. With her gaze locked on his, she soaped her hands then grasped the last remaining spot to be cleansed.

"It may require two washings," he said. "Possibly three."

"I could be mean and do what you did."

"You could be."

"I think one washing will probably take care of it," she said finally, her eyes sparkling.

"You could be right about—" What she was doing with her hands stole speech from him. He saw the small, triumphant smile on her face as he gave in to the sensations, concentrated and intense, a reward for his very long wait, until his body stiffened as release came in a long, satisfying explosion of completion.

He didn't let her bask in her triumph but went to his knees and pressed his mouth to her, enjoying her with long strokes of his tongue, then settling on her. She didn't protest. As with himself, it didn't take long to bring her to climax. He wasn't

satisfied. He wanted to be inside her, to feel her surround him, to bury himself deep and then take and take until they both were exhausted.

"Let's go back to bed," he said, kissing her.

"We have company."

"Who cares?"

"I do, Devlin."

The serious tone in her voice made him lift his head.

"There'll be time for more after she's gone," Nicole said.

"That's not until tomorrow."

"I know." She turned off the water.

At least she'd stopped hiding her body from him. She let him towel her dry and then dressed in front of him, which stirred him up again. She laughed as he tried to zip up his jeans, giving him a little pat as she returned to the bathroom to dry her hair.

"I'll go play host," he said, deciding to shave later. Or maybe not to shave at all. He couldn't remember a day since he'd graduated that he hadn't shaved.

She came back, put her hands on his face and kissed him. "You look a little dangerous."

Yeah. Maybe he wouldn't shave for a few days.

He found his sister in the kitchen, scarfing down a bowl of cereal.

"You've gone soft, sleeping in like that," she said, then focused on his unshaven face. "And lazy."

He started making coffee.

"I've already been for a run," she added. "You used to get up early to do that, too. And I've never seen you with a beard."

"I run after Nicole goes to work. She works the noon-to-eight shift. As for not shaving—it's none of your business, is it?"

"Nope." She cocked her head. "You look happier this morning than you did last night."

"I was tired last night."

"Uh-huh. So, will you answer questions this morning?"

"Like?"

"Like how you came to be an expectant father? And why you aren't married yet? And why you haven't told Mother and Father?"

He flipped the On switch to let the coffee start brewing. "I came to be an expectant father in the usual way. You did learn about the birds and the bees, didn't you?"

She stuck out her tongue.

"Takes more than that," he said, making her laugh. He *was* happier this morning. Lighter. He had hope for a smooth transition into marriage. "We're not married yet because we haven't had a wedding."

She groaned.

"And I haven't told Mother and Father because it has nothing to do with them."

Her brows arched. "Does that mean you're not inviting them to your wedding? That would never be tolerated. They would resent Nicole, you know. It would start things off on the wrong foot."

"It's my life. Mine and Nicole's."

"You have obligations, Dev."

"I know."

She rinsed out her cereal bowl, then leaned against the counter. "What's going on with you? You seem really different. More relaxed and yet more tense at the same time."

"I've got a lot on my plate."

"Are you going to help convince Father and Grandfather to take me on at the bank? It's time for you to move up the ladder, too. Maybe I could take over for you."

"You can't step into my job. You have to prove yourself."

"I've got a portfolio," she said. "I tried to show it to Father, but he brushed it off. I know it'll impress the hell out of them."

"Have you got it with you?"

"Yes."

"Show me after Nicole leaves. We'll see."

A few minutes later they were standing on the balcony overlooking Lake Tahoe, sipping coffee and enjoying the view, when Nicole appeared, her hair braided, makeup on and dressed for work. Dev made room for her in the shaft of sunlight warming the deck.

"I hope you slept well," she said to Izzy.

"I did. And you?"

"The same," Nicole said.

Dev slipped an arm around Nicole's waist and was pleased when she relaxed into him. "How about I fix breakfast?" he asked.

She looked at her watch. "I don't have much time. I wanted to stop by my cabin and pick up my violet to repot."

"I'll do that when I take Iz on a tour later."

"Really? That would be great, thanks."

"Iz? Breakfast?"

"The cereal I had was plenty, thanks."

"I'll leave you two to get to know each other," Dev said, a little worried about what Izzy would ask and what Nicole would answer....

Ten

Nicole tried not to panic. She didn't know what she was allowed to say. How much of the truth could she reveal to this sister of his, whom he trusted to keep his secrets?

"Dev hasn't been very generous with details about you," Isabel said. "Is he protecting you or himself?"

"Only he can answer that question. What would you like to know?"

"How you met."

"In Atlantic City. I used to work at the Sterling there."

"Your eyes met across a crowded casino floor and it was love at first sight?"

The memory made Nicole smile. "Exactly."

"Really?"

Nicole nodded. "Fate."

"You do realize you are completely different from the women he usually dates. Dated."

"He told me." He'd dated a lot of women…once. Women his parents would have deemed acceptable as his wife. "But he chose me."

"Did he? Or did the pregnancy?"

The blunt question caught Nicole off guard. She hadn't expected Isabel to be rude. Nicole didn't know what to say.

"I figured he's waiting for the birth to be sure it's his," Isabel said. "That's why he hasn't married you."

Her arrogant expression made Nicole want to retreat, but she didn't. "I assure you, this child is his."

"Something you planned, I imagine. The Campbell money must look awfully good to someone of your background."

"Money doesn't equal class."

Isabel's lips pursed, then she nodded slightly. "Touché."

Nicole switched subjects, wary of the other questions Isabel had. "Who is the girlfriend in San Francisco you're going to see?"

"Ashley and I roomed together through high school."

"High school?"

"We attended the same academy."

Ah, yes, a different life, indeed. She wondered if Devlin would expect their child to go away to school at a young age. She would never agree to that. Never.

"Ashley wants me to look for a job in San Francisco," Isabel added, "so that we could room together again."

"Why don't you? Wouldn't it be better to be hired by a company that really wants you than to force yourself somewhere you're not welcome?"

"You wouldn't understand."

"Why wouldn't I?"

"It has to do with entitlement. And tradition."

"And those are words I don't understand? I may have

been raised differently, but I have a sense of what you're talking about."

"You couldn't possibly, or you wouldn't need to ask the questions."

Maybe Isabel was right about that. Nicole had been trying to forge a relationship with a woman who would, at the very least, be an aunt to her child. Perhaps it was an impossible wish that they could become friends, too.

"I've worked hard for this," Isabel said, her voice harsh, revealing her emotions. "Harder than Golden Boy ever did. All he had to do was show up. He even got to spend his summers working at the bank. But I knew I had to prove myself."

"How could you stand working for someone who is so antifemale?" Nicole really didn't understand that need at all. Nor had she experienced that kind of ambition.

"It's *my* heritage as much as any man's in my family." She angled closer to Nicole and kept her voice low. "He's not going to marry you, you know. Or if he does, it'll only be temporary, for appearances. He knows his responsibility to the family. We all do. And it isn't marrying beneath him."

"You've come to a lot of conclusions about me, I see." She looked through the window, making sure Devlin wasn't near. "Your brother trusts you, you know. Please don't hurt him."

"My relationship with my brother is not something we're going to discuss," Isabel said. "I'll be gone by the time you get home from work. If I'd known Dev had company, I wouldn't have crashed his party. Ashley won't mind if I'm a day early. And I don't want to interrupt your…interlude."

Nicole chose not to sink to her level. "You're welcome here, Isabel."

"Your words are gracious, but your eyes tell a different story. Perhaps we'll meet again. Perhaps not."

Nicole had doubts now, too. She hated that the trust she'd been building with Devlin could be so easily shattered by a few words. And Devlin would think Nicole chased his sister off somehow. "I think you'll get what you set your mind to, Isabel."

"Are you saying I'm ruthless?"

"Your word. But a good one."

Isabel merely smiled.

"Breakfast is ready," Devlin said from behind them.

Nicole made sure her expression didn't reveal any emotional upheaval before she turned to face him. Isabel made the transition easily, smiling brightly.

His gaze slid from one woman to the other. "Everything okay?"

Isabel didn't let Nicole answer but looped her arm through Nicole's. "I've had a nice time getting to know my future sister-in-law."

Oh, she was a sly one, all right, and definitely capable of backstabbing her way to the top. Was Devlin blind to his sister's take-no-prisoners ambition?

Nicole was grateful she could escape to work. Even if Devlin accused her of saying something to scare off Isabel, Nicole would be glad to see the manipulative woman leave.

And Nicole could act just as innocent as Isabel.

A few hours later Dev watched his sister drive off, then he took a walk around the property. He hadn't been surprised that she'd left a day early, especially when she hinted that Nicole hadn't made her feel welcome. Something had transpired between the women that morning, but neither of them was owning up to it.

He wasn't sorry Izzy left. Things were too tenuous with

Nicole to have someone intruding, altering the path of discovery they were on, but if Nicole had somehow forced Iz to leave, it was a side of Nicole he hadn't seen. And wouldn't like. In his world, the game was always played. Civility and courtesy were expected. She'd told him stories about irate hotel guests and how'd she'd soothed them, so she certainly had the skills for keeping the peace with his family.

Giving up on understanding the female mind, Dev stopped to watch the activity on the lake, all the sailboats, speed boats, and the large paddleboats that carried tourists around the huge expanse and into the exquisite Emerald Bay, its green water shimmering in the sun. He'd traveled a lot, had visited some incredible places in the world, but the simplicity of the Tahoe area appealed to him in a different way, a straightforward, undemanding way. The scent of pine wrapped around him. No hustle and bustle, except in the casinos. Maybe that was part of what drew him there sometimes. He hadn't fully adapted to a slow and peaceful way of life.

He should get back to work, had taken a long break, considering he'd slipped away yesterday, too. Instead he let the memory of his shower with Nicole that morning play in his head.

Everything would be different now. He could start making wedding plans. The hotel had a nice wedding chapel. They would invite only a few people, closest friends and family. She could give a two-week notice at work, then at the end of his month, they would be free to move back home to Philadelphia. Perfect timing.

He pulled out his cell phone and called Nicole at work as he hiked back to the lodge.

"Is everything okay?" she asked.

"Yeah. I just wanted to let you know that Izzy left."

He couldn't interpret her long silence.

"That's too bad," she said at last.

"I can't say I minded."

"Okay."

Okay? What *had* they talked about? "I had a look at her portfolio."

"And?"

"It's not bad. There's potential."

"Will you talk her up to your father?"

"Yeah."

"I'll bet she was thrilled."

Was that sarcasm in her voice? "I didn't tell her. Didn't want to get her hopes up. I'll see you in a few hours."

When Dev let himself into her cabin later he stood just inside the door and studied the space she'd made her own, looking for clues about her. He didn't think there was a new piece of furniture in the place, but there was a certain charm to what she'd put together, although it was a far cry from the sharp, contemporary lines of his town house furnishings. He wondered what her reaction to it was going to be. She would look like a daisy in a steel planter.

He wasn't sure it was the right setting for her.

He found the potting soil under her sink, where she'd directed him, then grabbed the flower pot. As he headed back to the front door, he noticed the message light on her answering machine was blinking. He rubbed his fingers against his still-unshaven cheeks, contemplating the flashing red light.

He pressed the message button. Four messages in a row were from Mark, asking her to call him, each message a little more frantic. Then the last message, obviously left last night or today, after Dev had found them together.

"We left things up in the air, Nicki," Mark said. "My offer will be there forever, no matter what else happens. Please just

stay in touch with me. I just want to know what's happening. I don't like him. I don't think he's good to you. You know I would be good to you. Call me, please."

If Mark didn't mean anything to her, why hadn't she deleted the messages from the previous week?

Dev focused on the photographs on her mantel, pictures of her mom and dad, a couple with girlfriends, but no photos of Mark. That should've pleased Dev, but a man on a mission like Mark could break down barriers. It might take only one misstep from Dev to send her running.

It looked as if he was going to have to take matters into his own hands regarding Mark, make sure he understood that he needed to back away, not just for now but forever. No lovesick hulk was going to play knight in shining armor for his wife.

Dev decided to go to the casino and play a little blackjack, but he was in a foul mood by the time he reached the Sterling a half hour before Nicole's shift was up. He needed to hide the mood from her. Things were changing between them. He didn't want to damage what they were building. So a little playtime was in order, to get his mind off Mark, and Izzy's early departure. He wanted the night to be free of problems when he and Nicole got into bed later.

Tonight he would seal the deal with her. They would make love *and* a wedding date. She wouldn't consider Mark an option ever again.

He headed to the front desk first to let Nicole know he was there and where she could find him when she was ready. Since she'd never agreed to let him drive her to and from work, he'd occasionally used blackjack as an excuse to show up now and then. She didn't seem suspicious that he was really showing up so that he could make sure she made the half-hour trip home safely.

The bubbly Ann-Marie gave him a wave but continued talking with a guest. He didn't see Nicole, not even behind the glass door of the assistant manager's office.

"She's upstairs dealing with a guest," Ann-Marie told him as soon as she was free.

"Thanks. When she gets back, would you tell her I'm here? I'm going to try my luck at the blackjack table until she's ready."

"Sure. Maybe I should warn you, though." Ann-Marie looked around, then whispered. "She's on the warpath about something."

He couldn't imagine what Nicole looked like "on the warpath." He winked, as if it were all a joke. "I know how to take care of that."

She grinned. "I'll just bet you do."

He walked away, wondering what had happened to upset her. He found a table, bought himself some chips, played a few hands, lost a couple of hundred dollars.

Nicole approached the table a few minutes after eight.

"You're just in time, Ms. Fortune. I'm in need of a little luck."

She leaned close. "Your luck has run out."

He looked at her sharply. She was on the warpath be-cause of *him?*

He played out the last hand, betting everything he had left, then not just winning but also recouping his losses. "It seems you were wrong," he said coolly to Nicole. "You're still my lucky charm."

She waited until they got to her car before she let him have it with both barrels. "The next time you invade my privacy will be the last time."

"What'd I do?"

"You listened to my phone messages."

Caught. "What makes you say that?"

"Don't give me that innocent look. No one else has a key to my place. I called to check messages, and the machine said there were no new messages, yet there were five saved, not the four that were there yesterday. So I listened to them all, and what do you know? There was a message I hadn't heard before, yet apparently I had. It came at nine o'clock this morning. From Mark."

"Did you intend to keep it a secret?" he asked.

"Don't you dare deflect this onto me, Devlin Campbell. You had no business listening. You would be furious if I did that to you."

"I have no secrets from you."

"Bull."

He gave her a complacent look. "You may not like or understand any message you might overhear, but I wouldn't care if you heard them."

"Bull."

"You seem to have some trust issues, Nicole."

"I have— I seem to have trust issues? If you trusted me, you wouldn't have listened to my messages."

"If I hadn't listened to them, I wouldn't have known that Mark continues to call you *and* that you don't erase his messages. That speaks volumes to me. I don't trust you yet. Why should I? You haven't made a commitment to me."

"My making a commitment would make you trust me?"

"It would go a long way toward it."

Dev figured his anticipated night of sex was shot to hell now. He'd never worked so hard at a relationship before, yet he got nowhere, it seemed.

She used her remote to unlock her car. He opened her door.

"That's another thing," she said, gesturing broadly toward the car. "I'm perfectly capable of getting myself in and out of cars."

"That's part of being polite, Nicole. I was raised that way," he said, exasperated. "I hold coats and chairs and doors. I say please and thank you. I write thank-you notes. I don't like a woman to pay for any part of a date."

"You're a relic."

"And proud of it."

She got in her car and took off. It took him a few blocks to catch up. At the lodge she beat him to the front door and was halfway up the stairs by the time he'd gotten the potting soil and plant from the back of his car. She didn't stop at the great room but kept going up one more level, marching straight into the master bedroom. He was on her tail.

When she flung open a dresser drawer and grabbed an armful of lingerie, he understood that she was moving back to the guest room.

No way.

"Put that back," he said, low and steady.

"Make me."

They faced each other, two strong-willed people, both believing they were right. All the progress he'd made was about to disappear if he didn't do something different, didn't defuse the tension now.

"Make me," she said again, but with less heat.

"Nicole," he said softly, seeing something in her eyes that told him she didn't want to fight, either. He cupped her face, waited a second, then kissed her. He felt her let go of the lingerie, felt it land on his feet, a tempting heap of silk and lace.

She came at him hungrily, the heat of the argument transforming into passion.

"You can't move out of my bedroom," he said against her lips. "Ever. Please. Unless one of us is out of town, we will be sharing a bed for the rest of our lives."

Her eyes went bright. "Why are you making this so hard?" she asked, the words a rasp of sound.

"I'm not trying to. I'm trying to make this as easy on you as possible. Why can't *you* see that?"

"We're too different, Devlin."

He brushed her hair with his fingertips and tried to lighten the moment. "You don't have to be so formal, you know. Dev's fine. Or darling. Even, Hey, you."

She flattened her hands against his chest and leaned her forehead against him.

"So, we're different," he said. "What does it matter?" He was making light of it, but he knew she was right, to a degree. If he married a woman who shared his upbringing, it would be easier in some ways. They would have the same expectations, the same experiences. But he had no doubt that Nicole would figure out how to fit into his world. She was bright and competent and, well, friendly. She'd do fine.

The question was, could he fit into hers?

Nicole showered, unbraided her hair and changed into one of her new comfortable gowns. He'd finally left her alone after she assured him she wouldn't move her clothes out of the room.

Which didn't mean she still wouldn't move herself out, she thought rebelliously. What was it about him that made her want to do the opposite of everything he said?

She didn't like when he got possessive and bossy—and yet she did like it, too. No one had taken care of her since the day she'd hit the road after graduation. She'd always done the

caring for, even in her other relationships. She'd given and given, not ever receiving the equivalent in return. Even her job was all about service. Why couldn't she just enjoy the things he wanted to do for her?

Because it meant giving up control. And giving up control meant giving up a piece of herself. She would only give up a piece of herself when she knew she could fill the vacant spot with a piece of him, one that he gave her freely.

She padded down the stairs and into the great room, following the strains of quiet jazz and a crackling fire. She kept going into the kitchen, stopping as soon as she saw him. He'd spread a towel on the counter. On top of it was her African violet, the bag of potting mix and the new pot, only slightly larger than her old one. He'd changed into sweatpants and a T-shirt and was barefoot, as was she.

"Shall we do it?" he asked.

"Do it?" She felt heat rise in her face.

He laughed low. "I guess there are two meanings to that question, but I'm referring to the plant."

They worked side by side. He recited the instructions given by the nurseryman, and the job was done. She carried it to the bottom of the staircase and placed it on a pedestal where sunlight was diffused, perfect for the plant.

"Thank you," she said, hugging him.

He held her close, without turning it into something seductive, and she appreciated that he knew it was an emotional moment for her, that it was a memory of her mother. After a while they headed back up the stairs, hand in hand.

"We didn't get a chance to talk about your trip home," she said. So much had happened since he returned. It'd seemed like a week instead of a day. "I heard you talking about a party for Isabel's graduation?"

"We went to dinner, just the family and one of her oldest girlfriends."

"Does she have a boyfriend?"

"If so, he wasn't there. I don't stay in touch with Iz like I do Joan. Joan e-mails and sends photos of the kids and calls."

"Did you tell Joan about me? The baby?"

They settled on the sofa. The fire was perfect.

"There wasn't time or privacy."

Nicole wondered about that. You could always find time and a place if you really wanted to. "Is that why you didn't tell your parents, either?"

"As I said to Izzy last night, it was her party. Not the place to bring up my own news and steal away the attention. I'll let you know as soon as I break the news," he said, tugging on her hair a little.

Which meant she should drop the subject. "What about the business you were taking care of? The face time you needed?"

"I decided against one deal. Have to make up my mind about the others soon, before someone else grabs them."

"What's taking you so long to make a decision? You seem like the decisive type."

"Everything will fall into place soon." He gathered her to him. "You always smell good," he said, threading his fingers through her hair, nuzzling her. "Let's go upstairs. It can only help," he added softly.

Could it? Last night she'd been ready, so what was holding her back now?

Isabel, she decided. His sister had stolen whatever confidence Nicole had found, as well as her hope for a true, long lasting marriage.

But, oh, how she wanted him. And she was so tired of

denying her needs. She just didn't know what price she would pay…

"Devlin," she said tentatively.

"Nicole," he said, conveying his need in the single word. She knew he was waiting for her to say yes.

Nicole sat up. She looked him in the eyes.

"No more waiting," he said.

The freedom in his taking the decision out of her hands set her in motion. She straddled him, kissed him deeply, thoroughly, their mouths merging into one flaming entity. Down low she felt him, hard and strong, pressing against her own burning need.

Nicole tugged his shirt up and off him, then tossed it aside. She dragged her tongue down his neck and across his chest, sliding her fingers along the same path. A breath of air cooled her rising heat as he peeled off her gown, lobbing it on top of his shirt, then he maneuvered his sweatpants off. Face to face, skin to skin, they both paused. Looked. Enjoyed. Settled.

She arched her back and moaned as he sucked a nipple into his mouth.

"This is what I remembered about you," he said against her flesh. "How good you taste. How hard your nipples are. How perfect your body is."

"You really did go back to find me?"

"Oh, yeah." He met her gaze. "If I'd known you were an employee, I would've haunted the place."

"And broken your one-date rule?" She waited, almost breathless, for his answer, which mattered a lot to her.

"Yeah."

"But only for sex."

"The best sex I could remember."

It was a start, Nicole decided. A very good start. The fact that he'd admitted it pleased her, as well. "Me, too. I did things I'd never done before."

"I remember them all." His jaw tightened, his gaze burned into her, then his hands got into the action, stroking her first with long sweeps, then searching lower and lower. She raised herself up on her knees a little, giving him access. He slid a hand to the juncture of her thighs, caressed her tenderly, thoroughly, then slipped a finger inside her, leaving his thumb to rest where the ache had intensified.

"I remembered this, too," he said, his words like sandpaper.

Her breath had caught in her throat. "Remembered what?"

"How wet you get, how tight you are, how good you feel when I'm inside you."

"So, get inside, why don't you?" She gripped his shoulders to steady herself. "I don't think I can wait any longer."

He helped position her over him, to slide down him. "Don't move," he said harshly. "Don't move for a second."

She didn't, but she couldn't help but squeeze him tight. He made a long, low sound of ecstasy.

The sensations may have started where they were joined, but they shot like liquid fire everywhere, fast and overwhelming. It wasn't going to be one of those slow rolling climaxes but one that hit hard and didn't relent. Her own voice echoed in the vast room, not words but sounds she had no control over. She became aware of his helping her slide up and down on him, then his rising to meet her. Their mating was mutual, intense and primal, obliterating anything that had gone before. Waves rolled through her long after they'd collapsed against each other.

"Better than I remembered," she breathed against his shoulder.

"Yeah."

After a minute her legs cramped. He helped her shift onto the couch and rubbed her thighs until she could feel sensation again, then he laid his hands on her belly. She opened her eyes.

"Nicole."

She waited.

"Anytime you're in the mood, you don't hesitate to let me know. Don't hold back."

"You're pretty good at reading my mind." *Seeing into my soul.*

"I don't want to guess."

"Okay, it's a deal, provided you do the same."

"You turn me loose like that, and the only time you'll be dressed is when you're at work. I can't get enough of you."

She ran her thumb along his lower lip, let it dip inside. "There's something to be said for anticipation."

He bit her thumb lightly. "I've been anticipating too long already."

"Patience is a virtue."

"Patience is wasted energy."

She grinned.

"Were you comfortable enough?" he asked.

"Until the end when I couldn't move my legs."

"We'll have to get creative." He helped her up. "Let's go to bed."

"Perchance to sleep?" she asked.

"Perchance."

Eventually they did.

Eleven

The week passed, the routine of their days merely a way of killing time until the nights, in Dev's opinion. The ripples Nicole had felt in her abdomen turned into what she called tiny flutters instead, distinctly different but still too light for Dev to feel, frustrating him.

His month was winding down. Decisions about their future together couldn't be put off much longer, especially since she was approaching her fifth month. The wedding needed to happen *now*. Plus she would need to give notice at work. And put her cabin on the market. He wanted to take care of that for her, take the responsibility off her shoulders. She might not be able to fly much until after the baby was born, so he would fly her father to see her as often as they liked. That should help ease her concerns about leaving him.

Dev hoped he'd thought of everything. They had an appointment to see her obstetrician in a few days for a con-

sultation and ultrasound. Joan had shoved ultrasound photos in his face for all three of her children, including the one still tucked safely inside her, so he knew what to expect.

Nicole was still asleep on this Sunday morning, but Dev was wound tight. He'd awakened early, watched her sleep for a little while, then eased out of bed. While waiting for the coffee to finish brewing, he jogged up to the office to study the photos of the Samurai. Because he'd been looking at them every day, he'd started to feel a connection to them again. Memories of their time together came back in bits and pieces. He looked forward to the mass reunion in October, when they'd all served their time, as he'd begun to think of it.

"Well, Hunter, are you satisfied?" he asked, focusing on the man with the biggest smile and broadest gestures. "You wanted us to reassess our lives during our stays in the wilderness." There was very little he hadn't reassessed, personally and professionally.

The plans were set, he thought just as his cell phone rang. He saw on the screen that it was his father, the first call he'd made to Dev all month. Dev had always called *him*.

"Hello, Son."

"Morning, Father." He rubbed his cheeks, unshaven for days. He could only imagine how his father would feel about that.

"I understand you have news."

Dev's heart slammed into his chest. Since Izzy was the only one who could've told anyone—

"Ed Maguire says you're close to a deal," his father went on to say. "Yet you haven't even presented the property to the board. You don't have the authority to make the deal on your own."

Dev let go of the satisfying image of wringing Izzy's neck, although the way his father had chastised him didn't sit well,

either. Had he always spoken to Dev in that paternal, dictatorial voice, even after all these years of his doing his job beyond anyone's expectations?

"I'm not close to a deal with Maguire, Father. That's just wishful thinking on his part."

"He said you checked out the property when you were home last week."

Dev had already denied the claim, yet his father continued to push? "I did. I decided it was a bad risk."

"Fred Hayden and Ron Allister said you took meetings with them, too."

Cold, hard accusation coated the words. Dev shouldn't have been surprised that the men had spread the word to his father.

"What are you up to, Devlin?"

He sat in the desk chair, ready to explain. "I—"

"Before you answer with a lie or a half truth, you should know that your sister told your mother and me about a woman you apparently impregnated. Someone who works for a casino." The last word was said with disdain, as if that were worse than Dev getting a woman pregnant out of wedlock.

He would wring Izzy's neck, after all. What had she hoped to gain by violating his confidence?

"You have nothing to say?" his father asked.

"I have plenty to say."

Nicole appeared in the doorway, her hair mussed, her smile sleepy. She wore a flannel shirt of his that came to the tops of her thighs. He held out an arm to her, inviting her in.

"Well?" his father said impatiently.

Nicole took his hand and placed it on her belly. Apparently she was feeling kicks, but he felt nothing.

Dev had paid closer attention to his parents while he was home last week, trying to figure out what kind of relation-

ship they had. He couldn't imagine his father ever anxiously awaiting his children's first kicks. He and his mother had never once touched during the hours Dev had spent with them. Had they ever been hungry for each other, as he and Nicole were?

"I'm still waiting," came the stern voice on the other end.

Dev kept his gaze locked to Nicole's as he spoke into the phone. "I am going to be a father in September. My fiancée's name is Nicole. She doesn't work at a casino but a hotel. You'll meet her soon."

Nicole had jerked back when he'd called her his fiancée. He tightened his hold.

"I tolerated your taking a month off from work since you've been able to work from there, but I won't tolerate your marrying a woman I don't approve of. You'll bring her home tomorrow so that your mother and I can meet her."

"That won't be possible."

"If you value your position—"

"Don't threaten, Father," Dev said mildly. It felt freeing to take control of the conversation.

"I can't believe you let yourself get taken in by the oldest trick in the—"

Dev snapped his phone shut and set it aside. He pulled Nicole to stand between his thighs. "Good morning."

"Fiancée?"

"Just because you don't have a ring yet doesn't make it any less true."

"There's been no asking and answering that I know of."

"It's going to happen, Nicole. You know it and I know it."

"You don't allow a girl any fantasies, do you?" she asked. She moved away. He didn't understand what she meant,

and after the difficult conversation with his father, he didn't want to pursue why she was upset with him now, too.

"I want to go see my dad on my own today," she said.

"Why?"

"Because I'd like a little time alone with him. He's been acting strangely every time we've talked. I need to settle things with him."

He wanted to offer to drive her, even if only to drop her off and pick her up later, but he knew her by now. It wouldn't sit well with her, so he didn't even suggest it.

"You've got to start trusting me sometime, Devlin," she said, interpreting his silence incorrectly. "I'm not going to see Mark."

"Mark may come to see you."

"I can't stop him from doing that, since it's my father's house. Trust me. Please."

"I do." He just didn't trust Mark. Dev knew how men thought; Nicole didn't.

"Thank you." She gestured to his phone. "You told your father."

"Izzy did."

Nicole's face paled.

"I'm calling her the same names as you are in your head," he said. "I can't believe she did that. I can't imagine what she thought she might gain from it."

"To discredit you with your parents."

"Why?"

She hesitated. "You know, I hardly know her. This is between you and her."

"You have an opinion. I'd like to hear it."

"I'm angry. Very angry. It's bad enough when a friend plays you false. For a sibling to be disloyal is unforgivable. I mean, I don't have any siblings but…"

So she was championing him? "Thank you for your allegiance," he said.

"I believe in loyalty," she said, then she kissed him, surprising him with her intensity.

He slipped his hands under the shirt, curved his hands over her rear and drew her close, the discussion well and truly over. "You weren't planning to leave soon, were you?"

She smiled seductively. "I have time to let you have your way with me."

He stripped her shirt off, sat her in the desk chair and did, indeed, have his way with her, giving her a memory to take to Sacramento with her.

Nicole got an early start, arriving twenty minutes before her usual time. A strange car was parked in the driveway as she approached, a small red sedan. Just then her father and a woman came into view, walking arm in arm up the pathway from the house. The woman was as round as he was slender, and was younger, maybe by ten years. She looked up at him and smiled; he bent to give her a quick kiss.

Stunned, Nicole pulled over, blocking the driveway. She stared through the window until they noticed her. Nicole rolled down the window.

"Dad?" she asked, stunned.

He looked mildly uncomfortable but held tight to the woman's hand. "You're early," he said to Nicole. "This is Liz. Liz, my daughter, Nicole."

"What's going on?" Nicole asked, her voice raw. Her gaze drilled her father, then Liz.

"We'll talk in the house, Nicki."

"I was just leaving," Liz said quietly, then with a quick, sad look at Rob, she got in her car.

After a moment Nicole pulled out of the way and parked the car, not getting out until the red sedan was gone. Her father met her on the sidewalk, but she didn't look at him. Couldn't look at him. Hurt and bewilderment tumbled around her in an avalanche of emotion as they walked into the house and straight into the living room.

"Who is she?" Nicole asked hoarsely as her father sat in his big blue recliner.

"I met Liz a few weeks ago at the grocery store. She helped me pick out some…cantaloupe." His voice faded. "I was just standing there, staring at the bin, not knowing what to look for. I missed your mother so much, and I was mad at her, too, for putting me in that predicament. She always did the shopping."

"I know," Nicole said. "But it's too soon."

"By whose timetable? I'm lonely. Sometimes I'm lost. Liz helps."

"Are you sleeping with her?"

"That's none of your business."

He was right, of course. She'd just blurted it out, not even wanting to know if it was true. "It's only been five months," she said aloud finally, her voice shaking, tears burning her eyes.

"I'm sorry you're hurt, honey. But I like her. You would, too, if you gave her a chance."

"I can't, Dad."

"You're moving forward. I need to, too."

"There's a big difference. I'm having a baby. And you were married to Mom for thirty-five years."

"I know you won't understand this, but I'm honoring her. She wouldn't like that I've been sitting at home mourning rather than living. You know she wouldn't."

Nicole finally sat. "I know she would want you to keep living, Dad. But dating so soon?"

"I'm not saying I'm going to marry Liz. But she's a kind, cheerful, undemanding woman, and for now it's nice to have company. She's widowed, too, so she understands. And she has a lot of family and friends. She keeps me busy. She keeps me from thinking too much. She likes to cook."

And he didn't. Nicole knew that. He'd been relying on frozen dinners and whatever she made on Sundays, which she made in quantity to freeze extra portions for him.

"You can't take care of me forever, Nicki. You've got your own life. I imagine you'll be moving to Philadelphia."

It was one of the things Nicole had stuck her head in the sand about—moving. Moving meant giving up her cabin. Her job. Her proximity to her father. It meant cutting all ties and starting over, knowing only Devlin, becoming part of a family who would probably start off resenting her for "tricking" their son into marriage.

"I'm not asking you to accept Liz as anything other than a new friend in my life," her father said.

"I miss Mom." The ache that stayed with her day by day, hour by hour, became white-hot. She missed her mother like she never thought she could miss anyone. Nothing could ever replace her. It was a black hole of emptiness.

"I know, honey. I know." He pulled her out of her chair and into his arms. They cried together. Nicole wished she'd found it healing, but she felt even emptier, maybe because everything with Devlin was so complicated, too.

"Have you made wedding plans?" her father asked a little while later as they headed into the kitchen to make lunch.

"No."

His brows rose. "What's the holdup?"

"Time. Trust. Love." There it was, the biggest reason. She'd spent the past three weeks falling in love—maybe

because she wanted to so much. Devlin had rarely given any indication she was much more than the woman he got pregnant, who was now his responsibility. The woman he lusted after, yes, but loved? No. He could be tender at times, and kind, and even funny on occasion.

"Do you believe in love at first sight, Dad?"

"Yes, I do. I also believe love can grow out of a deep and abiding friendship to become something even better." He gave her a fatherly look. "*Mark* loves you."

Nicole laughed a little. "Dad, please."

"Well, he does."

"Do you seriously think Devlin would let another man raise his child? Besides, I don't love Mark."

"You love Devlin?"

"Yes." Yes, she did. Stupidly and wonderfully loved him. Maybe she'd let it happen because she carried his baby and they had a future because of that baby. But maybe she'd fallen for him that first night.

"But?" her father asked.

She needed to tell someone, talk to someone, so she opened up. "Do you know what it's like loving someone who doesn't love you in return?"

He shook his head.

"It's lonely. It's painful. You start to feel used, even though it's your own choice to give so much, *too* much. I've been through it in a much less harrowing way before, and I decided I wouldn't ever get myself into that position again. Yet here I am, in an even worse position, because I'm pregnant and my choices are limited."

"You're welcome to come live with me. I'll help raise the baby."

Nicole reached for his hand. "Thank you. I appreciate the

offer, Dad. But there's no way Devlin is going to let anyone else raise his child, not even just me. He's in my child's life— my life—forever. I just have to figure out what I can live with." She straightened her shoulders. "And that's enough about me. I'm ready for lunch."

She discovered a refrigerator full of food, and the bills paid and organized. He didn't need her anymore, not the way he had. Her life continued to change.

Nicole was tired enough to take a nap before she left for home, but she didn't want to stay at her father's house any longer. She needed time alone to think about him with a woman other than her mother, and to think about Devlin and where they would go from here. Her expectations had probably been too high when she'd agreed to spend the month with him. A month wasn't enough time, and she was fairly certain he wouldn't stay beyond the month. He seemed anxious to get on with his plan, whatever it was.

Instead of driving home right away, she took a sentimental journey around Sacramento. It had been a great place to grow up, a big city, an important one politically as the state capital, yet with a small-town atmosphere and lots of trees; in fact its nickname was "City of Trees."

She drove to Land Park. How many times had she visited the zoo and Fairytale Town? Nostalgia swept over her in agonizing waves. Reminders of her mother were everywhere here—picnics and summer escapes and fun. Mom would pack the car with kids and spend the day like a recreation director. Everyone would go home tired and dirty and satisfied.

What was Philadelphia like? Aside from being home to the Liberty Bell, she really didn't know much about the city, except that it was more sophisticated, probably, and histori-

cal. How easy would it be to make friends? Would Devlin's friends accept her? Would she find places to take her child where they would make the kind of memories she had?

Nicole realized she couldn't wait any longer to decide her future. It was make-or-break time. Tell him yes or no. She would either marry Devlin and move to Philadelphia, and find a way to make a good life with him—and hope he would come to love her...

Or she would move back to her cabin and find a way to fit him into her life without benefit of marriage. She had rights, too. Emotional, as well as legal.

By the time she got to the lodge she would have made her decision. She would tell him tonight.

Twelve

Pacing, Dev glared at his watch again. Why wasn't she home yet? He'd talked to her father, learned she'd left almost four hours ago. Dev wouldn't wait too much longer before he contacted the California Highway Patrol to see if there'd been any accidents.

His cell phone rang. He grabbed it, ground out a hello.

"You called?" Izzy asked leisurely.

Dev moved to stare out the window, where he could see the driveway. Anxiety over Nicole grabbed him by the throat, but it didn't stop the anger directed at his sister. "I trusted you, Iz. I can't believe you told Mother and Father about Nicole."

"It just slipped out."

"In what context?"

"I asked Father if you'd talked to him about me. He said no. Then it just slipped out."

Not a slip at all, but retaliation for his not acting fast

enough for her. "I had every intention of talking to him, Iz, but I wanted to do it in person and show him your portfolio, which would've earned you points."

A long pause, then, "I assumed since you hadn't said anything…"

"One of the first rules of business—don't assume. That little slip cost you. It cost you big-time."

"Why?" She sounded haughty and defensive. When had she turned into their father?

"Because now you're on your own, without my support. Second rule of business, Iz—trust matters. I don't trust you anymore."

"But, Dev—"

"I'm done." He ended the call. He couldn't deal with her and her ambitions right now.

He was about to dial 4ll to get the highway patrol's number when Nicole pulled into the driveway. Anger dynamited its way through relief as he hurried down the stairs and flung open the door.

"Where the hell have you been?" He shouted the words. Having never shouted at anyone before, he amazed himself that he was even capable of it.

She stopped in her tracks. "You know where I was."

"You left your father's house more than four hours ago. Four hours." He came within a foot of her, examining her, then her car. No damage that he could see.

"My father is dating…."

He almost couldn't make out her barely spoken words. "So?"

Her eyes went bright. "So, my mother has only been gone for five months."

"That's what made you late? That's why you didn't call

to say you'd be delayed? You scared the—" He stopped ranting when he saw her recoil. "What exactly took you so long?"

She walked past him and entered the house. "You wouldn't understand."

"Try me." He followed her upstairs and into the great room then on into the kitchen, where she dumped her purse on the counter, grabbed a glass and pressed it to the cold water lever in the refrigerator door.

"I needed some time alone," she said, eyeing him directly, then taking a long drink.

"Why?"

"To think. To remember my mother."

She'd put him through hell because she'd needed to *think?* He'd been scared to death something had happened to her or the baby. "Did you even once consider I might be worried when you didn't come home within a reasonable time frame?"

"Don't yell at me."

No apology? "You don't have a clue what you put me through."

"I needed time, Devlin. I needed—"

"Stop. Just stop. I'm through being patient. Here's what's going to happen." He watched her set down her water glass, her body going rigid. Where was the sexy woman he'd taken back to bed that very morning? The even-tempered woman he'd come to enjoy sharing space with? He should've taken charge weeks ago.

Control. He needed control back. Something had gone haywire today. He couldn't let that happen again. Couldn't be afraid like that again.

"First, I'll drive you to the Sterling tonight so that you can

give notice that you're leaving your job. It won't be a considerate two-week notice, but they'll have to manage. Second, we'll contact a real estate agent tomorrow to put your cabin on the market."

He saw her retreat, mentally and physically, but it didn't slow him down any. "Third, we'll get married at the Sterling's wedding chapel on Saturday. Invite as many people as you want, except your *friend,* Mark. Fourth, I'll hire a moving company to pack up your things and have them shipped to Philadelphia, although you won't need to take much. Your furnishings won't fit in my house anywhere. Fifth—"

"What an interesting way to win me over," Nicole interrupted, ice dripping from her words.

She grabbed her purse and walked away, taking long, slow strides, as if time was infinite. He started to follow, but she left the house without packing her things, so he knew she would be back after she cooled down. Surely she would be able to see how reasonable he was being. There weren't any options other than the ones he'd cited.

When she returned, they would have a reasonable discussion. She would apologize for putting him through hell while he waited for her to get home, and he would apologize for yelling.

To kill time Dev opened a bottle of beer, grabbed a bag of pretzels and turned on the television, catching a ballgame between the Giants and the Oakland A's. Night fell. Why wasn't she back? Surely she'd calmed down by now.

He called her cell phone. Turned off, as usual.

Needing to do something, Dev decided to go looking. He grabbed his keys, headed down the staircase. At the bottom he saw the pedestal. Empty. She'd taken her African violet. Her only possession that mattered.

He approached the pedestal slowly, placed his hand on the

empty stand. It said more than any words she could've thrown at him before she left.

Still, he needed to know where she was. That she was all right. He wouldn't think about anything else until he knew she was safe.

Dev didn't see her car along the route to the Sterling, or in the parking lot, so he drove to the only other place he figured she might be—her cabin. All the lights were out. Her car wasn't in the driveway. Then he saw a curtain move inside.

He stopped, got out, headed to her front door. He changed his mind, continuing on until he reached the detached garage. He pulled open the door a crack, saw her car inside.

He closed his eyes for a few seconds, then headed to her door. The crunch of leaves and pine needles on the dirt-and-rock path to her house reminded him of the first time he'd come, the night he'd found out she was pregnant—a lifetime ago yet not even three weeks. The air had warmed up considerably since then, when she'd been sitting on her porch swing watching him without alerting him she was there until he'd almost tripped over her.

She wasn't on the porch now. He would bet his stock portfolio that she wouldn't answer the door, but he knocked anyway. Waited. Knocked again and called her name. Waited.

"I know you're in there, Nicole," he said, hoping his voice wouldn't drift to the nearest cabin, about fifty yards away. "Your car is in your garage."

He laid a hand on the door frame. "You're being childish."

A soft thump hit the door. He pictured her throwing a pillow, which made him smile, even as he was torn by her leaving. He couldn't picture his mother ever tossing a pillow at his father. Nicole was certainly the liveliest woman he'd…

dated? He couldn't exactly define their relationship in those terms, but he didn't know what else to call it.

"Come on, Nicole. Open up. Let's talk." Women always wanted to talk to clear the air.

"Okay," he said. "I'll just sleep on your swing tonight. If I freeze to death, it'll be on your conscience."

He underestimated her, however. She didn't open the door, not then, not an hour later. The temperatures may have warmed during the month, but it was still only forty degrees.

He had a choice—go home or try to force her hand. She was too kindhearted to leave him there to freeze…wasn't she?

She took her violet.

Another hour passed and she still didn't open her door to him. He used his cell phone to call and talk to her answering machine.

"I don't know why you won't talk to me," he said after the beep. "Maybe I owe you an apology. I know you owe *me* one. But this kind of behavior accomplishes nothing but to keep us at an impasse." He paused, then added, "I'm going to miss you sleeping next to me. Good night, Ms. Fortune."

He waited a few seconds, hoping to hear the lock turn. He would come back early in the morning with breakfast, since he knew she had no food in the house. He'd be damned if she'd deny his child sustenance.

With that plan in mind he went home to his big, empty bed.

Nicole listened to his car fade into the night. What could have been a night of celebration when she told him she had decided to marry him and move to Philadelphia had been shattered by his chauvinistic attitude. Okay, maybe she'd been wrong not letting him know she would be late. That wasn't an excuse for his tirade. No excuse at all.

She was not going to give up her good job, her first home and her proximity to her father for a man who didn't even care enough about her to involve her in critical decisions. Her feelings for him had shifted during the seismic eruption of orders he'd inflicted on her. Obviously he had no idea what it meant to be a partner.

A tear slid down her cheek. She swiped hard at it, angry that he'd affected her enough to cry. She'd had such hopes, had truly thought they could make a go of it, even with the strikes against them of coming at the relationship backwards, of hardly knowing each other, and expecting a baby, and coming from two different worlds.

She realized how crazy she sounded. Why *had* she been hopeful? She'd been the one doing all the compromising, after all. He'd gotten his way about everything.

How could she have thought for even a second that she could marry him without his loving her, adoring her? Impossible.

Nicole moved from the sofa to her bedroom and climbed under the covers. Even though the bed was much smaller than the one she'd shared with Devlin, it had way too much empty space.

She would have to learn to live with it.

Thirteen

After an almost sleepless night, Nicole scanned her refrigerator the next morning. The contents included ketchup, mustard, pickle relish, salad dressing and three kinds of jam. The only item in the freezer was ice. She'd taken everything else to the lodge weeks ago.

The cupboards weren't much better, but at least there was soup. She poured a can of chicken noodle into a bowl and put it in the microwave, then sat at the kitchen table with a pad of paper. She needed a plan. She needed to present Devlin with orders of her own.

Nicole held the pen poised over the paper, but no words would come. The microwave beeped that the soup was done. Still she didn't move. After a few minutes she laid her arms on the table and put her head down.

She wanted a father for her baby. She wanted a husband for herself.

She wanted love.

As much as she'd proclaimed that it wouldn't bother her to be a single, unmarried mother, it did bother her. A lot.

But if she let him get his way about everything now, would she ever get her way about anything in the future—or even compromises? Would they ever have a meeting of the minds, find a way to be partners? Maybe he was used to a household where parents didn't show affection, but she wasn't. She hadn't known how deprived of touch she was until the past couple of weeks, when he'd been within touching range all the time. She'd only had to reach out. It had been wonderful.

But it had been all about sex for him. And being in charge.

The microwave continued to beep every so often. She grabbed a spoon and opened the microwave door, then heard a car approach. Already? It was only 7:30, and Devlin was already starting in on her? But when she moved to the window to peek out from behind the curtain, she saw instead a minivan with the words Lakeside Diner painted on the side.

A teenage boy hopped out and ran around to the back. She could see into the van, where he opened a hot pack and pulled out a white foam plastic container, then slammed the door shut and raced to her door, banging on it.

"Delivery!" he called out.

She tightened her robe sash and opened the door.

He shoved the box into her hands. "Morning."

"I didn't order—"

He snagged a piece of paper from his shirt pocket and looked at it. "Nicole Price?"

"Yes, but—"

"Breakfast is served." He grinned, then hopped down the stairs.

"Wait. I'll get a tip."

"Taken care of," he said with a wave, then he was gone.

Nicole set the package on the table as if it might contain explosives. The smell of something wonderful wafted up. Her stomach rumbled. She lifted the lid. Inside was a blueberry muffin, still warm, a bacon-and-avocado omelet, and a beautiful orange, peeled, sliced and sprinkled with powdered sugar. A note wrapped in plastic was tucked into the lid.

"Good morning," it read. "I've been jogging past this little diner almost daily without ever going inside. For some reason, today I did. Guess what I learned? The mayor of Hunter's Landing, whose family owns this place, married one of the Samurai—Nathan. Amazing coincidence. They're in Barbados at the moment, but apparently they are in and out of Hunter's Landing a lot. I'll try to catch him—or meet her. Figured you would be out of food. Dev."

Nicole stared at the note. No pressure. No demands.

What was he up to?

She devoured the food, made a shopping list instead of a game plan, then went to the grocery store. At least it was her day off, so she had time to get her cabin in order again. Everything needed dusting. Then she would start on the nursery curtains. Plus, somehow, she needed to get her clothes and toiletries from the lodge.

But later, as she carried her grocery sacks from her car into the cabin, two cars pulled into her driveway, Devlin's and a sleek black Cadillac with a rental agency sticker on the bumper. Nicole couldn't retreat into the house and shut the door because two more bags of perishable food were still in her trunk, including ice cream, so she just kept moving, ignoring them.

"Need some help?" Devlin asked, coming up to her.

"I've got it. Thanks." Out of the corner of her eye, she saw

a slender, elegant man get out of the Cadillac, reach inside it, then head toward them, a black leather briefcase in his hand. Another man, big and burly, climbed out of the driver's side and followed.

Everything about the thin man screamed *lawyer*. The bearer of the prenuptial agreement, she decided. Why it took two men to deliver one little document she didn't know, unless the big guy was supposed to strong-arm her into signing.

Nicole tried to grab the two remaining bags from her car at the same time, but she couldn't manage both at once. She heard Devlin pick up the other bag, then close her trunk. He followed her. She set her bag inside the house then turned and reached for his. Then she shut the door in his face.

"Thank you," she called from inside.

"Nicole." His tone of voice was patient, even indulgent.

"Thank you for breakfast, too." She put her ice cream in the freezer, along with the frozen vegetables. Milk into the refrigerator. Fruit. Salad fixings. Chicken breasts. All the while she was aware of Devlin right outside her door.

If only he would say he was sorry. If only he would say he loved her….

An anvil dropped on her chest, making it hard to breathe.

"I just want to show you something," he said through the door.

"What?"

"Open the door for a minute. Please."

"I'm not signing anything."

"I'm not asking you to. I just want to show you something."

She took her time washing her hands, then moved to the living room window and looked out. When he didn't spot her, she tapped on the glass.

"What do you think I'm going to do, kidnap you?" he asked, his earlier patience apparently being tested.

"You wanted to show me something?"

He gestured to the men waiting at the bottom of the steps, who joined Devlin. The attorney held up the briefcase and opened the lid.

"This is Mr. Sokoloff, who has been kind enough to fly in from Philadelphia so that you can choose from his selections."

The case held a display of probably fifty engagement rings, mostly with diamonds, but a few sapphires and other stones she couldn't name. So, the big guy was a bodyguard? She couldn't begin to imagine the total value of the rings.

"What do you like?" Devlin asked.

A hot lump formed in her throat. *I'd like to be proposed to. I'd like to hear you pledge your life to me.*

She didn't care about a ring, although her eye was drawn to a square-cut diamond with sapphire petals surrounding it. "It doesn't matter."

Mr. Sokoloff didn't even blink, yet he surely couldn't be accustomed to balky, belligerent recipients of his fine jewelry.

"It doesn't matter?" Devlin repeated. "So, *I* should choose?" When she didn't reply, he seemed to mull over the case, stroking his chin. He still hadn't shaved, and the last time she'd touched his face, his beard had finally gone from scratchy to soft.

"Personally, I like this one," he said, pulling out an enormous diamond in an intricate setting.

"Excellent choice, sir," Mr. Sokoloff said. "Five carats. Platinum setting. Perfect quality."

"Five carats? Are you crazy?" she asked. "I don't want five carats. It's…gaudy. It isn't me."

She caught Devlin smiling then, just a little satisfied smile. He'd gotten a rise out of her, which was apparently what he wanted.

"Tell me what appeals to you, Nicole."

"If you knew me at all, you wouldn't have to ask that." She yanked the curtains shut.

Nicole knew she was being a brat, but he was a conservative man, with old-fashioned values and actions. Why couldn't he see that she needed roses and candlelight as much as any woman did, maybe even more so because she was pregnant and they'd gone about everything backward. She didn't want to choose her own ring—at least not until after he'd proposed and she'd accepted.

A few minutes later she peeked through a crack in the curtains as the men left the porch and walked to the Cadillac. When Devlin glanced toward the house, she took a step back, out of sight. Then she heard a car start. The jeweler was leaving. Devlin, however, climbed the stairs, sat on the porch swing and stayed. Every time she peeked, he was there, sometimes making the swing move slowly, sometimes resting his head, his eyes closed, as if asleep.

Her neighbor's golden retriever, Alamo, came crashing up her stairs, waking him up, and the two played fetch with some twigs for a long time. Of course, Alamo liked everyone....

Around five o'clock Devlin had a pizza delivered, which made her laugh. Why had he all of a sudden become funny? Maybe he hadn't been much fun—or funny—because of their situation. Come to think of it, she hadn't been much fun, either. How could she expect him to love her when she'd never shown him the true Nicole?

Later he seemed to be playing a video game on his cell

phone, was putting his whole body into it and shouting at success or loss. Eventually he knocked on her door.

"Can I use your bathroom?" he asked.

She opened the door and let him in. He gave her a nod, went directly into the bathroom, came out a few minutes later, gave her another nod, then he went directly outside, shutting the door behind him.

Guilt grabbed her and shook hard.

By the time night settled, she'd accomplished nothing, had spent the whole day sneaking peeks of him, had constantly stopped herself from going out and sitting in his lap.

He finally knocked on her door, said good-night and left. Twenty minutes later her phone rang.

"I had a good time today, did you?" he asked.

She smiled. "It was different." She waited but he didn't say anything. "You didn't get any work done."

"I phoned my computer and told it I was taking a sick day."

"I bet you'll be up all night catching up."

"Maybe. Nicole?"

"Yes?"

"Are we going to be able to resolve this?"

"I hope so."

"You don't sound mad at me. I don't understand why you're not here trying to work things out."

His confusion gave her strength. He needed time without her. If they were together, they would be making love, and he would be focusing on what wasn't a problem between them—sex. She hoped he would miss her as much as she missed him.

"I'm sorry you don't understand," she said, twisting a tassel on one of her sofa pillows. "Sleep well."

His long silence seemed to shout at her. "You took your

plant," he said finally, sounding defeated by that action. Without hope. "Good night, Ms. Fortune."

Tears filled her eyes when she hung up. Was she being too hard on him? On them? On their future? Didn't she have a right to expect more than she'd gotten?

Because she was exhausted, she finally slept, then the next day he didn't show up in the morning, nor did he join her for lunch at work later. When she drove home after her shift, her driveway was empty.

The day after was the same. She didn't know what to do. Had something happened to him? She didn't want to call, so she drove to the lodge. The lights were on. She saw someone moving around the great room and assumed it was him. She kept going until she found a place to turn around.

At least he was okay.

The next day when she arrived for her appointment with her obstetrician, he was there, already seated. He came to the counter while she checked in, then took a seat next to her. He'd been thumbing through a parenting magazine but had put it aside. He didn't pick it up again.

She smiled at him, glad to see him but unsure. *Why did you disappear for two days?* "Hi."

"How are you feeling?" he asked.

She couldn't tell anything by his tone of voice. "Good. Fine. You?"

"Fine."

Was he angry? Had he given up? *Please don't give up.*

The inner door opened and a close-to-her-due-date woman came into the reception area. She led with her belly, one hand pressed against her lower back. A toddler held her other hand.

"Ain't life grand?" she said to Nicole, flashing a smile, seeming to mean her words.

Nicole smiled back. That would be her in a few months—well, minus the toddler. Would Devlin find her attractive then?

He looked at her just then, and she wondered if that was what was going through his mind, too. Would he resent her when the physical connection had to be put on hold?

"Nicole?" The doctor's assistant, Jennie, held the door for her to enter. Devlin followed.

Nicole stepped on the scale, and Jennie cheerfully announced her weight aloud as she recorded it, then directed Nicole to sit on the exam table to have her blood pressure taken.

"Slip off your skirt and put the drape over you. The doctor will be with you in a few minutes."

"Is that true?" Devlin asked after the door closed.

"Is what true?" Nicole climbed off the table, handed him the drape, kicked off her shoes and stepped out of her skirt. She was wearing the purple thong that he'd held up the first night she'd stayed at the lodge. She'd worn it on purpose, hoping he would be there, would see it and be reminded.

"Is your doctor prompt?" His slowness in responding made her look at him.

She caught him eyeing her legs and took her time getting back onto the table. "She's generally prompt. Would you hand me the drape, please?"

He stood and opened the paper fold by fold, then he laid it over her lap. He rested his hands on either side of her.

"You shaved," she said, realizing why he looked different.

"Yeah."

"Why?"

"It was time."

"Because it's time to go home and back to work?"

"Because the experiment is over."

The door opened then and the doctor entered. "You must be the dad," she said, extending her hand. "I'm Dr. Saxon."

"Dev Campbell."

They shook hands, then she sat on a stool and opened Nicole's file. "Your weight's good. Blood pressure is excellent. Any problems?"

My baby's father doesn't love me. "None."

They went through the usual routine of stethoscope listening and abdomen measuring. Devlin seemed fascinated, not speaking, hardly even blinking. Dr. Saxon got out the fetal heartbeat implements, and the sound soon resonated in the room, swooshing and beating, fast and furious. Devlin's face paled a little. He grasped Nicole's hand.

"Awesome, isn't it?" Dr. Saxon said. "I never get tired of hearing it." She tugged a different machine closer, shoved Nicole's drape out of the way then squirted some gel on her abdomen. "Watch the monitor."

"We don't want to know the baby's sex," Nicole said in a hurry.

"Speak for yourself," Devlin said.

"Uh-oh. I hear this all the time," the doctor said. "Should I leave the room and let you duke it out?"

Nicole made eye contact. After a moment he said, "No. We'll do it her way."

It seemed like a huge victory to Nicole.

"Okay. I can't guarantee you won't see something to give the secret away, you understand, but I'll do my best."

She put the device on Nicole's abdomen and slowly moved it around, pressing down every so often and taking a picture. Nicole saw blurs followed by things she could almost pick out, then blurs again. Devlin seemed hypnotized. He crushed Nicole's hand in his, his gaze on the screen.

"Have you felt movement?" the doctor asked.

"Yes. Flutters."

Dr. Saxon looked at Devlin. "Can you feel them yet?"

He shook his head.

"It may be a little while still. Firsts are sometimes more difficult to feel. Okay." She put away the wand, handed Nicole some cloths to wipe off the gel. "Here's your Broadway premiere."

She showed the pictures then, pointing out all the body parts. Fingers and toes. The spinal column. A beautiful little head. Arms and legs all tucked up close. The life-sustaining umbilical cord. Nicole's eyes welled, which made her mad. She wanted to see everything.

"He looks perfect," Devlin said.

"She," Nicole countered, wiping her eyes.

The doctor just laughed, then handed Devlin a piece of paper printed with four different photos, copies of the ones in which she'd pointed out the details. "Take good care of them, Papa. I'll see you in a month."

The door shut. Quiet settled in the room. He seemed as in awe as she was. She held out her hand. "Can I see those again?"

Nicole traced all the tiny features with her fingers. "Look," she said. "She has your nose."

He didn't laugh at her teasing. Instead he stared into her eyes for a long time. "I have to go," he said finally.

She called his name. He kept going. She climbed off the table, the drape clutched to her, the page of ultrasound photos clenched in her hand, totally bewildered. And maybe a little scared, too.

It seemed like a now-or-never moment. Like his leaving meant something huge and important. He hadn't been unpredictable before. She had no idea what his actions meant.

Nicole dressed, made her next appointment and then drove to work.

"If it's just you and me, kid," she said to the photographs, a lump in her throat, "we might as well start getting used to it."

Fourteen

Nicole woke from a sound sleep to banging coming from her front door. She looked at the clock, saw it was almost midnight. She was scared to get out of bed to such a ruckus. Then she heard him call her name. Devlin.

The pounding continued.

She slipped into her robe as she hurried into the living room, turned the lock with shaking fingers, then opened the door.

"What are you doing?" she asked, tempted to grab his arm and pull him in. He looked awful. His eyes were red and his hair uncombed. Once again he looked as if he hadn't shaved in the two days since she'd seen him at the doctor's office. Two long, devastating, horrible, crushing days when she'd felt lost and lonely. A look into her future, she feared. She'd cursed him, cried over him. She'd dialed all but the last digit of his number, then hung up, several times. She didn't think she could take much more, and now here he was, looking as miserable as she felt.

"Are you drunk?" she asked, studying him. She wished she could hug him and make whatever was hurting him go away. She wanted him to hug her back.

"Maybe a little."

"How little?"

"I've had a few. Not enough to leave me incapacitated."

"And you *drove* here?"

"I took a cab."

Which meant she had to deal with him. It was too cold to leave him outdoors. "Come in." She was still stunned by—and hopeful about—how horrible he looked. "Why were you drinking?"

He lifted a hand toward her hair then dropped it. "Because I ran out of other ideas."

"I think we'd better sit down." She tugged him along with her, was amazed how he let her take control. "What's going on?"

He sat bonelessly, his knees spread, his hands resting on his thighs. "I told my father I quit."

"Wow. I'm sure that came as a shock."

He snorted. This Devlin was so different from the one she'd known until now that she could hardly believe he was the same man.

"Yeah, which is why I let him rant for a while."

"About what?"

"Tradition. Responsibility. Obligation. Duty."

He said the word *duty* as if it were an obscenity.

"I had to hang up on him."

"Of course you did."

"He called back a couple hours later. Told me the board had decided to make me president of a new commercial real estate division. I'd have a lot more autonomy and authority."

"Good." When he glared at her she said, "Not good?"

"I have never worked anywhere other than my family's bank. I'm good, Nicole. I'm damn good. I want to prove it to myself and everyone else. I want to sink or swim on my own."

"Looks like you're going to do that." She patted his arm. "So, getting a little drunk was supposed to help you get ideas for the new job?"

"No. You. I ran out of ideas about *you*."

She shook her head, still not understanding.

"I don't know what else I can do. I don't want my child born out of wedlock. I told you I believe he's mine—"

"She," she said automatically.

He didn't crack a smile. "I wanted you to choose a ring. I've told you I would take care of you forever. I even stayed away, giving you the space you seemed to want." He dragged his hands down his face. "Then I saw the ultrasound. It made it so real, you know?"

"Real?"

"I see the changes in your body. I've felt them. I knew there was a child growing inside you. But when I heard the heartbeat and saw the images, saw his arms and legs moving, it was suddenly *real*. I wanted to protect him and love him and be a completely different kind of father than mine."

He looked straight at her. "And I realized I'd fallen in love with you. I didn't recognize it was love until it was walking away. *You* were walking away. And I don't know what else I can do to convince you to marry me beyond what I've already offered."

Joy swept through her like nothing she'd known. She could barely see him through her tears that began to well. "I fell in love with you in Atlantic City."

"Did you?" He reached out tentatively to touch her face.

"I think I did, too. All I knew was I'd never wanted a second date with anyone until you. And now I want a lifetime."

She tried to breathe. Words poured out of her. "You want a prenup, sweetheart, I'll sign a prenup. You want to live in Philadelphia, we'll live in Philadelphia. I'd like to keep this cabin, however. Maybe we could vacation here occasionally. Maybe my dad would like to use—"

He crushed her in his arms, emotion flowing from him like a palpable thing. He'd probably been storing it up for a lifetime but had never felt he could let his guard down with anyone before.

"I told you I will marry only once," he said close to her ear. "No prenup necessary for that. And if you want to stay on here, we can do that. I can work from anywhere. Except—" he leaned back "—we have to build another home. This is too—"

"Small. I know." She cupped his face, welcoming a kiss, his beard scratchy, but what did it matter? "We can live anywhere, Devlin. Sweetheart. Anywhere."

She pulled his hand to where their baby had started to kick.

"I feel him," he said quietly, then he smiled. "Her."

"*Him* is okay."

After the movement stopped, he dug into a pocket and pulled out a jeweler's box. "I've been carrying this around with me."

Before she could open the lid, he slid to a knee on the floor and faced her. "I love you, Nicole. You are my lucky charm. I want to have more children with you. I want to take care of you. I want to be your partner forever. Please, marry me."

After a proposal like that, she would never again think he married her because of the baby. She was his choice, even if they *had* gone about things backward. "I love you, Devlin. Yes, I'll marry you."

He pushed the lever to open the box. The ring she'd admired winked at her, a sparkly sapphire-and-diamond flower. She put a hand to her mouth. "How did you know?"

"It was the one I'd picked. The others were window dressing." He plucked the ring from the box and slid it onto her finger.

"It's beautiful."

"It had to match the setting, the very beautiful woman I love."

She barely recognized this gentle, besotted man, but she liked him. She also liked his old self-confidence as much as his new devotion. She hoped the two sides of him would merge and mingle.

"The wedding?" she asked.

"I don't think we should delay, do you? Can you put it together in a week? Next Saturday at the Sterling's wedding chapel?"

"I wouldn't have to do anything but make decisions. The wedding planners do all the work." Her head started to spin. "I want two of my girlfriends from Atlantic City to be my attendants. We'll have to figure out how to get their dresses. And my dress."

"Whatever you want."

"Hey, you're lucking out," she said, framing his face. "I only have a week to be a bridezilla, then it's over. Some women drag that out for months. You'll only have a week to worry if you made a mistake."

He smiled. "I haven't made a mistake."

She squeezed his hands when another thought struck her. "Your parents…"

"Will be invited."

"What if they don't come?"

"It doesn't matter who else is there, Ms. Fortune. You show up, and it's fine with me. I'm sure my sister Joan will come, and her husband, and their two and two-thirds offspring. You can even invite *Mark*."

She brushed his unruly hair, then linked her fingers at the back of his neck. "Rubbing it in, huh?"

"Maybe."

"I never slept with him," she said, then kissed him.

He didn't say anything, but she could tell he was glad.

"Would you like to go to bed?" she asked.

"Yeah." One word, but layered with so much meaning. "I missed you."

The words were music to her ears. "Let's go make up for lost time."

Dev lifted the frosty glass of ice-cold beer the bartender had just set in front of him. He scanned the casino's sports bar in time to see a man stride into the room. Beer sloshed onto Dev's hand in a déjà vu moment as he thumped the glass onto the bar. A grin stretched his mouth as the dark-haired, dark-eyed man approached, then stopped in front of Dev.

"I don't see a ball and chain," the man said. "But I hear you've got one."

Dev laughed, extended his hand, then pulled Ryan Sperling into a quick, hearty hug. "Man, you haven't changed a bit, Ryan. Not a bit."

"You have." He took the seat next to Dev's and ordered a beer. "What's that fuzz on your face?"

"It's coming off for the wedding. But I'm leaving it on until my father gets here tomorrow."

Ryan laughed, low. "I hear you."

One of the ties that had bound Dev and Ryan was their dif-

ficult relationships with their fathers. Apparently, that hadn't changed for Ryan, either. "Thanks for being my best man."

"I'm honored. When do I get to meet the miracle worker?"

"Nicole's working her last shift. She'll be done in an hour. Hey, we moved out of the lodge and into her cabin, but the caretaker, Mary, says I can't hand the keys over to you tonight. She'll clean the place in the morning and get the keys to you."

"No problem. Coming in a day early, I figured I'd get a room here anyway."

"Nicole got you a suite. It's on us."

"Yeah? Thanks."

"I hope you enjoy the lodge—the Love Shack—as much as I did. And Luke and Nathan, for that matter. You did hear they both got married, right?"

Ryan shuddered. "Yeah. Not me, though. No wedding. No hooking up. No *permanently* hooking up."

"Good luck with that. The lodge is magic. And, hey, if you find you do need a best man, after all, I'll be happy to return the favor."

"Bite your tongue."

Dev spied Nicole heading their way. The past few days had been a whirlwind as they prepared for the quick wedding. She hadn't even come close to a being a bridezilla, but a glowing woman who showed her love at every opportunity. He knew she was worried about meeting his parents. He tried to assure her that his first loyalty would always be to her, that *they* were a family now. It was something he was going to have to show her, not just tell her.

"Here's my beautiful bride." Dev introduced them.

"Are you sure you want to marry this guy?" Ryan asked her. "Do you have full disclosure about him? Maybe I should tell you about—"

Dev slapped his arm around Ryan's shoulders. "I think Nicole has to get back to work now."

"Not really. I—"

"Yeah. You do." He kissed her soundly, ending the discussion.

"So that's how you stop a woman from talking," Ryan said. "I'll have to remember that."

Nicole grinned, taking the kidding well. "Here's the key to your suite," she said. "It's got a view you won't believe. My bridesmaids, Lisa and DeeDee, are in the next room. They're both single," she added with a wink before she left.

"So," Ryan said, taking his seat again and lifting his glass in a toast. "You're going to be a father."

"A different kind from mine, Ryan. Completely different."

"Good."

Dev reached into his pocket and pulled out a piece of paper he'd been carrying around since his first night at the lodge, a note that had been taped to the bathroom mirror. He opened it, placed it on the bar and slid it in front of Ryan. "Luke left me this."

Ryan read it aloud. "'Remember the talk we had about women on New Year's Eve our senior year? We were wrong, man. So wrong. We didn't have a clue.'" Ryan frowned. "I'm not recalling that."

"Took me all month to figure it out myself. Remember the list we came up with? The universal truths about women?"

Ryan rapped the note with his fist. "Oh, yeah. They tie you down."

Dev grinned. "They cut off your freedom."

"Right! And they won't let you ever do anything dangerous again."

"Yeah." He hesitated. "Like what? What do you suppose we meant?"

"Like... Hell, I don't know. Become a Navy SEAL."

"Right," Dev said, trying not to smile, then adding another from their list. "Sex gets boring."

"The worst of all, man. Boring sex." Ryan took a long swig of his beer, then set the glass down carefully, contemplating Luke's note. "I don't get it. Why does he say we were wrong? All those things are true."

"Because we were talking about women. Plural. In general. Not a woman in particular. Maybe it is all true—except the boring sex part. I refuse to believe that one. But when it's the right woman, we want to be with her. We want to be there for a lifetime. None of the rest matters. Except the boring sex."

"Shoot, man. You're hopeless." Ryan tempered it with a grin, then clinked his glass to Dev's.

Dev nodded, but he knew the truth. He wasn't hopeless at all. He was the most hopeful he'd ever been in his life. The universal truth he'd learned was that love changed everything.

He studied Ryan, who'd turned his attention to the Giants game on the television, just as Dev had been doing a month ago. Before his life changed for good.

For *good*.

* * * * *

Look for the next installment in
THE MILLIONAIRE OF THE MONTH
series this June with
Anna DePalo's AN IMPROPER AFFAIR.

Mediterranean Nights

Join the guests and crew of Alexandra's Dream, *the newest luxury ship to set sail on the romantic Mediterranean, as they experience the glamorous world of cruising.*

A new Harlequin continuity series begins in June 2007 with FROM RUSSIA, WITH LOVE by Ingrid Weaver

Marina Artamova books a cabin on the luxurious cruise ship Alexandra's Dream, *when she finds out that her orphaned nephew and his adoptive father are aboard. She's determined to be reunited with the boy…but the romantic ambience of the ship and her undeniable attraction to a man she considers her enemy are about to interfere with her quest!*

Turn the page for a sneak preview!

Piraeus, Greece

"THERE SHE IS, Stefan. *Alexandra's Dream.*" David Anderson squatted beside his new son and pointed at the dark blue hull that towered above the pier. The cruise ship was a majestic sight, twelve decks high and as long as a city block. A circle of silver and gold stars, the logo of the Liberty Cruise Line, gleamed from the swept-back smokestack. Like some legendary sea creature born for the water, the ship emanated power from every sleek curve—even at rest it held the promise of motion. "That's going to be our home for the next ten days."

The child beside him remained silent, his cheeks working in and out as he sucked furiously on his thumb. Hair so blond

it appeared white ruffled against his forehead in the harbor breeze. The baby-sweet scent unique to the very young mingled with the tang of the sea.

"Ship," David said. "Uh, *parakhod*."

From beneath his bangs, Stefan looked at the *Alexandra's Dream*. Although he didn't release his thumb, the corners of his mouth tightened with the beginning of a smile.

David grinned. That was Stefan's first smile this afternoon, one of only two since they had left the orphanage yesterday. It was probably because of the boat—according to the orphanage staff, the boy loved boats, which was the main reason David had decided to book this cruise. Then again, there was a strong possibility the smile could have been a reaction to David's attempt at pocket-dictionary Russian. Whatever the cause, it was a good start.

The liaison from the adoption agency had claimed that Stefan had been taught some English, but David had yet to see evidence of it. David continued to speak, positive his son would understand his tone even if he couldn't grasp the words. "This is her maiden voyage. Her first trip, just like this is our first trip, and that makes it special." He motioned toward the stage that had been set up on the pier beneath the ship's bow. "That's why everyone's celebrating."

The ship's official christening ceremony had been held the day before and had been a closed affair, with only the cruise-line executives and VIP guests invited, but the stage hadn't yet been disassembled. Banners bearing the blue and white of the Greek flag of the ship's owner, as well as the Liberty circle of stars logo, draped the edges of the platform. In the center, a group of musicians and a dance troupe dressed in traditional white folk costumes performed for the benefit of the *Alexandra's Dream*'s first passengers. Their

audience was in a festive mood, snapping their fingers in time to the music while the dancers twirled and wove through their steps.

David bobbed his head to the rhythm of the mandolins. They were playing a folk tune that seemed vaguely familiar, possibly from a movie he'd seen. He hummed a few notes. "Catchy melody, isn't it?"

Stefan turned his gaze on David. His eyes were a striking shade of blue, as cool and pale as a winter horizon and far too solemn for a child not yet five. Still, the smile that hovered at the corners of his mouth persisted. He moved his head with the music, mirroring David's motion.

David gave a silent cheer at the interaction. Hopefully, this cruise would provide countless opportunities for more. "Hey, good for you," he said. "Do you like the music?"

The child's eyes sparked. He withdrew his thumb with a pop. *"Moozika!"*

"Music. Right!" David held out his hand. "Come on, let's go closer so we can watch the dancers."

Stefan grasped David's hand quickly, as if he feared it would be withdrawn. In an instant his budding smile was replaced by a look close to panic.

Did he remember the car accident that had killed his parents? It would be a mercy if he didn't. As far as David knew, Stefan had never spoken of it to anyone. Whatever he had seen had made him run so far from the crash that the police hadn't found him until the next day. The event had traumatized him to the extent that he hadn't uttered a word until his fifth week at the orphanage. Even now he seldom talked.

David sat back on his heels and brushed the hair from Stefan's forehead. That solemn, too-old gaze locked with

his, and for an instant, David felt as if he looked back in time at an image of himself thirty years ago.

He didn't need to speak the same language to understand exactly how this boy felt. He knew what it meant to be alone and powerless among strangers, trying to be brave and tough but wishing with every fiber of his being for a place to belong, to be safe, and most of all for someone to love him….

He knew in his heart he would be a good parent to Stefan. It was why he had never considered halting the adoption process after Ellie had left him. He hadn't balked when he'd learned of the recent claim by Stefan's spinster aunt, either; the absentee relative had shown up too late for her case to be considered. The adoption was meant to be. He and this child already shared a bond that went deeper than paperwork or legalities.

A seagull screeched overhead, making Stefan start and press closer to David.

"That's my boy," David murmured. He swallowed hard, struck by the simple truth of what he had just said.

That's my *boy*.

"I CAN'T BE PATIENT, Rudolph. I'm not going to stand by and watch my nephew get ripped from his country and his roots to live on the other side of the world."

Rudolph hissed out a slow breath. "Marina, I don't like the sound of that. What are you planning?"

"I'm going to talk some sense into this American kidnapper."

"No. Absolutely not. No offence, but diplomacy is not your strong suit."

"Diplomacy be damned. Their ship's due to sail at five o'clock."

"Then you wouldn't have an opportunity to speak with him even if his lawyer agreed to a meeting."

"I'll have ten days of opportunities, Rudolph, since I plan to be on board that ship."

* * * * *

Follow Marina and David as they join forces to uncover the reason behind little Stefan's unusual silence, and the secret behind the death of his parents....

Look for From Russia, With Love
by Ingrid Weaver
in stores June 2007.

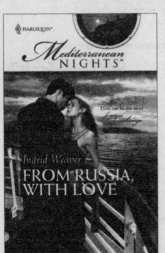

SPECIAL EDITION™

COMING IN JUNE

HER LAST FIRST DATE

by *USA TODAY* bestselling author

SUSAN MALLERY

After one too many bad dates, Crissy Phillips
finally swore off men. Recently widowed,
pediatrician Josh Daniels can't risk losing his
heart. With an intense attraction pulling them
together, will their fear keep them apart?
Or will one wild night change everything…?

**Sometimes the unexpected
is the best news of all….**

REQUEST YOUR FREE BOOKS!

2 FREE NOVELS PLUS 2 FREE GIFTS!

Passionate, Powerful, Provocative!

YES! Please send me 2 FREE Silhouette Desire® novels and my 2 FREE gifts. After receiving them, if I don't wish to receive any more books, I can return the shipping statement marked "cancel." If I don't cancel, I will receive 6 brand-new novels every month and be billed just $3.80 per book in the U.S., or $4.47 per book in Canada, plus 25¢ shipping and handling per book and applicable taxes, if any*. That's a savings of almost 15% off the cover price! I understand that accepting the 2 free books and gifts places me under no obligation to buy anything. I can always return a shipment and cancel at any time. Even if I never buy another book from Silhouette, the two free books and gifts are mine to keep forever.

225 SDN EEXJ 326 SDN EEXU

Name	(PLEASE PRINT)	
Address		Apt.
City	State/Prov.	Zip/Postal Code

Signature (if under 18, a parent or guardian must sign)

Mail to the Silhouette Reader Service™:
IN U.S.A.: P.O. Box 1867, Buffalo, NY 14240-1867
IN CANADA: P.O. Box 609, Fort Erie, Ontario L2A 5X3

Not valid to current Silhouette Desire subscribers.

Want to try two free books from another line?
Call 1-800-873-8635 or visit www.morefreebooks.com.

* Terms and prices subject to change without notice. NY residents add applicable sales tax. Canadian residents will be charged applicable provincial taxes and GST. This offer is limited to one order per household. All orders subject to approval. Credit or debit balances in a customer's account(s) may be offset by any other outstanding balance owed by or to the customer. Please allow 4 to 6 weeks for delivery.

Your Privacy: Silhouette is committed to protecting your privacy. Our Privacy Policy is available online at www.eHarlequin.com or upon request from the Reader Service. From time to time we make our lists of customers available to reputable firms who may have a product or service of interest to you. If you would prefer we not share your name and address, please check here. ☐

SDES07

HARLEQUIN®

American ROMANCE®

**is proud to present a special treat this
Fourth of July with three stories
to kick off your summer!**

SUMMER LOVIN'
by
Marin Thomas,
Laura Marie Altom
Ann Roth

This year, celebrating the Fourth of July in Silver Cliff,
Colorado, is going to be special. There's an all-year
high school reunion taking place before the old
school building gets torn down. As old flames find
each other and new romances begin, this small
town is looking like the perfect place
for some summer lovin'!

*Available June 2007
wherever Harlequin books are sold.*

www.eHarlequin.com   HAR75169

COMING NEXT MONTH

#1801 FORTUNE'S FORBIDDEN WOMAN—Heidi Betts
Dakota Fortunes
Can he risk the family honor to fulfill an unrequited passion with the one woman he's forbidden to have?

#1802 SIX-MONTH MISTRESS—Katherine Garbera
The Mistresses
She was contracted to be his mistress in exchange for his help in getting her struggling business off the ground. Now he's come to collect his prize.

#1803 AN IMPROPER AFFAIR—Anna DePalo
Millionaire of the Month
This ruthless businessman is on the verge of extracting the ultimate revenge…until he falls for the woman who could jeopardize his entire plan.

#1804 THE MILLIONAIRE'S INDECENT PROPOSAL—Emilie Rose
Monte Carlo Affairs
When an attractive stranger offers her a million euros to become his mistress, will she prove his theory that everyone has a price?

#1805 BETWEEN THE CEO'S SHEETS—Charlene Sands
She'd been paid off to leave him. Now he wants revenge and will stop at nothing until he settles the score…and gets her back in his bed.

#1806 RICH MAN'S REVENGE—Tessa Radley
He'd marry his enemy's daughter and extract his long-denied revenge—but his new bride has her own plan for him.

SDCNM0507